*Everyman, I will go with thee,
and be thy guide*

Joseph Conrad

TALES OF UNREST

Edited by
ANTHONY FOTHERGILL
University of Exeter

Consultant Editor for this volume
CEDRIC WATTS
University of Sussex

EVERYMAN
J. M. DENT · LONDON
CHARLES E. TUTTLE
VERMONT

Consultant editor for the Everyman Joseph Conrad Series
Cedric Watts

Selection, introduction and other critical apparatus
© J. M. Dent 2000

This edition first published by Everyman Paperbacks in 2000

J. M. Dent
Orion Publishing Group
Orion House, 5 Upper St Martin's Lane,
London WC2H 9EA
and
Charles E. Tuttle Co. Inc.
28 South Main Street,
Rutland, Vermont 05701, USA

Typeset by SetSystems Ltd, Saffron Walden, Essex
Printed in Great Britain by
The Guernsey Press Co. Ltd, Guernsey, Channel Islands

British Library Cataloguing-in-Publication Data
is available upon request.

ISBN 0 460 87656 2

CONTENTS

NOTE ON THE AUTHOR AND EDITOR

JOSEPH CONRAD (Józef Teodor Konrad Nałęcz Korzeniowski) was born in 1857, in the part of Poland annexed by Russia (now the Ukraine). His father, a fervent Polish nationalist, was placed in exile by the Russians in 1862 with his wife and son Joseph. Upon the early deaths of his parents, Conrad was brought up by relatives. In 1874 he left Poland, first for France and then for England (in 1878) to become a master mariner. He adopted British nationality in 1886. After twenty years at sea (voyaging to the Far East, the Congo and South America), he gave up that profession to become a writer, settling permanently in England with his wife, Jessie (née George), in 1896.

His first novels, *Almayer's Folly* (1895) and *An Outcast of the Islands* (1896), brought him critical acclaim but not financial stability. *The Nigger of the 'Narcissus'* (1897) and *Tales of Unrest* (1898) followed, and within the next fifteen years he produced what are now regarded as some of the finest works in English literature: *Lord Jim, Heart of Darkness, Nostromo, The Secret Agent* and *Under Western Eyes*. That English was his third language makes this an even more startling achievement. Conrad was never a writer for the popular market, and it was only with *Chance* (1914) that he attained a level of widespread success and fame matching his earlier critical renown. In his last years he produced such fine works as *Victory, The Shadow-Line* and *The Rescue*.

The individual voice in which he speaks of the problems and concerns of the modern age – political, philosophical, ethnic and ethical – has had an abiding influence. Later writers (Thomas Mann, T. S. Eliot, F. Scott Fitzgerald, Graham Greene, Chinua Achebe and V. S. Naipaul) as well as film-makers (Hitchcock, Welles, Wajda, Coppola and Roeg) have taken inspiration from and issue with him in their works. Even when, more recently, critics have argued with aspects of his writing, his remains an overwhelmingly important literary, critical and humane voice.

ANTHONY FOTHERGILL graduated from Sussex University. After research at the University of Heidelberg and a lectureship in the English Department there he was appointed as lecturer in English Studies at Exeter University. He has taught as Visiting Professor at Kenyon College, USA and also for the Open University. Author of a critical study on Joseph Conrad's *Heart of Darkness* (Open University Press) and articles on Conrad and other nineteenth- and twentieth-century writers, he is currently researching for a book on Conrad and Germany. Recently he has edited *Oscar Wilde: Plays, Prose Writings and Poems* for Everyman.

CHRONOLOGY OF CONRAD'S LIFE

Year	Age	Life
1857		Józef Teodor Konrad Nałęcz Korzeniowski (Joseph Conrad) born in the Ukraine on 3 December
1861	3	Conrad's father, Apollo Korzeniowski, arrested in Warsaw for patriotic conspiracy
1862	4	Conrad's parents exiled to Vologda, Russia; he goes with them
1863	5	Family moves to Chernigov, Ukraine
1865	7	Death of Conrad's mother, Ewelina Korzeniowska
1869	11	Death of his father. His maternal uncle, Tadeusz Bobrowski, becomes his guardian
1870	12	Taught by Adam Pulman in Kraków
1871	13	Also taught by Izydor Kopernicki
1872	14	Resolves to go to sea

CHRONOLOGY OF HIS TIMES

Year	Literary Context	Historical Events
1857	Flaubert, *Madame Bovary* Baudelaire, *Les Fleurs du mal*	Indian Mutiny begins
1859	Dickens, *A Tale of Two Cities*	Darwin, *Origin of Species*
1861	Dickens, *Great Expectations* George Eliot, *Silas Marner*	American Civil War begins Nansen born
1862	Turgenev, *Fathers and Sons* Hugo, *Les Misérables*	Bismarck gains power in Prussia
1863	Thackeray dies	American slaves freed Polish uprising
1865	Kipling and Yeats born	American Civil War ends
1866	Swinburne, *Poems and Ballads* Dostoyevsky, *Crime and Punishment*	Nobel invents dynamite
1867	Marx, *Das Kapital*, vol. 1	
1868		Gladstone becomes Prime Minister
1869	Tolstoy, *War and Peace* Gide born Arnold, *Culture and Anarchy*	Gandhi born Suez Canal opens
1870	Dickens dies	Franco-Prussian War (to 1871) Elementary Education Act
1871	Dostoyevsky, *The Devils* Zola begins the Rougon-Macquart novels	Paris Commune Trades Unions legalised
1872	George Eliot, *Middlemarch*	Mazzini dies Bertrand Russell born Edison's Telegraph invented

Year	Age	Life
1873	15	Tour of Austria, Germany and Switzerland with Adam Pulman
1874	16	Leaves Poland for Marseille to become apprentice seaman
1875	17	Sails Atlantic in *Mont-Blanc*
1876	18	Serves as steward in *Saint-Antoine*
1878	20	Shoots himself, recovers, and joins British ship *Mavis*
1879	21	Serves in clipper *Duke of Sutherland*
1880	22	Sails to Australia in *Loch Etive*
1881	23	Second mate of *Palestine*
1882	24	Storm-damaged *Palestine* repaired
1883	25	Shipwrecked when *Palestine* sinks
1884	26	Sailed to Madras in *Riversdale*; in *Narcissus* from Bombay to France

Year	Literary Context	Historical Events
1873	Ford Madox Hueffer born Pater, *Studies in the History of the Renaissance* Tolstoy, *Anna Karenina*	Livingstone dies
1874	Hardy, *Far From the Madding Crowd*	Churchill born Disraeli becomes Prime Minister
1875	Thomas Mann born	Albert Schweitzer born
1876	George Sand dies James, *Roderick Hudson*	Queen Victoria declared Empress of India
1878	Hardy, *The Return of the Native*	Second Afghan War Congress of Berlin London electric streetlighting established
1879	Ibsen, *A Doll's House* Meredith, *The Egoist*	Zulu War Einstein and Stalin born London telephone exchange established
1880	Dostoyevsky, *The Brothers Karamazov* George Eliot and Flaubert die Maupassant, *Boule de Suif*	Boer uprising in Transvaal
1881	Dostoyevsky and Carlyle die Henry James, *The Portrait of a Lady* Ibsen, *Ghosts* Flaubert, *Bouvard et Pécuchet*	Tsar Alexander II assassinated
1882	Virginia Woolf and James Joyce born	Darwin and Garibaldi die
1883	Nietzsche, *Thus Spake Zarathustra* R. L. Stevenson, *Treasure Island* Turgenev dies Kafka born	Marx dies Mussolini born
1884	Oxford English Dictionary (completed 1928)	

Year	Age	Life
1885	27	Sails to Calcutta in *Tilkhurst*
1886	28	Becomes a British subject; qualifies as captain
1887	29	Sails to Java in *Highland Forest*; hospitalised in Singapore, then first mate on the steamship *Vidar*, sailing in the Malay Archipelago
1888	30	Master of the *Otago*, his sole command
1889	31	Resigns from *Otago*; living in London, begins to write *Almayer's Folly*
1890	32	Works in Congo Free State
1891	33	Mate of *Torrens* (until 1893)
1892	34	Voyages to Australia, meeting John Galsworthy among his passengers
1893	35–6	Visits Bobrowski in Ukraine. Joins steamship *Adowa*
1894	36	*Almayer's Folly* accepted by Unwin. Meets Edward Garnett and Jessie George. Ends his sea career
1895	37	*Almayer's Folly* published. Completes *An Outcast of the Islands*

Year	Literary Context	Historical Events
1885	D. H. Lawrence born	'Congo Free State' recognised Berlin conference divides up Africa following European claims Gordon dies at Khartoum
1886	Stevenson, *Dr Jekyll and Mr Hyde* Hardy, *The Mayor of Casterbridge* James, *The Bostonians* and *The Princess Casamassima*	Salisbury becomes Premier R.C. Graham becomes MP Gladstone re-elected Irish Home Rule Bill defeated
1887	Marianne Moore born	'Bloody Sunday' riot in London
1888	T. S. Eliot born Matthew Arnold dies	Wilhelm II becomes Kaiser Eastman invents Kodak camera
1889	Browning and G. M. Hopkins die	Hitler born London Docker's Strike Parnell scandal
1890	Ibsen, *Hedda Gabler* James, *The Tragic Muse*	Bismarck resigns Fall of Parnell Electrification of London Underground railway begins
1891	Hardy, *Tess of the d'Urbervilles* Morris, *News from Nowhere*	Free elementary education
1892	Tennyson dies	Gladstone's fourth ministry
1893	Maupassant dies	Independent Labour Party formed
1894	Pater dies First issue of *The Yellow Book* Stevenson dies Huxley born	Dreyfus trial in Paris Nicholas II becomes Tsar Greenwich explosion
1895	Crane, *The Red Badge of Courage* Yeats, *Poems* Hardy, *Jude the Obscure* Wilde, *An Ideal Husband* and *The Importance of Being Earnest* Trials and imprisonment of Wilde	Marconi invents 'wireless' telegraphy Lumière brothers invent cinematography Jameson Raid into the Transvaal

Year	Age	Life
1896	38	*An Outcast of the Islands* published. Starts *The Rescue*. Marries Jessie George; honeymoons in Brittany where he starts and completes writing 'The Idiots', 'An Outpost Of Progress', and 'The Lagoon'
1897	39	Writes 'Karain' and 'The Return'. Meets Henry James and Stephen Crane. Befriended by Cunninghame Graham. *The Nigger of the 'Narcissus'* published
1898	40	First son (Borys) born. *Tales of Unrest* published. Collaborates with Ford Madox Hueffer (later surnamed Ford).
1899	41	*Heart of Darkness* serialised. Serialisation of *Lord Jim* begins
1900	42	*Lord Jim* as a book. J. B. Pinker becomes Conrad's agent
1901	43	*The Inheritors* (co-author Hueffer)
1902	44	*Youth* appears (including *Heart of Darkness*)
1903	45	*Typhoon* volume. *Romance* (co-author Hueffer)
1904	46	*Nostromo* published
1905	47	*One Day More* (play) fails
1906	48	Second son (John) born. *The Mirror of the Sea* (aided by Hueffer)
1907	49	*The Secret Agent* published
1908	50	*A Set of Six* (tales). Heavily indebted to Pinker. Involved in *English Review*
1909	51	Quarrels with Hueffer
1910	52	Nervous breakdown on completion of *Under Western Eyes*. Awarded a Civil List pension of £100 per year
1911	53	*Under Western Eyes* published
1912	54	*Some Reminiscences* (later known by the title of the American edition, *A Personal Record*). *'Twixt Land and Sea* (tales). *Chance* serialised in *New York Herald*

Year	Literary Context	Historical Events
1896	Morris and Verlaine die Chekhov, *The Seagull*	Nobel Prizes established
1897	Kipling, *Captains Courageous* James, *What Maisie Knew*	Queen Victoria's Diamond Jubilee
1898	Wilde, 'The Ballad of Reading Gaol' Wells, *The War of the Worlds* James, *The Turn of the Screw*	War between Spain and USA Bismarck and Gladstone die Fashoda incident The Curies discover radium
1899	Hemingway born	Dreyfus freed Boer War begins
1900	Ruskin, Wilde and Crane die Freud, *The Interpretation of* *Dreams*	Russia occupies Manchuria Relief of Ladysmith and Mafeking British Labour Party founded
1901	Kipling, *Kim*	Queen Victoria dies
1902	Zola dies	Boer War ends
1903	James, *The Ambassadors*	First powered aircraft flight
1904	Chekhov, *The Cherry Orchard*	Russo-Japanese War begins
1905	Wells, *Kipps*	Russia defeated by Japan; first Russian revolution
1906	Beckett born Ibsen dies	Liberals win British election
1907	Auden born	Lord Kelvin dies; Einstein, *General Theory of Relativity*
1908	Bennett, *The Old Wives' Tale* Forster, *A Room with a View*	Feminist agitation; Mrs Pankhurst jailed
1909	Swinburne dies	Blériot flies across Channel
1910	Forster, *Howards End* Yeats, *The Green Helmet*	King Edward VII dies; accession of George V
1911	Golding born	Industrial unrest in UK
1912	Patrick White born Pound, *Ripostes*	First Balkan War Sinking of *Titanic* Wilson elected U.S. President

Year	Literary Context	Historical Events
1913	Lawrence, *Sons and Lovers*	Second Balkan War
1914	Joyce, *Dubliners*	World War I begins
1915	Lawrence's *The Rainbow* banned	Italy enters war Gallipoli disaster
1916	James dies Joyce, *A Portrait of the Artist as a Young Man*	Battle of Jutland Battle of the Somme Easter Uprising; Casement trial and execution, Dublin
1917	T. S. Eliot, *Prufrock* Anthony Burgess born	USA enters war Russian October Revolution
1918	Rosenberg and Owen die Wyndham Lewis, *Tarr*	Armistice Polish Republic restored Women enfranchised in UK
1919	Virginia Woolf, *Night and Day* Hardy, *Poetical Works*	UK's first woman MP Versailles Treaty
1920	Lawrence, *Women in Love* Katherine Mansfield, *Bliss*	Poles rout Russian invaders League of Nations created
1921	Huxley, *Crome Yellow*	Irish Free State founded
1922	T. S. Eliot, *The Waste Land* Joyce, *Ulysses*	Mussolini gains power in Italy
1923	Yeats wins Nobel Prize Wells, *Men Like Gods*	Treaty of Lausanne
1924	Forster, *A Passage to India* Shaw, *St Joan* Anatole France and Franz Kafka die	Lenin dies MacDonald heads first Labour government in UK
1925	T. S. Eliot, *Poems 1909–25*	Hitler publishes *Mein Kampf*
1926	Kafka, *The Castle*	General Strike in UK Pilsudski seizes power in Poland
1927	Virginia Woolf, *To the Lighthouse*	Lindbergh flies Atlantic

INTRODUCTION

Unless it is produced by a Turgenev or a Maupassant, an Edgar Allan Poe or a Jorge Luis Borges, short fiction as a literary form can easily be regarded as a secondary effort, a trial run for greater works. Thus the fine short stories of Henry James, Virginia Woolf and James Joyce stand in the shadow of their major novels. The short tales of Joseph Conrad have also suffered under this crude rule of critical perception – that great size, length and scope are necessary for a work to be deemed great. *Tales of Unrest* like other early stories, particularly, have been looked at, and overlooked, as mere experimental trials for his later great novels.[1]

Certainly, elements of these early 'tales of unrest' provide a sort of artistic scaffolding or maquette for Conrad's building of more elaborated works. The geographical locations of the tales (the Malay Archipelago, an African colonial outpost, a rainy London) are obviously relevant to the novels. So, too, are their thematic preoccupations (memories of betrayal, the confrontation of 'civilisation' with the 'primitive', the power of belief and its discontents). Traces of ideas and styles of writing which Conrad perfects in *Lord Jim*, *Heart of Darkness*, *Nostromo*, *The Secret Agent*, and *Under Western Eyes* are clearly discernible in *Tales of Unrest*. But to think of them *only* in terms of what they contribute to later works is to underrate their achievement as short stories, for the subsequent great novels can *also* be seen to highlight the originality, the self-fashioning qualities of these fine though less well-known works.

When he wrote the stories, Conrad's literary status was not yet assured. He had received good critical reviews with his first two novels, both set in the Malay Archipelago: *Almayer's Folly* (1895) and *An Outcast of the Islands* (1896).[2] But despite this early critical acclaim,[3] real popular and financial success from his writing came only much later with *Chance* (1914), written years after his greatest novels had been published. In the 1890s he was still a literary newcomer, praised mainly for capturing the exotic local atmosphere of the Far East or Africa, with the spice of adventure thrown in. The popular writers of the day and of the genre, Kipling, Rider Haggard, R. L. Stevenson, Louis Becke, and Clark Russell, often came off better than Conrad in comparative reviews, although Conrad's was immediately recognised as a distinctive and unique (if not a fully acclimatised) literary voice.

In 1896 and 1897, when he was writing the stories contained in this volume, he was facing a major creative crisis, trying to complete his third novel, *The Rescuer*. (Renamed *The Rescue*, it in fact took him twenty more years to finish.) He intermittently took time off from working on it to write the stories which were to become *Tales of Unrest*, published as his first collection of stories in 1898. His correspondence at the time with Edward Garnett, a reader for Conrad's publisher, T. Fisher Unwin, and one of the great discoverers and enablers of modern English writers, gives a good sense of the stories' artistic incubation. As a new and in some ways innocent writer, Conrad was negotiating the rough frontier between being an independent artist and being a professional author, financially dependent on the publishing (particularly the periodical) market and the good will and patronage of others. Garnett gave him invaluable artistic and professional advice and guidance.[4]

Conrad first mentions the tales in a letter to Garnett, written while spending his honeymoon with his wife Jessie, in Brittany, France, in August 1896. By this time he had completed, almost as a diversion from his struggles with *The Rescue*, the writing of 'The Idiots' (May, 1896), 'An Outpost of Progress' (July, 1896) and 'The Lagoon' (August, 1896), and he was seeking to place them in English literary magazines. 'Karain: A Memory' was finished in April, 1897 and 'The Return' (the only story in the collection not to be serialised in magazines) was finished by September, 1897. In the letters, there is a guarded off-handedness in his referring to some of the tales, rather disparagingly, as 'magazine'ish'.[5] As Cedric Watts has pointed out, the magazines to which Conrad was alluding – particularly *Blackwood's*, which took 'Karain: A Memory' – were not avant-garde literary magazines.[6] They were rather aimed at the intelligent middle-class reader, pleased to be provided with adventure and romance stories and articles of a conservative, even jingoistic flavour.

Although the *Savoy* (edited by Arthur Symons, who published 'The Idiots') and *Cosmopolis* (which published 'An Outpost of Progress') were more sophisticated and internationally inclined in their literary and artistic commitments, Conrad temperamentally preferred the ambience of *Blackwood's*.[7] Furthermore, the early support its editors gave him was vital in the crucial threshold years from 1897 to 1902.

The stories in this volume were not conceived as a unity, although in retrospect we can see among them similarities of theme and a common engagement with experimental modes of story-telling. Thus, in 'An Outpost of Progress', 'The Idiots', and 'The Return', two narrative perspectives are juxtaposed: a sardonic external observation, which quickly and efficiently offers social comment along with natural description, and an isolated fictional consciousness, bewildered, limited, and driven by fraught needs. In 'Karain: A Memory' the framing-narrator is a self-confident and perhaps rather obtuse Englishman, through whose re-telling we must decipher the very different experience and attitude of the story's eponymous hero. The end of the story transposes us from the Eastern Archipelago to the Strand in London, where the narrator meets up again with his British shipmate. As they reminisce over Karain, they swap conflicting judgements about his superstitious fears. Early critics of the story tended to side with the complacently superior narrator. More recently, critics have focused on narrative voice as a problem raised by the use of the very *structure* of a framing narrative, with its interpretative possibilities and implicit equivocations. Must we concur with the narrator's judgements, or can we read them ironically? If the latter, what is at stake? Where, or with whom, are we meant to be standing? We confront these questions again in the narratives of Marlow in *Heart of Darkness*, Captain Mitchell in *Nostromo*, and the teacher of languages in *Under Western Eyes*. Political and cultural judgements follow on the heels of the answers we give, and much recent Conradian criticism has implicitly been trying to come to terms with them. The ironic is normally predicated on a notion of a consensus: we who 'get it' are all 'insiders'. But insiders of what? Conrad's Author's Note to *The Secret Agent* claims that the ironic is the appropriate mode for revealing the political and cultural impoverishment which that novel depicts. But is there a stable idea of community, a safe standpoint, from which to read Conrad's ironies? These tales too provide a searching challenge for the reader. And however we answer it, an argument can be made for saying of them that the ironic thrives within the confines of the short story, with its gaps and abbreviations. Moreover, extended irony can become tedious and monologic, thus losing its satirical effect. 'Everyone knows that the novel nowadays should be funny, brutalist, and short.'[8]

If the tales leave aesthetic and cultural loose ends, however, they powerfully demonstrate their own generic possibilities. In Conrad's hands, the advantages of scale which the short story characteristically offers – narrative shorthand, elision, and even brusqueness – are exploited to the utmost. The reader is left in a creative state of unrest by the marked condensation of plot and compression of narrated events; by abrupt switches from authorial commentary to fictional introspection; by the elaboration of isolated incidents and descriptions of physical place to the point that they take on symbolic weight. These are all qualities we find in the early tales. We do not expect from them the generic strengths of the novel, complex psychological portrayal or historical depth which delineates the nuances of experience as revealed through time. The strengths of the short story have to do rather with the stylistic possibilities of gaps and elisions, the suggested and the glanced-at. In these tales one nonetheless finds history, politics, and psychology powerfully, if concisely, realised. Conrad's vision in the stories is not confined to the realm of the private and personal; it encompasses the cultural and the political as well. Even when we cannot all agree with, or indeed *on*, what he is saying, it is this generosity of insight which makes his writing so powerful and historically interesting.

As a writer who was to become one of the great European literary figures of the century, Conrad's pedigree was unconventional. Józef Teodor Konrad Nałęcz Korzeniowski (as Conrad continued occasionally to sign himself throughout his life) came from a social and intellectual background that fostered a bonding of culture and public patriotic expression. He was born into a family of landowning Polish gentry in 1857, in that part of the Ukraine annexed since 1793 from Poland by Russia. Polish national awareness was as if inborn. Because of his nationalist political activities, Conrad's father, Apollo Korzeniowski, writer, literary translator, and fervent revolutionary activist, was put into internal exile with his wife, Ewa, and young son Joseph in northern Russia. Conrad's childhood was thus a hard and perforce stoic one. The family's exile was soon followed by the early death of Conrad's mother. His ailing and defeated father provided for Conrad a caring and cultured but sombre and isolated upbringing for two more years until his death in 1869. The orphaned Conrad lived his early teen years with relatives in Kraków, Poland, supported mainly by his less romantic, more pragmatic uncle and guardian, Tadeusz Bobrowski. At the age of sixteen, Conrad left Poland for Marseille, to fulfil his ambition of becoming a sailor. Historical cultural connections between Poland and France were, of course, well established and well fostered among the Polish intelligentsia. But Conrad's romantic desire to join the mercantile navy (a desire spurred on, perhaps, by his boyhood reading of English and French adventure literature) was less conventionally acceptable. His uncle did not approve.

This idiosyncratic turning-point in his life was described by Bobrowski as a terrible 'betrayal of patriotic duties'.[9] Conrad also talks of it in *A Personal Record* as 'the only case of a boy of my nationality and antecedents taking a, so to speak, standing jump, out of his racial surroundings and associations'.[10] It is too crude to see this early choice as definitively causal or even symptomatic of the rest of Conrad's lifework: when it comes to re-telling a life, it is impossible to distinguish with any certainty the shape of lives actually lived from the narrative shape of stories we tell ourselves about them. Nor do we have clear access to the desires, needs, and accidents that lead people to become who it is they do become. But we might agree with Conrad when in *The Secret Agent* he says simply and obscurely, 'We can never cease to be ourselves.'[11]

Some contemporary Polish commentators and other later critics have nevertheless read into Conrad's decision to leave Poland and go to sea a psychological 'jumping ship' (to put it paradoxically).[12] The metaphor, which sometimes becomes literal in Conrad's works, stands powerfully for the theme of betrayal, of turnings, which plays such a dominant role in *Tales of Unrest* and in other major works like *Lord Jim* (1900), *Heart of Darkness* (1902), *Nostromo* (1904), *The Secret Agent* (1907), and *Under Western Eyes* (1911). We need, however, to recall that *betrayal* is etymologically linked to *tradition*, which connotes belonging: for carrying on and passing over (to the other side) are not as alien to each other as one may think.[13]

English – which throughout his life he spoke with a heavy accent – was Conrad's third language, after Polish and French. It was necessary for him to learn it to pass his exams to qualify as chief mate (1884) and then as captain in the British Merchant Marine (1886). In that capacity he first started his literary writing, in English. Trips to the Far East, Australia, and the Congo in the 1880s and 1890s gave him much material. Only in 1894 did he jump ship again to give himself up to the more arduous task of writing.

It may be that the necessity to write in a language not native to him explains an abiding exploration of cultural estrangement in Conrad's works. The tales in this volume reveal his capacity to bring the absolutely familiar into a strange context, or vice versa, which challenges the reader to a critical re-visioning. In 'An Outpost of Progress', Kayerts and Carlier, the two heroic mainstays of a godforsaken[14] colonial outpost in the middle of Africa, find old 'home' newspapers. They then chat about the advance of civilisation to these wild parts in terms of the provision of 'Quays, and warehouses, and barracks, and – and – billiard-rooms' (73). The reader cannot *not* feel how much scorching irony is contained in the hesitant *and*s, the search for something more and the bathetic conclusion. Such is Empire, Conrad implies.

Another form of estrangement comes with Conrad's capacity for composing the one-liner. Conrad is not famed for his one-liners. Indeed, critics commenting on his style have often characterised (and sometimes criticised) him for his 'adjectival insistence'[15] – the piling up of long descriptive phrases, often producing an 'unEnglish' sentence structure, when a noun is followed by three adjectives sombre, resonant and obscure. This, however, is a one-sided view of Conrad's writerly qualities, intellectual insight and political clarity. He is supremely and painfully succinct in his observations and critique. Take the exchange between Kayerts and Carlier after they discover that Makola, effectively the African manager of their Company trading station, has sold off all the other hired African hands in

exchange for ivory. Briefly dubious about the propriety of
actually going along with this advantageous trade, Carlier says:

> 'This is a funny country. What will you do now?'
> 'We can't touch it, of course,' said Kayerts.
> 'Of course not,' assented Carlier.
> 'Slavery is an awful thing,' stammered out Kayerts in an unsteady
> voice.
> 'Frightful – the sufferings,' grunted Carlier, with conviction.
> They believed their words. Everybody shows a respectful defer-
> ence to certain sounds that he and his fellows can make. (80–1)

There is a masterly poise of style, even a sad grim humour, in
the choice of the verbs *assented*, *stammered*, *grunted*. This
casual exchange hovers between the comedy of Laurel and
Hardy and, in its everyday cliché-ridden absurdity, Samuel
Beckett's Vladimir and Estragon. Like the latter, Kayerts and
Carlier are also forever waiting for a returning god, the Managing Director of the Great Civilising Company. The banalities
of horror are registered, but the implications are not forced on
the reader. What follows from the omniscient narrator is at
once a critique of language and of political ethics. With an
urgency of authorial voice, a devastating indictment is made of
our capacity to hide within clichés our ignorance of others' real
pain:

> We talk with indignation or enthusiasm; we talk about oppression,
> cruelty, crime, devotion, self-sacrifice, virtue, and we know nothing
> real beyond the words. Nobody knows what suffering or sacrifice
> mean – except, perhaps, the victims of the mysterious purpose of
> these illusions. (81)

Much of the critical shock-effect in these stories comes, for
the reader, from the rhythms of sentences which culminate in
short, summary executions of judgement. The long-awaited
return of the Managing Director of the Great Civilising Company, bringing supplies to Kayerts and Carlier, is heralded by
estranging, impressionistically rendered noise:

> A shriek inhuman, vibrating and sudden, pierced like a sharp dart
> the white shroud of that land of sorrow. Three short, impatient
> screeches followed, and then, for a time, the fog-wreaths rolled on,
> undisturbed, through a formidable silence. Then many more shrieks,

rapid and piercing, like the yells of some exasperated and ruthless creature, rent the air. Progress was calling to Kayerts from the river. Progress and civilisation and all the virtues. (88)

Or take 'The Idiots', where the Breton farmer Jean-Pierre Baca- dou decides to marry Susan and raise a family of sons, who, he hopes, will one day inherit his farm. After first fathering twin 'idiot' boys, and then a third idiot son, Bacadou, though a fervent republican and anti-cleric, makes his peace with the local Catholic priest in the hope that this will bless his wife's third pregnancy. She gives birth – to a girl, and 'The child turned out an idiot too' (53). If not funny, the sentence is brutalist and short, coming as it does a few paragraphs after this other sentence, whose grim ironies the reader is left to work out: 'The world is to the young' (48).

In his introduction to *Letters from Conrad, 1895 to 1924*, Edward Garnett neatly captures the tonal complexity at play in Conrad's writing, whether in fiction or letters:

He was so perfect an artist in the expression of his moods and feelings that it needed a fine ear to seize the blended shapes of friendly derision, flattery, self-depreciation, sardonic criticism and affection in his tone. And so with his early letters, many of which show a wonderful chameleon-like quality [. . .] one must guard oneself against taking his moods, his flatteries, his cries of distress [. . .] either too absolutely or too lightly.[16]

This complexity can be felt in Conrad's response to Garnett's criticism of the story in the collection that gave him the greatest creative problems:

The Return! And you – you are jealous! Of what? The subject is yours as much as it has ever been. The work is vile – or else good. I don't know. I can't know. But I swear to you that I won't alter a line – a word – not a comma – for you. There! And this for the reason that I have a physical horror of that story. I simply won't look at it any more. It has embittered five months of my life. I hate it.
Now, as to selling the odious thing. It has 23,000 words – who would take it?[17]

There is something of the self-dramatising here. Indeed there is a performed, blasé rejection of his own artistic achievements in many of the more personal pronouncements made in his letters. Beneath them is a founded confidence in his chosen artistic project. Yet, with a sort of double bluff, the off-hand dismissals reveal a genuine anxiety about taking on, so relatively late in life, the peculiarly precarious profession of writer.

When the German poet Hölderlin asks, 'To what end be a poet in such needy times?', the question is, as such questions probably always have been, a powerful political and aesthetic one.[18] It deserves considered and multifarious answers. It would certainly have meant confronting the aesthetic, moral and metaphysical problems of which a late nineteenth-century sensibility such as Conrad's was fully aware: pessimistic arguments about the 'degeneration' of culture, about civilisation and its discontents, about scientific views even predicting the dying of the sun. How do you write poetry about the world, when the world weighs so heavy?[19] But more immediately for Conrad came the matter of having given up his profession as a maritime captain to pursue a writerly career. It is hard to imagine what such a change of direction of profession means, and words like *trust*, *physical commitment*, and *fortitude* can sound appropriate or melodramatic depending on whether the speaker is facing a death-threatening typhoon or the writing of a long short story. But it was in such idioms that in his letters Conrad described this challenging change of life as he wrote his tales.

His working title for what was to become *Tales of Unrest* was *Outpost of Progress and Other Stories*. 'Nice and proper,' Conrad thought it sounded; certainly better than another possibility he toyed with, *Idiots and Other Stories*.[20] Perhaps *The Return and Other Stories* would have served as well – not to give 'The Return' more emphasis (although it has been severely underrated by some critics), but rather to signal a recurrent and powerful motif both of these stories and of Conrad's major novels. All are chiefly based on the hope, or fear, of a return. In this respect, the early tales give us a foretaste of the later works not only in their topologies but more importantly in their aesthetic and psychological preoccupations. Turns and turning-points are, of course, the stuff of narrative, of novels and drama: a false identity revealed; a crisis (the word in Greek means 'turning') of recognition; a moral challenge which needs (or fails) to be met. But the turns and the returns which Conrad's stories treat are more like a haunting: the coming back again, and again, of what had been unresolved, forgotten or ignored, or denied and repressed. Such haunting is linked to a guilty need obsessively to repeat (in fact or in narration) some unresolved matter. Jim's jumping overboard in *Lord Jim* provides the obvious example, but we may also recall that the Marlow of *Heart of Darkness* becomes truly interested in Kurtz (the central, perplexing character in that novel) when, overhearing gossip about him, Marlow pictures Kurtz *turning back* up-river, away from the Central Station – turning his back, so to speak, on the civilisation and the economy it represents.

Coming some twenty years before Sigmund Freud wrote what was to become a powerfully influential essay on 'Das Unheimliche' ('The Uncanny'), the 'unrest' of these tales, particularly that of 'Karain: A Memory' and 'The Idiots', is very close to Freud's notion.[21] Conceptualised as the 'return of the repressed', Freud's idea of a haunting uncanny resonates with the anxiety-within-the-familiar dealt with in Conrad's stories. 'Das Unheimliche' literally means the *negation* of the homely and the familiar. In 'Karain: A Memory' there is a double haunting. Karain, a Malay prince, is haunted by the memory of murdering his best friend, whose ghost then returns to torment him. For a while Karain is protected from his own fears by the guarding presence of an old shamanic manservant. On *his* death, Karain's guilty fear returns and he can find release only in the compulsive retelling of his story to his white listeners. But the talking is no talking cure. Karain needs a new mythic token to protect himself. He finds the desired mythological effect in theatrical ceremony when his English sailor friends hand over to him a Jubilee silver sixpence bearing Queen Victoria's image.

It is easy to construe Conrad as setting up the 'simple' Eastern myth-believer against the superior rationality of the Westerners, as critics commonly have done. But should we be so complacent? The ironies of the passage reveal that the English are no less bound to magic tokens or theatricality than Karain. Do we not also go along with the theatricality of regal crownings? More to the point, it is the English sailors who carry unusable coins, mementoes and bits of ribbon into the wilderness. Finally, at an even more sceptical level, we might say that the circulation of currency, the very form of modern capitalist society, is hardly less ritualised or mythical. It, too, is phantasmagoric, relying on sheer belief, confidence in the coinage, which as a token, a sign, always carries a mythic power beyond its actual physical worth. That the silver coin is – fraudulently – gilded adds to the ironies. Once again, Conrad's demythologising strategies run deep.[22]

The idea of different kinds of history (moral, political, economic, sexual) returning and weighing on the present, and thus on the future, is a potent one in Conrad's writing, beyond and in addition to the level of the representing of individual psychology. On the surface, at plot level, the tales frequently posit protagonists empowered to command the future: in furthering colonial progress in Africa ('An Outpost of Progress'), farming rich fields in Brittany ('The Idiots'), or controlling imperial capital in the stockmarkets of London ('The Return'). These stories are initially coloured by a pervading confidence in future achievement, in advance and progress. But the projected future turns out to be anchored in a past, or in the recalcitrant facts of the present which will not relinquish it and which finally thwart its fulfilment. A Nietzschean model of genealogy and its discontents – what we might paradoxically call the forward pressure of history – determines these tales. In 'The Idiots' murder and suicide end Bacadou's future dreams when his children inherit not the family farm but poor family genes. The 'progress' in 'An Outpost of Progress' is revealed ironically to be a return to a more atavistic, 'primitive' state. Yet to confound late Victorian stereotypes of 'civilised' and 'primitive' even further, it is the family-loving, hard-working, pragmatic African Makola who most embodies 'Victorian' standards.

The opening paragraph of 'The Return' epitomises this movement of futurity and its illusions. It is a story which, in a far from simply naturalistic way, exploits images from the everyday urban world of modern London to reveal its bourgeois beastliness.[23] It is peopled by objects – and 'peopled' is precisely the right term. In an expressionistic manner, objects take on the attributes of human forms and psychologies, and humans are converted into things. Underground trains disgorge their rush-hour occupants. The mirrors in an upper-middle-class bedroom, in sudden and horrifying mimicry, turn their master into a puppet, reproducing him in all his economic, political and social uniformity. In a letter about the publication of 'The Return', Conrad clearly conveys this sense of human figures trapped in a nightmarish, inescapable vortex:

Inevitableness is the only certitude, it is the very essence of life – as it is of dreams. A picture of life is saved from failure by the merciless vividness of detail. Like a dream it must be startling, undeniable, absurd and appalling. Like a dream it may be ludicrous or tragic and like a dream pitiless and inevitable; a thing monstrous or sweet from which You cannot escape. Our captivity within the incomprehensible logic of accident is the only fact of the universe. From that reality flows deception and inspiration, error and faith, egoism and sacrifice, love and hate. (*CLJC* vol. 1, p. 303)

Another letter about 'The Return' reveals Conrad fluctuating between extreme self-doubt about his artistic achievement and a sublime sense of loyalty to his own writerly convictions.

I am hoist on my own petard. My dear fellow what I aimed at was just to produce the effect of cold water in every one of my man's speeches. I swear to you that was my intention. I wanted to produce the effect of insincerity, or artificiality. Yes! I wanted the reader to *see him think* and then to hear *him speak* – and shudder. The whole point of the joke is there. I wanted the truth to be first dimly seen through the fabulous untruth of that man's convictions – of his idea of life – and then to make its way out with a rush at the end. But if I have to explain that to you – to You! – then I've egregiously failed. I've tried with all my might to avoid just these trivialities of rage and distraction which you judge necessary to the true picture. I counted it a virtue and lo and behold! You say it is a sin. Well! Never more! It is evident that my fate is to be descriptive and descriptive only. There are things I *must* leave alone. (*CLJC* vol. 1, p. 387)

The letters of this period (the late 1890s) are consistently marked by Conrad's almost casual self-deprecation. Of 'Karain: A Memory', one of the finest and most complex stories in the collection, he writes: 'I am heartily ashamed of [it].'[24] Of 'The Lagoon' he complains that 'everything seems so abominably stupid'.[25] Yet, despite his constantly reiterated complaints of failure at his new-found profession, Conrad also evinces a clear conviction about his task: 'After all ['The Idiots'] is my work. The only lasting thing in the world. People die – affections die – all passes – but a man's work remains with him to the last.'[26] Conrad later concurs with Garnett's judgement that 'The Return' fails as a story, in part because of 'the unreality of the dialogue', which results in the faulty 'logic of melodrama'. But this judgement undervalues the powerfully revealed depths that a certain rendering of surface exposes. In a letter to the novelist John Galsworthy (whom Conrad first met while sailing as first officer from Australia, and who was to remain a close and life-long friend), Conrad suggests that the writer's business is not 'to invent depths – to invent depths is not art either' because 'most things and most natures have nothing but a surface'. What amounts to an aesthetics of surface is being proposed: 'The force of the book is in its fidelity to the surface of life – to the surface of events – to the surface of things and ideas. Now this is not being shallow.'[27] This sounds startlingly like the aesthetics of Oscar Wilde, perhaps an unlikely bedfellow for Conrad.[28] Wilde's argument, generally put, is that only super-ficial people fail to recognise the depths of superficiality. This comes close to Conrad's point in a letter to Cunninghame Graham, when he describes his attempt in *Heart of Darkness* to convey the truth of his vision by means of 'secondary notions' rather than the big theme.

Much of Conrad's strength lies in the detail, in the capturing of a carefully imagined moment which reveals much more than it tells. His style is not in any straightforward way merely 'descriptive', although his early writing has been blamed (or praised) for being just that. A fine balance of irony and psycho-logical revelation is captured in moments such as that in 'The Return' when Alvan Hervey, stockbroker and bourgeois cultural patron, first catches sight of the letter his wife has left for him. The letter will tell him she is leaving him for another man, the artistic publisher he has been financing. 'He muttered, "How very odd," and felt annoyed. [. . .] That she should write to him at all, when she knew he would be home for dinner, was perfectly ridiculous [. . .]'. (96) His reaction painfully captures the trivialy domestic, the customary response to the uncustom-ary, the homely reaction that comes just before a hurricane hits.

Hervey's (unnamed) wife chooses to leave him for another man, then goes back on her choice, so choosing not to choose. The anonymity and voicelessness that Conrad assigns to her may signal silently her resistance to any forced choice. Hervey then leaves – never to return. Properly speaking, there can be no choice without renunciation;[29] but perhaps the problem of real choice is even more complicated. Conrad, being both idealist and sceptic, identifies this complexity. In a moral world, moral

choices should *mean* something; but modern commodity culture
– that is, the bourgeois commercial world Alvan Hervey and his
wife inhabit – proposes choice without renunciation. 'The gospel
of the beastly bourgeois' is what Conrad calls its ethics.[30] In
many of Conrad's narratives, characters are not aware that they
are choosing: the choice is hardly made. Or if it is made, it is
made in (at best) a twilight of knowledge. The ethical, political
or psychological returns of these half-choices often come in the
form of hauntings – the Eternal Return with a vengeance, so to
speak.

The Author's Note to *Tales of Unrest* was written for the
Collected Edition some twenty-one years after Conrad first
published the volume. There is something doubled and haunting
about this essay, too. With all the apparent authenticity of
autobiographical fact, it is a literary performance in its own
right. As with Conrad's fictional writing, nothing in it is quite
straightforwardly true.[31] Casually conversational, adopting a
throwaway modesty, Conrad gives with one hand and takes
away with the other. It is a tricky performance. Unlike Henry
James's prefaces, Conrad's late prefaces are self-consciously
untheoretical.[32] But they are certainly self-fashioning. Sometimes
anecdotal, sometimes aphoristic ('We cannot escape from ourselves'), Conrad uses his prefaces to create for himself a writerly
persona and a literary history – thus initiating later critics think
they themselves discover. Continuity and narrative development
are crucial to this construed history. His writerly life, he implies,
comes in 'phases', for it has a narrative shape. Thus with 'The
Lagoon', his 'Malay phase' is over. For the continuity of his
career, Conrad provides in the Author's Note a convenient
symbol: the very pen he has used in writing his tales. He claims
to treasure it, superstitiously, rather as Karain treasures his
sixpence; it is a precious icon of his singular creative intent.
However, as in the doubling and returns of dreams and the
uncanny, there then comes an ironic twist. Conrad plays a
gentle trick on the reader. He confounds his own sentimental
historical account by revealing the discovery of two *identical*
pens – when writerly authenticity actually requires and permits
only one. What we and ostensibly he had been taking as the
singular truth gets re-written. Appropriately, both pens then get
thrown away in a flower bed, perhaps (we may speculate) to be

dug up again a couple of centuries later, material for yet another fictional archaeology. 'Another' – for Conrad has already dug them up once in writing his Author's Note. A writer of fiction, he is not unwise in the ways of creating convincing realities and convincing symbols. He talks in connection with 'The Return' of 'writing with both hands at once'. 'A left-handed production' is the way he describes the story, whose features 'produce a sinister effect'. The balanced ambiguities and uncertainties of his fiction, that is, return to haunt us in his Note. They are left finally for the reader to assess.

Conrad's *Tales of Unrest* represents a quality of artistic intelligence, aim and achievement that few modern writers can claim for their early work. The stories in this volume signal the strengths and the direction of Conrad's later great and more famous works. But they do more than that. They engage the reader in a complex and intense confrontation with a quality of experience, which in different ways carries the burdens of history and the promises of modernity – the dreams of progress and its corruption, the play of ritual against rationality, the force of memory over desire, and the drive of material possession against the self-possession of maturity.

ANTHONY FOTHERGILL

References

1. See, for example, Thomas Moser, *Joseph Conrad: Achievement and Decline* (1957; (repr. Hamden, Conn.: Archon Books, 1966), an extremely influential critical work, which traces a trajectory for Conrad's career as novelist from works of 'apprenticeship' (as he describes *Tales of Unrest*), through the creativity of the major novels, into later decline. 'Conrad wrote during the early period a number of short stories that are frankly potboilers' (50), Moser declares. See also, below, my chapter on 'Conrad and his Critics'.
2. Indispensable reading for early critical reviews of Conrad is to be found in *Conrad: The Critical Heritage*, ed. Norman Sherry (London and Boston: Routledge & Kegan Paul, 1973).
3. In January 1899, *Tales of Unrest* was declared to be one of the most promising books of the year by *The Academy*, and Conrad was 'crowned' with an award of fifty guineas, a sum not to be

sniffed at in 1898. In his extremely helpful *A Conrad Chronology* (London: Macmillan, 1989), p. xvii, Owen Knowles points out this would have been worth several hundred pounds. Zdzisław Najder has commented that Conrad's maid earned no more than twenty pounds per annum.

4. See *Letters from Conrad, 1895 to 1924*, ed. Edward Garnett, with introduction and notes (London: Nonesuch, 1928); and *The Collected Letters of Joseph Conrad*, eds. Frederick R. Karl and Laurence Davies (Cambridge: Cambridge University Press, 1983–), esp. Vols. 1 and 2 – henceforth referred to as *CLJC*. For a fuller account of the publishing history of the short stories, see J. D. Gordan, *Joseph Conrad: The Making of a Novelist* (Cambridge, Mass.: Harvard University Press, 1940), and Lawrence Graver, *Conrad's Short Fiction* (Berkeley: University of California Press, 1969), esp. Chapters 1 and 2.

5. Conrad so refers to 'Karain', which he wrote for *Blackwood's* magazine. See the letter to R. Cunninghame Graham, 14 April 1898 (*CLJC* vol. 2, p. 57).

6. See Watts's introduction to *Heart of Darkness and Other Tales* (Oxford: Oxford University Press, World's Classics, 1990), pp. viii–xii. His edition also provides extensive and illuminating notes on 'An Outpost of Progress' and 'Karain', to which I am indebted.

7. In the same volume in which 'An Outpost of Progress' appeared, *Cosmopolis* published edited letters of Nietzsche and Turgenev (in French) and articles by Lou Andreas-Salomé (in German). It should also be added that there were enthusiastic articles on 'The Reign of Queen Victoria', the Jubilee celebrations and the successes of British gunboat diplomacy.

8. The distinction between a playfully complex dialogic mode of writing, where competing voices never quite 'settle', and the uniformly monologic is drawn from the writing of the Russian critic Bakhtin. The quotation is from B. S. Johnson's fine (short) novel *Christie Malry's Own Double Entry* (London: Quartet, 1972, p. 106) in which the hero, in a chat with his author, agrees that the thousand-page blockbuster novel is anachronistic.

9. See *Conrad Under Familial Eyes*, ed. Z. Najder (Cambridge: Cambridge University Press, 1983), p. 141.

10. Joseph Conrad, *A Personal Record* (New York: Doubleday, Page, 1912), p. 194.

11. *The Secret Agent* (London: Methuen, 1907), 166. Compare this to

the statement made in the Author's Note to *Tales of Unrest*: 'We cannot escape from ourselves' (156).

12. For the early Polish debate around Conrad, see Andrzej Busza, 'Conrad's Polish Literary Background and Some Illustrations of the Influence of Polish Literature on his Work', *Antemurale*, 10 (1966) pp. 109–255. For later critics see, for example, Moser, pp. 19–22.

13. For a fuller argument, see my 'Conrad's "Nightmarish Meanings": Betraying the Tradition in *Nostromo* and *Under Western Eyes*' in *L'Epoque Conradienne*, 18 (1992) pp. 11–24.

14. The critique, in this story, of a failed Christianity and its links to and justification of European colonialism is figured in the recurrent motif of the toppling cross, from which, in grotesque parody of the Crucifixion, Kayerts hangs himself.

15. This phrase was famously coined by F. R. Leavis in his (otherwise laudatory) critique of Conrad, whom Leavis regards as one of the three members of *The Great Tradition* (1948; repr. Harmondsworth: Penguin, 1972). See especially 204–7.

16. See Garnett, op. cit., xxv.

17. *CLJC* vol. 1, p. 386. The editors' note, adds, 'No one would take it.' The story came out only within the collection.

18. Hölderlin, 'Brot und Wein', *Werke und Briefe* (Frankfurt: Insel, 1969), vol. 1, p. 118.

19. A very good general introduction to Conrad, and particularly this aspect of the prevailing culture, can be found in Cedric Watts, *A Preface to Conrad*, 2nd ed. (London: Longman, 1993).

20. See his letter to Edward Garnett, 14 August 1896 (*CLJC* vol. 1, p. 300).

21. See Sigmund Freud, 'The Uncanny', Penguin Freud Library (Harmondsworth: Penguin, 1990), vol. 14, p. 272 ff.

22. The complexities of such Western myths and 'material interests' are profoundly pursued in *Nostromo*. For an interesting recent treatment of the intersection of money and fictionality, see Kevin Barry, 'Paper Money and English Romanticism', *Times Literary Supplement* (21 February 1997), pp. 14–16. For the guilty Jubilee silver sixpence, see the note to 'Karain' below.

23. See Conrad's letter to Garnett, 11 October 1897 (*CLJC* vol. 1, p. 393).

24. Letter to Edward Garnett, 13 February 1897 (*CLJC* vol. 1, p. 339).

25. Letter to Garnett, 5 August 1896 (*CLJC* vol. 1, p. 297).

26. Letter to T. Fisher Unwin, 22 July 1896 (*CLJC* vol. 1, p. 293).

27. Letter of 16 January 1898 (*CLJC* vol. 2, p. 22).

28. Wilde and Conrad both lived in a period of radical cultural and political change, which they experienced as outsiders. They had in common, as well as shared acquaintances, a colonial and colonised experience; the awareness of speaking literally or figuratively in a foreign language; an 'aristocratic' disdain for the merely bourgeois; an interest in – and simultaneous scepticism towards – an individualist anarchist political alternative; and a keen cosmopolitan awareness of the ideas surrounding *fin de siècle* decadence. For more on these aspects of Wilde, see my introduction to *Oscar Wilde: Plays, Prose Writings and Poems* (London: Everyman, 1996). See also Hans Mayer, *Outsiders* (Cambridge, Mass.: MIT, 1982) and his afterword to a German translation of *The Secret Agent* (Munich: C. H. Beck, 1987).

29. See Gabriel Josipovici, 'Death of the Word' in *Four Stories* (London: Menard, 1977): 'That is the pathos of memory and of the sentimentality it engenders, which is the belief that one can have choice without renunciation' (21).

30. See note 20 above.

31. Conrad's autobiographical account is by no means always accurate: he mistakes the chronology of his writing of the stories for instance.

32. In his introduction to *Letters from Conrad*, Garnett notes that Conrad had *not*, as one critic argued, ' "thrashed out for himself theories and convictions on the art of fiction through years of concentrated lonely thoughts at sea." Conrad worked by intuition after a preliminary meditation, just as his criticism of other men's work was intuitive and not the fruit of considered theory [. . .] He never theorized about it' (xxix–xxx). Despite this assertion, we need to remember that theory takes many forms, sometimes moving in mysterious ways. We cannot take Conrad's or Garnett's words as the truth about Conrad and theory.

NOTE ON THE TEXT

For this Everyman edition of *Tales of Unrest*, I have followed
the first British edition, published by T. Fisher Unwin (London,
1898). *Tales* was also published in the same year by Scribner's
(New York) and by Tauchnitz (Leipzig), in its famous British
Authors series. I have compared the first edition with the first
magazine publications of the tales where these exist, with the
first collected editions of Conrad's works in 1923 by Doubleday,
Page (New York) and Dent (London), and Dent's later Collected
Edition (London, 1947). In the latter, *Tales of Unrest* appeared
in a volume along with *Almayer's Folly*. J. H. Stape and Gordon
Lindstrand have convincingly argued that the plates for the
Doubleday edition were used for the Dent editions. The
Author's Note follows that which was published with the
Doubleday, Page Collected Edition (1923).

As other scholars commenting on the publication history of
Tales of Unrest have noted, relatively few changes were made
from serial publication to the first edition, or from the first edition
to the collected edition.[1] It is generally agreed that Conrad
regarded the serial versions of these tales as polished enough to go
virtually unchanged into their book publications. When there are
interesting verbal changes between the magazine publication and
the first book edition, I have commented on them in my notes.
Apparent errors in the first edition which have been corrected for
the later Collected Editions have been silently amended in the
body of the present text, but the changes are noted below.

This Everyman text is editorially conservative; changes have
been limited to the correction of clear errors. The text does,
however, follow the conventional Everyman house style, which
sometimes alters the style of punctuation adopted by T. Fisher

---

[1] For details see, George Whiting, 'Conrad's Revisions of Six Stories', *PMLA*,
XLVIII (1933), pp. 552–7, and Elmer A. Ordoñez, *The Early Joseph Conrad*
(Quezon City: University of the Philippines Press, 1969), esp. Chap. 3.

Unwin. With the exception of the few emendations listed, this Everyman text gives the reader an accurate sense of the original, even when awkwardnesses of expression, grammar or punctuation are perceptible. Sometimes, when the Collected Edition has not changed a mispelling or has remained internally inconsistent (e.g. 'pier-glass' and 'pier glass' both occur in 'The Return'), I have kept the inconsistencies.

Other occasional stylistic idiosyncrasies – particularly Gallicisms or unconventional word-order – have been preserved. Seeing the odd blemish along with the brilliance allows us to appreciate Conrad's authentic voice and the remarkable fluency of language and imagination which he was already commanding at this early stage in his writing career.

Textual Emendations

Page numbers to the emendations refer to this Everyman edition; the 1898 version is in square brackets. An asterisk in the text indicates an editorial note.

'Karain: A Memory':

p. 12, 42	cortège	[cortége]
p. 20	hills.	[hills,]
p. 32	in the forest.	[in the forest?]
p. 41	beach. 'I	[beach. I]

'The Idiots':

p. 45	'Ah! There's	['Ah! there's]
p. 53	quarry.	[quarry,]
p. 54	near by	[near-by]
p. 58	Madame!'	[madame!']
p. 64	you wait. . . .	[You wait. . . .]

'An Outpost of Progress':

p. 85	he could	[he. could]

'The Return':

p. 92	again. The	[again The]
p. 100	real feelings, of	[real feelings of]
p. 106	open-mouthed	[openmouthed]
p. 109	someone	[some-one]
p. 110, 120	breadth	[breath]
p. 123	'Words?	[Words?]

'Author's Note':

p. 158	in me	[in the]

TALES OF UNREST

'Be it thy course to busy giddy minds
With foreign quarrels.'

SHAKESPEARE

To

For the sake of
old days

Karain: A Memory

I

We knew him in those unprotected days when we were content to hold in our hands our lives and our property. None of us, I believe, has any property now, and I hear that many, negligently, have lost their lives; but I am sure that the few who survive are not yet so dim-eyed as to miss in the befogged respectability of their newspapers the intelligence of various native risings in the Eastern Archipelago.* Sunshine gleams between the lines of those short paragraphs – sunshine and the glitter of the sea. A strange name wakes up memories; the printed words scent the smoky atmosphere of to-day faintly, with the subtle and penetrating perfume as of land breezes breathing through the starlight of bygone nights; a signal fire gleams like a jewel on the high brow of a sombre cliff; great trees, the advanced sentries of immense forests, stand watchful and still over sleeping stretches of open water; a line of white surf thunders on an empty beach, the shallow water foams on the reefs; and green islets scattered through the calm of noonday lie upon the level of a polished sea, like a handful of emeralds on a buckler of steel.

There are faces too – faces dark, truculent, and smiling; the frank audacious faces of men barefooted, well armed and noiseless. They thronged the narrow length of our schooner's decks with their ornamented and barbarous crowd, with the variegated colours of checkered sarongs, red turbans, white jackets, embroideries; with the gleam of scabbards, gold rings, charms, armlets, lance blades, and jewelled handles of their weapons. They had an independent bearing, resolute eyes, a restrained manner; and we seem yet to hear their soft voices speaking of battles, travels, and escapes; boasting with composure, joking quietly; sometimes in well-bred murmurs extolling their own valour, our generosity; or celebrating with loyal enthusiasm the virtues of their ruler. We remember the faces, the eyes, the voices, we see again the gleam of silk and metal; the murmuring stir of that crowd, brilliant, festive, and martial;

and we seem to feel the touch of friendly brown hands that, after one short grasp, return to rest on a chased hilt. They were Karain's* people – a devoted following. Their movements hung on his lips; they read their thoughts in his eyes; he murmured to them nonchalantly of life and death, and they accepted his words humbly, like gifts of fate. They were all free men, and when speaking to him said, 'Your slave.' On his passage voices died out as though he had walked guarded by silence; awed whispers followed him. They called him their war-chief. He was the ruler of three villages on a narrow plain; the master of an insignificant foothold on the earth – of a conquered foothold that, shaped like a young moon, lay ignored between the hills and the sea.

From the deck of our schooner, anchored in the middle of the bay,* he indicated by a theatrical sweep of his arm along the jagged outline of the hills the whole of his domain; and the ample movement seemed to drive back its limits, augmenting it suddenly into something so immense and vague that for a moment it appeared to be bounded only by the sky. And really, looking at that place, landlocked from the sea and shut off from the land by the precipitous slopes of mountains, it was difficult to believe in the existence of any neighbourhood. It was still, complete, unknown, and full of a life that went on stealthily with a troubling effect of solitude; of a life that seemed unaccountably empty of anything that would stir the thought, touch the heart, give a hint of the ominous sequence of days. It appeared to us a land without memories, regrets, and hopes; a land where nothing could survive the coming of the night, and where each sunrise, like a dazzling act of special creation, was disconnected from the eve and the morrow.

Karain swept his hand over it. 'All mine!' He struck the deck with his long staff; the gold head flashed like a falling star; very close behind him a silent old fellow in a richly embroidered black jacket alone of all the Malays around did not follow the masterful gesture with a look. He did not even lift his eyelids. He bowed his head behind his master, and without stirring held hilt up over his right shoulder a long blade in a silver scabbard. He was there on duty, but without curiosity, and seemed weary, not with age, but with the possession of a burdensome secret of existence. Karain, heavy and proud, had a lofty pose and breathed calmly. It was our first visit, and we looked about curiously.

The bay was like a bottomless pit of intense light. The circular sheet of water reflected a luminous sky, and the shores enclosing it made an opaque ring of earth floating in an emptiness of transparent blue. The hills, purple and arid, stood out heavily on the sky: their summits seemed to fade into a coloured tremble as of ascending vapour; their steep sides were streaked with the green of narrow ravines; at their foot lay rice-fields, plantain-patches, yellow sands. A torrent wound about like a dropped thread. Clumps of fruit-trees marked the villages; slim palms put their nodding heads together above the low houses; dried palm-leaf roofs shone afar, like roofs of gold, behind the dark colonnades of tree-trunks; figures passed vivid and vanishing; the smoke of fires stood upright above the masses of flowering bushes; bamboo fences glittered, running away in broken lines between the fields. A sudden cry on the shore sounded plaintive in the distance, and ceased abruptly, as if stifled in the down-pour of sunshine; a puff of breeze made a flash of darkness on the smooth water, touched our faces, and became forgotten. Nothing moved. The sun blazed down into a shadowless hollow of colours and stillness.

It was the stage where, dressed splendidly for his part, he strutted, incomparably dignified, made important by the power he had to awaken an absurd expectation of something heroic going to take place – a burst of action or song – upon the vibrating tone of a wonderful sunshine. He was ornate and disturbing, for one could not imagine what depth of horrible void such an elaborate front could be worthy to hide. He was not masked – there was too much life in him, and a mask is only a lifeless thing; but he presented himself essentially as an actor, as a human being aggressively disguised. His smallest acts were prepared and unexpected, his speeches grave, his sentences ominous like hints and complicated like arabesques. He was treated with a solemn respect accorded in the irreverent West only to the monarchs of the stage, and he accepted the profound homage with a sustained dignity seen nowhere else but behind the footlights and in the condensed falseness of some grossly tragic situation. It was almost impossible to remember who he was – only a petty chief of a conveniently isolated corner of Mindanao,* where we could in comparative safety break the law against the traffic in firearms and ammunition with the natives. What would happen should one of the moribund

Spanish gun-boats* be suddenly galvanised into a flicker of active life did not trouble us, once we were inside the bay – so completely did it appear out of the reach of a meddling world; and besides, in those days we were imaginative enough to look with a kind of joyous equanimity on any chance there was of being quietly hanged somewhere out of the way of diplomatic remonstrance. As to Karain, nothing could happen to him unless what happens to all – failure and death; but his quality was to appear clothed in the illusion of unavoidable success. He seemed too effective, too necessary there, too much of an essential condition for the existence of his land and his people, to be destroyed by anything short of an earthquake. He summed up his race, his country, the elemental force of ardent life, of tropical nature. He had its luxuriant strength, its fascination; and, like it, he carried the seed of peril within.

In many successive visits we came to know his stage well – the purple semicircle of hills, the slim trees leaning over houses, the yellow sands, the streaming green of ravines. All that had the crude and blended colouring, the appropriateness almost excessive, the suspicious immobility of a painted scene; and it enclosed so perfectly the accomplished acting of his amazing pretences that the rest of the world seemed shut out for ever from the gorgeous spectacle. There could be nothing outside. It was as if the earth had gone on spinning, and had left that crumb of its surface alone in space. He appeared utterly cut off from everything but the sunshine, and that even seemed to be made for him alone. Once when asked what was on the other side of the hills, he said, with a meaning smile, 'Friends and enemies – many enemies; else why should I buy your rifles and powder?' He was always like this – word-perfect in his part, playing up faithfully to the mysteries and certitudes of his surroundings. 'Friends and enemies' – nothing else. It was impalpable and vast. The earth had indeed rolled away from under his land, and he, with his handful of people, stood surrounded by a silent tumult as of contending shades. Certainly no sound came from outside. 'Friends and enemies!' He might have added, 'and memories,' at least as far as he himself was concerned; but he neglected to make that point then. It made itself later on, though; but it was after the daily performance – in the wings, so to speak, and with the lights out. Meantime he filled the stage with barbarous dignity. Some ten years ago he had led his people – a scratch lot of wandering Bugis* – to the conquest of the bay, and now in his august care they had forgotten all the past, and had lost all concern for the future. He gave them wisdom, advice, reward, punishment, life or death, with the same serenity of attitude and voice. He understood irrigation and the art of war – the qualities of weapons and the craft of boat-building. He could conceal his heart; had more endurance; he could swim longer, and steer a canoe better than any of his people; he could shoot straighter, and negotiate more tortuously than any man of his race I knew. He was an adventurer of the sea, an outcast, a ruler – and my very good friend. I wish him a quick death in a stand-up fight, a death in sunshine; for he had known remorse and power, and no man can demand more from life. Day after day he appeared before us, incomparably faithful to the illusions of the stage, and at sunset the night descended upon him quickly, like a falling curtain. The seamed hills became black shadows towering high upon a clear sky; above them the glittering confusion of stars resembled a mad turmoil stilled by a gesture; sounds ceased, men slept, forms vanished – and the reality of the universe alone remained – a marvellous thing of darkness and glimmers.

II

But it was at night that he talked openly, forgetting the exactions of his stage. In the daytime there were affairs to be discussed in state. There were at first between him and me his own splendour, my shabby suspicions, and the scenic landscape that intruded upon the reality of our lives by its motionless fantasy of outline and colour. His followers thronged round him; above his head the broad blades of their spears made a spiked halo of iron points, and they hedged him from humanity by the shimmer of silks, the gleam of weapons, the excited and respectful hum of eager voices. Before sunset he would take leave with ceremony, and go off sitting under a red umbrella, and escorted by a score of boats. All the paddles flashed and struck together with a mighty splash that reverberated loudly in the monumental amphitheatre of hills. A broad stream of dazzling foam trailed behind the flotilla. The canoes appeared very black on the white hiss of water; turbaned heads swayed back and forth; a multitude of arms in crimson and yellow rose and fell with one movement; the spearmen upright in the bows of canoes had variegated sarongs and gleaming shoulders like bronze statues; the muttered strophes of the paddlers' song ended periodically in a plaintive shout. They diminished in the distance; the song ceased; they swarmed on the beach in the long shadows of the western hills. The sunlight lingered on the purple crests, and we could see him leading the way to his stockade, a burly bareheaded figure walking far in advance of a straggling *cortège*, and swinging regularly an ebony staff taller than himself. The darkness deepened fast; torches gleamed fitfully, passing behind bushes; a long hail or two trailed in the silence of the evening; and at last the night stretched its smooth veil over the shore, the lights, and the voices.

Then, just as we were thinking of repose, the watchmen of the schooner would hail a splash of paddles away in the starlit gloom of the bay; a voice would respond in cautious tones, and our serang, putting his head down the open skylight, would inform us without surprise, 'That Rajah, he coming. He here now.' Karain appeared noiselessly in the doorway of the little cabin. He was simplicity itself then; all in white; muffled about his head; for arms only a kriss with a plain buffalo-horn handle,

which he would politely conceal* within a fold of his sarong
before stepping over the threshold. The old sword-bearer's face,
the worn-out and mournful face so covered with wrinkles that
it seemed to look out through the meshes of a fine dark net,
could be seen close above his shoulder. Karain never moved
without that attendant, who stood or squatted close at his back.
He had a dislike of an open space behind him. It was more than
a dislike – it resembled fear, a nervous preoccupation of what
went on where he could not see. This, in view of the evident
and fierce loyalty that surrounded him, was inexplicable. He
was there alone in the midst of devoted men; he was safe from
neighbourly ambushes, from fraternal ambitions; and yet more
than one of our visitors had assured us that their ruler could
not bear to be alone. They said, 'Even when he eats and sleeps
there is always one on the watch near him who has strength
and weapons.' There was indeed always one near him, though
our informants had no conception of that watcher's strength
and weapons, which were both shadowy and terrible. We knew,
but only later on, when we had heard the story. Meantime we
noticed that, even during the most important interviews, Karain
would often give a start, and interrupting his discourse, would
sweep his arm back with a sudden movement, to feel whether
the old fellow was there. The old fellow, impenetrable and
weary, was always there. He shared his food, his repose, and
his thoughts; he knew his plans, guarded his secrets; and,
impassive behind his master's agitation, without stirring the
least bit, murmured above his head in a soothing tone some
words difficult to catch.

It was only on board the schooner, when surrounded by
white faces, by unfamiliar sights and sounds, that Karain seemed
to forget the strange obsession that wound like a black thread
through the gorgeous pomp of his public life. At night we
treated him in a free and easy manner, which just stopped short
of slapping him on the back, for there are liberties one must not
take with a Malay. He said himself that on such occasions he
was only a private gentleman coming to see other gentlemen
whom he supposed as well born as himself. I fancy that to the
last he believed us to be emissaries of Government, darkly
official persons furthering by our illegal traffic some dark
scheme of high statecraft. Our denials and protestations were
unavailing. He only smiled with discreet politeness and inquired

about the Queen. Every visit began with that inquiry; he was insatiable of details; he was fascinated by the holder of a sceptre the shadow of which, stretching from the westward over the earth and over the seas, passed far beyond his own hand's-breadth of conquered land. He multiplied questions; he could never know enough of the Monarch of whom he spoke with wonder and chivalrous respect – with a kind of affectionate awe! Afterwards, when we had learned that he was the son of a woman who had many years ago ruled a small Bugis state,* we came to suspect that the memory of his mother (of whom he spoke with enthusiasm) mingled somehow in his mind with the image he tried to form for himself of the far-off Queen whom he called Great, Invincible, Pious, and Fortunate. We had to invent details at last to satisfy his craving curiosity; and our loyalty must be pardoned, for we tried to make them fit for his august and resplendent ideal. We talked. The night slipped over us, over the still schooner, over the sleeping land, and over the sleepless sea that thundered amongst the reefs outside the bay. His paddlers, two trustworthy men, slept in the canoe at the foot of our side-ladder. The old confidant, relieved from duty, dozed on his heels, with his back against the companion-doorway; and Karain sat squarely in the ship's wooden arm-chair, under the slight sway of the cabin lamp, a cheroot between his dark fingers, and a glass of lemonade before him. He was amused by the fizz of the thing, but after a sip or two would let it get flat, and with a courteous wave of his hand ask for a fresh bottle. He decimated our slender stock; but we did not begrudge it to him, for, when he began, he talked well. He must have been a great Bugis dandy in his time, for even then (and when we knew him he was no longer young) his splendour was spotlessly neat, and he dyed his hair a light shade of brown. The quiet dignity of his bearing transformed the dim-lit cuddy of the schooner into an audience-hall. He talked of inter-island politics with an ironic and melancholy shrewdness. He had travelled much, suffered not a little, intrigued, fought. He knew native Courts, European Settlements, the forests, the sea, and, as he said himself, had spoken in his time to many great men. He liked to talk with me because I had known some of these men: he seemed to think that I could understand him, and, with a fine confidence, assumed that I, at least, could appreciate how much greater he was himself. But he preferred to talk of his native country – a small Bugis state on the island of Celebes. I had visited it some time before, and he asked eagerly for news. As men's names came up in conversation he would say, 'We swam against one another when we were boys;' or, 'We had hunted the deer together – he could use the noose and the spear as well as I.' Now and then his big dreamy eyes would roll restlessly; he frowned or smiled, or he would become pensive, and, staring in silence, would nod slightly for a time at some regretted vision of the past.

His mother had been the ruler of a small semi-independent state on the sea-coast at the head of the Gulf of Boni.* He spoke of her with pride. She had been a woman resolute in affairs of state and of her own heart. After the death of her first husband, undismayed by the turbulent opposition of the chiefs, she married a rich trader, a Korinchi man* of no family. Karain was her son by that second marriage, but his unfortunate descent had apparently nothing to do with his exile. He said nothing as to its cause, though once he let slip with a sigh, 'Ha! my land will not feel any more the weight of my body.' But he related willingly the story of his wanderings, and told us all about the conquest of the bay. Alluding to the people beyond the hills, he would murmur gently, with a careless wave of the hand, 'They came over the hills once to fight us, but those who got away never came again.' He thought for a while, smiling to himself. 'Very few got away,' he added, with proud serenity. He cherished the recollections of his successes; he had an exulting eagerness for endeavour; when he talked, his aspect was warlike, chivalrous, and uplifting. No wonder his people admired him. We saw him once walking in daylight amongst the houses of the settlement. At the doors of huts groups of women turned to look after him, warbling softly, and with gleaming eyes; armed men stood out of the way, submissive and erect; others approached from the side, bending their backs to address him humbly; an old woman stretched out a draped lean arm – 'Blessings on thy head!' she cried from a dark doorway; a fiery-eyed man showed above the low fence of a plantain-patch a streaming face, a bare breast scarred in two places, and bellowed out pantingly after him, 'God give victory to our master!' Karain walked fast, and with firm long strides; he answered greetings right and left by quick piercing glances. Children ran forward between the houses, peeped fearfully round corners; young boys

kept up with him, gliding between bushes: their eyes gleamed
through the dark leaves. The old sword-bearer, shouldering the
silver scabbard, shuffled hastily at his heels with bowed head,
and his eyes on the ground. And in the midst of a great stir they
passed swift and absorbed, like two men hurrying through a
great solitude.

In his council hall he was surrounded by the gravity of armed
chiefs, while two long rows of old headmen dressed in cotton
stuffs squatted on their heels, with idle arms hanging over their
knees. Under the thatch roof supported by smooth columns, of
which each one had cost the life of a straight-stemmed young
palm, the scent of flowering hedges drifted in warm waves. The
sun was sinking. In the open courtyard suppliants walked
through the gate, raising, when yet far off, their joined hands
above bowed heads, and bending low in the bright stream of
sunlight. Young girls, with flowers in their laps, sat under the
wide-spreading boughs of a big tree. The blue smoke of wood
fires spread in a thin mist above the high-pitched roofs of houses
that had glistening walls of woven reeds, and all round them
rough wooden pillars under the sloping eaves. He dispensed
justice in the shade; from a high seat he gave orders, advice,
reproof. Now and then the hum of approbation rose louder,
and idle spearmen that lounged listlessly against the posts,
looking at the girls, would turn their heads slowly. To no man
had been given the shelter of so much respect, confidence, and
awe. Yet at times he would lean forward and appear to listen as
for a far-off note of discord, as if expecting to hear some faint
voice, the sound of light footsteps; or he would start half up in
his seat, as though he had been familiarly touched on the
shoulder. He glanced back with apprehension; his aged follower
whispered inaudibly at his ear; the chiefs turned their eyes away
in silence, for the old wizard, the man who could command
ghosts and send evil spirits against enemies, was speaking low
to their ruler. Around the short stillness of the open place the
trees rustled faintly, the soft laughter of girls playing with the
flowers rose in clear bursts of joyous sound. At the end of
upright spear-shafts the long tufts of dyed horse-hair waved
crimson and filmy in the gust of wind; and beyond the blaze of
hedges the brook of limpid quick water ran invisible and loud
under the drooping grass of the bank, with a great murmur,
passionate and gentle.

After sunset, far across the fields and over the bay, clusters of torches could be seen burning under the high roofs of the council shed. Smoky red flames swayed on high poles, and the fiery blaze flickered over faces, clung to the smooth trunks of palm-trees, kindled bright sparks on the rims of metal dishes standing on fine floor-mats. That obscure adventurer feasted like a king. Small groups of men crouched in tight circles round the wooden platters; brown hands hovered over snowy heaps of rice. Sitting upon a rough couch apart from the others, he leaned on his elbow with inclined head; and near him a youth improvised in a high tone a song that celebrated his valour and wisdom. The singer rocked himself to and fro, rolling frenzied eyes; old women hobbled about with dishes, and men, squatting low, lifted their heads to listen gravely without ceasing to eat. The song of triumph vibrated in the night, and the stanzas rolled out mournful and fiery like the thoughts of a hermit. He silenced it with a sign, 'Enough!' An owl hooted far away, exulting in the delight of deep gloom in dense foliage; overhead lizards ran in the attap thatch, calling softly; the dry leaves of the roof rustled; the rumour of mingled voices grew louder suddenly. After a circular and startled glance, as of a man waking up abruptly to the sense of danger, he would throw himself back, and under the downward gaze of the old sorcerer take up, wide-eyed, the slender thread of his dream. They watched his moods; the swelling rumour of animated talk subsided like a wave on a sloping beach. The chief is pensive. And above the spreading whisper of lowered voices only a light rattle of weapons would be heard, a single louder word distinct and alone, or the grave ring of a big brass tray.

III

For two years at short intervals we visited him. We came to like him, to trust him, almost to admire him. He was plotting and preparing a war with patience, with foresight – with a fidelity to his purpose and with a steadfastness of which I would have thought him racially incapable. He seemed fearless of the future, and in his plans displayed a sagacity that was only limited by his profound ignorance of the rest of the world. We tried to enlighten him, but our attempts to make clear the irresistible nature of the forces which he desired to arrest failed to discourage his eagerness to strike a blow for his own primitive ideas. He did not understand us, and replied by arguments that almost drove one to desperation by their childish shrewdness. He was absurd and unanswerable. Sometimes we caught glimpses of a sombre, glowing fury within him – a brooding and vague sense of wrong, and a concentrated lust of violence which is dangerous in a native. He raved like one inspired. On one occasion, after we had been talking to him late in his campong, he jumped up. A great, clear fire blazed in the grove; lights and shadows danced together between the trees; in the still night bats flitted in and out of the boughs like fluttering flakes of denser darkness. He snatched the sword from the old man, whizzed it out of the scabbard, and thrust the point into the earth. Upon the thin, upright blade the silver hilt, released, swayed before him like something alive. He stepped back a pace, and in a deadened tone spoke fiercely to the vibrating steel: 'If there is virtue in the fire, in the iron, in the hand that forged thee, in the words spoken over thee, in the desire of my heart, and in the wisdom of thy makers, – then we shall be victorious together!' He drew it out, looked along the edge. 'Take,' he said over his shoulder to the old sword-bearer. The other, unmoved on his hams, wiped the point with a corner of his sarong, and returning the weapon to its scabbard, sat nursing it on his knees without a single look upwards. Karain, suddenly very calm, reseated himself with dignity. We gave up remonstrating after this, and let him go his way to an honourable disaster. All we could do for him was to see to it that the powder was good for the money and the rifles serviceable, if old.

But the game was becoming at last too dangerous; and if we,

who had faced it pretty often, thought little of the danger, it was decided for us by some very respectable people sitting safely in counting-houses that the risks were too great, and that only one more trip could be made. After giving in the usual way many misleading hints as to our destination, we slipped away quietly, and after a very quick passage entered the bay. It was early morning, and even before the anchor went to the bottom the schooner was surrounded by boats.

The first thing we heard was that Karain's mysterious sword-bearer had died a few days ago. We did not attach much importance to the news. It was certainly difficult to imagine Karain without his inseparable follower; but the fellow was old, he had never spoken to one of us, we hardly ever had heard the sound of his voice; and we had come to look upon him as upon something inanimate, as a part of our friend's trappings of state – like that sword he had carried, or the fringed red umbrella displayed during an official progress. Karain did not visit us in the afternoon as usual. A message of greeting and a present of fruit and vegetables came off for us before sunset. Our friend paid us like a banker, but treated us like a prince. We sat up for him till midnight. Under the stern awning bearded Jackson jingled an old guitar and sang, with an execrable accent, Spanish love-songs; while young Hollis and I, sprawling on the deck, had a game of chess by the light of a cargo lantern. Karain did not appear. Next day we were busy unloading, and heard that the Rajah was unwell. The expected invitation to visit him ashore did not come. We sent friendly messages, but, fearing to intrude upon some secret council, remained on board. Early on the third day we had landed all the powder and rifles, and also a six-pounder brass gun with its carriage, which we had sub-scribed together for a present to our friend. The afternoon was sultry. Ragged edges of black clouds peeped over the hills, and invisible thunderstorms circled outside, growling like wild beasts. We got the schooner ready for sea, intending to leave next morning at daylight. All day a merciless sun blazed down into the bay, fierce and pale, as if at white heat. Nothing moved on the land. The beach was empty, the villages seemed deserted; the trees far off stood in unstirring clumps, as if painted; the white smoke of some invisible bush-fire spread itself low over the shores of the bay like a settling fog. Late in the day three of Karain's chief men, dressed in their best and armed to the teeth, came off in a canoe, bringing a case of dollars. They were gloomy and languid, and told us they had not seen their Rajah for five days. No one had seen him! We settled all accounts, and after shaking hands in turn and in profound silence, they descended one after another into their boat, and were paddled to the shore, sitting close together, clad in vivid colours, with hanging heads: the gold embroideries of their jackets flashed dazzlingly as they went away gliding on the smooth water, and not one of them looked back once. Before sunset the growling clouds carried with a rush the ridge of hills, and came tumbling down the inner slopes. Everything disappeared; black whirling vapours filled the bay, and in the midst of them the schooner swung here and there in the shifting gusts of wind. A single clap of thunder detonated in the hollow with a violence that seemed capable of bursting into small pieces the ring of high land, and a warm deluge descended. The wind died out. We panted in the close cabin; our faces streamed; the bay outside hissed as if boiling; the water fell in perpendicular shafts as heavy as lead; it swished about the deck, poured off the spars, gurgled, sobbed, splashed, murmured in the blind night. Our lamp burned low. Hollis, stripped to the waist, lay stretched out on the lockers, with closed eyes and motionless like a despoiled corpse; at his head Jackson twanged the guitar, and gasped out in sighs a mournful dirge about hopeless love and eyes like stars. Then we heard startled voices on deck crying in the rain, hurried footsteps overhead, and suddenly Karain appeared in the doorway of the cabin. His bare breast and his face glistened in the light; his sarong, soaked, clung about his legs; he had his sheathed kriss in his left hand; and wisps of wet hair, escaping from under his red kerchief, stuck over his eyes and down his cheeks. He stepped in with a headlong stride and looking over his shoulder like a man pursued. Hollis turned on his side quickly and opened his eyes. Jackson clapped his big hand over the strings and the jingling vibration died suddenly. I stood up.

'We did not hear your boat's hail!' I exclaimed.

'Boat! The man's swum off,' drawled out Hollis from the locker. 'Look at him!'

He breathed heavily, wild-eyed, while we looked at him in silence. Water dripped from him, made a dark pool, and ran crookedly across the cabin floor. We could hear Jackson, who had gone out to drive away our Malay seamen from the

doorway of the companion; he swore menacingly in the patter
of a heavy shower, and there was a great commotion on deck.
The watchmen, scared out of their wits by the glimpse of a
shadowy figure leaping over the rail, straight out of the night as
it were, had alarmed all hands.

Then Jackson, with glittering drops of water on his hair and
beard, came back looking angry, and Hollis, who, being the
youngest of us, assumed an indolent superiority, said without
stirring, 'Give him a dry sarong – give him mine; it's hanging up
in the bathroom.' Karain laid the kriss on the table, hilt inwards,
and murmured a few words in a strangled voice.

'What's that?' asked Hollis, who had not heard.

'He apologises for coming in with a weapon in his hand,' I
said, dazedly.

'Ceremonious beggar. Tell him we forgive a friend . . . on
such a night,' drawled out Hollis. 'What's wrong?'

Karain slipped the dry sarong over his head, dropped the wet
one at his feet, and stepped out of it. I pointed to the wooden
armchair – his armchair. He sat down very straight, said 'Ha!'
in a strong voice; a short shiver shook his broad frame. He
looked over his shoulder uneasily, turned as if to speak to us,
but only stared in a curious blind manner, and again looked
back. Jackson bellowed out, 'Watch well on deck there!' heard
a faint answer from above, and reaching out with his foot
slammed-to the cabin door.

'All right now,' he said.

Karain's lips moved slightly. A vivid flash of lightning made
the two round sternports facing him glimmer like a pair of cruel
and phosphorescent eyes. The flame of the lamp seemed to
wither into brown dust for an instant, and the looking-glass
over the little sideboard leaped out behind his back in a smooth
sheet of livid light. The roll of thunder came near, crashed over
us; the schooner trembled, and the great voice went on, threatening terribly, into the distance. For less than a minute a furious
shower rattled on the decks. Karain looked slowly from face to
face, and then the silence became so profound that we all could
hear distinctly the two chronometers in my cabin ticking along
with unflagging speed against one another.

And we three, strangely moved, could not take our eyes from
him. He had become enigmatical and touching, in virtue of that
mysterious cause that had driven him through the night and

through the thunderstorm to the shelter of the schooner's cuddy. Not one of us doubted that we were looking at a fugitive, incredible as it appeared to us. He was haggard, as though he had not slept for weeks; he had become lean, as though he had not eaten for days. His cheeks were hollow, his eyes sunk, the muscles of his chest and arms twitched slightly as if after an exhausting contest. Of course, it had been a long swim off to the schooner; but his face showed another kind of fatigue, the tormented weariness, the anger and the fear of a struggle against a thought, an idea – against something that cannot be grappled, that never rests – a shadow, a nothing, unconquerable and immortal, that preys upon life. We knew it as though he had shouted it at us. His chest expanded time after time, as if it could not contain the beating of his heart. For a moment he had the power of the possessed – the power to awaken in the beholders wonder, pain, pity, and a fearful near sense of things invisible, of things dark and mute, that surround the loneliness of mankind. His eyes roamed about aimlessly for a moment, then became still. He said with effort—

'I came here . . . I leaped out of my stockade as after a defeat. I ran in the night. The water was black. I left him calling on the edge of black water . . . I left him standing alone on the beach. I swam . . . he called out after me . . . I swam . . .'

He trembled from head to foot, sitting very upright and gazing straight before him. Left whom? Who called? We did not know. We could not understand. I said at all hazards—*

'Be firm.'

The sound of my voice seemed to steady him into a sudden rigidity, but otherwise he took no notice. He seemed to listen, to expect something for a moment, then went on—

'He cannot come here – therefore I sought you. You men with white faces who despise the invisible voices. He cannot abide your unbelief and your strength.'

He was silent for a while, then exclaimed softly—

'Oh! the strength of unbelievers!'

'There's no one here but you – and we three,' said Hollis, quietly. He reclined with his head supported on elbow and did not budge.

'I know,' said Karain. 'He has never followed me here. Was not the wise man ever by my side? But since the old wise man, who knew of my trouble, has died, I have heard the voice every night. I shut myself up – for many days – in the dark. I can hear the sorrowful murmurs of women, the whisper of the wind, of the running waters; the clash of weapons in the hands of faithful men, their footsteps – and his voice! ... Near ... So! In my ear! I felt him near ... His breath passed over my neck. I leaped out without a cry. All about me men slept quietly. I ran to the sea. He ran by my side without footsteps, whispering, whispering old words – whispering into my ear in his old voice. I ran into the sea; I swam off to you, with my kriss between my teeth. I, armed, I fled before a breath – to you. Take me away to your land. The wise old man has died, and with him is gone the power of his words and charms. And I can tell no one. No one. There is no one here faithful enough and wise enough to know. It is only near you, unbelievers, that my trouble fades like a mist under the eye of day.'

He turned to me.

'With you I go!' he cried in a contained voice. 'With you, who know so many of us. I want to leave this land – my people ... and him – there!'

He pointed a shaking finger at random over his shoulder. It was hard for us to bear the intensity of that undisclosed distress. Hollis stared at him hard. I asked gently—

'Where is the danger?'

'Everywhere outside this place,' he answered, mournfully. 'In every place where I am. He waits for me on the paths, under the trees, in the place where I sleep – everywhere but here.'

He looked round the little cabin, at the painted beams, at the tarnished varnish of bulkheads; he looked round as if appealing to all its shabby strangeness, to the disorderly jumble of unfamiliar things that belong to an inconceivable life of stress, of power, of endeavour, of unbelief – to the strong life of white men, which rolls on irresistible and hard on the edge of outer darkness. He stretched out his arms as if to embrace it and us. We waited. The wind and rain had ceased, and the stillness of the night round the schooner was as dumb and complete as if a dead world had been laid to rest in a grave of clouds. We expected him to speak. The necessity within him tore at his lips. There are those who say that a native will not speak to a white man. Error. No man will speak to his master; but to a wanderer and a friend, to him who does not come to teach or to rule, to him who asks for nothing and accepts all things, words are spoken by the camp-fires, in the shared solitude of the sea, in riverside villages, in resting-places surrounded by forests – words are spoken that take no account of race or colour. One heart speaks – another one listens; and the earth, the sea, the sky, the passing wind and the stirring leaf, hear also the futile tale of the burden of life.

He spoke at last. It is impossible to convey the effect of his story. It is undying, it is but a memory, and its vividness cannot be made clear to another mind any more than the vivid emotions of a dream. One must have seen his innate splendour, one must have known him before – looked at him then. The wavering gloom of the little cabin; the breathless stillness outside, through which only the lapping of water against the schooner's sides could be heard; Hollis's pale face, with steady dark eyes; the energetic head of Jackson held up between two big palms, and with the long yellow hair of his beard flowing over the strings of the guitar lying on the table; Karain's upright and motionless pose, his tone – all this made an impression that cannot be forgotten. He faced us across the table. His dark head and bronze torso appeared above the tarnished slab of wood, gleaming and still as if cast in metal. Only his lips moved, and his eyes glowed, went out, blazed again, or stared mournfully. His expressions came straight from his tormented heart. His words sounded low, in a sad murmur as of running water;* at times they rang loud like the clash of a war-gong – or trailed slowly like weary travellers – or rushed forward with the speed of fear.

IV

This is, imperfectly, what he said—

'It was after the great trouble that broke the alliance of the four states of Wajo.* We fought amongst ourselves, and the Dutch watched from afar till we were weary. Then the smoke of their fire-ships was seen at the mouth of our rivers, and their great men came in boats full of soldiers to talk to us of protection and peace. We answered with caution and wisdom, for our villages were burnt, our stockades weak, the people weary, and the weapons blunt. They came and went; there had been much talk, but after they went away everything seemed to be as before, only their ships remained in sight from our coast, and very soon their traders came amongst us under a promise of safety. My brother was a Ruler, and one of those who had given the promise. I was young then, and had fought in the war, and Pata Matara* had fought by my side. We had shared hunger, danger, fatigue, and victory. His eyes saw my danger quickly, and twice my arm had preserved his life. It was his destiny. He was my friend. And he was great amongst us – one of those who were near my brother, the Ruler. He spoke in council, his courage was great, he was the chief of many villages round the great lake that is in the middle of our country as the heart is in the middle of a man's body. When his sword was carried into a campong in advance of his coming, the maidens whispered wonderingly under the fruit-trees, the rich men consulted together in the shade, and a feast was made ready with rejoicing and songs. He had the favour of the Ruler and the affection of the poor. He loved war, deer hunts, and the charms of women. He was the possessor of jewels, of lucky weapons, and of men's devotion. He was a fierce man; and I had no other friend.

'I was the chief of a stockade at the mouth of the river, and collected tolls for my brother from the passing boats. One day I saw a Dutch trader go up the river. He went up with three boats, and no toll was demanded from him, because the smoke of Dutch warships stood out from the open sea, and we were too weak to forget treaties. He went up under the promise of safety, and my brother gave him protection. He said he came to trade. He listened to our voices, for we are men who speak openly and without fear; he counted the number of our spears, he examined the trees, the running waters, the grasses of the bank, the slopes of our hills. He went up to Matara's country and obtained permission to build a house. He traded and planted. He despised our joys, our thoughts, and our sorrows. His face was red, his hair like flame, and his eyes pale, like a river mist; he moved heavily, and spoke with a deep voice; he laughed aloud like a fool, and knew no courtesy in his speech. He was a big, scornful man, who looked into women's faces and put his hand on the shoulders of free men as though he had been a noble-born chief. We bore with him. Time passed.

'Then Pata Matara's sister fled from the campong and went to live in the Dutchman's house. She was a great and wilful lady: I had seen her once carried high on slaves' shoulders amongst the people, with uncovered face, and I had heard all men say that her beauty was extreme, silencing the reason and ravishing the heart of the beholders. The people were dismayed; Matara's face was blackened with that disgrace, for she knew she had been promised to another man. Matara went to the Dutchman's house, and said, "Give her up to die – she is the daughter of chiefs." The white man refused, and shut himself up, while his servants kept guard night and day with loaded guns. Matara raged. My brother called a council. But the Dutch ships were near, and watched our coast greedily. My brother said, "If he dies now our land will pay for his blood. Leave him alone till we grow stronger and the ships are gone." Matara was wise; he waited and watched. But the white man feared for her life and went away.

'He left his house, his plantations, and his goods! He departed, armed and menacing, and left all – for her! She had ravished his heart! From my stockade I saw him put out to sea in a big boat. Matara and I watched him from the fighting platform behind the pointed stakes. He sat cross-legged, with his gun in his hands, on the roof at the stern of his prau. The barrel of his rifle glinted aslant before his big red face. The broad river was stretched under him – level, smooth, shining, like a plain of silver; and his prau, looking very short and black from the shore, glided along the silver plain and over into the blue of the sea.

'Thrice Matara, standing by my side, called aloud her name with grief and imprecations. He stirred my heart. It leaped three

times; and three times with the eye of my mind I saw in the
gloom within the enclosed space of the prau a woman with
streaming hair going away from her land and her people. I was
angry – and sorry. Why? And then I also cried out insults and
threats. Matara said, "Now they have left our land their lives
are mine. I shall follow and strike – and, alone, pay the price of
blood." A great wind was sweeping towards the setting sun
over the empty river. I cried, "By your side I will go!" He
lowered his head in sign of assent. It was his destiny. The sun
had set, and the trees swayed their boughs with a great noise
above our heads.

'On the third night we two left our land together in a trading
prau.

'The sea met us – the sea, wide, pathless, and without voice.
A sailing prau leaves no track. We went south. The moon was
full; and, looking up, we said to one another, "When the next
moon shines as this one, we shall return and they will be dead."
It was fifteen years ago. Many moons have grown full and
withered, and I have not seen my land since. We sailed south;
we overtook many praus; we examined the creeks and the bays;
we saw the end of our coast, of our island – a steep cape over a
disturbed strait, where drift the shadows of shipwrecked praus
and drowned men clamour in the night. The wide sea was all
round us now. We saw a great mountain burning in the midst
of water;* we saw thousands of islets scattered like bits of iron
fired from a big gun; we saw a long coast of mountain and
lowlands stretching away in sunshine from west to east. It was
Java. We said, "They are there; their time is near, and we shall
return or die cleansed from dishonour."

'We landed. Is there anything good in that country? The paths
run straight and hard and dusty. Stone campongs, full of white
faces, are surrounded by fertile fields, but every man you meet
is a slave. The rulers live under the edge of a foreign sword. We
ascended mountains, we traversed valleys; at sunset we entered
villages. We asked every one, "Have you seen such a white
man?" Some stared; others laughed; women gave us food,
sometimes, with fear and respect, as though we had been
distracted by the visitation of God; but some did not understand
our language, and some cursed us, or, yawning, asked with
contempt the reason of our quest. Once, as we were going away,
an old man called after us, "Desist!"

'We went on. Concealing our weapons, we stood humbly aside before the horsemen on the road; we bowed low in the courtyards of chiefs who were no better than slaves. We lost ourselves in the fields, in the jungle; and one night, in a tangled forest, we came upon a place where crumbling old walls had fallen amongst the trees, and where strange stone idols – carved images of devils with many arms and legs, with snakes twined round their bodies, with twenty heads and holding a hundred swords – seemed to live and threaten in the light of our camp-fire. Nothing dismayed us. And on the road, by every fire, in resting-places, we always talked of her and of him. Their time was near. We spoke of nothing else. No! not of hunger, thirst, weariness, and faltering hearts. No! we spoke of him and her? Of her! And we thought of them – of her! Matara brooded by the fire. I sat and thought and thought, till suddenly I could see again the image of a woman, beautiful, and young, and great, and proud, and tender, going away from her land and her people. Matara said, "When we find them we shall kill her first to cleanse the dishonour – then the man must die." I would say, "It shall be so; it is your vengeance." He stared long at me with his big sunken eyes.

'We came back to the coast. Our feet were bleeding, our bodies thin. We slept in rags under the shadow of stone enclosures; we prowled, soiled and lean, about the gateways of white men's courtyards. Their hairy dogs barked at us, and their servants shouted from afar, "Begone!" Low-born wretches, that keep watch over the streets of stone campongs, asked us who we were. We lied, we cringed, we smiled with hate in our hearts, and we kept looking here, looking there, for them – for the white man with hair like flame, and for her, for the woman who had broken faith, and therefore must die. We looked. At last in every woman's face I thought I could see hers. We ran swiftly. No! Sometimes Matara would whisper, "Here is the man," and we waited, crouching. He came near. It was not the man – those Dutchmen are all alike.* We suffered the anguish of deception. In my sleep I saw her face, and was both joyful and sorry. . . . Why? . . . I seemed to hear a whisper near me. I turned swiftly. She was not there! And as we trudged wearily from stone city to stone city I seemed to hear a light footstep near me. A time came when I heard it always, and I was glad. I thought, walking dizzy and weary in sunshine on the hard paths of white men – I thought, She is there – with us! . . . Matara was sombre. We were often hungry.

'We sold the carved sheaths of our krisses – the ivory sheaths with golden ferules. We sold the jewelled hilts. But we kept the blades – for them. The blades that never touch but kill – we kept the blades for her. . . . Why? She was always by our side. . . . We starved. We begged. We left Java at last.

'We went West, we went East. We saw many lands, crowds of strange faces, men that live in trees and men who eat their old people. We cut rattans in the forest for a handful of rice, and for a living swept the decks of big ships and heard curses heaped upon our heads. We toiled in villages; we wandered upon the seas with the Bajow people, who have no country.* We fought for pay; we hired ourselves to work for Goram men,* and were cheated; and under the orders of rough white-faces we dived for pearls in barren bays, dotted with black rocks, upon a coast of sand and desolation. And everywhere we watched, we listened, we asked. We asked traders, robbers, white men. We heard jeers, mockery, threats – words of wonder and words of contempt. We never knew rest; we never thought of home, for our work was not done. A year passed, then another. I ceased to count the number of nights, of moons, of years. I watched over Matara. He had my last handful of rice; if there was water enough for one he drank it; I covered him up when he shivered with cold; and when the hot sickness came upon him I sat sleepless through many nights and fanned his face. He was a fierce man, and my friend. He spoke of her with fury in the daytime, with sorrow in the dark; he remembered her in health, in sickness. I said nothing; but I saw her every day – always! At first I saw only her head, as of a woman walking in the low mist on a river bank. Then she sat by our fire. I saw her! I looked at her! She had tender eyes and a ravishing face. I murmured to her in the night. Matara said sleepily sometimes, "To whom are you talking? Who is there?" I answered quickly, "No one" . . . It was a lie! She never left me. She shared the warmth of our fire, she sat on my couch of leaves, she swam on the sea to follow me. . . . I saw her! . . . I tell you I saw her long black hair spread behind her upon the moonlit water as she struck out with bare arms by the side of a swift prau. She was beautiful, she was faithful, and in the silence of foreign countries she spoke to me very low in the language of my people. No one

saw her; no one heard her; she was mine only! In daylight she
moved with a swaying walk before me upon the weary paths;
her figure was straight and flexible like the stem of a slender
tree; the heels of her feet were round and polished like shells of
eggs; with her round arm she made signs. At night she looked
into my face. And she was sad! Her eyes were tender and
frightened; her voice soft and pleading. Once I murmured to
her, "You shall not die," and she smiled ... ever after she
smiled! ... She gave me courage to bear weariness and hard-
ships. Those were times of pain, and she soothed me. We
wandered patient in our search. We knew deception, false
hopes; we knew captivity, sickness, thirst, misery, despair. . . .
Enough! We found them! . . .'

He cried out the last words and paused. His face was impassive, and he kept still like a man in a trance. Hollis sat up
quickly, and spread his elbows on the table. Jackson made a
brusque movement, and accidentally touched the guitar. A
plaintive resonance filled the cabin with confused vibrations and
died out slowly. Then Karain began to speak again. The
restrained fierceness of his tone seemed to rise like a voice from
outside, like a thing unspoken but heard; it filled the cabin and
enveloped in its intense and deadened murmur the motionless
figure in the chair.

'We were on our way to Atjeh,* where there was war; but
the vessel ran on a sandbank, and we had to land in Delli.* We
had earned a little money, and had bought a gun from some
Selangore* traders; only one gun, which was fired by the spark
of a stone: Matara carried it. We landed. Many white men lived
there, planting tobacco on conquered plains,* and Matara ...
But no matter. He saw him! . . . The Dutchman! . . . At last! . . .
We crept and watched. Two nights and a day we watched. He
had a house – a big house in a clearing in the midst of his fields;
flowers and bushes grew around; there were narrow paths of
yellow earth between the cut grass, and thick hedges to keep
people out. The third night we came armed, and lay behind a
hedge.

'A heavy dew seemed to soak through our flesh and made our
very entrails cold. The grass, the twigs, the leaves, covered with
drops of water, were grey in the moonlight. Matara, curled up
in the grass, shivered in his sleep. My teeth rattled in my head
so loud that I was afraid the noise would wake up all the land.

Afar, the watchmen of white men's houses struck wooden clappers and hooted in the darkness. And, as every night, I saw her by my side. She smiled no more! . . . The fire of anguish burned in my breast, and she whispered to me with compassion, with pity, softly – as women will; she soothed the pain of my mind; she bent her face over me – the face of a woman who ravishes the hearts and silences the reason of men. She was all mine, and no one could see her – no one of living mankind! Stars shone through her bosom, through her floating hair. I was overcome with regret, with tenderness, with sorrow. Matara slept . . . Had I slept? Matara was shaking me by the shoulder, and the fire of the sun was drying the grass, the bushes, the leaves. It was day. Shreds of white mist hung between the branches of trees.

'Was it night or day? I saw nothing again till I heard Matara breathe quickly where he lay, and then outside the house I saw her. I saw them both. They had come out. She sat on a bench under the wall, and twigs laden with flowers crept high above her head, hung over her hair. She had a box on her lap, and gazed into it, counting the increase of her pearls. The Dutchman stood by looking on; he smiled down at her; his white teeth flashed; the hair on his lip was like two twisted flames. He was big and fat, and joyous, without fear. Matara tipped fresh priming from the hollow of his palm, scraped the flint with his thumb-nail,* and gave the gun to me. To me! I took it . . . O fate!

'He whispered into my ear, lying on his stomach, "I shall creep close and then amok . . . let her die by my hand. You take aim at the fat swine there. Let him see me strike my shame off the face of the earth – and then . . . you are my friend – kill with a sure shot." I said nothing; there was no air in my chest – there was no air in the world. Matara had gone suddenly from my side. The grass nodded. Then a bush rustled. She lifted her head.

'I saw her! The consoler of sleepless nights, of weary days; the companion of troubled years! I saw her! She looked straight at the place where I crouched. She was there as I had seen her for years – a faithful wanderer by my side. She looked with sad eyes and had smiling lips; she looked at me . . . Smiling lips! Had I not promised that she should not die!

'She was far off and I felt her near. Her touch caressed me, and her voice murmured, whispered above me, around me, "Who shall be thy companion, who shall console thee if I die?" I saw a flowering thicket to the left of her stir a little . . . Matara was ready . . . I cried aloud – "Return!"

'She leaped up; the box fell; the pearls streamed at her feet. The big Dutchman by her side rolled menacing eyes through the still sunshine. The gun went up to my shoulder. I was kneeling and I was firm – firmer than the trees, the rocks, the mountains. But in front of the steady long barrel the fields, the house, the earth, the sky swayed to and fro like shadows in a forest on a windy day. Matara burst out of the thicket; before him the petals of torn flowers whirled high as if driven by a tempest. I heard her cry; I saw her spring with open arms in front of the white man. She was a woman of my country and of noble blood. They are so! I heard her shriek of anguish and fear – and all stood still! The fields, the house, the earth, the sky stood still – while Matara leaped at her with uplifted arm. I pulled the trigger, saw a spark, heard nothing; the smoke drove back into my face, and then I could see Matara roll over head first and lie with stretched arms at her feet. Ha! A sure shot! The sunshine fell on my back colder than the running water. A sure shot! I flung the gun after the shot. Those two stood over the dead man as though they had been bewitched by a charm. I shouted at her, "Live and remember!" Then for a time I stumbled about in a cold darkness.

'Behind me there were great shouts, the running of many feet; strange men surrounded me, cried meaningless words into my face, pushed me, dragged me, supported me . . . I stood before the big Dutchman: he stared as if bereft of his reason. He wanted to know, he talked fast, he spoke of gratitude, he offered me food, shelter, gold – he asked many questions. I laughed in his face. I said, "I am a Korinchi traveller from Perak* over there, and know nothing of that dead man. I was passing along the path when I heard a shot, and your senseless people rushed out and dragged me here." He lifted his arms, he wondered, he could not believe, he could not understand, he clamoured in his own tongue! She had her arms clasped round his neck, and over her shoulder stared back at me with wide eyes. I smiled and looked at her; I smiled and waited to hear the sound of her voice. The white man asked her suddenly, "Do you know him?" I listened – my life was in my ears! She looked at me long, she

looked at me with unflinching eyes, and said aloud, "No! I
never saw him before." ... What! Never before? Had she
forgotten already? Was it possible? Forgotten already – after so
many years – so many years of wandering, of companionship,
of trouble, of tender words! Forgotten already! ... I tore myself
out from the hands that held me and went away without a word
... They let me go.

'I was weary. Did I sleep? I do not know. I remember walking
upon a broad path under a clear starlight; and that strange
country seemed so big, the rice-fields so vast, that, as I looked
around, my head swam with the fear of space. Then I saw
a forest. The joyous starlight was heavy upon me. I turned off
the path and entered the forest, which was very sombre and
very sad.'

V

Karain's tone had been getting lower and lower, as though he had been going away from us, till the last words sounded faint but clear, as if shouted on a calm day from a very great distance. He moved not. He stared fixedly past the motionless head of Hollis, who faced him, as still as himself. Jackson had turned sideways, and with elbow on the table shaded his eyes with the palm of his hand. And I looked on, surprised and moved; I looked at that man, loyal to a vision, betrayed by his dream, spurned by his illusion, and coming to us unbelievers for help – against a thought. The silence was profound; but it seemed full of noiseless phantoms, of things sorrowful, shadowy, and mute, in whose invisible presence the firm, pulsating beat of the two ship's chronometers ticking off steadily the seconds of Greenwich Time* seemed to me a protection and a relief. Karain stared stonily; and looking at his rigid figure, I thought of his wanderings, of that obscure Odyssey of revenge, of all the men that wander amongst illusions; of the illusions as restless as men; of the illusions faithful, faithless; of the illusions that give joy, that give sorrow, that give pain, that give peace; of the invincible illusions that can make life and death appear serene, inspiring, tormented, or ignoble.

A murmur was heard; that voice from outside seemed to flow out of a dreaming world into the lamplight of the cabin. Karain was speaking.

'I lived in the forest.

'She came no more. Never! Never once! I lived alone. She had forgotten. It was well. I did not want her; I wanted no one. I found an abandoned house in an old clearing. Nobody came near. Sometimes I heard in the distance the voices of people going along a path. I slept; I rested; there was wild rice, water from a running stream – and peace! Every night I sat alone by my small fire before the hut. Many nights passed over my head.

'Then, one evening, as I sat by my fire after having eaten, I looked down on the ground and began to remember my wanderings. I lifted my head. I had heard no sound, no rustle, no footsteps – but I lifted my head. A man was coming towards me across the small clearing. I waited. He came up without a greeting and squatted down into the firelight. Then he turned his face to me. It was Matara. He stared at me fiercely with his big sunken eyes. The night was cold; the heat died suddenly out of the fire, and he stared at me. I rose and went away from there, leaving him by the fire that had no heat.

'I walked all that night, all next day, and in the evening made up a big blaze and sat down – to wait for him. He did not come into the light. I heard him in the bushes here and there, whispering, whispering. I understood at last – I had heard the words before, "You are my friend – kill with a sure shot."

'I bore it as long as I could – then leaped away, as on this very night I leaped from my stockade and swam to you. I ran – I ran crying like a child left alone and far from the houses. He ran by my side, without footsteps, whispering, whispering – invisible and heard. I sought people – I wanted men around me! Men who had not died! And again we two wandered. I sought danger, violence, and death. I fought in the Atjeh war, and a brave people wondered at the valiance of a stranger. But we were two; he warded off the blows . . . Why? I wanted peace, not life. And no one could see him; no one knew – I dared tell no one. At times he would leave me, but not for long; then he would return and whisper or stare. My heart was torn with a strange fear, but could not die. Then I met an old man.

'You all knew him. People here called him my sorcerer, my servant and sword-bearer; but to me he was father, mother, protection, refuge, and peace. When I met him he was returning from a pilgrimage, and I heard him intoning the prayer of sunset. He had gone to the holy place with his son, his son's wife, and a little child; and on their return, by the favour of the Most High, they all died: the strong man, the young mother, the little child – they died; and the old man reached his country alone. He was a pilgrim serene and pious, very wise and very lonely. I told him all. For a time we lived together. He said over me words of compassion, of wisdom, of prayer. He warded from me the shade of the dead. I begged him for a charm that would make me safe. For a long time he refused; but at last, with a sigh and a smile, he gave me one. Doubtless he could command a spirit stronger than the unrest of my dead friend, and again I had peace; but I had become restless, and a lover of turmoil and danger. The old man never left me. We travelled together. We were welcomed by the great; his wisdom and my courage are remembered where your strength, O white men, is

forgotten! We served the Sultan of Sula.* We fought the Span-
iards. There were victories, hopes, defeats, sorrow, blood,
women's tears . . . What for? . . . We fled. We collected wanderers of a warlike race and came here to fight again. The rest you
know. I am the ruler of a conquered land, a lover of war and
danger, a fighter and a plotter. But the old man has died, and I
am again the slave of the dead. He is not here now to drive
away the reproachful shade – to silence the lifeless voice! The
power of his charm has died with him. And I know fear; and I
hear the whisper, "Kill! kill! kill!" . . . Have I not killed
enough? . . .'

For the first time that night a sudden convulsion of madness
and rage passed over his face. His wavering glances darted here
and there like scared birds in a thunderstorm. He jumped up,
shouting—

'By the spirits that drink blood: by the spirits that cry in the
night: by all the spirits of fury, misfortune, and death, I swear –
some day I will strike into every heart I meet – I . . .'

He looked so dangerous that we all three leaped to our feet,
and Hollis, with the back of his hand, sent the kriss flying off
the table. I believe we shouted together. It was a short scare,
and the next moment he was again composed in his chair, with
three white men standing over him in rather foolish attitudes.
We felt a little ashamed of ourselves. Jackson picked up the
kriss, and, after an inquiring glance at me, gave it to him. He
received it with a stately inclination of the head and stuck it in
the twist of his sarong, with punctilious care to give his weapon
a pacific position. Then he looked up at us with an austere
smile. We were abashed and reproved. Hollis sat sideways on
the table and, holding his chin in his hand, scrutinised him in
pensive silence. I said—

'You must abide with your people. They need you. And there
is forgetfulness in life. Even the dead cease to speak in time.'

'Am I a woman, to forget long years before an eyelid has had
the time to beat twice?' he exclaimed, with bitter resentment.
He startled me. It was amazing. To him his life – that cruel
mirage of love and peace, seemed as real, as undeniable, as
theirs would be to any saint, philosopher, or fool of us all.
Hollis muttered—

'You won't soothe him with your platitudes.'

Karain spoke to me.

'You know us. You have lived with us. Why? – we cannot
know; but you understand our sorrows and our thoughts. You
have lived with my people, and you understand our desires and
our fears. With you I will go. To your land – to your people.
To your people, who live in unbelief; to whom day is day, and
night is night – nothing more, because you understand all things
seen, and despise all else! To your land of unbelief, where the
dead do not speak, where every man is wise, and alone – and at
peace!'

'Capital description,' murmured Hollis, with the flicker of a
smile.

Karain hung his head.

'I can toil, and fight – and be faithful,' he whispered, in a
weary tone, 'but I cannot go back to him who waits for me on
the shore. No! Take me with you . . . Or else give me some of
your strength – of your unbelief . . . A charm! . . .'

He seemed utterly exhausted.

'Yes, take him home,' said Hollis, very low, as if debating
with himself. 'That would be one way. The ghosts there are in
society, and talk affably to ladies and gentlemen, but would
scorn a naked human being – like our princely friend. . . . Naked
. . . Flayed! I should say. I am sorry for him. Impossible – of
course. The end of all this shall be,' he went on, looking up at
us – 'the end of this shall be, that some day he will run amuck
amongst his faithful subjects and send *ad patres* ever so many
of them before they make up their minds to the disloyalty of
knocking him on the head.'

I nodded. I thought it more than probable that such would be
the end of Karain. It was evident that he had been hunted by
his thought along the very limit of human endurance, and very
little more pressing was needed to make him swerve over into
the form of madness peculiar to his race. The respite he had
during the old man's life made the return of the torment
unbearable. That much was clear.

He lifted his head suddenly; we had imagined for a moment
that he had been dozing.

'Give me your protection – or your strength!' he cried. 'A
charm . . . a weapon!'

Again his chin fell on his breast. We looked at him, then
looked at one another with suspicious awe in our eyes, like men
who come unexpectedly upon the scene of some mysterious

disaster. He had given himself up to us; he had thrust into our hands his errors and his torment, his life and his peace; and we did not know what to do with that problem from the outer darkness. We three white men, looking at that Malay, could not find one word to the purpose amongst us – if indeed there existed a word that could solve that problem. We pondered, and our hearts sank. We felt as though we three had been called to the very gate of Infernal Regions to judge, to decide the fate of a wanderer coming suddenly from a world of sunshine and illusions.

'By Jove, he seems to have a great idea of our power,' whispered Hollis, hopelessly. And then again there was a silence, the feeble plash of water, the steady tick of chronometers. Jackson, with bare arms crossed, leaned his shoulders against the bulkhead of the cabin. He was bending his head under the deck beam; his fair beard spread out magnificently over his chest; he looked colossal, ineffectual, and mild. There was something lugubrious in the aspect of the cabin; the air in it seemed to become slowly charged with the cruel chill of help-lessness, with the pitiless anger of egoism against the incompre-hensible form of an intruding pain. We had no idea what to do; we began to resent bitterly the hard necessity to get rid of him.

Hollis mused, muttered suddenly with a short laugh, 'Strength . . . Protection . . . Charm.' He slipped off the table and left the cuddy without a look at us. It seemed a base desertion. Jackson and I exchanged indignant glances. We could hear him rummag-ing in his pigeon-hole of a cabin. Was the fellow actually going to bed? Karain sighed. It was intolerable!

Then Hollis reappeared, holding in both hands a small leather box. He put it down gently on the table and looked at us with a queer gasp, we thought, as though he had from some cause become speechless for a moment, or were ethically uncertain about producing that box. But in an instant the insolent and unerring wisdom of his youth gave him the needed courage. He said, as he unlocked the box with a very small key, 'Look as solemn as you can, you fellows.'

Probably we looked only surprised and stupid, for he glanced over his shoulder, and said angrily—

'This is no play; I am going to do something for him. Look serious. Confound it! . . . Can't you lie a little . . . for a friend!'

Karain seemed to take no notice of us, but when Hollis threw open the lid of the box his eyes flew to it – and so did ours. The quilted crimson satin of the inside put in a violent patch of colour into the sombre atmosphere; it was something positive to look at – it was fascinating.

VI

Hollis looked smiling into the box. He had lately made a dash home through the Canal.* He had been away six months, and only joined us again just in time for this last trip. We had never seen the box before. His hands hovered above it; and he talked to us ironically, but his face became as grave as though he were pronouncing a powerful incantation over the things inside.

'Every one of us,' he said, with pauses that somehow were more offensive than his words – 'every one of us, you'll admit, has been haunted by some woman . . . And . . . as to friends . . . dropped by the way . . . Well! . . . ask yourselves . . .'

He paused. Karain stared. A deep rumble was heard high up under the deck. Jackson spoke seriously—

'Don't be so beastly cynical.'

'Ah! You are without guile,' said Hollis, sadly. 'You will learn . . . Meantime this Malay has been our friend . . .'

He repeated several times thoughtfully, 'Friend . . . Malay. Friend, Malay,' as though weighing the words against one another, then went on more briskly—

'A good fellow – a gentleman in his way. We can't, so to speak, turn our backs on his confidence and belief in us. Those Malays are easily impressed – all nerves, you know – therefore . . .'

He turned to me sharply.

'You know him best,' he said, in a practical tone. 'Do you think he is fanatical – I mean very strict in his faith?'

I stammered in profound amazement that 'I did not think so.'

'It's on account of its being a likeness – an engraved image,'* muttered Hollis, enigmatically, turning to the box. He plunged his fingers into it. Karain's lips were parted and his eyes shone. We looked into the box.

There were there a couple of reels of cotton, a packet of needles, a bit of silk ribbon, dark blue; a cabinet photograph, at which Hollis stole a glance before laying it on the table face downwards. A girl's portrait, I could see. There were, amongst a lot of various small objects, a bunch of flowers, a narrow white glove with many buttons, a slim packet of letters carefully tied up. Amulets of white men! Charms and talismans! Charms that keep them straight, that drive them crooked, that have the power to make a young man sigh, an old man smile. Potent things that procure dreams of joy, thoughts of regret; that soften hard hearts, and can temper a soft one to the hardness of steel. Gifts of heaven – things of earth . . .

Hollis rummaged in the box.

And it seemed to me, during that moment of waiting, that the cabin of the schooner was becoming filled with a stir invisible and living as of subtle breaths. All the ghosts driven out of the unbelieving West by men who pretend to be wise and alone and at peace – all the homeless ghosts of an unbelieving world – appeared suddenly round the figure of Hollis bending over the box; all the exiled and charming shades of loved women; all the beautiful and tender ghosts of ideals, remembered, forgotten, cherished, execrated; all the cast-out and reproachful ghosts of friends admired, trusted, traduced, betrayed, left dead by the way – they all seemed to come from the inhospitable regions of the earth to crowd into the gloomy cabin, as though it had been a refuge and, in all the unbelieving world, the only place of avenging belief . . . It lasted a second – all disappeared. Hollis was facing us alone with something small that glittered between his fingers. It looked like a coin.

'Ah! here it is,' he said.

He held it up. It was a sixpence – a Jubilee sixpence.* It was gilt; it had a hole punched near the rim. Hollis looked towards Karain.

'A charm for our friend,' he said to us. 'The thing itself is of great power – money, you know – and his imagination is struck. A loyal vagabond; if only his puritanism doesn't shy at a likeness . . .'

We said nothing. We did not know whether to be scandalised, amused, or relieved. Hollis advanced towards Karain, who stood up as if startled, and then, holding the coin up, spoke in Malay.

'This is the image of the Great Queen, and the most powerful thing the white men know,' he said, solemnly.

Karain covered the handle of his kriss in sign of respect, and stared at the crowned head.

'The Invincible, the Pious,' he muttered.

'She is more powerful than Suleiman the Wise,* who commanded the genii, as you know,' said Hollis, gravely. 'I shall give this to you.'

He held the sixpence in the palm of his hand, and looking at it thoughtfully, spoke to us in English.

'She commands a spirit, too – the spirit of her nation; a masterful, conscientious, unscrupulous, unconquerable devil . . . that does a lot of good – incidentally . . . a lot of good . . . at times – and wouldn't stand any fuss from the best ghost out for such a little thing as our friend's shot. Don't look thunderstruck, you fellows. Help me to make him believe – everything's in that.'

'His people will be shocked,' I murmured.

Hollis looked fixedly at Karain, who was the incarnation of the very essence of still excitement. He stood rigid, with head thrown back; his eyes rolled wildly, flashing; the dilated nostrils quivered.

'Hang it all!' said Hollis at last, 'he is a good fellow. I'll give him something that I shall really miss.'

He took the ribbon out of the box, smiled at it scornfully, then with a pair of scissors cut out a piece from the palm of the glove.

'I shall make him a thing like those Italian peasants wear, you know.'

He sewed the coin in the delicate leather, sewed the leather to the ribbon, tied the ends together. He worked with haste. Karain watched his fingers all the time.

'Now then,' he said – then stepped up to Karain. They looked close into one another's eyes. Those of Karain stared in a lost glance, but Hollis's seemed to grow darker and looked out masterful and compelling. They were in violent contrast together – one motionless and the colour of bronze, the other dazzling white and lifting his arms, where the powerful muscles rolled slightly under a skin that gleamed like satin. Jackson moved near with the air of a man closing up to a chum in a tight place. I said impressively, pointing to Hollis—

'He is young, but he is wise. Believe him!'

Karain bent his head: Hollis threw lightly over it the dark-blue ribbon and stepped back.

'Forget, and be at peace!' I cried.

Karain seemed to wake up from a dream. He said, 'Ha!' shook himself as if throwing off a burden. He looked round with assurance. Some one on deck dragged off the skylight cover, and a flood of light fell into the cabin. It was morning already.

'Time to go on deck,' said Jackson.

Hollis put on a coat, and we went up, Karain leading.

The sun had risen beyond the hills, and their long shadows stretched far over the bay in the pearly light. The air was clear, stainless, and cool. I pointed at the curved line of yellow sands.

'He is not there,' I said, emphatically, to Karain. 'He waits no more. He has departed for ever.'

A shaft of bright hot rays darted into the bay between the summits of two hills, and the water all round broke out as if by magic into a dazzling sparkle.

'No! He is not there waiting,' said Karain, after a long look over the beach. 'I do not hear him,' he went on, slowly. 'No!'

He turned to us.

'He has departed again – for ever!' he cried.

We assented vigorously, repeatedly, and without compunction. The great thing was to impress him powerfully; to suggest absolute safety – the end of all trouble. We did our best; and I hope we affirmed our faith in the power of Hollis's charm efficiently enough to put the matter beyond the shadow of a doubt. Our voices rang around him joyously in the still air, and above his head the sky, pellucid, pure, stainless, arched its tender blue from shore to shore and over the bay, as if to envelop the water, the earth, and the man in the caress of its light.

The anchor was up, the sails hung still, and half-a-dozen big boats were seen sweeping over the bay to give us a tow out. The paddlers in the first one that came alongside lifted their heads and saw their ruler standing amongst us. A low murmur of surprise arose – then a shout of greeting.

He left us, and seemed straightway to step into the glorious splendour of his stage, to wrap himself in the illusion of unavoidable success. For a moment he stood erect, one foot over the gangway, one hand on the hilt of his kriss, in a martial pose; and, relieved from the fear of outer darkness, he held his head high, he swept a serene look over his conquered foothold on the earth. The boats far off took up the cry of greeting; a great clamour rolled on the water; the hills echoed it, and seemed to toss back at him the words invoking long life and victories.

He descended into a canoe, and as soon as he was clear of the side we gave him three cheers. They sounded faint and

orderly after the wild tumult of his loyal subjects, but it was the
best we could do. He stood up in the boat, lifted up both his
arms, then pointed to the infallible charm. We cheered again;
and the Malays in the boats stared – very much puzzled and
impressed. I wonder what they thought; what he thought; . . .
what the reader thinks?

We towed out slowly. We saw him land and watch us from
the beach. A figure approached him humbly but openly – not
at all like a ghost with a grievance. We could see other men
running towards him. Perhaps he had been missed? At any rate
there was a great stir. A group formed itself rapidly near him,
and he walked along the sands, followed by a growing *cortège*,
and kept nearly abreast of the schooner. With our glasses we
could see the blue ribbon on his neck and a patch of white
on his brown chest. The bay was waking up. The smoke of
morning fires stood in faint spirals higher than the heads of
palms; people moved between the houses; a herd of buffaloes
galloped clumsily across a green slope; the slender figures
of boys brandishing sticks appeared black and leaping in the
long grass; a coloured line of women, with water bamboos on
their heads, moved swaying through a thin grove of fruit-
trees. Karain stopped in the midst of his men and waved his
hand; then, detaching himself from the splendid group, walked
alone to the water's edge and waved his hand again. The
schooner passed out to sea between the steep headlands that
shut in the bay, and at the same instant Karain passed out of
our life for ever.

But the memory remains. Some years afterwards I met Jackson,
in the Strand. He was magnificent as ever. His head was high
above the crowd. His beard was gold, his face red, his eyes blue;
he had a wide-brimmed grey hat and no collar or waistcoat; he
was inspiring; he had just come home – had landed that very
day! Our meeting caused an eddy in the current of humanity.
Hurried people would run against us, then walk round us, and
turn back to look at that giant. We tried to compress seven
years of life into seven exclamations; then, suddenly appeased,
walked sedately along, giving one another the news of yesterday.
Jackson gazed about him, like a man who looks for landmarks,
then stopped before Bland's window.* He always had a passion
for firearms; so he stopped short and contemplated the row of

weapons, perfect and severe, drawn up in a line behind the black-framed panes. I stood by his side. Suddenly he said—

'Do you remember Karain?'

I nodded.

'The sight of all this made me think of him,' he went on, with his face near the glass . . . and I could see another man, powerful and bearded, peering at him intently from amongst the dark and polished tubes that can cure so many illusions. 'Yes; it made me think of him,' he continued, slowly. 'I saw a paper this morning; they are fighting over there again. He's sure to be in it. He will make it hot for the caballeros.* Well, good luck to him, poor devil! He was perfectly stunning.'

We walked on.

'I wonder whether the charm worked – you remember Hollis's charm, of course. If it did . . . never was a sixpence wasted to better advantage! Poor devil! I wonder whether he got rid of that friend of his. Hope so . . . Do you know, I sometimes think that——'

I stood still and looked at him.

'Yes . . . I mean, whether the thing was so, you know . . . whether it really happened to him . . . What do you think?'

'My dear chap,' I cried, 'you have been too long away from home. What a question to ask! Only look at all this.'

A watery gleam of sunshine flashed from the west and went out between two long lines of walls; and then the broken confusion of roofs, the chimney-stacks, the gold letters sprawling over the fronts of houses, the sombre polish of windows, stood resigned and sullen under the falling gloom. The whole length of the street, deep as a well and narrow like a corridor, was full of a sombre and ceaseless stir. Our ears were filled by a headlong shuffle and beat of rapid footsteps and an underlying rumour – a rumour vast, faint, pulsating, as of panting breaths, of beating hearts, of gasping voices. Innumerable eyes stared straight in front, feet moved hurriedly, blank faces flowed, arms swung. Over all, a narrow ragged strip of smoky sky wound about between the high roofs, extended and motionless, like a soiled streamer flying above the rout of a mob.

'Ye-e-e-s,' said Jackson, meditatively.

The big wheels of hansoms turned slowly along the edge of side-walks; a pale-faced youth strolled, overcome by weariness, by the side of his stick and with the tails of his overcoat flapping

gently near his heels; horses stepped gingerly on the greasy
pavement, tossing their heads; two young girls passed by, talking vivaciously and with shining eyes; a fine old fellow strutted,
red-faced, stroking a white moustache; and a line of yellow
boards* with blue letters on them approached us slowly, tossing
on high behind one another like some queer wreckage adrift
upon a river of hats.

'Ye-e-es,' repeated Jackson. His clear blue eyes looked about,
contemptuous, amused and hard, like the eyes of a boy. A
clumsy string of red, yellow, and green omnibuses rolled swaying, monstrous and gaudy; two shabby children ran across the
road; a knot of dirty men with red neckerchiefs round their bare
throats lurched along, discussing filthily; a ragged old man with
a face of despair yelled horribly in the mud the name of a paper;
while far off, amongst the tossing heads of horses, the dull flash
of harnesses, the jumble of lustrous panels and roofs of car-
riages, we could see a policeman, helmeted and dark, stretching
out a rigid arm at the crossing of the streets.

'Yes; I see it,' said Jackson, slowly. 'It is there; it pants, it
runs, it rolls; it is strong and alive; it would smash you if you
didn't look out; but I'll be hanged if it is yet as real to me as . . .
as the other thing . . . say, Karain's story.'

I think that, decidedly, he had been too long away from
home.

The Idiots

We were driving along the road from Treguier to Kervanda.*
We passed at a smart trot between the hedges topping an earth
wall on each side of the road; then at the foot of the steep
ascent before Ploumar the horse dropped into a walk, and the
driver jumped down heavily from the box. He flicked his whip
and climbed the incline, stepping clumsily uphill by the side of
the carriage, one hand on the footboard, his eyes on the ground.
After a while he lifted his head, pointed up the road with the
end of the whip, and said—

'The idiot!'

The sun was shining violently upon the undulating surface of
the land.* The rises were topped by clumps of meagre trees,
with their branches showing high on the sky as if they had been
perched upon stilts. The small fields, cut up by hedges and stone
walls that zigzagged over the slopes, lay in rectangular patches
of vivid greens and yellows, resembling the unskilful daubs of a
naïve picture. And the landscape was divided in two by the
white streak of a road stretching in long loops far away, like a
river of dust crawling out of the hills on its way to the sea.

'Here he is,' said the driver, again.

In the long grass bordering the road a face glided past the
carriage at the level of the wheels as we drove slowly by. The
imbecile face was red, and the bullet head with close-cropped
hair seemed to lie alone, its chin in the dust. The body was lost
in the bushes growing thick along the bottom of the deep ditch.

It was a boy's face. He might have been sixteen, judging from
the size – perhaps less, perhaps more. Such creatures are forgotten by time, and live untouched by years till death gathers them
up into its compassionate bosom; the faithful death that never
forgets in the press of work the most insignificant of its children.

'Ah! There's another,' said the man, with a certain satisfaction
in his tone, as if he had caught sight of something expected.

There was another. That one stood nearly in the middle of
the road in the blaze of sunshine at the end of his own short
shadow. And he stood with hands pushed into the opposite
sleeves of his long coat, his head sunk between the shoulders,

all hunched up in the flood of heat. From a distance he had the aspect of one suffering from intense cold.

'Those are twins,' explained the driver.

The idiot shuffled two paces out of the way and looked at us over his shoulder when we brushed past him. The glance was unseeing and staring, a fascinated glance; but he did not turn to look after us. Probably the image passed before the eyes without leaving any trace on the misshapen brain of the creature. When we had topped the ascent I looked over the hood. He stood in the road just where we had left him.

The driver clambered into his seat, clicked his tongue, and we went down hill. The brake squeaked horribly from time to time. At the foot he eased off the noisy mechanism and said, turning half round on his box—

'We shall see some more of them by-and-by.'

'More idiots? How many of them are there, then?' I asked.

'There's four of them – children of a farmer near Ploumar here. . . . The parents are dead now,' he added, after a while. 'The grandmother lives on the farm. In the daytime they knock about on this road, and they come home at dusk along with the cattle. . . . It's a good farm.'

We saw the other two: a boy and a girl, as the driver said. They were dressed exactly alike, in shapeless garments with petticoat-like skirts. The imperfect thing that lived within them moved those beings to howl at us from the top of the bank, where they sprawled amongst the tough stalks of furze. Their cropped black heads stuck out from the bright yellow wall of countless small blossoms. The faces were purple with the strain of yelling; the voices sounded blank and cracked like a mechanical imitation of old people's voices; and suddenly ceased when we turned into a lane.

I saw them many times in my wandering about the country. They lived on that road, drifting along its length here and there, according to the inexplicable impulses of their monstrous darkness. They were an offence to the sunshine, a reproach to empty heaven, a blight on the concentrated and purposeful vigour of the wild landscape. In time the story of their parents shaped itself before me out of the listless answers to my questions, out of the indifferent words heard in wayside inns or on the very road those idiots haunted. Some of it was told by an emaciated and sceptical old fellow with a tremendous whip, while we trudged together over the sands by the side of a two-wheeled cart loaded with dripping seaweed. Then at other times other people confirmed and completed the story: till it stood at last before me, a tale formidable and simple, as they always are, those disclosures of obscure trials endured by ignorant hearts.

When he returned from his military service Jean-Pierre Bacadou found the old people very much aged. He remarked with pain that the work of the farm was not satisfactorily done. The father had not the energy of old days. The hands did not feel over them the eye of the master. Jean-Pierre noted with sorrow that the heap of manure in the courtyard before the only entrance to the house was not so large as it should have been. The fences were out of repair, and the cattle suffered from neglect. At home the mother was practically bedridden, and the girls chattered loudly in the big kitchen, unrebuked, from morning to night. He said to himself: 'We must change all this.' He talked the matter over with his father one evening when the rays of the setting sun entering the yard between the outhouses ruled the heavy shadows with luminous streaks. Over the manure heap floated a mist, opal-tinted and odorous, and the marauding hens would stop in their scratching to examine with a sudden glance of their round eye the two men, both lean and tall, talking in hoarse tones. The old man, all twisted with rheumatism and bowed with years of work, the younger bony and straight, spoke without gestures in the indifferent manner of peasants, grave and slow. But before the sun had set the father had submitted to the sensible arguments of the son. 'It is not for me that I am speaking,' insisted Jean-Pierre. 'It is for the land. It's a pity to see it badly used. I am not impatient for myself.' The old fellow nodded over his stick. 'I dare say; I dare say,' he muttered. 'You may be right. Do what you like. It's the mother* that will be pleased.'

The mother was pleased with her daughter-in-law. Jean-Pierre brought the two-wheeled spring-cart* with a rush into the yard. The grey horse galloped clumsily, and the bride and bridegroom, sitting side by side, were jerked backwards and forwards by the up and down motion of the shafts, in a manner regular and brusque. On the road the distanced wedding guests straggled in pairs and groups.* The men advanced with heavy steps, swinging their idle arms. They were clad in town clothes: jackets cut with clumsy smartness, hard black hats, immense boots, polished highly. Their women all in simple black, with white caps and shawls of faded tints folded triangularly on the back, strolled lightly by their side. In front the violin sang a strident tune, and the biniou* snored and hummed, while the player capered solemnly, lifting high his heavy clogs. The sombre procession drifted in and out of the narrow lanes, through sunshine and through shade, between fields and hedgerows, scaring the little birds that darted away in troops right and left. In the yard of Bacadou's farm the dark ribbon wound itself up into a mass of men and women pushing at the door with cries and greetings. The wedding dinner was remembered for months. It was a splendid feast in the orchard. Farmers of considerable means and excellent repute were to be found sleeping in ditches, all along the road to Treguier, even as late as the afternoon of the next day. All the countryside participated in the happiness of Jean-Pierre. He remained sober, and, together with his quiet wife, kept out of the way, letting father and mother reap their due of honour and thanks. But the next day he took hold strongly, and the old folks felt a shadow – precursor of the grave – fall upon them finally. The world is to the young.

When the twins were born there was plenty of room in the house, for the mother of Jean-Pierre had gone away to dwell under a heavy stone in the cemetery of Ploumar. On that day, for the first time since his son's marriage, the elder Bacadou, neglected by the cackling lot of strange women who thronged the kitchen, left in the morning his seat under the mantel of the fireplace, and went into the empty cow-house, shaking his white locks dismally. Grandsons were all very well, but he wanted his soup at midday. When shown the babies, he stared at them with a fixed gaze, and muttered something like: 'It's too much.' Whether he meant too much happiness, or simply commented upon the number of his descendants, it is impossible to say. He looked offended – as far as his old wooden face could express anything; and for days afterwards could be seen, almost any time of the day, sitting at the gate, with his nose over his knees, a pipe between his gums, and gathered up into a kind of raging concentrated sulkiness. Once he spoke to his son, alluding to the newcomers with a groan: 'They will quarrel over the land.' 'Don't bother about that, father,' answered Jean-Pierre, stolidly, and passed, bent double, towing a recalcitrant cow over his shoulder.

He was happy, and so was Susan, his wife. It was not an ethereal joy welcoming new souls to struggle, perchance to victory. In fourteen years both boys would be a help; and, later on, Jean-Pierre pictured two big sons striding over the land from patch to patch, wringing tribute from the earth beloved and fruitful. Susan was happy too, for she did not want to be spoken of as the unfortunate woman, and now she had children no one could call her that. Both herself and her husband had seen something of the larger world – he during the time of his service; while she had spent a year or so in Paris with a Breton family; but had been too home-sick to remain longer away from the hilly and green country, set in a barren circle of rocks and sands, where she had been born. She thought that one of the boys ought perhaps to be a priest, but said nothing to her husband, who was a republican, and hated the 'crows', as he called the ministers of religion. The christening was a splendid affair. All the commune came to it, for the Bacadous were rich and influential, and, now and then, did not mind the expense. The grandfather had a new coat.

Some months afterwards, one evening when the kitchen had been swept, and the door locked, Jean-Pierre, looking at the cot, asked his wife: 'What's the matter with those children?' And, as if these words, spoken calmly, had been the portent of misfortune, she answered with a loud wail that must have been heard across the yard in the pig-sty; for the pigs (the Bacadous had the finest pigs in the country) stirred and grunted complainingly in the night. The husband went on grinding his bread and butter slowly, gazing at the wall, the soup-plate smoking under his chin. He had returned late from the market, where he had overheard (not for the first time) whispers behind his back. He revolved the words in his mind as he drove back. 'Simple! Both of them. . . . Never any use! . . . Well! May be, may be. One must see. Would ask his wife.' This was her answer. He felt like a blow on his chest, but said only: 'Go, draw me some cider. I am thirsty!'

She went out moaning, an empty jug in her hand. Then he arose, took up the light, and moved slowly towards the cradle. They slept. He looked at them sideways, finished his mouthful there, went back heavily, and sat down before his plate. When his wife returned he never looked up, but swallowed a couple of spoonfuls noisily, and remarked, in a dull manner—

'When they sleep they are like other people's children.'

She sat down suddenly on a stool near by, and shook with a silent tempest of sobs, unable to speak. He finished his meal, and remained idly thrown back in his chair, his eyes lost amongst the black rafters of the ceiling. Before him the tallow candle flared red and straight, sending up a slender thread of smoke. The light lay on the rough, sunburnt skin of his throat; the sunk cheeks were like patches of darkness, and his aspect was mournfully stolid, as if he had ruminated with difficulty endless ideas. Then he said, deliberately—

'We must see . . . consult people. Don't cry. . . . They won't be all like that . . . surely! We must sleep now.'

After the third child, also a boy, was born, Jean-Pierre went about his work with tense hopefulness. His lips seemed more narrow, more tightly compressed than before; as if for fear of letting the earth he tilled hear the voice of hope that murmured within his breast. He watched the child, stepping up to the cot with a heavy clang of sabots* on the stone floor, and glanced in, along his shoulder, with that indifference which is like a deformity of peasant humanity. Like the earth they master and serve, those men, slow of eye and speech, do not show the inner fire; so that, at last, it becomes a question with them as with the earth, what there is in the core: heat, violence, a force mysterious and terrible – or nothing but a clod, a mass fertile and inert, cold and unfeeling, ready to bear a crop of plants that sustain life or give death.

The mother watched with other eyes; listened with otherwise expectant ears. Under the high hanging shelves supporting great sides of bacon overhead, her body was busy by the great fire-place, attentive to the pot swinging on iron gallows, scrubbing the long table where the field hands would sit down directly to their evening meal. Her mind remained by the cradle, night and day on the watch, to hope and suffer. That child, like the other two, never smiled, never stretched its hands to her, never spoke; never had a glance of recognition for her in its big black eyes, which could only stare fixedly at any glitter, but failed hope-lessly to follow the brilliance of a sun-ray slipping slowly along the floor. When the men were at work she spent long days between her three idiot children and the childish grandfather, who sat grim, angular, and immovable, with his feet near the warm ashes of the fire. The feeble old fellow seemed to suspect that there was something wrong with his grandsons. Only once, moved either by affection or by the sense of proprieties, he attempted to nurse the youngest. He took the boy up from the floor, clicked his tongue at him, and essayed a shaky gallop of his bony knees. Then he looked closely with his misty eyes at the child's face and deposited him down gently on the floor again. And he sat, his lean shanks crossed, nodding at the steam escaping from the cooking-pot with a gaze senile and worried.

Then mute affliction dwelt in Bacadou's farmhouse, sharing the breath and the bread of its inhabitants; and the priest of the Ploumar parish had great cause for congratulation. He called upon the rich landowner, the Marquis de Chavanes,* on purpose to deliver himself with joyful unction of solemn platitudes about the inscrutable ways of Providence. In the vast dimness of the curtained drawing-room, the little man, resembling a black bolster, leaned towards a couch, his hat on his knees, and gesticulated with a fat hand at the elongated, gracefully-flowing lines of the clear Parisian toilette* from within which the half-amused, half-bored marquise listened with gracious languor. He was exulting and humble, proud and awed. The impossible had come to pass. Jean-Pierre Bacadou, the enraged republican farmer,* had been to mass last Sunday – had proposed to entertain the visiting priests at the next festival of Ploumar! It was a triumph for the Church and for the good cause. 'I thought I would come at once to tell Monsieur le Marquis. I know how anxious he is for the welfare of our country,' declared the priest, wiping his face. He was asked to stay to dinner.

The Chavanes returning that evening, after seeing their guest to the main gate of the park, discussed the matter while they strolled in the moonlight, trailing their long shadows up the straight avenue of chestnuts. The marquis, a royalist of course, had been mayor of the commune which includes Ploumar, the scattered hamlets of the coast, and the stony islands that fringe the yellow flatness of the sands. He had felt his position insecure, for there was a strong republican element in that part of the country; but now the conversion of Jean-Pierre made him safe. He was very pleased. 'You have no idea how influential those people are,' he explained to his wife. 'Now, I am sure, the next communal election will go all right. I shall be re-elected.' 'Your ambition is perfectly insatiable, Charles,' exclaimed the marquise, gaily. 'But, ma chère amie,' argued the husband, seriously, 'it's most important that the right man should be mayor this year, because of the elections to the Chamber. If you think it amuses me . . .'

Jean-Pierre had surrendered to his wife's mother. Madame Levaille was a woman of business, known and respected within a radius of at least fifteen miles. Thick-set and stout, she was seen about the country, on foot or in an acquaintance's cart, perpetually moving, in spite of her fifty-eight years, in steady pursuit of business. She had houses in all the hamlets, she worked quarries of granite, she freighted coasters with stone – even traded with the Channel Islands.* She was broad-cheeked, wide-eyed, persuasive in speech: carrying her point with the placid and invincible obstinacy of an old woman who knows her own mind. She very seldom slept for two nights together in the same house; and the wayside inns were the best places to inquire in as to her whereabouts. She had either passed, or was expected to pass there at six; or somebody, coming in, had seen her in the morning, or expected to meet her that evening. After the inns that command the roads, the churches were the build-ings she frequented most. Men of liberal* opinions would induce small children to run into sacred edifices to see whether Madame Levaille was there, and to tell her that so-and-so was in the road waiting to speak to her – about potatoes, or flour, or stones, or houses; and she would curtail her devotions, come out blinking and crossing herself into the sunshine; ready to discuss business matters in a calm, sensible way across a table in the kitchen of the inn opposite. Latterly she had stayed for a few days several times with her son-in-law, arguing against sorrow and misfortune with composed face and gentle tones. Jean-Pierre felt the convictions imbided in the regiment torn out of his breast – not by arguments, but by facts. Striding over his fields he thought it over. There were three of them. Three! All alike! Why? Such things did not happen to everybody – to nobody he ever heard of. One yet* – it might pass. But three! All three. For ever useless, to be fed while he lived and . . . What would become of the land when he died? This must be seen to. He would sacrifice his convictions. One day he told his wife—

'See what your God will do for us. Pay for some masses.'

Susan embraced her man. He stood unbending, then turned on his heels and went out. But afterwards, when a black *soutane** darkened his doorway, he did not object; even offered some cider himself to the priest. He listened to the talk meekly; went to mass between the two women; accomplished what the priest called 'his religious duties' at Easter. That morning he felt like a man who had sold his soul. In the afternoon he fought ferociously with an old friend and neighbour who had remarked that the priests had the best of it and were now going to eat the priest-eater. He came home dishevelled and bleeding, and happening to catch sight of his children (they were kept generally out of the way), cursed and swore incoherently, banging the table. Susan wept. Madame Levaille sat serenely unmoved. She assured her daughter that 'It will pass'; and taking up her thick umbrella, departed in haste to see after a schooner she was going to load with granite from her quarry.

A year or so afterwards the girl was born. A girl. Jean-Pierre heard of it in the fields, and was so upset by the news that he sat down on the boundary wall and remained there till the evening, instead of going home as he was urged to do. A girl! He felt half cheated. However, when he got home he was partly reconciled to his fate. One could marry her to a good fellow – not to a good for nothing, but to a fellow with some understanding and a good pair of arms. Besides, the next may be a boy, he thought. Of course they would be all right. His new credulity knew of no doubt. The ill luck was broken. He spoke cheerily to his wife. She was also hopeful. Three priests came to that christening, and Madame Levaille was godmother. The child turned out an idiot too.

Then on market days Jean-Pierre was seen bargaining bitterly, quarrelsome and greedy; then getting drunk with taciturn earnestness; then driving home in the dusk at a rate fit for a wedding, but with a face gloomy enough for a funeral. Sometimes he would insist for* his wife to come with him; and they would drive in the early morning, shaking side by side on the narrow seat above the helpless pig, that, with tied legs, grunted a melancholy sigh at every rut. The morning drives were silent; but in the evening, coming home, Jean-Pierre, tipsy, was viciously muttering,* and growled at the confounded woman who could not rear children that were like anybody else's. Susan, holding on against the erratic swayings of the cart, pretended not to hear. Once, as they were driving through Ploumar, some obscure and drunken impulse caused him to pull up sharply opposite the church. The moon swam amongst light white clouds. The tombstones gleamed pale under the fretted shadows of the trees in the churchyard. Even the village dogs slept. Only the nightingales, awake, spun out the thrill of their song above the silence of graves. Jean-Pierre said thickly to his wife—

'What do you think is there?'

He pointed his whip at the tower – in which the big dial of the clock appeared high in the moonlight like a pallid face without eyes – and getting out carefully, fell down at once by the wheel. He picked himself up and climbed one by one the few steps to the iron gate of the churchyard. He put his face to the bars and called out indistinctly—

'Hey there! Come out!'

'Jean! Return! Return!' entreated his wife in low tones.

He took no notice, and seemed to wait there. The song of nightingales beat on all sides against the high walls of the church, and flowed back between stone crosses and flat grey slabs, engraved with words of hope and sorrow.

'Hey! Come out!' shouted Jean-Pierre loudly.

The nightingales ceased to sing.

'Nobody?' went on Jean-Pierre. 'Nobody there. A swindle of the crows.* That's what this is. Nobody anywhere. I despise it. Allez! Houp!'*

He shook the gate with all his strength, and the iron bars rattled with a frightful clanging, like a chain dragged over stone steps. A dog near by barked hurriedly. Jean-Pierre staggered back, and after three successive dashes got into his cart. Susan sat very quiet and still. He said to her with drunken severity—

'See? Nobody. I've been made a fool! Malheur!* Somebody will pay for it. The next one I see near the house I will lay my whip on . . . on the black spine . . . I will. I don't want him in there . . . he only helps the carrion crows to rob poor folk. I am a man. . . . We will see if I can't have children like anybody else . . . now you mind. . . . They won't be all . . . all . . . we see. . . .'

She burst out through the fingers that hid her face—

'Don't say that, Jean; don't say that, my man!'

He struck her a swinging blow on the head with the back of his hand and knocked her into the bottom of the cart, where she crouched, thrown about lamentably by every jolt. He drove furiously, standing up, brandishing his whip, shaking the reins over the grey horse that galloped ponderously, making the heavy

harness leap upon his broad quarters. The country rang clam-
orous in the night with the irritated barking of farm dogs, that
followed the rattle of wheels all along the road. A couple of
belated wayfarers had only just time to step into the ditch. At
his own gate he caught the post and was shot out of the cart
head first. The horse went on slowly to the door. At Susan's
piercing cries the farm hands rushed out. She thought him dead,
but he was only sleeping where he fell, and cursed his men, who
hastened to him, for disturbing his slumbers.

Autumn came. The clouded sky descended low upon the
black contours of the hills; and the dead leaves danced in spiral
whirls under naked trees, till the wind, sighing profoundly, laid
them to rest in the hollows of bare valleys. And from morning
till night one could see all over the land black denuded boughs,
the boughs gnarled and twisted, as if contorted with pain,
swaying sadly between the wet clouds and the soaked earth.
The clear and gentle streams of summer days rushed discoloured
and raging at the stones that barred the way to the sea, with the
fury of madness bent upon suicide. From horizon to horizon the
great road to the sands lay between the hills in a dull glitter of
empty curves, resembling an unnavigable river of mud.

Jean-Pierre went from field to field, moving blurred and tall
in the drizzle, or striding on the crests of rises, lonely and high
upon the grey curtain of drifting clouds, as if he had been pacing
along the very edge of the universe. He looked at the black
earth, at the earth mute and promising, at the mysterious earth
doing its work of life in death-like stillness under the veiled
sorrow of the sky. And it seemed to him that to a man worse
than childless there was no promise in the fertility of fields, that
from him the earth escaped, defied him, frowned at him like the
clouds, sombre and hurried above his head. Having to face
alone* his own fields, he felt the inferiority of man who passes
away before the clod that remains. Must he give up the hope of
having by his side a son who would look at the turned-up sods
with a master's eye? A man that would think as he thought,
that would feel as he felt; a man who would be part of himself,
and yet remain to trample masterfully on that earth when he
was gone! He thought of some distant relations, and felt savage
enough to curse them aloud. They! Never! He turned home-
wards, going straight at the roof of his dwelling visible between
the enlaced skeletons of trees. As he swung his legs over the stile

a cawing flock of birds settled slowly on the field; dropped
down behind his back, noiseless and fluttering, like flakes of
soot.

That day Madame Levaille had gone early in the afternoon
to the house she had near Kervanion. She had to pay some of
the men who worked in her granite quarry there, and she went
in good time because her little house contained a shop where
the workmen could spend their wages without the trouble of
going to town. The house stood alone amongst rocks. A lane
of mud and stones ended at the door. The sea-winds coming
ashore on Stonecutter's point, fresh from the fierce turmoil of
the waves, howled violently at the unmoved heaps of black
boulders holding up steadily short-armed, high crosses against
the tremendous rush of the invisible. In the sweep of gales the
sheltered dwelling stood in a calm resonant and disquieting,
like the calm in the centre of a hurricane. On stormy nights,*
when the tide was out, the bay of Fougère, fifty feet below the
house, resembled an immense black pit, from which ascended
mutterings and sighs as if the sands down there had been alive
and complaining. At high tide the returning water assaulted the
ledges of rock in short rushes, ending in bursts of livid light
and columns of spray, that flew inland, stinging to death the
grass of pastures.

The darkness came from the hills, flowed over the coast, put
out the red fires of sunset, and went on to seaward pursuing the
retiring tide. The wind dropped with the sun, leaving a maddened sea and a devastated sky. The heavens above the house
seemed to be draped in black rags, held up here and there by
pins of fire. Madame Levaille, for this evening the servant of her
own workmen, tried to induce them to depart. 'An old woman
like me ought to be in bed at this late hour,' she good-
humouredly repeated. The quarrymen drank, asked for more.
They shouted over the table as if they had been talking across a
field. At one end four of them played cards, banging the wood
with their hard knuckles, and swearing at every lead. One sat
with a lost gaze, humming a bar of some song, which he
repeated endlessly. Two others, in a corner, were quarrelling
confidentially and fiercely over some woman, looking close into
one another's eyes as if they had wanted to tear them out, but
speaking in whispers that promised violence and murder dis-
creetly, in a venomous sibilation of subdued words. The atmos-

phere in there was thick enough to slice with a knife. Three candles burning about the long room glowed red and dull like sparks expiring in ashes.

The slight click of the iron latch was at that late hour as unexpected and startling as a thunder-clap. Madame Levaille put down a bottle she held above a liqueur glass; the players turned their heads; the whispered quarrel ceased; only the singer, after darting a glance at the door, went on humming with a stolid face. Susan appeared in the doorway, stepped in, flung the door to, and put her back against it, saying, half aloud—

'Mother!'

Madame Levaille, taking up the bottle again, said calmly: 'Here you are, my girl. What a state you are in!' The neck of the bottle rang on the rim of the glass, for the old woman was startled, and the idea that the farm had caught fire had entered her head. She could think of no other cause for her daughter's appearance.

Susan, soaked and muddy, stared the whole length of the room towards the men at the far end. Her mother asked—

'What has happened? God guard us from misfortune!'

Susan moved her lips. No sound came. Madame Levaille stepped up to her daughter, took her by the arm, looked into her face.

'In God's name,' she said shakily, 'what's the matter? You have been rolling in mud ... Why did you come? ... Where's Jean?'

The men had all got up and approached slowly, staring with dull surprise. Madame Levaille jerked her daughter away from the door, swung her round upon a seat close to the wall. Then she turned fiercely to the men—

'Enough of this! Out you go – you others! I close.'

One of them observed, looking down at Susan collapsed on the seat: 'She is – one may say – half dead.'

Madame Levaille flung the door open.

'Get out! March!' she cried, shaking nervously.

They dropped out into the night, laughing stupidly. Outside, the two Lotharios* broke out into loud shouts. The others tried to soothe them, all talking at once. The noise went away up the lane with the men, who staggered together in a tight knot, remonstrating with one another foolishly.

'Speak, Susan. What is it? Speak!' entreated Madame Levaille, as soon as the door was shut.

Susan pronounced some incomprehensible words, glaring at the table. The old woman clapped her hands above her head, let them drop, and stood looking at her daughter with disconsolate eyes. Her husband* had been 'deranged in his head' for a few years before he died, and now she began to suspect her daughter was going mad. She asked, pressingly—

'Does Jean know where you are? Where is Jean?'

Susan pronounced with difficulty—

'He knows . . . he is dead.'

'What!' cried the old woman. She came up near, and peering at her daughter, repeated three times: 'What do you say? What do you say? What do you say?'

Susan sat dry-eyed and stony before Madame Levaille, who contemplated her, feeling a strange sense of inexplicable horror creep into the silence of the house. She had hardly realised the news, further than to understand that she had been brought in one short moment face to face with something unexpected and final. It did not even occur to her to ask for any explanation. She thought: accident – terrible accident – blood to the head – fell down a trap door in the loft. . . . She remained there, distracted and mute, blinking her old eyes.

Suddenly, Susan said—

'I have killed him.'

For a moment the mother stood still, almost unbreathing, but with composed face. The next second she burst out into a shout—

'You miserable madwoman . . . they will cut your neck. . . .'

She fancied the gendarmes entering the house, saying to her: 'We want your daughter; give her up:' the gendarmes with the severe, hard faces of men on duty. She knew the brigadier well – and old friend, familiar and respectful, saying heartily, 'To your good health, Madame!' before lifting to his lips the small glass of cognac – out of the special bottle she kept for friends. And now! . . . She was losing her head. She rushed here and there, as if looking for something urgently needed – gave that up, stood stock still in the middle of the room, and screamed at her daughter—

'Why? Say! Say! Why?'

The other seemed to leap out of her strange apathy.

'Do you think I am made of stone?' she shouted back, striding towards her mother.

'No! It's impossible. . . .' said Madame Levaille, in a convinced tone.

'You go and see, mother,' retorted Susan, looking at her with blazing eyes. 'There's no mercy in heaven – no justice. No! . . . I did not know. . . . Do you think I have no heart? Do you think I have never heard people jeering at me, pitying me, wondering at me? Do you know how some of them were calling me? The mother of idiots – that was my nickname! And my children never would know me, never speak to me. They would know nothing; neither men – nor God. Haven't I prayed! But the Mother of God herself would not hear me. A mother! . . . Who is accursed – I, or the man who is dead? Eh? Tell me. I took care of myself. Do you think I would defy the anger of God and have my house full of those things – that are worse than animals who know the hand that feeds them? Who blasphemed in the night at the very church door? Was it I? . . . I only wept and prayed for mercy . . . and I feel the curse at every moment of the day – I see it round me from morning to night . . . I've got to keep them alive – to take care of my misfortune and shame. And he would come. I begged him and Heaven for mercy . . . No! . . . Then we shall see. . . . He came this evening. I thought to myself: "Ah! again!" . . . I had my long scissors. I heard him shouting. . . . I saw him near. . . . I must – must I? . . . Then take! . . . And I struck him in the throat above the breastbone. . . . I never heard him even sigh. . . . I left him standing. . . . It was a minute ago. How did I come here?'

Madame Levaille shivered. A wave of cold ran down her back, down her fat arms under her tight sleeves, made her stamp gently where she stood. Quivers ran over the broad cheeks, across the thin lips, ran amongst the wrinkles at the corners of her steady old eyes. She stammered—

'You wicked woman – you disgrace me. But there! You always resembled your father. What do you think will become of you . . . in the other world? In this . . . Oh misery!'

She was very hot now. She felt burning inside. She wrung her perspiring hands – and suddenly, starting in great haste, began to look for her big shawl and umbrella, feverishly, never once glancing at her daughter, who stood in the middle of the room following her with a gaze distracted and cold.

'Nothing worse than in this,' said Susan.

Her mother, umbrella in hand and trailing the shawl over the floor, groaned profoundly.

'I must go to the priest,' she burst out passionately. 'I do not know whether you even speak the truth! You are a horrible woman. They will find you anywhere. You may stay here – or go. There is no room for you in this world.'

Ready now to depart, she yet wandered aimlessly about the room, putting the bottles on the shelf, trying to fit with trembling hands the covers on cardboard boxes. Whenever the real sense of what she had heard emerged for a second from the haze of her thoughts she would fancy that something had exploded in her brain without, unfortunately, bursting her head to pieces – which would have been a relief. She blew the candles out one by one without knowing it, and was horribly startled by the darkness. She fell on a bench and began to whimper. After a while she ceased, and sat listening to the breathing of her daughter, whom she could hardly see, still and upright, giving no other sign of life. She was becoming old rapidly at last, during those minutes. She spoke in tones unsteady, cut about by the rattle of teeth, like one shaken by a deadly cold fit of ague.

'I wish you had died little. I will never dare to show my old head in the sunshine again. There are worse misfortunes than idiot children. I wish you had been born to me simple – like your own. . . .'

She saw the figure of her daughter pass before the faint and livid clearness of a window. Then it appeared in the doorway for a second, and the door swung to with a clang. Madame Levaille, as if awakened by the noise from a long nightmare, rushed out.

'Susan!' she shouted from the doorstep.

She heard a stone roll a long time down the declivity of the rocky beach above the sands. She stepped forward cautiously, one hand on the wall of the house, and peered down into the smooth darkness of the empty bay. Once again she cried—

'Susan! You will kill yourself there.'

The stone had taken its last leap in the dark, and she heard nothing now. A sudden thought seemed to strangle her, and she called no more. She turned her back upon the black silence of the pit and went up the lane towards Ploumar, stumbling along with sombre determination, as if she had started on a desperate journey that would last, perhaps, to the end of her life. A sullen and periodic clamour of waves rolling over reefs followed her far inland between the high hedges sheltering the gloomy solitude of the fields.

Susan had run out, swerving sharp to the left at the door, and on the edge of the slope crouched down behind a boulder. A dislodged stone went on downwards, rattling as it leaped. When Madame Levaille called out, Susan could have, by stretching her hand, touched her mother's skirt, had she had the courage to move a limb. She saw the old woman go away, and she remained still, closing her eyes and pressing her side to the hard and rugged surface of the rock. After a while a familiar face with fixed eyes and an open mouth became visible in the intense obscurity amongst the boulders. She uttered a low cry and stood up. The face vanished, leaving her to gasp and shiver alone in the wilderness of stone heaps. But as soon as she had crouched down again to rest, with her head against the rock, the face returned, came very near, appeared eager to finish the speech that had been cut short by death, only a moment ago. She scrambled quickly to her feet and said: 'Go away, or I will do it again.' The thing wavered, swung to the right, to the left. She moved this way and that, stepped back, fancied herself screaming at it, and was appalled by the unbroken stillness of the night. She tottered on the brink, felt the steep declivity under her feet, and rushed down blindly to save herself from a headlong fall. The shingle seemed to wake up; the pebbles began to roll before her, pursued her from above, raced down with her on both sides, rolling past with an increasing clatter. In the peace of the night the noise grew, deepening to a rumour, continuous and violent, as if the whole semicircle of the stony beach had started to tumble down into the bay. Susan's feet hardly touched the slope that seemed to run down with her. At the bottom she stumbled, shot forward, throwing her arms out, and fell heavily. She jumped up at once and turned swiftly to look back, her clenched hands full of sand she had clutched in her fall. The face was there, keeping its distance, visible in its own sheen that made a pale stain in the night. She shouted, 'Go away' – she shouted at it with pain, with fear, with all the rage of that useless stab that could not keep him quiet, keep him out of her sight. What did he want now? He was dead. Dead men have no children. Would he never leave her alone? She shrieked at it – waved her outstretched hands. She seemed to feel the breath of parted lips, and, with a long cry of discouragement, fled across the level bottom of the bay.

She ran lightly, unaware of any effort of her body. High sharp rocks that, when the bay is full, show above the glittering plain of blue water like pointed towers of submerged churches, glided past her, rushing to the land at a tremendous pace. To the left, in the distance, she could see something shining: a broad disc of light in which narrow shadows pivoted round the centre like the spokes of a wheel. She heard a voice calling, 'Hey! There!' and answered with a wild scream. So, he could call yet! He was calling after her to stop. Never! . . . She tore through the night, past the startled group of seaweed-gatherers who stood round their lantern paralysed with fear at the unearthly screech coming from that fleeing shadow. The men leaned on their pitchforks staring fearfully. A woman fell on her knees, and, crossing herself, began to pray aloud. A little girl with her ragged skirt full of slimy seaweed began to sob despairingly, lugging her soaked burden close to the man who carried the light. Somebody said: 'The thing ran out towards the sea.' Another voice exclaimed: 'And the sea is coming back! Look at the spreading puddles. Do you hear – you woman – there! Get up!' Several voices cried together. 'Yes, let us be off! Let the accursed thing go to the sea!' They moved on, keeping close round the light. Suddenly a man swore loudly. He would go and see what was the matter. It had been a woman's voice. He would go. There were shrill protests from women – but his high form detached itself from the group and went off running. They sent an unanimous call of scared voices after him. A word, insulting and mocking, came back, thrown at them through darkness. A woman moaned. An old man said gravely: 'Such things ought to be left alone.' They went on slower, shuffling in the yielding sand and whispering to one another that Millot feared nothing, having no religion, but that it would end badly some day.

Susan met the incoming tide by the Raven islet and stopped, panting, with her feet in the water. She heard the murmur and felt the cold caress* of the sea, and, calmer now, could see the sombre and confused mass of the Raven on one side and on the other the long white streak of Molène sands* that are left high above the dry bottom of Fougère Bay at every ebb. She turned round and saw far away, along the starred background of the sky, the ragged outline of the coast. Above it, nearly facing her, appeared the tower of Ploumar Church; a slender and tall pyramid shooting up dark and pointed into the clustered glitter of the stars. She felt strangely calm. She knew where she was, and began to remember how she came there – and why. She peered into the smooth obscurity near her. She was alone. There was nothing there; nothing near her, either living or dead.

The tide was creeping in quietly, putting out long impatient arms of strange rivulets that ran towards the land between ridges of sand. Under the night the pools grew bigger with mysterious rapidity, while the great sea, yet far off, thundered in a regular rhythm along the indistinct line of the horizon. Susan splashed her way back for a few yards without being able to get clear of the water that murmured tenderly all around and, suddenly, with a spiteful gurgle, nearly took her off her feet. Her heart thumped with fear. This place was too big and too empty to die in. To-morrow they would do with her what they liked. But before she died she must tell them – tell the gentlemen in black clothes that there are things no woman can bear. She must explain how it happened. . . . She splashed through a pool, getting wet to the waist, too preoccupied to care. . . . She must explain. 'He came in the same way as ever and said, just so: "Do you think I am going to leave the land to those people from Morbihan* that I do not know? Do you? We shall see! Come along, you creature of mischance!" And he put his arms out. Then, Messieurs, I said: "Before God – never!" And he said, striding at me with open palms: "There is no God to hold me! Do you understand, you useless carcase. I will do what I like." And he took me by the shoulders. Then I, Messieurs, called to God for help, and next minute, while he was shaking me, I felt my long scissors in my hand. His shirt was unbuttoned, and, by the candle-light, I saw the hollow of his throat. I cried: "Let go!" He was crushing my shoulders. He was strong, my man was! Then I thought: No! . . . Must I? . . . Then take! – and I struck in the hollow place. I never saw him fall. Never! Never! . . . Never saw him fall. . . . The old father never turned his head. He is deaf and childish, gentlemen. . . . Nobody saw him fall. I ran out . . . Nobody saw. . . .'

She had been scrambling amongst the boulders of the Raven

and now found herself, all out of breath, standing amongst the heavy shadows of the rocky islet. The Raven is connected with the main land by a natural pier of immense and slippery stones. She intended to return home that way. Was he still standing there? At home. Home! Four idiots and a corpse. She must go back and explain. Anybody would understand. . . .

Below her the night or the sea seemed to pronounce distinctly—

'Aha! I see you at last!'

She started, slipped, fell; and without attempting to rise, listened, terrified. She heard heavy breathing, a clatter of wooden clogs. It stopped.

'Where the devil did you pass?' said an invisible man, hoarsely.

She held her breath. She recognised the voice. She had not seen him fall. Was he pursuing her there dead, or perhaps . . . alive?

She lost her head. She cried from the crevice where she lay huddled, 'Never, never!'

'Ah! You are still there. You led me a fine dance. Wait, my beauty, I must see how you look after all this. You wait. . . .'

Millot was stumbling, laughing, swearing meaninglessly out of pure satisfaction, pleased with himself for having run down that fly-by-night. 'As if there were such things as ghosts! Bah! It took an old African soldier to show those clodhoppers. . . . But it was curious. Who the devil was she?'

Susan listened, crouching. He was coming for her, this dead man. There was no escape. What a noise he made amongst the stones. . . . She saw his head rise up, then the shoulders. He was tall – her own man! His long arms waved about, and it was his own voice sounding a little strange . . . because of the scissors. She scrambled out quickly, rushed to the edge of the causeway, and turned round. The man stood still on a high stone, detaching himself in dead black on the glitter of the sky.

'Where are you going to?' he called roughly.

She answered, 'Home!' and watched him intensely. He made a striding, clumsy leap on to another boulder, and stopped again, balancing himself, then said—

'Ha! ha! Well, I am going with you. It's the least I can do. Ha! ha! ha!'

She stared at him till her eyes seemed to become glowing

coals that burned deep into her brain, and yet she was in mortal fear of making out the well-known features. Below her the sea lapped softly against the rock with a splash, continuous and gentle.

The man said, advancing another step—

'I am coming for you. What do you think?'

She trembled. Coming for her! There was no escape, no peace, no hope. She looked round despairingly. Suddenly the whole shadowy coast, the blurred islets, the heaven itself, swayed about twice, then came to a rest. She closed her eyes and shouted—

'Can't you wait till I am dead!'

She was shaken by a furious hate for that shade that pursued her in this world, unappeased even by death in its longing for an heir that would be like other people's children.

'Hey! What?' said Millot, keeping his distance prudently. He was saying to himself: 'Look out! Some lunatic. An accident happens soon.'

She went on, wildly—

'I want to live. To live alone – for a week – for a day. I must explain to them. . . . I would tear you to pieces, I would kill you twenty times over rather than let you touch me while I live. How many times must I kill you – you blasphemer! Satan sends you here. I am damned too!'

'Come,' said Millot, alarmed and conciliating. 'I am perfectly alive! . . . Oh, my God!'

She had screamed, 'Alive!' and at once vanished before his eyes, as if the islet itself had swerved aside from under her feet. Millot rushed forward, and fell flat with his chin over the edge. Far below he saw the water whitened by her struggles, and heard one shrill cry for help that seemed to dart upwards along the perpendicular face of the rock, and soar past, straight into the high and impassive heaven.

Madame Levaille sat, dry-eyed, on the short grass of the hill side, with her thick legs stretched out, and her old feet turned up in their black cloth shoes. Her clogs stood near by, and further off the umbrella lay on the withered sward like a weapon dropped from the grasp of a vanquished warrior. The Marquis of Chavanes, on horseback, one gloved hand on thigh, looked down at her as she got up laboriously, with groans. On the narrow track of the seaweed-carts four men were carrying inland Susan's body on a hand-barrow, while several others straggled listlessly behind. Madame Levaille looked after the procession. 'Yes, Monsieur le Marquis,' she said dispassionately, in her usual calm tone of a reasonable old woman. 'There are unfortunate people on this earth. I had only one child. Only one! And they won't bury her in consecrated ground!'*

Her eyes filled suddenly, and a short shower of tears rolled down the broad cheeks. She pulled the shawl close about her. The Marquis leaned slightly over in his saddle, and said—

'It is very sad. You have all my sympathy. I shall speak to the Curé. She was unquestionably insane, and the fall was accidental. Millot says so distinctly. Good-day, Madame.'

And he trotted off, thinking to himself: I must get this old woman appointed guardian of those idiots, and administrator of the farm. It would be much better than having here one of those other Bacadous, probably a red republican, corrupting my commune.

An Outpost of Progress

I

There were two white men in charge of the trading station. Kayerts, the chief, was short and fat; Carlier,* the assistant, was tall, with a large head and a very broad trunk perched upon a long pair of thin legs. The third man on the staff was a Sierra Leone nigger,* who maintained that his name was Henry Price.* However, for some reason or other, the natives down the river had given him the name of Makola, and it stuck to him through all his wanderings about the country.* He spoke English and French with a warbling accent, wrote a beautiful hand, understood book-keeping, and cherished in his innermost heart the worship of evil spirits. His wife was a negress from Loanda,* very large and very noisy. Three children rolled about in sunshine before the door of his low, shed-like dwelling. Makola, taciturn and impenetrable, despised the two white men. He had charge of a small clay storehouse with a dried-grass roof,* and pretended to keep a correct account of beads, cotton cloth, red kerchiefs, brass wire, and other trade goods it contained. Besides the storehouse and Makola's hut, there was only one large building in the cleared ground of the station. It was built neatly of reeds, with a verandah on all the four sides. There were three rooms in it. The one in the middle was the living room, and had two rough tables and a few stools in it. The other two were the bedrooms for the white men. Each had a bedstead and a mosquito net for all furniture. The plank floor was littered with the belongings of the white men; open half-empty boxes, torn wearing apparel,* old boots; all the things dirty, and all the things broken, that accumulate mysteriously round untidy men. There was also another dwelling-place some distance away from the buildings. In it, under a tall cross much out of the perpendicular, slept the man who had seen the beginning of all this; who had planned and had watched the construction of this outpost of progress. He had been, at home, an unsuccessful painter who, weary of pursuing fame on an empty stomach, had gone out there through high protections. He had been the first chief of that station. Makola had watched the energetic artist die of fever in the just finished house with his usual kind of 'I told you so' indifference. Then, for a time, he dwelt alone with his family, his account books, and the Evil Spirit that rules the lands under the equator. He got on very well with his god. Perhaps he had propitiated him by a promise of more white men to play with, by and by. At any rate the director of the Great Trading Company, coming up in a steamer that resembled an enormous sardine box* with a flat-roofed shed erected on it, found the station in good order, and Makola as usual quietly diligent. The director had the cross put up over the first agent's grave, and appointed Kayerts to the post. Carlier was told off* as second in charge. The director was a man ruthless and efficient, who at times, but very imperceptibly, indulged in grim humour. He made a speech* to Kayerts and Carlier, pointing out to them the promising aspect of their station. The nearest trading-post was about three hundred miles away. It was an exceptional opportunity for them to distinguish themselves and to earn percentages on the trade. This appointment was a favour done to beginners. Kayerts was moved almost to tears by his director's kindness. He would, he said, by doing his best, try to justify the flattering confidence, etc., etc. Kayerts had been in the Administration of the Telegraphs, and knew how to express himself correctly. Carlier, an ex-non-commissioned officer of cavalry in an army guaranteed from harm by several European Powers,* was less impressed. If there were commissions to get, so much the better; and, trailing a sulky glance over the river, the forests, the impenetrable bush that seemed to cut off the station from the rest of the world, he muttered between his teeth, 'We shall see, very soon.'

Next day, some bales of cotton goods and a few cases of provisions having been thrown on shore, the sardine-box steamer went off, not to return for another six months. On the deck the director touched his cap to the two agents, who stood on the bank waving their hats, and turning to an old servant of the Company on his passage to headquarters, said, 'Look at those two imbeciles. They must be mad at home to send me such specimens. I told those fellows to plant a vegetable garden, build new storehouses and fences, and construct a landing-stage. I bet nothing will be done! They won't know how to begin.* I always thought the station on this river useless, and they just fit the station!'

'They will form themselves there,' said the old stager with a quiet smile.

'At any rate, I am rid of them for six months,' retorted the director.

The two men watched the steamer round the bend, then, ascending arm in arm the slope of the bank, returned to the station. They had been in this vast and dark country only a very short time, and as yet always in the midst of other white men, under the eye and guidance of their superiors. And now, dull as they were to the subtle influences of surroundings, they felt themselves very much alone, when suddenly left unassisted to face the wilderness; a wilderness rendered more strange, more incomprehensible by the mysterious glimpses of the vigorous life it contained. They were two perfectly insignificant and incapable individuals, whose existence is only rendered possible through the high organisation of civilised crowds. Few men realise that their life, the very essence of their character, their capabilities and their audacities, are only the expression of their belief in the safety of their surroundings. The courage, the composure, the confidence; the emotions and principles; every great and every insignificant thought belongs not to the individual but to the crowd: to the crowd that believes blindly in the irresistible force of its institutions and of its morals, in the power of its police and of its opinion. But the contact with pure unmitigated savagery, with primitive nature and primitive man, brings sudden and profound trouble into the heart. To the sentiment of being alone of one's kind, to the clear perception of the loneliness of one's thoughts, of one's sensations – to the negation of the habitual, which is safe, there is added the affirmation of the unusual, which is dangerous; a suggestion of things vague, uncontrollable, and repulsive, whose discomposing intrusion excites the imagination and tries the civilised nerves of the foolish and the wise alike.

Kayerts and Carlier walked arm in arm, drawing close to one another as children do in the dark; and they had the same, not altogether unpleasant, sense of danger which one half suspects to be imaginary. They chatted persistently in familiar tones. 'Our station is prettily situated,' said one. The other assented with enthusiasm, enlarging volubly on the beauties of the situ-

ation. Then they passed near the grave. 'Poor devil!' said
Kayerts. 'He died of fever, didn't he?' muttered Carlier, stopping
short. 'Why,' retorted Kayerts, with indignation, 'I've been told
that the fellow exposed himself recklessly to the sun. The climate
here, everybody says, is not at all worse than at home, as long
as you keep out of the sun. Do you hear that, Carlier? I am
chief here, and my orders are that you should not expose
yourself to the sun!' He assumed his superiority jocularly, but
his meaning was serious. The idea that he would, perhaps, have
to bury Carlier and remain alone, gave him an inward shiver.
He felt suddenly that this Carlier was more precious to him
here, in the centre of Africa, than a brother could be anywhere
else. Carlier, entering into the spirit of the thing, made a military
salute and answered in a brisk tone, 'Your orders shall be
attended to, chief!' Then he burst out laughing, slapped Kayerts
on the back, and shouted, 'We shall let life run easily here! Just
sit still and gather in the ivory those savages will bring. This
country has its good points, after all!' They both laughed loudly
while Carlier thought: That poor Kayerts; he is so fat and
unhealthy. It would be awful if I had to bury him here. He is a
man I respect. . . . Before they reached the verandah of their
house they called one another 'my dear fellow'.

The first day they were very active,* pottering about with
hammers and nails and red calico, to put up curtains, make
their house habitable and pretty; resolved to settle down
comfortably to their new life. For them an impossible task. To
grapple effectually with even purely material problems requires
more serenity of mind and more lofty courage than people
generally imagine. No two beings could have been more unfitted
for such a struggle. Society, not from any tenderness, but
because of its strange needs, had taken care of those two men,
forbidding them all independent thought, all initiative, all departure from routine; and forbidding it under pain of death. They
could only live on condition of being machines. And now,
released from the fostering care of men with pens behind the
ears, or of men with gold lace on the sleeves, they were like
those lifelong prisoners who, liberated after many years, do not
know what use to make of their freedom. They did not know
what use to make of their faculties, being both, through want
of practice, incapable of independent thought.

At the end of two months Kayerts often would say, 'If it was not for my Melie, you wouldn't catch me here.' Melie was his daughter. He had thrown up his post in the Administration of the Telegraphs, though he had been for seventeen years perfectly happy there, to earn a dowry for his girl. His wife was dead, and the child was being brought up by his sisters. He regretted the streets,* the pavements, the cafés, his friends of many years; all the things he used to see, day after day; all the thoughts suggested by familiar things – the thoughts effortless, monotonous, and soothing of a Government clerk; he regretted all the gossip, the small enmities, the mild venom, and the little jokes of Government offices. 'If I had had a decent brother-in-law,' Carlier would remark, 'a fellow with a heart, I would not be here.' He had left the army and had made himself so obnoxious to his family by his laziness and impudence, that an exasperated brother-in-law had made superhuman efforts to procure him an appointment in the Company as a second-class agent. Having not a penny in the world, he was compelled to accept this means of livelihood as soon as it became quite clear to him that there was nothing more to squeeze out of his relations. He, like Kayerts, regretted his old life. He regretted the clink of sabre and spurs on a fine afternoon, the barrack-room witticisms, the girls of garrison towns; but, besides, he had also a sense of grievance. He was evidently a much ill-used man. This made him moody, at times. But the two men got on well together in the fellowship of their stupidity and laziness. Together they did nothing, absolutely nothing, and enjoyed the sense of the idleness* for which they were paid. And in time they came to feel something resembling affection for one another.

They lived like blind men in a large room, aware only of what came in contact with them (and of that only imperfectly), but unable to see the general aspect of things. The river, the forest, all the great land throbbing with life, were like a great emptiness. Even the brilliant sunshine disclosed nothing intelligible. Things appeared and disappeared before their eyes in an unconnected and aimless kind of way. The river seemed to come from nowhere and flow nowhither.* It flowed through a void. Out of that void, at times, came canoes, and men with spears in their hands* would suddenly crowd the yard of the station. They were naked, glossy black, ornamented with snowy shells and glistening brass wire, perfect of limb. They made an uncouth babbling noise when they spoke, moved in a stately manner, and sent quick, wild glances out of their startled, never-resting eyes. Those warriors would squat in long rows, four or more deep, before the verandah, while their chiefs bargained for hours with Makola over an elephant tusk. Kayerts sat on his chair and looked down on the proceedings, understanding nothing. He stared at them with his round blue eyes, called out to Carlier, 'Here, look! look at that fellow there – and that other one, to the left. Did you ever see such a face? Oh, the funny brute!'

Carlier, smoking native tobacco in a short wooden pipe, would swagger up twirling his moustaches, and, surveying the warriors with haughty indulgence, would say—

'Fine animals. Brought any bone? Yes? It's not any too soon. Look at the muscles of that fellow – third from the end. I wouldn't care to get a punch on the nose from him. Fine arms, but legs no good below the knee. Couldn't make cavalry men of them.' And after glancing down complacently at his own shanks, he always concluded: 'Pah! Don't they stink! You, Makola! Take that herd over to the fetish'* (the storehouse was in every station called the fetish, perhaps because of the spirit of civilisation it contained) 'and give them up some of the rubbish you keep there. I'd rather see it full of bone than full of rags.'

Kayerts approved.

'Yes, yes! Go and finish that palaver* over there, Mr Makola. I will come round when you are ready, to weigh the tusk. We must be careful.' Then, turning to his companion: 'This is the tribe that lives down the river; they are rather aromatic. I remember, they had been once before here. D'ye hear that row? What a fellow has got to put up with in this dog of a country! My head is split.'

Such profitable visits were rare. For days the two pioneers of trade and progress would look on their empty courtyard in the vibrating brilliance of vertical sunshine. Below the high bank, the silent river flowed on glittering and steady. On the sands in the middle of the stream, hippos and alligators sunned themselves side by side. And stretching away in all directions, surrounding the insignificant cleared spot of the trading post, immense forests, hiding fateful complications of fantastic life, lay in the eloquent silence of mute greatness. The two men understood nothing, cared for nothing but for the passage of days that separated them from the steamer's return. Their predecessor had left some torn books. They took up these

wrecks of novels, and, as they had never read anything of the
kind before, they were surprised and amused. Then during long
days there were interminable and silly discussions about plots
and personages. In the centre of Africa they made the acquaintance of Richelieu and of d'Artagnan, of Hawk's Eye and of
Father Goriot, and of many other people.* All these imaginary
personages became subjects for gossip as if they had been living
friends. They discounted their virtues, suspected their motives,
decried their successes; were scandalised at their duplicity or
were doubtful about their courage. The accounts of crimes filled
them with indignation, while tender or pathetic passages moved
them deeply. Carlier cleared his throat and said in a soldierly
voice, 'What nonsense!' Kayerts, his round eyes suffused with
tears, his fat cheeks quivering, rubbed his bald head, and
declared, 'This is a splendid book. I had no idea there were such
clever fellows in the world.' They also found some old copies of
a home paper. That print discussed what it was pleased to call
'Our Colonial Expansion' in high-flown language.* It spoke
much of the rights and duties of civilisation, of the sacredness
of the civilising work, and extolled the merits of those who went
about bringing light, and faith, and commerce to the dark places
of the earth. Carlier and Kayerts read, wondered, and began to
think better of themselves. Carlier said one evening, waving his
hand about, 'In a hundred years, there will be perhaps a town
here. Quays, and warehouses, and barracks, and – and –
billiard-rooms. Civilisation, my boy, and virtue – and all. And
then, chaps will read that two good fellows, Kayerts and Carlier,
were the first civilised men to live in this very spot!' Kayerts
nodded, 'Yes, it is a consolation to think of that.' They seemed
to forget their dead predecessor; but, early one day, Carlier
went out and replanted the cross firmly. 'It used to make me
squint whenever I walked that way,' he explained to Kayerts
over the morning coffee. 'It made me squint, leaning over so
much. So I just planted it upright. And solid, I promise you! I
suspended myself with both hands to the cross-piece. Not a
move. Oh, I did that properly.'

At times Gobila* came to see them. Gobila was the chief of
the neighbouring villages. He was a grey-headed savage, thin
and black, with a white cloth round his loins and a mangy
panther skin hanging over his back. He came up with long
strides of his skeleton legs, swinging a staff as tall as himself,

and, entering the common room of the station, would squat on his heels to the left of the door. There he sat, watching Kayerts, and now and then making a speech which the other did not understand. Kayerts, without interrupting his occupation, would from time to time say in a friendly manner: 'How goes it, you old image?' and they would smile at one another. The two whites had a liking for that old and incomprehensible creature, and called him Father Gobila. Gobila's manner was paternal, and he seemed really to love all white men. They all appeared to him very young, indistinguishably alike (except for stature), and he knew that they were all brothers, and also immortal. The death of the artist, who was the first white man whom he knew intimately, did not disturb this belief, because he was firmly convinced that the white stranger had pretended to die and got himself buried for some mysterious purpose of his own, into which it was useless to inquire. Perhaps it was his way of going home to his own country? At any rate, these were his brothers, and he transferred his absurd affection to them. They returned it in a way. Carlier slapped him on the back, and recklessly struck off matches for his amusement. Kayerts was always ready to let him have a sniff at the ammonia bottle. In short, they behaved just like that other white creature that had hidden itself in a hole in the ground. Gobila considered them attentively. Perhaps they were the same being with the other – or one of them was. He couldn't decide – clear up that mystery; but he remained always very friendly. In consequence of that friendship the women of Gobila's village walked in single file through the reedy grass, bringing every morning to the station, fowls, and sweet potatoes, and palm wine, and sometimes a goat. The Company never provisions the stations fully, and the agents required those local supplies to live. They had them through the good-will of Gobila, and lived well. Now and then one of them had a bout of fever, and the other nursed him with gentle devotion. They did not think much of it. It left them weaker, and their appearance changed for the worse. Carlier was hollow-eyed and irritable. Kayerts showed a drawn, flabby face above the rotundity of his stomach, which gave him a weird aspect. But being constantly together, they did not notice the change that took place gradually in their appearance, and also in their dispositions.

Five months passed in that way.

Then, one morning, as Kayerts and Carlier, lounging in their chairs under the verandah, talked about the approaching visit of the steamer, a knot of armed men came out of the forest and advanced towards the station. They were strangers to that part of the country. They were tall, slight, draped classically from neck to heel in blue fringed clothes, and carried percussion muskets over their bare right shoulders. Makola showed signs of excitement, and ran out of the storehouse (where he spent all his days) to meet these visitors. They came into the courtyard and looked about them with steady, scornful glances. Their leader, a powerful and determined-looking negro with blood-shot eyes, stood in front of the verandah and made a long speech. He gesticulated much, and ceased very suddenly.

There was something in his intonation, in the sounds of the long sentences he used, that startled the two whites. It was like a reminiscence of something not exactly familiar, and yet resembling the speech of civilised men. It sounded like one of those impossible languages which sometimes we hear in our dreams.

'What lingo is that?' said the amazed Carlier. 'In the first moment I fancied the fellow was going to speak French. Anyway, it is a different kind of gibberish to what we ever heard.'

'Yes,' replied Kayerts. 'Hey, Makola, what does he say? Where do they come from? Who are they?'

But Makola, who seemed to be standing on hot bricks, answered hurriedly, 'I don't know. They come from very far. Perhaps Mrs Price will understand. They are perhaps bad men.'

The leader, after waiting for a while, said something sharply to Makola, who shook his head. Then the man, after looking round, noticed Makola's hut and walked over there. The next moment Mrs Makola was heard speaking with great volubility. The other strangers – they were six in all – strolled about with an air of ease, put their heads through the door of the store-room, congregated round the grave, pointed understandingly at the cross, and generally made themselves at home.

'I don't like those chaps – and, I say, Kayerts, they must be from the coast; they've got firearms,' observed the sagacious Carlier.

Kayerts also did not like those chaps. They both, for the first time, became aware that they lived in conditions where the unusual may be dangerous, and that there was no power on earth outside of themselves to stand between them and the unusual. They became uneasy, went in and loaded their revolvers. Kayerts said, 'We must order Makola to tell them to go away before dark.'

The strangers left in the afternoon, after eating a meal prepared for them by Mrs Makola. The immense woman was excited, and talked much with the visitors. She rattled away shrilly, pointing here and pointing there at the forests and at the river. Makola sat apart and watched. At times he got up and whispered to his wife. He accompanied the strangers across the ravine at the back of the station-ground, and returned slowly looking very thoughtful. When questioned by the white men he was very strange, seemed not to understand, seemed to have forgotten French – seemed to have forgotten how to speak altogether. Kayerts and Carlier agreed that the nigger had had too much palm wine.

There was some talk about keeping a watch in turn, but in the evening everything seemed so quiet and peaceful that they retired as usual. All night they were disturbed by a lot of drumming in the villages. A deep, rapid roll near by would be followed by another far off – then all ceased. Soon short appeals would rattle out here and there, then all mingle together, increase, become vigorous and sustained, would spread out over the forest, roll through the night, unbroken and ceaseless, near and far, as if the whole land had been one immense drum booming out steadily an appeal to heaven. And through the deep and tremendous noise sudden yells that resembled snatches of songs from a mad-house darted shrill and high in discordant jets of sound which seemed to rush far above the earth and drive all peace from under the stars.

Carlier and Kayerts slept badly. They both thought they had heard shots fired during the night – but they could not agree as to the direction. In the morning Makola was gone somewhere. He returned about noon with one of yesterday's strangers, and eluded all Kayerts' attempts to close with him: had become deaf apparently. Kayerts wondered. Carlier, who had been fishing off the bank, came back and remarked while he showed his catch, 'The niggers seem to be in a deuce of a stir; I wonder what's up. I saw about fifteen canoes cross the river during the two hours I was there fishing.' Kayerts, worried, said, 'Isn't this Makola very queer to-day?' Carlier advised, 'Keep all our men together in case of some trouble.'

II

There were ten station men who had been left by the Director. Those fellows, having engaged themselves to the Company for six months (without having any idea of a month in particular and only a very faint notion of time in general), had been serving the cause of progress for upwards of two years. Belonging to a tribe from a very distant part of this land of darkness and sorrow, they did not run away, naturally supposing that as wandering strangers they would be killed by the inhabitants of the country; in which they were right. They lived in straw huts on the slope of a ravine overgrown with reedy grass, just behind the station buildings. They were not happy, regretting the festive incantations, the sorceries, the human sacrifices of their own land; where they also had parents, brothers, sisters, admired chiefs, respected magicians, loved friends, and other ties supposed generally to be human. Besides, the rice rations served out by the Company did not agree with them, being a food unknown to their land, and to which they could not get used. Consequently they were unhealthy and miserable. Had they been of any other tribe they would have made up their minds to die – for nothing is easier to certain savages than suicide – and so have escaped from the puzzling difficulties of existence. But belonging, as they did, to a warlike tribe with filed teeth, they had more grit, and went on stupidly living through disease and sorrow. They did very little work, and had lost their splendid physique. Carlier and Kayerts doctored them assiduously without being able to bring them back into condition again. They were mustered every morning and told off to* different tasks – grass-cutting, fence-building, tree-felling, etc., etc., which no power on earth could induce them to execute efficiently. The two whites had practically very little control over them.

In the afternoon Makola came over to the big house and found Kayerts watching three heavy columns of smoke rising above the forests. 'What is that?' asked Kayerts. 'Some villages burn,' answered Makola, who seemed to have regained his wits. Then he said abruptly: 'We have got very little ivory; bad six months' trading. Do you like get a little more ivory?'

'Yes,' said Kayerts eagerly. He thought of percentages which were low.

'Those men who came yesterday are traders from Loanda who have got more ivory than they can carry home. Shall I buy? I know their camp.'

'Certainly,' said Kayerts. 'What are those traders?'

'Bad fellows,' said Makola indifferently. 'They fight with people, and catch women and children. They are bad men, and got guns. There is a great disturbance in the country. Do you want ivory?'

'Yes,' said Kayerts. Makola said nothing for a while. Then: 'Those workmen of ours are no good at all,' he muttered, looking round. 'Station in very bad order, sir. Director will growl. Better get a fine lot of ivory, then he say nothing.'

'I can't help it; the men won't work,' said Kayerts. 'When will you get that ivory?'

'Very soon,' said Makola. 'Perhaps to-night. You leave it to me, and keep indoors, sir. I think you had better give some palm wine to our men to make a dance this evening. Enjoy themselves. Work better to-morrow. There's plenty palm wine – gone a little sour.'

Kayerts said yes, and Makola, with his own hands, carried the big calabashes* to the door of his hut. They stood there till the evening, and Mrs Makola looked into every one. The men got them at sunset. When Kayerts and Carlier retired, a big bonfire was flaring before the men's huts. They could hear their shouts and drumming. Some men from Gobila's village had joined the station hands, and the entertainment was a great success.

In the middle of the night, Carlier waking suddenly, heard a man shout loudly; then a shot was fired. Only one. Carlier ran out and met Kayerts on the verandah. They were both startled. As they went across the yard to call Makola, they saw shadows moving in the night. One of them cried, 'Don't shoot! It's me, Price.' Then Makola appeared close to them. 'Go back, go back, please,' he urged, 'you spoil all.' 'There are strange men about,' said Carlier. 'Never mind; I know,' said Makola. Then he whispered, 'All right. Bring ivory. Say nothing! I know my business.' The two white men reluctantly went back to the house, but did not sleep. They heard footsteps, whispers, some groans. It seemed as if a lot of men came in, dumped heavy things on the ground, squabbled a long time, then went away. They lay on their hard beds and thought: 'This Makola is invaluable.' In the morning Carlier came out, very sleepy, and pulled at the cord of the big bell. The station hands mustered every morning to the sound of the bell. That morning nobody came. Kayerts turned out also, yawning. Across the yard they saw Makola come out of his hut, a tin basin of soapy water in his hand. Makola, a civilised nigger, was very neat in his person. He threw the soapsuds skilfully over a wretched little yellow cur he had, then turning his face to the agent's house, he shouted from the distance, 'All the men gone last night!'

They heard him plainly, but in their surprise they both yelled out together: 'What!' Then they stared at one another. 'We are in a proper fix now,' growled Carlier. 'It's incredible!' muttered Kayerts. 'I will go to the huts and see,' said Carlier, striding off. Makola coming up found Kayerts standing alone.

'I can hardly believe it,' said Kayerts tearfully. 'We took care of them as if they had been our children.'

'They went with the coast people,' said Makola after a moment of hesitation.

'What do I care with whom they went – the ungrateful brutes!' exclaimed the other. Then with sudden suspicion, and looking hard at Makola, he added: 'What do you know about it?'

Makola moved his shoulders, looking down on the ground. 'What do I know? I think only. Will you come and look at the ivory I've got there? It is a fine lot. You never saw such.'

He moved towards the store. Kayerts followed him mechanically, thinking about the incredible desertion of the men. On the ground before the door of the fetish lay six splendid tusks.

'What did you give for it?' asked Kayerts, after surveying the lot with satisfaction.

'No regular trade,' said Makola. 'They brought the ivory and gave it to me. I told them to take what they most wanted in the station. It is a beautiful lot. No station can show such tusks. Those traders wanted carriers badly, and our men were no good here. No trade, no entry in books; all correct.'

Kayerts nearly burst with indignation. 'Why!' he shouted, 'I believe you have sold our men for these tusks!' Makola stood impassive and silent. 'I – I – will – I,' stuttered Kayerts. 'You fiend!' he yelled out.

'I did the best for you and the Company,' said Makola imperturbably. 'Why you shout so much? Look at this tusk.'

'I dismiss you! I will report you – I won't look at the tusk. I forbid you to touch them. I order you to throw them into the river. You – you!'

'You very red, Mr Kayerts. If you are so irritable in the sun, you will get fever and die – like the first chief!' pronounced Makola impressively.

They stood still, contemplating one another with intense eyes, as if they had been looking with effort across immense distances. Kayerts shivered. Makola had meant no more than he said, but his words seemed to Kayerts full of ominous menace! He turned sharply and went away to the house. Makola retired into the bosom of his family; and the tusks, left lying before the store, looked very large and valuable in the sunshine.

Carlier came back on the verandah. 'They're all gone, hey?' asked Kayerts from the far end of the common room in a muffled voice. 'You did not find anybody?'

'Oh, yes,' said Carlier, 'I found one of Gobila's people lying dead before the huts – shot through the body. We heard that shot last night.'

Kayerts came out quickly. He found his companion staring grimly over the yard at the tusks, away by the store. They both sat in silence for a while. Then Kayerts related his conversation with Makola. Carlier said nothing. At the midday meal they ate very little. They hardly exchanged a word that day. A great silence seemed to lie heavily over the station and press on their lips. Makola did not open the store; he spent the day playing with his children. He lay full-length on a mat outside his door, and the youngsters sat on his chest and clambered all over him. It was a touching picture. Mrs Makola was busy cooking all day as usual. The white men made a somewhat better meal in the evening. Afterwards, Carlier smoking his pipe strolled over to the store; he stood for a long time over the tusks, touched one or two with his foot, even tried to lift the largest one by its small end. He came back to his chief, who had not stirred from the verandah, threw himself in the chair and said—

'I can see it! They were pounced upon while they slept heavily after drinking all that palm wine you've allowed Makola to give them. A put-up job! See? The worst is, some of Gobila's people were there, and got carried off too, no doubt. The least drunk woke up, and got shot for his sobriety. This is a funny country. What will you do now?'

'We can't touch it, of course,' said Kayerts.

'Of course not,' assented Carlier.

'Slavery is an awful thing,' stammered out Kayerts in an unsteady voice.

'Frightful – the sufferings,' grunted Carlier, with conviction.

They believed their words. Everybody shows a respectful deference to certain sounds that he and his fellows can make. But about feelings people really know nothing. We talk with indignation or enthusiasm; we talk about oppression, cruelty, crime, devotion, self-sacrifice, virtue, and we know nothing real beyond the words. Nobody knows what suffering or sacrifice mean – except, perhaps, the victims of the mysterious purpose of these illusions.

Next morning they saw Makola very busy setting up in the yard the big scales used for weighing ivory. By and by Carlier said: 'What's that filthy scoundrel up to?' and lounged out into the yard. Kayerts followed. They stood by watching. Makola took no notice. When the balance was swung true, he tried to lift a tusk into the scale. It was too heavy. He looked up helplessly without a word, and for a minute they stood round that balance as mute and still as three statues. Suddenly Carlier said: 'Catch hold of the other end, Makola – you beast!' and together they swung the tusk up. Kayerts trembled in every limb. He muttered, 'I say! O! I say!' and putting his hand in his pocket found there a dirty bit of paper and the stump of a pencil. He turned his back on the others, as if about to do something tricky, and noted stealthily the weights which Carlier shouted out to him with unnecessary loudness. When all was over Makola whispered to himself: 'The sun's very strong here for the tusks.' Carlier said to Kayerts in a careless tone: 'I say, chief, I might just as well give him a lift with this lot into the store.'

As they were going back to the house Kayerts observed with a sigh: 'It had to be done.' And Carlier said: 'It's deplorable, but, the men being Company's men, the ivory is Company's ivory. We must look after it.' 'I will report to the Director, of course,' said Kayerts. 'Of course; let him decide,' approved Carlier.

At mid-day they made a hearty meal. Kayerts sighed from time to time. Whenever they mentioned Makola's name they always added to it an opprobrious epithet. It eased their conscience.

Makola gave himself a half-holiday, and bathed his children in the river. No one from Gobila's villages came near the station that day. No one came the next day, and the next, nor for a whole week. Gobila's people might have all been dead and buried for any sign of life they gave. But they were only mourning for those they had lost by the witchcraft of white men, who had brought wicked people into their country. The wicked people were gone, but fear remained. Fear always remains. A man may destroy everything within himself, love and hate and belief, and even doubt; but as long as he clings to life he cannot destroy fear: the fear, subtle, indestructible, and terrible, that pervades his being; that tinges his thoughts; that lurks in his heart; that watches on his lips the struggle of his last breath. In his fear, the mild old Gobila offered extra human sacrifices to all the Evil Spirits that had taken possession of his white friends. His heart was heavy. Some warriors spoke about burning and killing, but the cautious old savage dissuaded them. Who could foresee the woe those mysterious creatures, if irritated, might bring? They should be left alone. Perhaps in time they would disappear into the earth as the first one had disappeared. His people must keep away from them, and hope for the best.

Kayerts and Carlier did not disappear, but remained above on this earth, that, somehow, they fancied had become bigger and very empty. It was not the absolute and dumb solitude of the post that impressed them so much as an inarticulate feeling that something from within them was gone, something that worked for their safety, and had kept the wilderness from interfering with their hearts. The images of home; the memory of people like them, of men that thought and felt as they used to think and feel, receded into distances made indistinct by the glare of unclouded sunshine. And out of the great silence of the surrounding wilderness, its very hopelessness and savagery seemed to approach them nearer, to draw them gently, to look upon them, to envelop them with a solicitude irresistible, familiar, and disgusting.

Days lengthened into weeks, then into months. Gobila's people drummed and yelled to every new moon, as of yore, but kept away from the station. Makola and Carlier tried once in a canoe to open communications, but were received with a shower of arrows, and had to fly back to the station for dear life. That attempt set the country up and down the river into an uproar that could be very distinctly heard for days. The steamer was late. At first they spoke of delay jauntily, then anxiously, then gloomily. The matter was becoming serious. Stores were running short. Carlier cast his lines off the bank, but the river was low, and the fish kept out in the stream. They dared not stroll far away from the station to shoot. Moreover, there was no game in the impenetrable forest. Once Carlier shot a hippo in the river. They had no boat to secure it, and it sank. When it floated up it drifted away, and Gobila's people secured the carcase. It was the occasion for a national holiday, but Carlier had a fit of rage over it, and talked about the necessity of exterminating all the niggers before the country could be made habitable.* Kayerts mooned about silently; spent hours looking at the portrait of his Melie.* It represented a little girl with long bleached tresses and a rather sour face. His legs were much swollen, and he could hardly walk. Carlier, undermined by fever, could not swagger any more, but kept tottering about, still with a devil-may-care air, as became a man who remembered his crack regiment. He had become hoarse, sarcastic, and inclined to say unpleasant things. He called it 'being frank with you'. They had long ago reckoned their percentages on trade, including in them that last deal of 'this infamous Makola'. They had also concluded not to say anything about it. Kayerts hesitated at first – was afraid of the Director.

'He has seen worse things done on the quiet,' maintained Carlier, with a hoarse laugh. 'Trust him! He won't thank you if you blab. He is no better than you or me. Who will talk if we hold our tongues? There is nobody here.'

That was the root of the trouble! There was nobody there; and being left there alone with their weakness, they became daily more like a pair of accomplices than like a couple of devoted friends. They had heard nothing from home for eight months. Every evening they said, 'To-morrow we shall see the steamer.' But one of the Company's steamers had been wrecked, and the Director was busy with the other, relieving very distant and important stations on the main river. He thought that the useless station, and the useless men, could wait. Meantime Kayerts and Carlier lived on rice boiled without salt, and cursed the Company, all Africa, and the day they were born. One must have lived on such diet to discover what ghastly trouble the necessity of swallowing one's food may become. There was

literally nothing else in the station but rice and coffee; they
drank the coffee without sugar. The last fifteen lumps Kayerts
had solemnly locked away in his box, together with a half-
bottle of Cognac, 'in case of sickness,' he explained. Carlier
approved. 'When one is sick,' he said, 'any little extra like that
is cheering.'

They waited. Rank grass began to sprout over the courtyard.
The bell never rang now. Days passed, silent, exasperating, and
slow. When the two men spoke, they snarled; and their silences
were bitter, as if tinged by the bitterness of their thoughts.

One day after a lunch of boiled rice, Carlier put down his cup
untasted, and said: 'Hang it all! Let's have a decent cup of
coffee for once. Bring out that sugar, Kayerts!'

'For the sick,' muttered Kayerts, without looking up.

'For the sick,' mocked Carlier. 'Bosh! . . . Well! I am sick.'

'You are no more sick than I am, and I go without,' said
Kayerts in a peaceful tone.

'Come! out with that sugar, you stingy old slave-dealer.'

Kayerts looked up quickly. Carlier was smiling with marked
insolence. And suddenly it seemed to Kayerts that he had never
seen that man before. Who was he? He knew nothing about
him. What was he capable of? There was a surprising flash of
violent emotion within him, as if in the presence of something
undreamt-of, dangerous, and final. But he managed to pronounce with composure—

'That joke is in very bad taste. Don't repeat it.'

'Joke!' said Carlier, hitching himself forward on his seat. 'I
am hungry – I am sick – I don't joke! I hate hypocrites. You are
a hypocrite. You are a slave-dealer. I am a slave-dealer. There's
nothing but slave-dealers in this cursed country. I mean to have
sugar in my coffee to-day, anyhow!'

'I forbid you to speak to me in that way,' said Kayerts with a
fair show of resolution.

'You! – What?' shouted Carlier, jumping up.

Kayerts stood up also. 'I am your chief,' he began, trying to
master the shakiness of his voice.

'What?' yelled the other. 'Who's chief? There's no chief here.
There's nothing here: there's nothing but you and I. Fetch the
sugar – you pot-bellied ass.'

'Hold your tongue. Go out of this room,' screamed Kayerts.
'I dismiss you – you scoundrel!'

Carlier swung a stool. All at once he looked dangerously in earnest. 'You flabby, good-for-nothing civilian – take that!' he howled.

Kayerts dropped under the table, and the stool struck the grass inner wall of the room. Then, as Carlier was trying to upset the table, Kayerts in desperation made a blind rush, head low, like a cornered pig would do, and overturning his friend, bolted along the verandah, and into his room. He locked the door, snatched his revolver, and stood panting. In less than a minute Carlier was kicking at the door furiously, howling, 'If you don't bring out that sugar, I will shoot you at sight, like a dog. Now then – one – two – three. You won't? I will show you who's the master.'

Kayerts thought the door would fall in, and scrambled through the square hole that served for a window in his room. There was then the whole breadth of the house between them. But the other was apparently not strong enough to break in the door, and Kayerts heard him running round. Then he also began to run laboriously on his swollen legs. He ran as quickly as he could, grasping the revolver, and unable yet to understand what was happening to him. He saw in succession Makola's house, the store, the river, the ravine, and the low bushes; and he saw all those things again as he ran for the second time round the house. Then again they flashed past him. That morning he could not have walked a yard without a groan.

And now he ran. He ran fast enough to keep out of sight of the other man.

Then as, weak and desperate, he thought, 'Before I finish the next round I shall die,' he heard the other man stumble heavily, then stop. He stopped also. He had the back and Carlier the front of the house, as before. He heard him drop into a chair cursing, and suddenly his own legs gave way, and he slid down into a sitting posture with his back to the wall. His mouth was as dry as a cinder, and his face was wet with perspiration – and tears. What was it all about? He thought it must be a horrible illusion; he thought he was dreaming; he thought he was going mad! After a while he collected his senses. What did they quarrel about? That sugar! How absurd! He would give it to him – didn't want it himself. And he began scrambling to his feet with a sudden feeling of security. But before he had fairly stood upright, a common-sense reflection occurred to him and drove

him back into despair. He thought: If I give way now to that
brute of a soldier, he will begin this horror again to-morrow –
and the day after – every day – raise other pretensions, trample
on me, torture me, make me his slave – and I will be lost! Lost!
The steamer may not come for days – may never come. He
shook so that he had to sit down on the floor again. He shivered
forlornly. He felt he could not, would not move any more. He
was completely distracted by the sudden perception that the
position was without issue – that death and life had in a moment
become equally difficult and terrible.

All at once he heard the other push his chair back; and he
leaped to his feet with extreme facility. He listened and got
confused. Must run again! Right or left? He heard footsteps. He
darted to the left, grasping his revolver, and at the very same
instant, as it seemed to him, they came into violent collision.
Both shouted with surprise. A loud explosion took place
between them; a roar of red fire, thick smoke; and Kayerts,
deafened and blinded, rushed back thinking: I am hit – it's all
over. He expected the other to come round – to gloat over his
agony. He caught hold of an upright of the roof – 'All over!'
Then he heard a crashing fall on the other side of the house, as
if somebody had tumbled headlong over a chair – then silence.
Nothing more happened. He did not die. Only his shoulder felt
as if it had been badly wrenched, and he had lost his revolver.
He was disarmed and helpless! He waited for his fate. The other
man made no sound. It was a stratagem. He was stalking him
now! Along what side? Perhaps he was taking aim this very
minute!

After a few moments of an agony frightful and absurd, he
decided to go and meet his doom. He was prepared for every
surrender. He turned the corner, steadying himself with one
hand on the wall; made a few paces, and nearly swooned.* He
had seen on the floor, protruding past the other corner, a pair
of turned-up feet. A pair of white naked feet in red slippers. He
felt deadly sick, and stood for a time in profound darkness.
Then Makola appeared before him, saying quietly: 'Come along,
Mr Kayerts. He is dead.'* He burst into tears of gratitude; a
loud, sobbing fit of crying. After a time he found himself sitting
in a chair and looking at Carlier, who lay stretched on his back.
Makola was kneeling over the body.

'Is this your revolver?' asked Makola, getting up.

'Yes,' said Kayerts; then he added very quickly, 'He ran after me to shoot me – you saw!'

'Yes, I saw,' said Makola. 'There is only one revolver; where's his?'

'Don't know,' whispered Kayerts in a voice that had suddenly become very faint.

'I will go and look for it,' said the other gently. He made the round along the verandah, while Kayerts sat still and looked at the corpse. Makola came back empty-handed, stood in deep thought, then stepped quietly into the dead man's room, and came out directly with a revolver, which he held up before Kayerts. Kayerts shut his eyes. Everything was going round. He found life more terrible and difficult than death. He had shot an unarmed man.

'After meditating for a while, Makola said softly, pointing at the dead man who lay there with his right eye blown out— *

'He died of fever.' Kayerts looked at him with a stony stare. 'Yes,' repeated Makola thoughtfully, stepping over the corpse. 'I think he died of fever. Bury him to-morrow.'

And he went away slowly to his expectant wife, leaving the two white men alone on the verandah.

Night came, and Kayerts sat unmoving on his chair. He sat quiet as if he had taken a dose of opium. The violence of the emotions he had passed through produced a feeling of exhausted serenity. He had plumbed in one short afternoon the depths of horror and despair, and now found repose in the conviction that life had no more secrets for him: neither had death! He sat by the corpse thinking; thinking very actively, thinking very new thoughts. He seemed to have broken loose from himself altogether. His old thoughts, convictions, likes and dislikes, things he respected and things he abhorred, appeared in their true light at last! Appeared contemptible and childish, false and ridiculous. He revelled in his new wisdom while he sat by the man he had killed. He argued with himself about all things under heaven with that kind of wrong-headed lucidity which may be observed in some lunatics. Incidentally he reflected that the fellow dead there had been a noxious beast anyway; that men died every day in thousands; perhaps in hundreds of thousands – who could tell? – and that in the number, that one death could not possibly make any difference; couldn't have any importance, at least to a thinking creature. He, Kayerts, was a thinking creature. He had been all his life, till that moment, a believer in a lot of nonsense like the rest of mankind – who are fools; but now he thought! He knew! He was at peace; he was familiar with the highest wisdom! Then he tried to imagine himself dead, and Carlier sitting in his chair watching him; and his attempt met with such unexpected success, that in a very few moments he became not at all sure who was dead and who was alive. This extraordinary achievement of his fancy startled him, however, and by a clever and timely effort of mind he saved himself just in time from becoming Carlier. His heart thumped, and he felt hot all over at the thought of that danger. Carlier! What a beastly thing! To compose his now disturbed nerves – and no wonder! – he tried to whistle a little. Then, suddenly, he fell asleep, or thought he had slept; but at any rate there was a fog, and somebody had whistled in the fog.

He stood up. The day had come, and a heavy mist* had descended upon the land: the mist penetrating, enveloping, and silent; the morning mist of tropical lands; the mist that clings and kills; the mist white and deadly, immaculate and poisonous. He stood up, saw the body, and threw his arms above his head with a cry like that of a man who, waking from a trance, finds himself immured for ever in a tomb. '*Help! . . . My God!*'

A shriek inhuman, vibrating and sudden, pierced like a sharp dart the white shroud of that land of sorrow. Three short, impatient screeches followed, and then, for a time, the fog-wreaths rolled on, undisturbed, through a formidable silence. Then many more shrieks, rapid and piercing, like the yells of some exasperated and ruthless creature, rent the air. Progress was calling to Kayerts from the river. Progress and civilisation and all the virtues. Society was calling to its accomplished child to come, to be taken care of, to be instructed, to be judged, to be condemned; it called him to return to that rubbish heap from which he had wandered away, so that justice could be done.

Kayerts heard and understood. He stumbled out of the veran-dah, leaving the other man quite alone for the first time since they had been thrown there together. He groped his way through the fog, calling in his ignorance upon the invisible heaven to undo its work. Makola flitted by in the mist, shouting as he ran —

'Steamer! Steamer! They can't see. They whistle for the station. I go ring the bell. Go down to the landing, sir. I ring.'

He disappeared. Kayerts stood still. He looked upwards; the fog rolled low over his head. He looked round like a man who has lost his way; and he saw a dark smudge, a cross-shaped stain, upon the shifting purity of the mist. As he began to stumble towards it, the station bell rang in a tumultuous peal its answer to the impatient clamour of the steamer.

The Managing Director of the Great Civilising Company (since we know that civilisation follows trade) landed first, and incontinently* lost sight of the steamer. The fog down by the river was exceedingly dense; above, at the station, the bell rang unceasing and brazen.

The Director shouted loudly to the steamer.

'There is nobody down to meet us; there may be something wrong, though they are ringing. You had better come, too!'

And he began to toil up the steep bank. The captain and the engine-driver of the boat followed behind. As they scrambled up the fog thinned, and they could see their Director a good way ahead. Suddenly they saw him start forward, calling to them over his shoulder: – Run! Run to the house! I've found one of them. Run, look for the other!'

He had found one of them! And even he, the man of varied and startling experience, was somewhat discomposed by the manner of this finding. He stood and fumbled in his pockets (for a knife) while he faced Kayerts, who was hanging by a leather strap from the cross. He had evidently climbed the grave, which was high and narrow, and after tying the end of the strap to the arm, had swung himself off. His toes* were only a couple of inches above the ground; his arms hung stiffly down; he seemed to be standing rigidly at attention, but with one purple cheek playfully posed on the shoulder. And, irreverently, he was putting out a swollen tongue at his Managing Director.

The Return

The inner circle train* from the City rushed impetuously out of a black hole and pulled up with a discordant, grinding racket in the smirched twilight of a West-End* station. A line of doors flew open and a lot of men stepped out headlong. They had high hats, healthy pale faces, dark overcoats and shiny boots; they held in their gloved hands thin umbrellas and hastily folded evening papers that resembled stiff, dirty rags of greenish, pinkish, or whitish colour.* Alvan Hervey stepped out with the rest, a smouldering cigar between his teeth. A disregarded little woman in rusty black, with both arms full of parcels, ran along in distress, bolted suddenly into a third-class compartment and the train went on. The slamming of carriage doors burst out sharp and spiteful like a fusillade; an icy draught mingled with acrid fumes swept the whole length of the platform and made a tottering old man, wrapped up to his ears in a woollen comforter, stop short in the moving throng to cough violently over his stick. No one spared him a glance.

Alvan Hervey passed through the ticket gate. Between the bare walls of a sordid staircase men clambered rapidly; their backs appeared alike – almost as if they had been wearing a uniform; their indifferent faces were varied but somehow suggested kinship, like the faces of a band of brothers* who through prudence, dignity, disgust, or foresight would resolutely ignore each other; and their eyes, quick or slow; their eyes gazing up the dusty steps; their eyes, brown, black, grey, blue, had all the same stare, concentrated and empty, satisfied and unthinking.

Outside the big doorway of the street they scattered in all directions, walking away fast from one another with the hurried air of men fleeing from something compromising; from familiarity or confidences; from something suspected and concealed – like truth or pestilence. Alvan Hervey hesitated, standing alone in the doorway for a moment; then decided to walk home.

He strode firmly. A misty rain settled like silvery dust on clothes, on moustaches; wetted the faces, varnished the flagstones, darkened the walls, dripped from umbrellas. And he moved on in the rain with careless serenity, with the tranquil ease of some one successful, and disdainful, very sure of himself – a man with lots of money and friends. He was tall, well set up, good-looking and healthy; and his clear pale face had under its commonplace refinement that slight tinge of overbearing brutality which is given by the possession of only partly difficult accomplishments; by excelling in games, or in the art of making money; by the easy mastery over animals and over needy men.

He was going home much earlier than usual, straight from the City and without calling at his club. He considered himself well connected, well educated, and intelligent. Who doesn't? But his connections, education, and intelligence were strictly on a par with those of the men with whom he did business or amused himself. He had married five years ago. At the time all his acquaintances had said he was very much in love; and he had said so himself, frankly, because it is very well understood that every man falls in love once in his life – unless his wife dies, when it may be quite praiseworthy to fall in love again. The girl was healthy, tall, fair, and, in his opinion, was well connected, well educated and intelligent. She was also intensely bored with her home where, as if packed in a tight box, her individuality – of which she was very conscious – had no play. She strode like a grenadier, was strong and upright like an obelisk, had a beautiful face, a candid brow, pure eyes, and not a thought of her own in her head. He surrendered quickly to all those charms, and she appeared to him so unquestionably of the right sort that he did not hesitate for a moment to declare himself in love. Under the cover of that sacred and poetical fiction he desired her masterfully, for various reasons; but principally for the satisfaction of having his own way. He was very dull and solemn about it – for no earthly reason, unless to conceal his feelings – which is an eminently proper thing to do. Nobody however would have been shocked had he neglected that duty, for the feeling he experienced really was a longing – a longing stronger and a little more complex no doubt, but no more reprehensible in its nature than a hungry man's appetite for his dinner.

After their marriage they busied themselves, with marked success, in enlarging the circle of their acquaintance. Thirty people knew them by sight; twenty more with smiling demonstrations tolerated their occasional presence within hospitable thresholds; at least fifty others became aware of their existence. They moved in their enlarged world amongst perfectly delightful men and women who feared emotion, enthusiasm, or failure, more than fire, war, or mortal disease; who tolerated only the commonest formulas of commonest thoughts, and recognised only profitable facts. It was an extremely charming sphere, the abode of all the virtues, where nothing is realised and where all joys and sorrows are cautiously toned down into pleasures and annoyances. In that serene region, then, where noble sentiments are cultivated in sufficient profusion to conceal the pitiless materialism of thoughts and aspirations Alvan Hervey and his wife spent five years of prudent bliss unclouded by any doubt as to the moral propriety of their existence. She, to give her individuality fair play, took up all manner of philanthropic work and became a member of various rescuing and reforming societies patronised or presided over by ladies of title. He took an active interest in politics; and having met quite by chance a literary man – who nevertheless was related to an earl – he was induced to finance a moribund society paper. It was a semi-political, and wholly scandalous publication, redeemed by excessive dulness; and as it was utterly faithless, as it contained no new thought, as it never by any chance had a flash of wit, satire, or indignation in its pages, he judged it respectable enough, at first sight. Afterwards, when it paid, he promptly perceived that upon the whole it was a virtuous undertaking. It paved the way of his ambition; and he enjoyed also the special kind of importance he derived from this connection with what he imagined to be literature.

This connection still further enlarged their world. Men who wrote or drew prettily for the public came at times to their house, and his editor came very often. He thought him rather an ass because he had such big front teeth (the proper thing is to have small, even teeth) and wore his hair a trifle longer than most men do. However, some dukes wear their hair long, and the fellow indubitably knew his business. The worst was that his gravity, though perfectly portentous, could not be trusted. He sat, elegant and bulky, in the drawing-room, the head of his stick hovering in front of his big teeth, and talked for hours with a thick-lipped smile (he said nothing that could be considered objectionable and not quite the thing) talked in an unusual manner – not obviously – irritatingly. His forehead was too lofty – unusually so – and under it there was a straight nose, lost between the hairless cheeks, that in a smooth curve ran into a chin shaped like the end of a snow-shoe. And in this face that resembled the face of a fat and fiendishly knowing baby there glittered a pair of clever, peering, unbelieving black eyes. He wrote verses too. Rather an ass. But the band of men* who trailed at the skirts of his monumental frock-coat seemed to perceive wonderful things in what he said. Alvan Hervey put it down to affectation. Those artist chaps, upon the whole, were so affected. Still, all this was highly proper – very useful to him – and his wife seemed to like it – as if she also had derived some distinct and secret advantage from this intellectual connection. She received her mixed and decorous guests with a kind of tall, ponderous grace, peculiarly her own and which awakened in the mind of intimidated strangers incongruous and improper reminiscences of an elephant, a giraffe, a gazelle; of a gothic tower – of an overgrown angel. Her Thursdays were becoming famous in their world; and their world grew steadily, annexing street after street. It included also Somebody's Gardens, a Crescent – a couple of Squares.

Thus Alvan Hervey and his wife for five prosperous years lived by the side of one another. In time they came to know each other sufficiently well for all the practical purposes of such an existence, but they were no more capable of real intimacy than two animals feeding at the same manger, under the same roof, in a luxurious stable. His longing was appeased and became a habit; and she had her desire – the desire to get away from under the paternal roof, to assert her individuality, to move in her own set (so much smarter than the parental one); to have a home of her own, and her own share of the world's respect, envy, and applause. They understood each other warily, tacitly, like a pair of cautious conspirators in a profitable plot; because they were both unable to look at a fact, a sentiment, a principle, or a belief otherwise than in the light of their own dignity, of their own glorification, of their own advantage. They skimmed over the surface of life hand in hand, in a pure and frosty atmosphere – like two skilful skaters cutting figures on thick ice for the admiration of the beholders, and disdainfully ignoring the hidden stream, the stream restless and dark; the stream of life, profound and unfrozen.

*

Alvan Hervey turned twice to the left, once to the right, walked along two sides of a square, in the middle of which groups of tame-looking trees stood in respectable captivity behind iron railings, and rang at his door. A parlourmaid opened. A fad of his wife's, this, to have only women servants. That girl, while she took his hat and overcoat, said something which made him look at his watch. It was five o'clock, and his wife not at home. There was nothing unusual in that. He said 'No; no tea,' and went upstairs.

He ascended without footfalls. Brass rods glimmered all up the red carpet. On the first-floor landing a marble woman, decently covered from neck to instep with stone draperies, advanced a row of lifeless toes to the edge of the pedestal, and thrust out blindly a rigid white arm holding a cluster of lights.* He had artistic tastes – at home. Heavy curtains caught back, half concealed dark corners. On the rich, stamped paper of the walls hung sketches, water-colours, engravings. His tastes were distinctly artistic. Old church towers peeped above green masses of foliage; the hills were purple, the sands yellow, the seas sunny, the skies blue. A young lady sprawled with dreamy eyes in a moored boat, in company of a lunch basket, a champagne bottle, and an enamoured man in a blazer. Bare-legged boys flirted sweetly with ragged maidens, slept on stone steps, gambolled with dogs. A pathetically lean girl flattened against a blank wall, turned up expiring eyes and tendered a flower for sale; while, near by, the large photographs of some famous and mutilated bas-reliefs seemed to represent a massacre turned into stone.

He looked, of course, at nothing, ascended another flight of stairs and went straight into the dressing room. A bronze dragon nailed by the tail to a bracket writhed away from the wall in calm convolutions, and held, between the conventional fury of its jaws, a crude gas flame that resembled a butterfly. The room was empty, of course; but, as he stepped in, it became filled all at once with a stir of many people; because the strips of glass on the doors of wardrobes and his wife's large pier-glass* reflected him from head to foot, and multiplied his image into a crowd of gentlemanly and slavish imitators, who were dressed exactly like himself; had the same restrained and rare gestures; who moved when he moved, stood still with him in an obsequious immobility, and had just such appearances of life and feeling as he thought it dignified and safe for any man to manifest. And like real people who are slaves of common thoughts, that are not even their own, they affected a shadowy independence by the superficial variety of their movements. They moved together with him; but they either advanced to meet him, or walked away from him; they appeared, disappeared; they seemed to dodge behind walnut furniture, to be seen again, far within the polished panes, stepping about distinct and unreal in the convincing illusion of a room. And like the men he respected they could be trusted to do nothing individual, original, or startling – nothing unforeseen and nothing improper.

He moved for a time aimlessly in that good company, humming a popular but refined tune, and thinking vaguely of a business letter from abroad, which had to be answered on the morrow with cautious prevarication. Then, as he walked towards a wardrobe, he saw appearing at his back, in the high mirror, the corner of his wife's dressing-table, and, amongst the glitter of silver-mounted objects on it, the square white patch of an envelope. It was such an unusual thing to be seen there that he spun round almost before he realised his surprise; and all the sham men about him pivoted on their heels; all appeared surprised; and all moved rapidly towards envelopes on dressing-tables.

He recognised his wife's handwriting and saw that the envelope was addressed to himself. He muttered, 'How very odd,' and felt annoyed. Apart from any odd action being essentially an indecent thing in itself, the fact of his wife indulging in it made it doubly offensive. That she should write to him at all, when she knew he would be home for dinner, was perfectly ridiculous; but that she should leave it like this – in evidence for chance discovery – struck him as so outrageous that, thinking of it, he experienced suddenly a staggering sense of insecurity, an absurd and bizarre flash of a notion that the house had moved a little under his feet. He tore the envelope open, glanced at the letter, and sat down in a chair near by.

He held the paper before his eyes and looked at half a dozen lines scrawled on the page, while he was stunned by a noise meaningless and violent, like the clash of gongs or the beating of drums; a great aimless uproar that, in a manner, prevented him from hearing himself think and made his mind an absolute blank. This absurd and distracting tumult seemed to ooze out of the written words, to issue from between his very fingers that trembled, holding the paper. And suddenly he dropped the letter as though it had been something hot, or venomous, or filthy; and rushing to the window with the unreflecting precipitation of a man anxious to raise an alarm of fire or murder, he threw it up and put his head out.

A chill gust of wind, wandering through the damp and sooty obscurity over the waste of roofs and chimney-pots, touched his face with a clammy flick. He saw an illimitable darkness, in which stood a black jumble of walls, and, between them, the many rows of gaslights stretched far away in long lines, like strung-up beads of fire. A sinister loom* as of a hidden conflagration lit up faintly from below the mist, falling upon a billowy and motionless sea of tiles and bricks. At the rattle of the opened window the world seemed to leap out of the night and confront him, while floating up to his ears there came a sound vast and faint; the deep mutter of something immense and alive. It penetrated him with a feeling of dismay and he gasped silently. From the cab-stand in the square came distinct hoarse voices and a jeering laugh which sounded ominously harsh and cruel. It sounded threatening. He drew his head in, as if before an aimed blow and flung the window down quickly. He made a few steps, stumbled against a chair, and, with a great effort, pulled himself together to lay hold of a certain thought that was whizzing about loose in his head.

He got it at last, after more exertion than he expected; he was flushed and puffed a little as though he had been catching it with his hands, but his mental hold on it was weak, so weak that he judged it necessary to repeat it aloud – to hear it spoken firmly – in order to insure a perfect measure of possession. But he was unwilling to hear his own voice – to hear any sound whatever – owing to a vague belief, shaping itself slowly within him, that solitude and silence are the greatest felicities of mankind. The next moment it dawned upon him that they are perfectly unattainable – that faces must be seen, words spoken, thoughts heard. All the words – all the thoughts!

He said very distinctly, and looking at the carpet, 'She's gone.'

It was terrible – not the fact but the words; the words charged with the shadowy might of a meaning, that seemed to possess the tremendous power to call Fate down upon the earth, like those strange and appalling words that sometimes are heard in sleep. They vibrated round him in a metallic atmosphere, in a space that had the hardness of iron and the resonance of a bell of bronze. Looking down between the toes of his boots he seemed to listen thoughtfully to the receding wave of sound; to the wave spreading out in a widening circle, embracing streets, roofs, church-steeples, fields – and travelling away, widening endlessly, far, very far, where he could not hear – where he could not imagine anything – where . . .

'And – with that . . . ass,' he said again without stirring in the least. And there was nothing but humiliation. Nothing else. He could derive no moral solace from any aspect of the situation, which radiated pain only on every side. Pain. What kind of pain? It occurred to him that he ought to be heart-broken; but in an exceedingly short moment he perceived that his suffering was nothing of so trifling and dignified a kind. It was altogether a more serious matter, and partook rather of the nature of those subtle and cruel feelings which are awakened by a kick or a horsewhipping.

He felt very sick – physically sick – as though he had bitten through something nauseous. Life, that to a well-ordered mind should be a matter of congratulation, appeared to him, for a second or so, perfectly intolerable. He picked up the paper at his feet, and sat down with the wish to think it out, to understand why his wife – his wife! – should leave him, should throw away respect, comfort, peace, decency, position – throw away everything for nothing! He set himself to think out the hidden logic of her action – a mental undertaking fit for the leisure hours of a madhouse, though he couldn't see it. And he thought of his wife in every relation except the only fundamental one. He thought of her as a well-bred girl, as a wife, as a cultured person, as the mistress of a house, as a lady; but he never for a moment thought of her simply as a woman.

Then a fresh wave, a raging wave of humiliation, swept through his mind, and left nothing there but a personal sense of undeserved abasement. Why should he be mixed up with such a horrid exposure! It annihilated all the advantages of his well-ordered past, by a truth effective and unjust like a calumny – and the past was wasted. Its failure was disclosed – a distinct failure, on his part, to see, to guard, to understand. It could not be denied; it could not be explained away, hustled out of sight. He could not sit on it and look solemn. Now – if she had only died!

If she had only died! He was driven to envy such a respectable bereavement, and one so perfectly free from any taint of misfortune that even his best friend or his best enemy would not have felt the slightest thrill of exultation. No one would have cared. He sought comfort in clinging to the contemplation of the only fact of life that the resolute efforts of mankind had never failed to disguise in the clatter and glamour of phrases. And nothing lends itself more to lies than death. If she had only died! Certain words would have been said to him in a sad tone, and he, with proper fortitude, would have made appropriate answers. There were precedents for such an occasion. And no one would have cared. If she had only died! The promises, the terrors, the hopes of eternity, are the concern of the corrupt dead; but the obvious sweetness of life belongs to living, healthy men. And life was his concern: that sane and gratifying existence untroubled by too much love or by too much regret. She had interfered with it; she had defaced it. And suddenly it occurred to him he must have been mad to marry. It was too much in the nature of giving yourself away, of wearing – if for a moment – your heart on your sleeve. But every one married. Was all mankind mad!

In the shock of that startling thought he looked up, and saw to the left, to the right, in front, men sitting far off in chairs and looking at him with wild eyes – emissaries of a distracted mankind intruding to spy upon his pain and his humiliation. It was not to be borne. He rose quickly, and the others jumped up too on all sides. He stood still in the middle of the room as if discouraged by their vigilance. No escape! He felt something akin to despair. Everybody must know. All the world must know to-morrow. The servants must know to-night. He ground his teeth. . . . And he had never noticed, never guessed anything. Every one will know. He thought: The woman's a monster, but everybody will think me a fool; and standing still in the midst of severe walnut-wood furniture, he felt such a tempest of anguish within him that he seemed to see himself rolling on the carpet, beating his head against the wall. He was disgusted with himself, with the loathsome rush of emotion breaking through all the reserves that guarded his manhood. Something unknown, withering and poisonous, had entered his life, passed near him, touched him, and he was deteriorating. He was appalled. What was it? She was gone. Why? His head was ready to burst with the endeavour to understand her act and his subtle horror of it.

Everything was changed. Why? Only a woman gone, after all; and yet he had a vision, a vision quick and distinct as a dream: the vision of everything he had thought indestructible and safe in this world crashing down about him, like solid walls do before the fierce breath of a hurricane. He stared, shaking in every limb, while he felt the destructive breath, the mysterious breath, the breath of passion, stir the profound peace of the house. He looked round in fear. Yes. Crime may be forgiven; uncalculating sacrifice, blind trust, burning faith, other follies, may be turned to account; suffering, death itself, may with a grin or a frown be explained away; but passion is the unpardonable and secret infamy of our hearts, a thing to curse, to hide and to deny; a shameless and forlorn thing that tramples upon the smiling promises, that tears off the placid mask, that strips naked the body of life. And it had come to him! It had laid its unclean hand upon the spotless draperies of his existence, and he had to face it alone with all the world looking on. All the world! And he thought that even the bare suspicion of such an adversary within his house carried with it a taint and a condemnation. He put both his hands out as if to ward off the approach of a defiling truth; and, instantly, the appalled conclave of unreal men, standing about mutely beyond the clear lustre of mirrors, made at him the same gesture of rejection and horror.

He glanced vainly here and there, like a man looking in desperation for a weapon or for a hiding place, and understood at last that he was disarmed and cornered by an enemy that, without any squeamishness, would strike so as to lay open his heart. He could get help nowhere, or even take counsel with himself, because in the sudden shock of her desertion the sentiments which he knew that in fidelity to his bringing up, to his prejudices and his surroundings, he ought to experience, were so mixed up with the novelty of real feelings, of fundamental feelings that know nothing of creed, class, or education, that he was unable to distinguish clearly between what is and what ought to be; between the inexcusable truth and the valid pretences. And he knew instinctively that truth would be of no use to him. Some kind of concealment seemed a necessity because one cannot explain. Of course not! Who would listen? One had simply to be without stain and without reproach to keep one's place in the forefront of life.

He said to himself, 'I must get over it the best I can,' and

began to walk up and down the room. What next? What ought
to be done? He thought: I will travel – no I won't. I shall face it
out. And after that resolve he was greatly cheered by the
reflection that it would be a mute and an easy part to play, for
no one would be likely to converse with him about the abominable conduct of – that woman. He argued to himself that
decent people – and he knew no others – did not care to talk
about such indelicate affairs. She had gone off – with that
unhealthy, fat ass of a journalist. Why? He had been all a
husband ought to be. He had given her a good position – she
shared his prospects – he had treated her invariably with great
consideration. He reviewed his conduct with a kind of dismal
pride. It had been irreproachable. Then, why? For love? Profa-
nation! There could be no love there. A shameful impulse of
passion. Yes, passion. His own wife! Good God! ... And the
indelicate aspect of his domestic misfortune struck him with
such shame that, next moment, he caught himself in the act of
pondering absurdly over the notion whether it would not be
more dignified for him to induce a general belief that he had
been in the habit of beating his wife. Some fellows do ... and
anything would be better than the filthy fact; for it was clear he
had lived with the root of it for five years – and it was too
shameful. Anything! Anything! Brutality ... But he gave it up
directly, and began to think of the Divorce Court. It did not
present itself to him, notwithstanding his respect for law and
usage, as a proper refuge for dignified grief. It appeared rather
as an unclean and sinister cavern where men and women are
haled by adverse fate to writhe ridiculously in the presence of
uncompromising truth. It should not be allowed. That woman!
Five ... years ... married five years ... and never to see
anything. Not to the very last day ... not till she coolly went
off. And he pictured to himself all the people he knew engaged
in speculating as to whether all that time he had been blind,
foolish, or infatuated. What a woman! Blind! ... Not at all.
Could a clean-minded man imagine such depravity? Evidently
not. He drew a free breath. That was the attitude to take; it was
dignified enough; it gave him the advantage, and he could not
help perceiving that it was moral. He yearned unaffectedly to
see morality (in his person) triumphant before the world. As to
her – she would be forgotten. Let her be forgotten – buried in
oblivion – lost! No one would allude ... Refined people – and

every man and woman he knew could be so described – had, of course, a horror of such topics. Had they? Oh, yes. No one would allude to her . . . in his hearing. He stamped his foot, tore the letter across, then again and again. The thought of sympathising friends excited in him a fury of mistrust. He flung down the small bits of paper. They settled, fluttering, at his feet, and looked very white on the dark carpet, like a scattered handful of snow-flakes.

This fit of hot anger was succeeded by a sudden sadness, by the darkening passage of a thought that ran over the scorched surface of his heart, like upon a barren plain, and after a fiercer assault of sunrays, the melancholy and cooling shadow of a cloud. He realised that he had had a shock – not a violent or rending blow, that can be seen, resisted, returned, forgotten, but a thrust, insidious and penetrating, that had stirred all those feelings, concealed and cruel, which the arts of the devil, the fears of mankind – God's infinite compassion, perhaps – keep chained deep down in the inscrutable twilight of our breasts. A dark curtain seemed to rise before him, and for less than a second he looked upon the mysterious universe of moral suffering. As a landscape is seen complete, and vast, and vivid, under a flash of lightning, so he could see disclosed in a moment, all the immensity of pain that can be contained in one short moment of human thought. Then the curtain fell again, but his rapid vision left in Alvan Hervey's mind a trail of invincible sadness, a sense of loss and bitter solitude, as though he had been robbed and exiled. For a moment he ceased to be a member of society with a position, a career, and a name attached to all this, like a descriptive label of some complicated compound. He was a simple human being removed from the delightful world of crescents and squares. He stood alone, naked and afraid, like the first man on the first day of evil. There are in life events, contacts, glimpses, that seem brutally to bring all the past to a close. There is a shock and a crash, as of a gate flung to behind one by the perfidious hand of fate. Go and seek another paradise, fool or sage. There is a moment of dumb dismay, and the wanderings must begin again; the painful explaining away of facts, the feverish raking up of illusions, the cultivation of a fresh crop of lies in the sweat of one's brow, to sustain life, to make it supportable, to make it fair, so as to hand intact to another generation of blind wanderers the charm-

ing legend of a heartless country, of a promised land, all flowers
and blessings. . . .

He came to himself with a slight start, and became aware of
an oppressive, crushing desolation. It was only a feeling, it is
true, but it produced on him a physical effect, as though his
chest had been squeezed in a vice. He perceived himself so
extremely forlorn and lamentable, and was moved so deeply by
the oppressive sorrow, that another turn of the screw, he felt,
would bring tears out of his eyes. He was deteriorating. Five
years of life in common had appeased his longing. Yes, long-
time ago.* The first five months did that – but . . . There was
the habit – the habit of her person, of her smile, of her gestures,
of her voice, of her silence. She had a pure brow, and good hair.
How utterly wretched all this was. Good hair and fine eyes –
remarkably fine. He was surprised by the number of details that
intruded upon his unwilling memory. He could not help remem-
bering her footsteps, the rustle of her dress, her way of holding
her head, her decisive manner of saying 'Alvan,' the quiver of
her nostrils when she was annoyed. All that had been so much
his property, so intimately and specially his! He raged in a
mournful, silent way, as he took stock of his losses. He was like
a man counting the cost of an unlucky speculation – irritated,
depressed – exasperated with himself and with others, with the
fortunate, with the indifferent, with the callous; yet the wrong
done him appeared so cruel that he would perhaps have
dropped a tear over that spoliation if it had not been for his
conviction that men do not weep. Foreigners do; they also kill
sometimes in such circumstances. And to his horror he felt
himself driven to regret almost that the usages of a society ready
to forgive the shooting of a burglar forbade him, under the
circumstances, even as much as a thought of murder. Nevertheless, he clenched his fists and set his teeth hard. And he was
afraid at the same time. He was afraid with that penetrating
faltering fear that seems, in the very middle of a beat, to turn
one's heart into a handful of dust.* The contamination of her
crime spread out, tainted the universe, tainted himself; woke up
all the dormant infamies of the world; caused a ghastly kind of
clairvoyance in which he could see the towns and fields of the
earth, its sacred places, its temples and its houses, peopled by
monsters* – by monsters of duplicity, lust, and murder. She was
a monster – he himself was thinking monstrous thoughts . . .

and yet he was like other people. How many men and women
at this very moment were plunged in abominations – meditated
crimes. It was frightful to think of. He remembered all the
streets – the well-to-do streets he had passed on his way home;
all the innumerable houses with closed doors and curtained
windows. Each seemed now an abode of anguish and folly. And
his thought, as if appalled, stood still, recalling with dismay the
decorous and frightful silence that was like a conspiracy; the
grim, impenetrable silence of miles of walls concealing passions,
misery, thoughts of crime. Surely he was not the only man; his
was not the only house ... and yet no one knew – no one
guessed. But he knew. He knew with unerring certitude that
could not be deceived by the correct silence of walls, of closed
doors, of curtained windows. He was beside himself with a
despairing agitation, like a man informed of a deadly secret –
the secret of a calamity threatening the safety of mankind – the
sacredness, the peace of life.

  He caught sight of himself in one of the looking-glasses. It
was a relief. The anguish of his feeling had been so powerful
that he more than half expected to see some distorted wild face
there, and he was pleasantly surprised to see nothing of the
kind. His aspect, at any rate, would let no one into the secret of
his pain. He examined himself with attention. His trousers were
turned up, and his boots a little muddy, but he looked very
much as usual. Only his hair was slightly ruffled, and that
disorder, somehow, was so suggestive of trouble that he went
quickly to the table, and began to use the brushes, in an anxious
desire to obliterate the compromising trace, that only vestige of
his emotion. He brushed with care, watching the effect of his
smoothing; and another face, slightly pale and more tense than
was perhaps desirable, peered back at him from the toilet glass.
He laid the brushes down, and was not satisfied. He took them
up again and brushed, brushed mechanically – forgot himself in
that occupation. The tumult of his thoughts ended in a sluggish
flow of reflection, such as, after the outburst of a volcano, the
almost imperceptible progress of a stream of lava, creeping
languidly over a convulsed land and pitilessly obliterating any
landmark left by the shock of the earthquake. It is a destructive but, by comparison, it is a peaceful phenomenon. Alvan
Hervey was almost soothed by the deliberate pace of his
thoughts. His moral landmarks were going one by one, con-

sumed in the fire of his experience, buried in hot mud, in ashes. He was cooling – on the surface; but there was enough heat left somewhere to make him slap the brushes on the table, and turning away, say in a fierce whisper: 'I wish him joy . . . Damn the woman.'

He felt himself utterly corrupted by her wickedness, and the most significant symptom of his moral downfall was the bitter, acrid satisfaction with which he recognised it. He, deliberately, swore in his thoughts; he meditated sneers; he shaped in profound silence words of cynical unbelief, and his most cherished convictions stood revealed finally as the narrow prejudices of fools. A crowd of shapeless, unclean thoughts crossed his mind in a stealthy rush, like a band of veiled malefactors* hastening to a crime. He put his hands deep into his pockets. He heard a faint ringing somewhere, and muttered to himself: 'I am not the only one . . . not the only one.' There was another ring. Front door!

His heart leaped up into his throat, and forthwith descended as low as his boots. A call! Who? Why? He wanted to rush out on the landing and shout to the servant: 'Not at home! Gone away abroad!' . . . Any excuse. He could not face a visitor. Not this evening. No. To-morrow. . . . Before he could break out of the numbness, that enveloped him like a sheet of lead, he heard far below, as if in the entrails of the earth, a door close heavily. The house vibrated to it more than to a clap of thunder. He stood still, wishing himself invisible. The room was very chilly. He did not think he would ever feel like that. But people must be met – they must be faced – talked to – smiled at. He heard another door, much nearer – the door of the drawing-room – being opened and flung too again. He imagined for a moment he would faint. How absurd! That kind of thing had to be gone through. A voice spoke. He could not catch the words. Then the voice spoke again, and footsteps were heard on the first floor landing. Hang it all! Was he to hear that voice and those footsteps whenever any one spoke or moved. He thought: 'This is like being haunted – I suppose it will last for a week or so, at least. Till I forget. Forget! Forget!' Some one was coming up the second flight of stairs. Servant? He listened, then, suddenly, as though an incredible, frightful revelation had been shouted to him from a distance, he bellowed out in the empty room: 'What! What!' in such a fiendish tone as to astonish himself. The footsteps stopped outside the door. He stood open-mouthed, maddened and still, as if in the midst of a catastrophe. The door-handle rattled lightly. It seemed to him that the walls were coming apart, that the furniture swayed at him; the ceiling slanted queerly for a moment, a tall wardrobe tried to topple over. He caught hold of something, and it was the back of a chair. So he had reeled against a chair! Oh! Confound it! He gripped hard.

The flaming butterfly poised between the jaws of the bronze dragon radiated a glare, a glare that seemed to leap up all at once into a crude, blinding fierceness, and made it difficult for him to distinguish plainly the figure of his wife standing upright with her back to the closed door. He looked at her and could not detect her breathing. The harsh and violent light was beating on her, and he was amazed to see her preserve so well the composure of her upright attitude in that scorching brilliance which, to his eyes, enveloped her like a hot and consuming mist. He would not have been surprised if she had vanished in it as suddenly as she had appeared. He stared and listened; listened for some sound, but the silence round him was absolute – as though he had in a moment grown completely deaf as well as dim-eyed. Then his hearing returned, preternaturally sharp. He heard the patter of a rain-shower on the window panes behind the lowered blinds, and below, far below, in the artificial abyss of the square, the deadened roll of wheels and the splashy trotting of a horse. He heard a groan also – very distinct – in the room – close to his ear.

He thought with alarm: 'I must have made that noise myself'; and at the same instant the woman left the door, stepped firmly across the floor before him, and sat down in a chair. He knew that step. There was no doubt about it. She had come back! And he very nearly said aloud 'Of course!' – such was his sudden and masterful perception of the indestructible character of her being. Nothing could destroy her – and nothing but his own destruction could keep her away. She was the incarnation of all the short moments which every man spares out of his life for dreams, for precious dreams that concrete the most cherished, the most profitable of his illusions. He peered at her with inward trepidation. She was mysterious, significant, full of obscure meaning – like a symbol. He peered, bending forward, as though he had been discovering about her things he had never seen before. Unconsciously he made a step towards her – then another. He saw her arm make an ample, decided movement – and he stopped. She had lifted her veil.* It was like the lifting of a vizor.

The spell was broken. He experienced a shock as though he had been called out of a trance by the sudden noise of an explosion. It was even more startling and more distinct; it was an infinitely more intimate change, for he had the sensation of having come into this room only that very moment; of having returned from very far; he was made aware that some essential part of himself had in a flash returned into his body, returned finally from a fierce and lamentable region, from the dwelling-place of unveiled hearts. He woke up to an amazing infinity of contempt, to a droll bitterness of wonder, to a disenchanted conviction of safety. He had a glimpse of the irresistible force, and he saw also the barrenness of his convictions – of her convictions. It seemed to him that he could never make a mistake as long as he lived. It was morally impossible to go wrong. He was not elated by that certitude; he was dimly uneasy about its price; there was a chill as of death in this triumph of sound principles, in this victory snatched under the very shadow of disaster.

The last trace of his previous state of mind vanished, as the instantaneous and elusive trail of a bursting meteor vanishes on the profound blackness of the sky; it was the faint flicker of a painful thought, gone as soon as perceived, that nothing but her presence – after all – had the power to recall him to himself. He stared at her. She sat with her hands on her lap, looking down; and he noticed that her boots were dirty, her skirts wet and splashed, as though she had been driven back there by a blind fear through a waste of mud. He was indignant, amazed and shocked, but in a natural, healthy way now; so that he could control those unprofitable sentiments by the dictates of cautious self-restraint. The light in the room had no unusual brilliance now; it was a good light in which he could easily observe the expression of her face. It was that of dull fatigue. And the silence that surrounded them was the normal silence of any quiet house, hardly disturbed by the faint noises of a respectable quarter of the town. He was very cool – and it was quite coolly that he thought how much better it would be if neither of them ever spoke again. She sat with closed lips, with an air of lassitude in the stony forgetfulness of her pose, but after a moment she lifted her drooping eyelids and met his tense and inquisitive stare by a look that had all the formless eloquence of a cry. It penetrated, it stirred without informing; it was the very essence of anguish stripped of words that can be smiled at, argued away, shouted down, disdained. It was anguish naked and unashamed, the bare pain of existence let loose upon the world in the fleeting unreserve of a look that had in it an immensity of fatigue, the scornful sincerity, the black impudence of an extorted confession. Alvan Hervey was seized with wonder, as though he had seen something inconceivable; and some obscure part of his being was ready to exclaim with him: 'I would never have believed it!' but an instantaneous revulsion of wounded susceptibilities checked the unfinished thought. He felt full of rancorous indignation against the woman who could look like this at one. This look probed him; it tampered with him. It was dangerous to one as would be a hint of unbelief whispered by a priest in the august decorum of a temple; and at the same time it was impure, it was disturbing, like a cynical consolation muttered in the dark, tainting the sorrow, corroding the thought, poisoning the heart. He wanted to ask her furiously: 'Who do you take me for? How dare you look at me like this?' He felt himself helpless before the hidden meaning of that look; he resented it with pained and futile violence as an injury so secret that it could never, never be redressed. His wish was to crush her by a single sentence. He was stainless. Opinion was on his side; morality, men and gods were on his side; law, conscience – all the world! She had nothing but that look. And he could only say:

'How long do you intend to stay here?'

Her eyes did not waver, her lips remained closed; and for any effect of his words he might have spoken to a dead woman, only that this one breathed quickly. He was profoundly disappointed by what he had said. It was a great deception, something in the nature of a treason. He had deceived himself. It should have been altogether different – other words – another sensation. And before his eyes, so fixed that at times they saw nothing, she sat apparently as unconscious as though she had been alone, sending that look of brazen confession straight at him – with an air of staring into empty space. He said significantly:

'Must I go then?' And he knew he meant nothing of what he implied.

One of her hands on her lap moved slightly as though his words had fallen there and she had thrown them off on the floor. But her silence encouraged him. Possibly it meant remorse – perhaps fear. Was she thunderstruck by his attitude? . . . Her eyelids dropped. He seemed to understand ever so much – everything! Very well – but she must be made to suffer. It was due to him. He understood everything, yet he judged it indispensable to say with an obvious affection of civility:

'I don't understand – be so good as to . . .'

She stood up. For a second he believed she intended to go away, and it was as though someone had jerked a string attached to his heart. It hurt. He remained open-mouthed and silent. But she made an irresolute step towards him, and instinctively he moved aside. They stood before one another, and the fragments of the torn letter lay between them – at their feet – like an insurmountable obstacle, like a sign of eternal separation! Around them three other couples stood still and face to face, as if waiting for a signal to begin some action – a struggle, a dispute, or a dance.

She said: 'Don't – Alvan!' and there was something that resembled a warning in the pain of her tone. He narrowed his eyes as if trying to pierce her with his gaze. Her voice touched him. He had aspirations after magnanimity, generosity, superiority – interrupted, however, by flashes of indignation and anxiety – frightful anxiety to know how far she had gone. She looked down at the torn paper. Then she looked up, and their eyes met again, remained fastened together, like an unbreakable bond, like a clasp of eternal complicity; and the decorous silence, the pervading quietude of the house which enveloped this meeting of their glances became for a moment inexpressibly vile, for he was afraid she would say too much and make magnanimity impossible, while behind the profound mournfulness of her face there was a regret – a regret of things done – the regret of delay – the thought that if she had only turned back a week sooner – a day sooner – only an hour sooner. . . . They were afraid to hear again the sound of their voices; they did not know what they might say – perhaps something that could not be recalled; and words are more terrible than facts. But the tricky fatality that lurks in obscure impulses spoke through Alvan Hervey's lips suddenly; and he heard his own voice with the excited and sceptical curiosity with which one listens to actors' voices speaking on the stage in the strain of a poignant situation.

'If you have forgotten anything . . . of course . . . I . . .'

Her eyes blazed at him for an instant; her lips trembled – and then she also became the mouthpiece of the mysterious force for ever hovering near us; of that perverse inspiration, wandering capricious and uncontrollable, like a gust of wind.

'What is the good of this, Alvan? . . . You know why I came back. . . . You know that I could not . . .'

He interrupted her with irritation.

'Then – what's this?' he asked, pointing downwards at the torn letter.

'That's a mistake,' she said hurriedly, in a muffled voice.

This answer amazed him. He remained speechless, staring at her. He had half a mind to burst into a laugh. It ended in a smile as involuntary as a grimace of pain.

'A mistake . . .' he began slowly, and then found himself unable to say another word.

'Yes . . . it was honest,' she said very low, as if speaking to the memory of a feeling in a remote past.

He exploded.

'Curse your honesty! . . . Is there any honesty in all this! . . . When did you begin to be honest? Why are you here? What are you now? . . . Still honest? . . .'

He walked at her, raging, as if blind; during these three quick strides he lost touch of the material world and was whirled interminably through a kind of empty universe made up of nothing but fury and anguish, till he came suddenly upon her face – very close to his. He stopped short, and all at once seemed to remember something heard ages ago.

'You don't know the meaning of the word,' he shouted.

She did not flinch. He perceived with fear that everything around him was still. She did not move a hair's breadth; his own body did not stir. An imperturbable calm enveloped their two motionless figures, the house, the town, all the world – and the trifling tempest of his feelings. The violence of the short tumult within him had been such as could well have shattered all creation; and yet nothing was changed. He faced his wife in the familiar room in his own house. It had not fallen. And right and left all the innumerable dwellings, standing shoulder to shoulder, had resisted the shock of his passion, had presented, unmoved, to the loneliness of his trouble, the grim silence of walls, the impenetrable and polished discretion of closed doors and curtained windows. Immobility and silence pressed on him, assailed him, like two accomplices of the immovable and mute woman before his eyes. He was suddenly vanquished. He was shown his impotence. He was soothed by the breath of a corrupt resignation coming to him through the subtle irony of the surrounding peace.

He said with villainous composure:

'At any rate it isn't enough for me. I want to know more – if you're going to stay.'

'There is nothing more to tell,' she answered sadly.

It struck him as so very true that he did not say anything. She went on:

'You wouldn't understand. . . .'

'No?' he said quietly. He held himself tight not to burst out into howls and imprecations.

'I tried to be faithful . . .' she began again.

'And this?' he exclaimed, pointing at the fragments of her letter.

'This – this is a failure,' she said.

'I should think so,' he muttered bitterly.

'I tried to be faithful to myself – Alvan – and . . . and honest to you. . . .'

'If you had tried to be faithful to me it would have been more to the purpose,' he interrupted angrily. 'I've been faithful to you – and you have spoiled my life – both our lives . . .' Then after a pause the unconquerable preoccupation of self came out, and he raised his voice to ask resentfully, 'And, pray, for how long have you been making a fool of me?'

She seemed horribly shocked by that question. He did not wait for an answer, but went on moving about all the time; now and then coming up to her, then wandering off restlessly to the other end of the room.

'I want to know. Everybody knows, I suppose, but myself – and that's your honesty!'

'I have told you there is nothing to know,' she said, speaking unsteadily as if in pain. 'Nothing of what you suppose. You don't understand me. This letter is the beginning – and the end.'

'The end – this thing has no end,' he clamoured unexpectedly. 'Can't you understand that? I can. . . . The beginning . . .'

He stopped and looked into her eyes with concentrated intensity, with a desire to see, to penetrate, to understand, that made him positively hold his breath till he gasped.

'By Heavens!' he said, standing perfectly still in a peering attitude and within less than a foot from her. 'By Heavens!' he repeated slowly, and in a tone whose involuntary strangeness was a complete mystery to himself. 'By Heavens – I could believe you – I could believe anything – now!'

He turned short on his heel and began to walk up and down the room with an air of having disburdened himself of the final pronouncement of his life – of having said something on which he would not go back, even if he could. She remained as if rooted to the carpet. Her eyes followed the restless movements of the man, who avoided looking at her. Her wide stare clung to him, inquiring, wondering and doubtful.

'But the fellow was for ever sticking in here,' he burst out distractedly. 'He made love to you,* I suppose – and, and . . .' He lowered his voice. 'And – you let him.'

'And I let him,' she murmured, catching his intonation, so that her voice sounded unconscious, sounded far off and slavish, like an echo.

He said twice, 'You! You!' violently, then calmed down. 'What could you see in the fellow?' he asked, with unaffected wonder. 'An effeminate, fat ass. What could you . . . Weren't you happy? Didn't you have all you wanted? Now – frankly; did I deceive your expectations in any way? Were you disappointed with our position – or with our prospects – perhaps? You know you couldn't be – they are much better than you could hope for when you married me. . . .'

He forgot himself so far as to gesticulate a little while he went on with animation.

'What could you expect from such a fellow? He's an outsider – a rank outsider. . . . If it hadn't been for my money . . . do you hear? . . . for my money, he wouldn't know where to turn. His people won't have anything to do with him. The fellow's no class – no class at all. He's useful, certainly, that's why I . . . I thought you had enough intelligence to see it. . . . And you . . . No! It's incredible! What did he tell you? Do you care for no one's opinion – is there no restraining influence in the world for you – women? Did you ever give me a thought? I tried to be a good husband. Did I fail? Tell me – what have I done?'

Carried away by his feelings he took his head in both his hands and repeated wildly:

'What have I done? . . . Tell me! What? . . .'

'Nothing,' she said.

'Ah! You see . . . you can't . . .' he began, triumphantly walking away; then suddenly, as though he had been flung back at her by something invisible he had met, he spun round and shouted with exasperation:

'What on earth did you expect me to do?'

Without a word she moved slowly towards the table, and, sitting down, leaned on her elbow, shading her eyes with her hand. All that time he glared at her watchfully as if expecting every moment to find in her deliberate movements an answer to his question. But he could not read anything, he could gather no hint of her thought. He tried to suppress his desire to shout, and, after waiting awhile, said with incisive scorn:

'Did you want me to write absurd verses; to sit and look at you for hours – to talk to you about your soul? You ought to have known I wasn't that sort. . . . I had something better to do. But if you think I was totally blind . . .'

He perceived in a flash that he could remember an infinity of enlightening occurrences. He could recall ever so many distinct occasions when he came upon them; he remembered the absurdly interrupted gesture of his fat, white hand, the rapt expression of her face, the glitter of unbelieving eyes; snatches of incomprehensible conversations not worth listening to, silences that had meant nothing at the time and seemed now illuminating like a burst of sunshine. He remembered all that. He had not been blind. Oh! No! And to know this was an exquisite relief; it brought back all his composure.

'I thought it beneath me to suspect you,' he said loftily.

The sound of that sentence evidently possessed some magical power, because, as soon as he had spoken, he felt wonderfully at ease; and directly afterwards he experienced a flash of joyful amazement at the discovery that he could be inspired to such noble and truthful utterance. He watched the effect of his words. They caused her to glance at him quickly over her shoulder. He caught a glimpse of wet eye-lashes, of a red cheek with a tear running down swiftly; and then she turned away again and sat as before, covering her face with her hands.

'You ought to be perfectly frank with me,' he said slowly.

'You know everything,' she answered indistinctly through her fingers.

'This letter. . . . Yes . . . but . . .'

'And I came back,' she exclaimed in a stifled voice; 'you know everything.'

'I am glad of it – for your sake,' he said with impressive gravity. He listened to himself with solemn emotion. It seemed to him that something inexpressibly momentous was in progress within the room, that every word and every gesture had the importance of events preordained from the beginning of all things, and summing up in their finality the whole purpose of creation.

'For your sake,' he repeated.

Her shoulders shook as though she had been sobbing, and he forgot himself in the contemplation of her hair. Suddenly he gave a start, as if waking up, and asked very gently and not much above a whisper—

'Have you been meeting him often?'

'Never!' she cried into the palms of her hands.

This answer seemed for a moment to take from him the power of speech. His lips moved for some time before any sound came.

'You preferred to make love here – under my very nose,' he said furiously. He calmed down instantly, and felt regretfully uneasy, as though he had let himself down in her estimation by that outburst. She rose, and with her hand on the back of the chair confronted him with eyes that were perfectly dry now. There was a red spot on each of her cheeks.

'When I made up my mind to go to him – I wrote,' she said.

'But you didn't go to him,' he took up in the same tone. 'How far did you go? What made you come back?'

'I didn't know myself,' she murmured. Nothing of her moved but the lips. He fixed her sternly.

'Did he expect this? Was he waiting for you?' he asked.

She answered him by an almost imperceptible nod, and he continued to look at her for a good while without making a sound. Then, at last—

'And I suppose he is waiting yet?' he asked quickly.

Again she seemed to nod at him. For some reason he felt he must know the time. He consulted his watch gloomily. Half-past seven.

'Is he?' he muttered, putting the watch in his pocket. He looked up at her, and, as if suddenly overcome by a sense of sinister fun, gave a short, harsh laugh, directly repressed.

'No! It's the most unheard! . . .' he mumbled while she stood before him biting her lower lip, as if plunged in deep thought. He laughed again in one low burst that was as spiteful as an imprecation. He did not know why he felt such an overpowering and sudden distaste for the facts of existence – for facts in general – such an immense disgust at the thought of all the many days already lived through. He was wearied. Thinking seemed a labour beyond his strength. He said—

'You deceived me – now you make a fool of him. . . . It's awful! Why?'

'I deceived myself!' she exclaimed.

'Oh! Nonsense!' he said impatiently.

'I am ready to go if you wish it,' she went on quickly. 'It was due to you – to be told – to know. No! I could not!' she cried, and stood still wringing her hands stealthily.

'I am glad you repented before it was too late,' he said in a dull tone and looking at his boots. 'I am glad . . . some spark of better feeling,' he muttered, as if to himself. He lifted up his head after a moment of brooding silence. 'I am glad to see that there is some sense of decency left in you,' he added a little louder. Looking at her he appeared to hesitate, as if estimating the possible consequences of what he wished to say, and at last blurted out—

'After all, I loved you. . . .'

'I did not know,' she whispered.

'Good God!' he cried. 'Why do you imagine I married you?'

The indelicacy of his obtuseness angered her.

'Ah – why?' she said through her teeth.

He appeared overcome with horror, and watched her lips intently as though in fear.

'I imagined many things,' she said slowly, and paused. He watched, holding his breath. At last she went on musingly, as if thinking aloud. 'I tried to understand. I tried honestly. . . . Why? . . . To do the usual thing – I suppose. . . . To please yourself.'

He walked away smartly, and when he came back, close to her, he had a flushed face.

'You seemed pretty well pleased too – at the time,' he hissed, with scathing fury. 'I needn't ask whether you loved me.'

'I know now I was perfectly incapable of such a thing,' she said calmly. 'If I had, perhaps you would not have married me.'

'It's very clear I would not have done it if I had known you – as I know you now.'

He seemed to see himself proposing to her – ages ago. They were strolling up the slope of a lawn. Groups of people were scattered in sunshine. The shadows of leafy boughs lay still on the short grass. The coloured sunshades far off, passing between trees, resembled deliberate and brilliant butterflies moving without a flutter. Men smiling amiably, or else very grave, within the impeccable shelter of their black coats, stood by the side of women who, clustered in clear summer toilettes,* recalled all the fabulous tales of enchanted gardens where animated flowers smile at bewitched knights. There was a sumptuous serenity in it all, a thin, vibrating excitement, the perfect security, as of an invincible ignorance, that evoked within him a transcendent belief in felicity as the lot of all mankind, a recklessly picturesque desire to get promptly something for himself only, out of that splendour unmarred by any shadow of a thought. The girl walked by his side across an open space; no one was near, and suddenly he stood still, as if inspired, and spoke. He remembered looking at her pure eyes, at her candid brow; he remembered glancing about quickly to see if they were being observed, and thinking that nothing could go wrong in a world of so much charm, purity, and distinction. He was proud of it. He was one of its makers, of its possessors, of its guardians, of its extollers. He wanted to grasp it solidly, to get as much gratification as he could out of it; and in view of its incomparable quality, of its unstained atmosphere, of its nearness to the heaven of its choice, this gust of brutal desire seemed the most noble of aspirations. In a second he lived again through all these moments, and then all the pathos of his failure presented itself to him with such vividness that there was a suspicion of tears in his tone when he said almost unthinkingly, 'My God! I did love you!'

She seemed touched by the emotion of his voice. Her lips quivered a little, and she made one faltering step towards him, putting out her hands in a beseeching gesture, when she perceived, just in time, that being absorbed by the tragedy of his life he had absolutely forgotten her very existence. She stopped, and her outstretched arms fell slowly. He, with his features distorted by the bitterness of his thought, saw neither her movement nor her gesture. He stamped his foot in vexation, rubbed his head – then exploded.

'What the devil am I to do now?'

He was still again. She seemed to understand, and moved to the door firmly.

'It's very simple – I'm going,' she said aloud.

At the sound of her voice he gave a start of surprise, looked at her wildly, and asked in a piercing tone—

'You. . . . Where? To him?'

'No – alone – goodbye.'

The door-handle rattled under her groping hand as though she had been trying to get out of some dark place.

'No – stay!' he cried.

She heard him faintly. He saw her shoulder touch the lintel* of the door. She swayed as if dazed. There was less than a second of suspense while they both felt as if poised on the very edge of moral annihilation, ready to fall into some devouring nowhere. Then, almost simultaneously, he shouted, 'Come back!' and she let go the handle of the door. She turned round in peaceful desperation like one who deliberately has thrown away the last chance of life; and, for a moment, the room she faced appeared terrible, and dark, and safe – like a grave.

He said, very hoarse and abrupt: 'It can't end like this. . . . Sit down'; and while she crossed the room again to the low-backed chair before the dressing-table, he opened the door and put his head out to look and listen. The house was quiet. He came back pacified, and asked—

'Do you speak the truth?'

She nodded.

'You have lived a lie, though,' he said suspiciously.

'Ah! You made it so easy,' she answered.

'You reproach me – me!'

'How could I?' she said; 'I would have you no other – now.'

'What do you mean by . . .' he began, then checked himself, and without waiting for an answer went on, 'I won't ask any questions. Is this letter the worst of it?'

She had a nervous movement of her hands.

'I must have a plain answer,' he said hotly.

'Then, no! The worst is my coming back.'

There followed a period of dead silence, during which they exchanged searching glances.

He said authoritatively—

'You don't know what you are saying. Your mind is unhinged. You are beside yourself, or you would not say such things. You can't control yourself. Even in your remorse . . .' He paused a moment, then said with a doctoral air: 'Self-restraint is everything in life, you know. It's happiness, it's dignity . . . it's everything.'

She was pulling nervously at her handkerchief while he went on watching anxiously to see the effect of his words. Nothing satisfactory happened. Only, as he began to speak again, she covered her face with both her hands.

'You see where the want of self-restraint leads to. Pain – humiliation – loss of respect – of friends, of everything that ennobles life, that . . . All kinds of horrors,' he concluded abruptly.

She made no stir. He looked at her pensively for some time as though he had been concentrating the melancholy thoughts evoked by the sight of that abased woman. His eyes became fixed and dull. He was profoundly penetrated by the solemnity of the moment; he felt deeply the greatness of the occasion. And more than ever the walls of his house seemed to enclose the sacredness of ideals to which he was about to offer a magnificent sacrifice. He was the high priest of that temple, the severe guardian of formulas, of rites, of the pure ceremonial concealing the black doubts of life. And he was not alone. Other men too – the best of them – kept watch and ward by the hearthstones that were the altars of that profitable persuasion. He understood confusedly that he was part of an immense and beneficent power, which had a reward ready for every discretion. He dwelt within the invincible wisdom of silence; he was protected by an indestructible faith that would last for ever, that would withstand unshaken all the assaults – the loud execrations of apostates, and the secret weariness of its confessors! He was in league with a universe of untold advantages. He represented the moral strength of a beautiful reticence that could vanquish all the deplorable crudities of life – fear, disaster, sin – even death itself. It seemed to him he was on the point of sweeping triumphantly away all the illusory mysteries of existence. It was simplicity itself.

'I hope you see now the folly – the utter folly of wickedness,' he began in a dull, solemn manner. 'You must respect the conditions of your life or lose all it can give you. All! Everything!'

He waved his arm once, and three exact replicas of his face, of his clothes, of his dull severity, of his solemn grief, repeated the wide gesture that in its comprehensive sweep indicated an infinity of moral sweetness, embraced the walls, the hangings, the whole house, all the crowd of houses outside, all the flimsy and inscrutable graves of the living, with their doors numbered like the doors of prison-cells, and as impenetrable as the granite of tombstones.

'Yes! Restraint, duty, fidelity – unswerving fidelity to what is expected of you. This – only this – secures the reward, the peace. Everything else we should labour to subdue – to destroy. It's misfortune; it's disease. It is terrible – terrible. We must not know anything about it – we needn't. It is our duty to ourselves – to others. You do not live all alone in the world – and if you have no respect for the dignity of life, others have. Life is a serious matter. If you don't conform to the highest standards you are no one – it's a kind of death. Didn't this occur to you? You've only to look round you to see the truth of what I am saying. Did you live without noticing anything, without under-standing anything? From a child you had examples before your eyes – you could see daily the beauty, the blessings of morality, of principles. . . .'

His voice rose and fell pompously in a strange chant. His eyes were still, his stare exalted and sullen; his face was set, was hard, was woodenly exulting over the grim inspiration that secretly possessed him, seethed within him, lifted him up into a stealthy frenzy of belief. Now and then he would stretch out his right arm over her head, as it were, and he spoke down at that sinner from a height, and with a sense of avenging virtue, with a profound and pure joy as though he could from his steep pinnacle see every weighty word strike and hurt like a punishing stone.

'Rigid principles – adherence to what is right,' he finished after a pause.

'What is right?' she said indistinctly, without uncovering her face.

'Your mind is diseased!' he cried, upright and austere. 'Such a question is rot – utter rot. Look round you – there's your answer, if you only care to see. Nothing that outrages the received beliefs can be right. Your conscience tells you that. They are the received beliefs because they are the best, the noblest, the only possible. They survive. . . .'

He could not help noticing with pleasure the philosophic breadth of his view, but he could not pause to enjoy it, for his inspiration, the call of august truth, carried him on.

'You must respect the moral foundations of a society that has made you what you are. Be true to it. That's duty – that's honour – that's honesty.'

He felt a great glow within him, as though he had swallowed something hot. He made a step nearer. She sat up and looked at him with an ardour of expectation that stimulated his sense of the supreme importance of that moment. And as if forgetting himself he raised his voice very much.

' "What's right?" you ask me. Think only. What would you have been if you had gone off with that infernal vagabond? . . . What would you have been? . . . You! My wife! . . .'

He caught sight of himself in the pier glass, drawn up to his full height, and with a face so white that his eyes, at the distance, resembled the black cavities in a skull. He saw himself as if about to launch imprecations, with his arms uplifted above her bowed head. He was ashamed of that unseemly posture, and put his hands in his pockets hurriedly. She murmured faintly, as if to herself—

'Ah! What am I now?'

'As it happens you are still Mrs Alvan Hervey – uncommonly lucky for you, let me tell you,' he said in a conversational tone. He walked up to the furthest corner of the room, and, turning back, saw her sitting very upright, her hands clasped on her lap, and with a lost, unswerving gaze of her eyes which stared unwinking, like the eyes of the blind, at the crude gas flame, blazing and still, between the jaws of the bronze dragon.

He came up quite close to her, and straddling his legs a little, stood looking down at her face for some time without taking his hands out of his pockets. He seemed to be turning over in his mind a heap of words, piecing his next speech out of an overpowering abundance of thoughts.

'You've tried me to the utmost,' he said at last; and as soon as he said these words he lost his moral footing, and felt himself swept away from his pinnacle by a flood of passionate resentment against the bungling creature that had come so near to spoiling his life. 'Yes; I've been tried more than any man ought to be,' he went on with righteous bitterness. 'It was unfair. What possessed you to? . . . What possessed you? . . . Write such a . . . After five years of perfect happiness! 'Pon my word, no one would believe. . . . Didn't you feel you couldn't? Because you couldn't . . . it was impossible – you know. Wasn't it? Think. Wasn't it?'

'It was impossible,' she whispered obediently.

This submissive assent given with such readiness did not soothe him, did not elate him; it gave him, inexplicably, that sense of terror we experience when in the midst of conditions we had learned to think absolutely safe we discover all at once the presence of a near and unsuspected danger. It was impossible, of course! He knew it. She knew it. She confessed it. It was impossible! That man knew it too – as well as any one; couldn't help knowing it. And yet those two had been engaged in a conspiracy against his peace – in a criminal enterprise for which there could be no sanction of belief within themselves. There could not be! There could not be! And yet how near to . . . With a short thrill he saw himself an exiled, forlorn figure in a realm of ungovernable, of unrestrained folly. Nothing could be foreseen, foretold – guarded against. And the sensation was intolerable, had something of the withering horror that may be conceived as following upon the utter extinction of all hope. In the flash of thought the dishonouring episode seemed to disengage itself from everything actual, from earthly conditions, and even from earthly suffering; it became purely a terrifying knowledge, an annihilating knowledge of a blind and infernal force. Something desperate and vague, a flicker of an insane desire to abase himself before the mysterious impulses of evil, to ask for mercy in some way, passed through his mind; and then came the idea, the persuasion, the certitude, that the evil must be forgotten – must be resolutely ignored to make life possible; that the knowledge must be kept out of mind, out of sight, like the knowledge of certain death is kept out of the daily existence of men. He stiffened himself inwardly for the effort, and next moment it appeared very easy, amazingly feasible, if one only kept strictly to facts, gave one's mind to their perplexities and not to their meaning. Becoming conscious of a long silence, he cleared his throat warningly, and said in a steady voice—

'I am glad you feel this . . . uncommonly glad . . . you felt this in time. For, don't you see . . .' Unexpectedly he hesitated.

'Yes . . . I see,' she murmured.

'Of course you would,' he said, looking at the carpet and speaking like one who thinks of something else. He lifted his head. 'I cannot believe – even after this – even after this – that you are altogether – altogether . . . other than what I thought you. It seems impossible – to me.'

'And to me,' she breathed out.

'Now – yes,' he said, 'but this morning? And to-morrow? . . . This is what . . .'

He started at the drift of his words and broke off abruptly. Every train of thought seemed to lead into the hopeless realm of ungovernable folly, to recall the knowledge and the terror of forces that must be ignored. He said rapidly—

'My position is very painful – difficult . . . I feel . . .'

He looked at her fixedly with a pained air, as though frightfully oppressed by a sudden inability to express his pent-up ideas.

'I am ready to go,' she said very low. 'I have forfeited everything . . . to learn . . . to learn . . .'

Her chin fell on her breast; her voice died out in a sigh. He made a slight gesture of impatient assent.

'Yes! Yes! It's all very well . . . of course. Forfeited – ah! Morally forfeited – only morally forfeited . . . if I am to believe you . . .'

She startled him by jumping up.

'Oh! I believe, I believe,' he said hastily, and she sat down as suddenly as she had got up. He went on gloomily—

'I've suffered – I suffer now. You can't understand how much. So much that when you propose a parting I almost think . . . But no. There is duty. You've forgotten it; I never did. Before heaven, I never did. But in a horrid exposure like this the judgment of mankind goes astray – at least for a time. You see, you and I – at least I feel that – you and I are one before the world. It is as it should be. The world is right – in the main – or else it couldn't be – couldn't be – what it is. And we are part of it. We have our duty to – to our fellow beings who don't want to . . . to . . . er.'

He stammered. She looked up at him with wide eyes, and her lips were slightly parted. He went on mumbling—

'. . . Pain. . . . Indignation. . . . Sure to misunderstand. I've suffered enough. And if there has been nothing irreparable – as you assure me . . . then . . .'

'Alvan!' she cried.

'What?' he said morosely. He gazed down at her for a moment with a sombre stare, as one looks at ruins, at the devastation of some natural disaster.

'Then,' he continued after a short pause, 'the best thing is . . . the best for us . . . for every one. . . . Yes . . . least pain – most unselfish. . . .' His voice faltered, and she heard only detached words. '. . . Duty . . . Burden . . . Ourselves . . . Silence.'

A moment of perfect stillness ensued.

'This is an appeal I am making to your conscience,' he said suddenly, in an explanatory tone, 'not to add to the wretchedness of all this: to try loyally and help me to live it down somehow. Without any reservations – you know. Loyally! You can't deny I've been cruelly wronged and – after all – my affection deserves . . .' He paused with evident anxiety to hear her speak.

'I make no reservations,' she said mournfully. 'How could I? I found myself out and came back to . . .' her eyes flashed scornfully for an instant '. . . to what – to what you propose. You see . . . I . . . I can be trusted . . . now.'

He listened to every word with profound attention, and when she ceased seemed to wait for more.

'Is that all you've got to say?' he asked.

She was startled by his tone, and said faintly—

'I spoke the truth. What more can I say?'

'Confound it! You might say something human,' he burst out. 'It isn't being truthful; it's being brazen – if you want to know. Not a word to show you feel your position, and – and mine. Not a single word of acknowledgment, or regret – or remorse . . . or . . . something.'

'Words!' she whispered in a tone that irritated him. He stamped his foot.

'This is awful!' he exclaimed. 'Words? Yes, words. Words

mean something – yes – they do – for all this infernal affectation.
They mean something to me – to everybody – to you. What the
devil else did you use to express those sentiments – sentiments –
pah! – which made you forget me, duty, shame!' . . . He foamed
at the mouth while she stared at him, appalled by this sudden
fury. 'Did you two talk only with your eyes?' he spluttered
savagely. She rose.

'I can't bear this,' she said, trembling from head to foot. 'I am
going.'

They stood facing one another for a moment.

'Not you,' he said, with conscious roughness, and began to
walk up and down the room. She remained very still with an air
of listening anxiously to her own heart-beats, then sank down
on the chair slowly, and sighed, as if giving up a task beyond
her strength.

'You misunderstand everything I say,' he began quietly, 'but I
prefer to think that – just now – you are not accountable for
your actions.' He stopped again before her. 'Your mind is
unhinged,' he said, with unction. 'To go now would be adding
crime – yes, crime – to folly. I'll have no scandal in my life, no
matter what's the cost. And why? You are sure to misunderstand me – but I'll tell you. As a matter of duty. Yes. But you're
sure to misunderstand me – recklessly. Women always do – they
are too – too narrow-minded.'

He waited for a while, but she made no sound, didn't even
look at him; he felt uneasy, painfully uneasy, like a man who
suspects he is unreasonably mistrusted. To combat that exasperating sensation he recommenced talking very fast. The sound of
his words excited his thoughts, and in the play of darting
thoughts he had glimpses now and then of the inexpugnable
rock of his convictions, towering in solitary grandeur above the
unprofitable waste of errors and passions.

'For it is self-evident,' he went on, with anxious vivacity, 'it is
self-evident that, on the highest ground, we haven't the right –
no, we haven't the right to intrude our miseries upon those who
– who naturally expect better things from us. Every one wishes
his own life and the life around him to be beautiful and pure.
Now, a scandal amongst people of our position is disastrous for
the morality – a fatal influence – don't you see – upon the
general tone of the class – very important – the most important,
I verily believe, in – in the community. I feel this – profoundly.

This is the broad view. In time you'll give me ... when you become again the woman I loved – and trusted. ...'

He stopped short, as though unexpectedly suffocated, then in a completely changed voice said, 'For I did love and trust you' – and again was silent for a moment. She put her handkerchief to her eyes.

'You'll give me credit for – for – my motives. It's mainly loyalty to – to the larger conditions of our life – where you – you! of all women – failed. One doesn't usually talk like this – of course – but in this case you'll admit ... And consider – the innocent suffer with the guilty. The world is pitiless in its judgments. Unfortunately there are always those in it who are only too eager to misunderstand. Before you and before my conscience I am guiltless, but any – any disclosure would impair my usefulness in the sphere – in the larger sphere in which I hope soon to ... I believe you fully shared my views in that matter – I don't want to say any more ... on – on that point – but, believe me, true unselfishness is to bear one's burdens in – in silence. The ideal must – must be preserved – for others, at least. It's clear as daylight. If I've a – a loathsome sore, to gratuitously display it would be abominable – abominable! And often in life – in the highest conception of life – outspokenness in certain circumstances is nothing less than criminal. Temptation, you know, excuses no one. There is no such thing really if one looks steadily to one's welfare – which is grounded in duty. But there are the weak.' ... His tone became ferocious for an instant ... 'And there are the fools and the envious – especially for people in our position. I am guiltless of this terrible – terrible ... estrangement; but if there has been nothing irreparable.' ... Something gloomy, like a deep shadow passed over his face. ... 'Nothing irreparable – you see even now I am ready to trust you implicitly – then our duty is clear.'

He looked down. A change came over his expression, and straightway from the outward impetus of his loquacity he passed into the dull contemplation of all the appeasing truths that, not without some wonder, he had so recently been able to discover within himself. During this profound and soothing communion with his innermost beliefs he remained staring at the carpet, with a portentously solemn face and with a dull vacuity of eyes that seemed to gaze into the blankness of an empty hole. Then, without stirring in the least, he continued:

'Yes. Perfectly clear. I've been tried to the utmost, and I can't pretend that, for a time, the old feelings – the old feelings are not . . .' He sighed . . . 'But I forgive you. . . .'

She made a slight movement without uncovering her eyes. In his profound scrutiny of the carpet he noticed nothing. And there was silence, silence within and silence without, as though his words had stilled the beat and tremor of all the surrounding life, and the house had stood alone – the only dwelling upon a deserted earth.

He lifted his head and repeated solemnly:

'I forgive you . . . from a sense of duty – and in the hope . . .'

He heard a laugh, and it not only interrupted his words but also destroyed the peace of his self-absorption with the vile pain of a reality intruding upon the beauty of a dream. He couldn't understand whence the sound came. He could see, foreshortened, the tear-stained, dolorous face of the woman stretched out, and with her head thrown over the back of the seat. He thought the piercing noise was a delusion. But another shrill peal followed by a deep sob and succeeded by another shriek of mirth positively seemed to tear him out from where he stood. He bounded to the door. It was closed. He turned the key and thought: that's no good. . . . 'Stop this!' he cried, and perceived with alarm that he could hardly hear his own voice in the midst of her screaming. He darted back with the idea of stifling that unbearable noise with his hands, but stood still distracted, finding himself as unable to touch her as though she had been on fire. He shouted, 'Enough of this!' like men shout in the tumult of a riot, with a red face and starting eyes; then, as if swept away before another burst of laughter, he disappeared in a flash out of three looking-glasses, vanished suddenly from before her. For a time the woman gasped and laughed at no one in the luminous stillness of the empty room.

He reappeared, striding at her, and with a tumbler of water in his hand. He stammered: 'Hysterics – Stop – They will hear – Drink this.' She laughed at the ceiling. 'Stop this!' he cried. 'Ah!'

He flung the water in her face, putting into the action all the secret brutality of his spite, yet still felt that it would have been perfectly excusable – in any one – to send the tumbler after the water. He restrained himself, but at the same time was so convinced nothing could stop the horror of those mad shrieks that, when the first sensation of relief came, it did not even occur to him to doubt the impression of having become suddenly deaf. When, next moment, he became sure that she was sitting up, and really very quiet, it was as though everything – men, things, sensations, had come to a rest. He was prepared to be grateful. He could not take his eyes off her, fearing, yet unwilling to admit, the possibility of her beginning again; for, the experience, however contemptuously he tried to think of it, had left the bewilderment of a mysterious terror. Her face was streaming with water and tears; there was a wisp of hair on her forehead, another stuck to her cheek; her hat was on one side, undecorously tilted; her soaked veil resembled a sordid rag festooning her forehead. There was an utter unreserve in her aspect, an abandonment of safeguards, that ugliness of truth which can only be kept out of daily life by unremitting care for appearances. He did not know why, looking at her, he thought suddenly of to-morrow, and why the thought called out a deep feeling of unutterable, discouraged weariness – a fear of facing the succession of days. To-morrow! It was as far as yesterday. Ages elapsed between sunrises – sometimes. He scanned her features like one looks at a forgotten country. They were not distorted – he recognised landmarks, so to speak; but it was only a resemblance that he could see, not the woman of yesterday – or was it, perhaps, more than the woman of yesterday? Who could tell? Was it something new? A new expression – or a new shade of expression? or something deep – an old truth unveiled, a fundamental and hidden truth – some unnecessary, accursed certitude? He became aware that he was trembling very much, that he had an empty tumbler in his hand – that time was passing. Still looking at her with lingering mistrust he reached towards the table to put the glass down and was startled to feel it apparently go through the wood. He had missed the edge. The surprise, the slight jingling noise of the accident annoyed him beyond expression. He turned to her irritated.

'What's the meaning of this?' he asked grimly.

She passed her hand over her face and made an attempt to get up.

'You're not going to be absurd again,' he said. ''Pon my soul, I did not know you could forget yourself to that extent.' He didn't try to conceal his physical disgust, because he believed it to be a purely moral reprobation of every unreserve, of anything in the nature of a scene. 'I assure you – it was revolting,' he went on. He stared for a moment at her. 'Positively degrading,' he added with insistence.

She stood up quickly as if moved by a spring and tottered. He started forward instinctively. She caught hold of the back of the chair and steadied herself. This arrested him, and they faced each other wide-eyed, uncertain, and yet coming back slowly to the reality of things with relief and wonder, as though just awakened after tossing through a long night of fevered dreams.

'Pray, don't begin again,' he said hurriedly, seeing her open her lips. 'I deserve some little consideration – and such unaccountable behaviour is painful to me. I expect better things. . . . I have the right. . . .'

She pressed both her hands to her temples.

'Oh, nonsense!' he said sharply. 'You are perfectly capable of coming down to dinner. No one should even suspect; not even the servants. No one! No one! . . . I am sure you can.'

She dropped her arms; her face twitched. She looked straight into his eyes and seemed incapable of pronouncing a word. He frowned at her.

'I – wish – it,' he said tyrannically. 'For your own sake also. . . .' He meant to carry that point without any pity. Why didn't she speak? He feared passive resistance. She must. . . . Make her come. His frown deepened, and he began to think of some effectual violence, when most unexpectedly she said in a firm voice, 'Yes, I can,' and clutched the chair-back again. He was relieved, and all at once her attitude ceased to interest him. The important thing was that their life would begin again with an everyday act – with something that could not be misunderstood, that, thank God, had no moral meaning, no perplexity – and yet was symbolic of their uninterrupted communion in the past – in all the future. That morning, at that table, they had breakfast together; and now they would dine. It was all over! What had happened between could be forgotten – must be forgotten, like things that can only happen once – death for instance.

'I will wait for you,' he said, going to the door. He had some difficulty with it, for he did not remember he had turned the key. He hated that delay, and his checked impatience to be gone out of the room made him feel quite ill as, with the consciousness of her presence behind his back, he fumbled at the lock. He managed it at last; then in the doorway he glanced over his shoulder to say, 'It's rather late – you know – ' and saw her standing where he had left her, with a face white as alabaster and perfectly still, like a woman in a trance.

He was afraid she would keep him waiting, but without any breathing time, he hardly knew how, he found himself sitting at table with her. He had made up his mind to eat, to talk, to be natural. It seemed to him necessary that deception should begin at home. The servants must not know – must not suspect. This intense desire of secrecy; of secrecy dark, destroying, profound, discreet like a grave, possessed him with the strength of a hallucination – seemed to spread itself to inanimate objects that had been the daily companions of his life, affected with a taint of enmity every single thing within the faithful walls that would stand for ever between the shamelessness of facts and the indignation of mankind. Even when – as it happened once or twice – both the servants left the room together he remained carefully natural, industriously hungry, laboriously at his ease, as though he had wanted to cheat the black oak sideboard, the heavy curtains, the stiff-backed chairs, into the belief of an unstained happiness. He was mistrustful of his wife's self-control, unwilling to look at her and reluctant to speak, for, it seemed to him inconceivable that she should not betray herself by the slightest movement, by the very first word spoken. Then he thought the silence in the room was becoming dangerous, and so excessive as to produce the effect of an intolerable uproar. He wanted to end it, as one is anxious to interrupt an indiscreet confession; but with the memory of that laugh upstairs he dared not give her an occasion to open her lips. Presently he heard her voice pronouncing in a calm tone some unimportant remark. He detached his eyes from the centre of his plate and felt excited as if on the point of looking at a wonder. And nothing could be more wonderful than her composure. He was looking at the candid eyes, at the pure brow, at what he had seen every evening for years in that place; he listened to the voice that for five years he had heard every day. Perhaps she was a little pale – but a healthy pallor had always been for him one of her chief attractions. Perhaps her face was rigidly set – but that marmoreal impassiveness, that magnificent stolidity, as of a wonderful statue by some great sculptor

working under the curse of the gods;* that imposing, unthinking
stillness of her features, had till then mirrored for him the
tranquil dignity of a soul of which he had thought himself – as
a matter of course – the inexpugnable possessor. Those were the
outward signs of her difference from the ignoble herd that feels,
suffers, fails, errs – but has no distinct value in the world except
as a moral contrast to the prosperity of the elect. He had been
proud of her appearance. It had the perfectly proper frankness
of perfection – and now he was shocked to see it unchanged.
She looked like this, spoke like this, exactly like this, a year ago,
a month ago – only yesterday when she ... What went on
within made no difference. What did she think? What meant
the pallor, the placid face, the candid brow, the pure eyes? What
did she think during all these years? What did she think
yesterday – to-day; what would she think to-morrow? He must
find out. . . . And yet how could he get to know? She had been
false to him, to that man, to herself; she was ready to be false –
for him. Always false. She looked lies, breathed lies, lived lies –
would tell lies – always – to the end of life! And he would never
know what she meant. Never! Never! No one could. Impossible
to know.

He dropped his knife and fork, brusquely, as though by the
virtue of a sudden illumination he had been made aware of
poison in his plate, and became positive in his mind that he
could never swallow another morsel of food as long as he lived.
The dinner went on in a room that had been steadily growing,
from some cause, hotter than a furnace. He had to drink. He
drank time after time, and, at last, recollecting himself, was
frightened at the quantity, till he perceived that what he had
been drinking was water – out of two different wine glasses;
and the discovered unconsciousness of his actions affected him
painfully. He was disturbed to find himself in such an
unhealthy state of mind. Excess of feeling – excess of feeling;
and it was part of his creed that any excess of feeling was
unhealthy – morally unprofitable; a taint on practical manhood. Her fault. Entirely her fault. Her sinful self-forgetfulness
was contagious. It made him think thoughts he had never had
before; thoughts disintegrating, tormenting, sapping to the very
core of life – like mortal disease; thoughts that bred the fear of
air, of sunshine, of men – like the whispered news of a
pestilence.

The maids served without noise; and to avoid looking at his wife and looking within himself, he followed with his eyes first one and then the other without being able to distinguish between them. They moved silently about, without one being able to see by what means, for their skirts touched the carpet all round; they glided here and there, receded, approached, rigid in black and white, with precise gestures, and no life in their faces, like a pair of marionettes in mourning; and their air of wooden unconcern struck him as unnatural, suspicious, irremediably hostile. That such people's feelings or judgment could affect one in any way, had never occurred to him before. He understood they had no prospects, no principles – no refinement and no power. But now he had become so debased that he could not even attempt to disguise from himself his yearning to know the secret thoughts of his servants. Several times he looked up covertly at the faces of those girls. Impossible to know. They changed his plates and utterly ignored his existence. What impenetrable duplicity. Women – nothing but women round him. Impossible to know. He experienced that heart-probing, fiery sense of dangerous loneliness, which sometimes assails the courage of a solitary adventurer in an unexplored country. The sight of a man's face – he felt – of any man's face, would have been a profound relief. One would know then – something – could understand. . . . He decided he must have men servants. He would engage a butler as soon as possible. And then the end of that dinner – which had seemed to have been going on for hours – the end came, taking him violently by surprise, as though he had expected in the natural course of events to sit at that table for ever and ever.

But upstairs in the drawing-room he became the victim of a restless fate, that would, on no account, permit him to sit down. She had sunk on a low easy-chair, and taking up from a small table at her elbow a fan with ivory leaves, shaded her face from the fire. The coals glowed without a flame; and upon the red glow the vertical bars of the grate stood out at her feet, black and curved, like the charred ribs of a consumed sacrifice. Far off, a lamp perched on a slim brass rod, burned under a wide shade of crimson silk: the centre, within the shadows of the large room, of a fiery twilight that had in the warm quality of its tint something delicate, refined and infernal. His soft footfalls and the subdued beat of the clock on the high mantel-piece answered each other regularly – as if time and himself, engaged in a measured contest, had been pacing together through the infernal delicacy of twilight towards a mysterious goal.

He walked from one end of the room to the other without a pause, like a traveller who, at night, hastens doggedly upon an interminable journey. Now and then he glanced at her. Impossible to know. The gross precision of that thought expressed to his practical mind something illimitable and infinitely profound, the all-embracing subtlety of a feeling, the eternal origin of his pain. This woman had accepted him, had abandoned him – had returned to him. And of all this he would never know the truth. Never. Not till death – not after – not on judgment day when all shall be disclosed, thoughts and deeds, rewards and punishments, but the secret of hearts alone shall return, for ever unknown, to the Inscrutable Creator of good and evil, to the Master of doubts and impulses.

He stood still to look at her. Thrown back and with her face turned away from him, she did not stir – as if asleep. What did she think? What did she feel? And in the presence of her perfect stillness, in the breathless silence, he felt himself insignificant and powerless before her, like a prisoner in chains. The fury of his impotence called out sinister images, that faculty of tormenting vision, which in a moment of anguishing sense of wrong induces a man to mutter threats or make a menacing gesture in the solitude of an empty room. But the gust of passion passed at once, left him trembling a little, with the wondering, reflective fear of a man who has paused on the very verge of suicide. The serenity of truth and the peace of death can be only secured through a largeness of contempt embracing all the profitable servitudes of life. He found he did not want to know. Better not. It was all over. It was as if it hadn't been. And it was very necessary for both of them, it was morally right, that nobody should know.

He spoke suddenly, as if concluding a discussion.

'The best thing for us is to forget all this.'

She started a little and shut the fan with a click.

'Yes, forgive – and forget' he repeated, as if to himself.

'I'll never forget' she said in a vibrating voice. 'And I'll never forgive myself. . . .'

'But I, who have nothing to reproach myself . . .' he began, making a step towards her. She jumped up.

'I did not come back for your forgiveness,' she exclaimed passionately, as if clamouring against an unjust aspersion.

He only said 'oh!' and became silent. He could not understand this unprovoked aggressiveness of her attitude, and certainly was very far from thinking that an unpremeditated hint of something resembling emotion in the tone of his last words had caused that uncontrollable burst of sincerity. It completed his bewilderment, but he was not at all angry now. He was as if benumbed by the fascination of the incomprehensible. She stood before him, tall and indistinct, like a black phantom in the red twilight. At last poignantly uncertain as to what would happen if he opened his lips, he muttered:

'But if my love is strong enough . . .' and hesitated.

He heard something snap loudly in the fiery stillness. She had broken her fan. Two thin pieces of ivory fell, one after another, without a sound, on the thick carpet, and instinctively he stooped to pick them up. While he groped at her feet it occurred to him that the woman there had in her hands an indispensable gift which nothing else on earth could give; and when he stood up he was penetrated by an irresistible belief in an enigma, by the conviction that within his reach, and passing away from him was the very secret of existence – its certitude, immaterial and precious! She moved to the door, and he followed at her elbow, casting about for a magic word that would make the enigma clear, that would compel the surrender of the gift. And there is no such word! The enigma is only made clear by sacrifice, and the gift of heaven is in the hands of every man. But they had lived in a world that abhors enigmas, and cares for no gifts but such as can be obtained in the street. She was nearing the door. He said hurriedly:

''Pon my word, I loved you – I love you now.'

She stopped for an almost imperceptible moment to give him an indignant glance, and then moved on. That feminine penetration – so clever and so tainted by the eternal instinct of self-defence, so ready to see an obvious evil in everything it cannot understand – filled her with bitter resentment against both the men who could offer to the spiritual and tragic strife of her feelings nothing but the coarseness of their abominable materialism. In her anger against her own ineffectual self-deception she found hate enough for them both. What did they want? What more did this one want? And as her husband faced her again, with his hand on the door-handle, she asked herself whether he was unpardonably stupid, or simply ignoble.

She said, nervously, and very fast:

'You are deceiving yourself. You never loved me. You wanted a wife – some woman – any woman that would think, speak, and behave in a certain way – in a way you approved. You loved yourself.'

'You won't believe me?' he asked slowly.

'If I had believed you loved me,' she began passionately, then drew in a long breath; and during that pause he heard the steady beat of blood in his ears. 'If I had believed it . . . I would never have come back,' she finished recklessly.

He stood looking down as though he had not heard. She waited. After a moment he opened the door, and, on the landing, the sightless woman of marble appeared, draped to the chin, thrusting blindly at them a cluster of lights.

He seemed to have forgotten himself in a meditation so deep that on the point of going out she stopped to look at him in surprise. While she had been speaking he had wandered on the track of the enigma, out of the world of senses into the region of feeling. What did it matter what she had done, what she had said, if through the pain of her acts and words he had obtained the word of the enigma! There can be no life without faith and love – faith in a human heart, love of a human being! That touch of grace, whose help once in life is the privilege of the most undeserving, flung open for him the portals of beyond, and in contemplating there the certitude immaterial and precious he forgot all the meaningless accidents of existence: the bliss of getting, the delight of enjoying; all the protean and enticing forms of the cupidity that rules a material world of foolish joys, of contemptible sorrows. Faith! – Love! – the undoubting, clear faith in the truth of a soul – the great tenderness, deep as the ocean, serene and eternal, like the infinite peace of space above the short tempests of the earth. It was what he had wanted all his life – but he understood it only then for the first time. It was through the pain of losing her that the knowledge had come. She had the gift! She had the gift! And in all the world she was the only human being that could surrender it to his immense desire. He made a step forward, putting his arms out, as if to take her to his breast, and, lifting his head, was met by such a look of blank consternation that his arms fell as though they had been struck down by a blow. She started away from him, stumbled over the threshold, and once on the landing turned, swift and crouching. The train of her gown swished as it flew round her feet. It was an undisguised panic. She panted, showing her teeth, and the hate of strength, the disdain of weakness, the eternal preoccupation of sex came out like a toy demon out of a box.

'This is odious,' she screamed.

He did not stir; but her look, her agitated movements, the sound of her voice were like a mist of facts thickening between him and the vision of love and faith. It vanished; and looking at that face triumphant and scornful, at that white face, stealthy and unexpected, as if discovered staring from an ambush, he was coming back slowly to the world of senses. His first clear thought was: I am married to that woman; and the next: she will give nothing but what I see. He felt the need not to see. But the memory of the vision, the memory that abides for ever within the seer made him say to her with the naïve austerity of a convert awed by the touch of a new creed, 'You haven't the gift.' He turned his back on her, leaving her completely mystified. And she went upstairs slowly, struggling with a distasteful suspicion of having been confronted by something more subtle than herself – more profound than the misunderstood and tragic contest of her feelings.

He shut the door of the drawing-room and moved at hazard, alone amongst the heavy shadows and in the fiery twilight as of an elegant place of perdition. She hadn't the gift – no one had. ... He stepped on a book that had fallen off one of the crowded little tables. He picked up the slender volume, and holding it, approached the crimson-shaded lamp. The fiery tint deepened of the cover, and contorted gold letters sprawling all over it in an intricate maze, came out, gleaming redly. 'Thorns and Arabesques.' He read it twice, 'Thorns and Ar . . . .' The other's book of verses. He dropped it at his feet, but did not feel the slightest pang of jealousy or indignation. What did he know? ... What? ... The mass of hot coals tumbled down in the grate, and he turned to look at them. ... Ah! That one was ready to give up everything he had for that woman – who did not come – who had not the faith, the love, the courage to come. What did that man expect, what did he hope, what did he want? The woman – or the certitude immaterial and precious! The first unselfish thought he had ever given to any human being was for that man who had tried to do him a terrible wrong. He was not angry. He was saddened by an impersonal sorrow, by a vast melancholy as of all mankind longing for what cannot be attained. He felt his fellowship with every man – even with that man – especially with that man. What did he think now? Had he ceased to wait – and hope? Would he ever cease to wait and hope? Would he understand that the woman, who had no courage, had not the gift – had not the gift!

The clock began to strike, and the deep-toned vibration filled the room as though with the sound of an enormous bell tolling far away. He counted the strokes. Twelve. Another day had begun. To-morrow had come; the mysterious and lying to-morrow that lures men, disdainful of love and faith, on and on through the poignant futilities of life to the fitting reward of a grave. He counted the strokes, and gazing at the grate seemed to wait for more. Then, as if called out, left the room, walking firmly.

When outside he heard footsteps in the hall and stood still. A bolt was shot – then another. They were locking up – shutting out his desire and his deception from the indignant criticism of a world full of noble gifts for those who proclaim themselves without stain and without reproach. He was safe; and on all sides of his dwelling servile fears and servile hopes slept, dreaming of success, behind the severe discretion of doors as impenetrable to the truth within as the granite of tombstones. A lock snapped – a short chain rattled. Nobody shall know!

Why was this assurance of safety heavier than a burden of fear, and why the day that began presented itself obstinately like the last day of all – like a to-day without a to-morrow? Yet nothing was changed, for nobody would know; and all would go on as before – the getting, the enjoying, the blessing of hunger that is appeased every day; the noble incentives of unappeasable ambitions. All – all the blessings of life. All – but the certitude immaterial and precious – the certitude of love and faith. He believed the shadow of it had been with him as long as he could remember; that invisible presence had ruled his life. And now the shadow had appeared and faded he could not extinguish his longing for the truth of its substance. His desire of it was naïve; it was masterful like the material aspirations that are the groundwork of existence, but, unlike these, it was unconquerable. It was the subtle despotism of an idea that suffers no rivals, that is lonely, inconsolable, and dangerous. He went slowly up the stairs. Nobody shall know. The days would go on and he would go far – very far. If the idea could not be mastered, fortune could be, men could be – the whole world. He was dazzled by the greatness of the prospect; the brutality of a practical instinct shouted to him that only that which could be had was worth having. He lingered on the steps. The lights were out in the hall, and a small yellow flame flitted about down there. He felt a sudden contempt for himself which braced him up. He went on, but at the door of their room and with his arm advanced to open it, he faltered. On the flight of stairs below the head of the girl who had been locking up appeared. His arm fell. He thought, 'I'll wait till she is gone' – and stepped back within the perpendicular folds of a *portière.* *

He saw her come up gradually, as if ascending from a well. At every step the feeble flame of the candle swayed before her tired, young face, and the darkness of the hall seemed to cling to her black skirt, followed her, rising like a silent flood, as though the great night of the world had broken through the discreet reserve of walls, of closed doors, of curtained windows. It rose over the steps, it leaped up the walls like an angry wave, it flowed over the blue skies, over the yellow sands, over the sunshine of landscapes, and over the pretty pathos of ragged innocence and of meek starvation. It swallowed up the delicious idyll in a boat and the mutilated immortality of famous bas-reliefs. It flowed from outside – it rose higher, in a destructive silence. And, above it, the woman of marble, composed and blind on the high pedestal, seemed to ward off the devouring night with a cluster of lights.

He watched the rising tide of impenetrable gloom with impatience, as if anxious for the coming of a darkness black enough to conceal a shameful surrender. It came nearer. The cluster of lights went out. The girl ascended facing him. Behind her the shadow of a colossal woman danced lightly on the wall. He held his breath while she passed by, noiseless and with heavy eyelids. And on her track the flowing tide of a tenebrous sea filled the house, seemed to swirl about his feet, and rising unchecked, closed silently above his head.

The time had come but he did not open the door. All was still; and instead of surrendering to the reasonable exigencies of life he stepped out, with a rebelling heart, into the darkness of the house. It was the abode of an impenetrable night; as though indeed the last day had come and gone, leaving him alone in a darkness that has no to-morrow. And looming vaguely below the woman of marble, livid and still like a patient phantom, held out in the night a cluster of extinguished lights.

His obedient thought traced for him the image of an uninterrupted life, the dignity and the advantages of an uninterrupted success; while his rebellious heart beat violently within his breast, as if maddened by the desire of a certitude immaterial and precious – the certitude of love and faith. What of the night within his dwelling if outside he could find the sunshine in which men sow, in which men reap! Nobody would know. The days, the years would pass, and . . . He remembered that he had loved her. The years would pass . . . And then he thought of her as we think of the dead – in a tender immensity of regret, in a passionate longing for the return of idealised perfections. He had loved her – he had loved her – and he never knew the truth. . . . The years would pass in the anguish of doubt. . . . He remembered her smile, her eyes, her voice, her silence, as though he had lost her for ever. The years would pass and he would always mistrust her smile, suspect her eyes; he would always misbelieve her voice, he would never have faith in her silence. She had no gift – she had no gift! What was she? Who was she? . . . The years would pass; the memory of this hour would grow faint – and she would share the material serenity of an unblemished life. She had no love and no faith for any one. To give her your thought, your belief, was like whispering your confession over the edge of the world. Nothing came back – not even an echo.

In the pain of that thought was born his conscience;* not that fear of remorse which grows slowly, and slowly decays amongst the complicated facts of life, but a Divine wisdom springing full-grown, armed and severe out of a tried heart, to combat the secret baseness of motives. It came to him in a flash that morality is not a method of happiness. The revelation was terrible. He saw at once that nothing of what he knew mattered in the least. The acts of men and women, success, humiliation, dignity, failure – nothing mattered. It was not a question of more or less pain, of this joy, of that sorrow. It was a question of truth or falsehood – it was a question of life or death.

He stood in the revealing night – in the darkness that tries the hearts, in the night useless for the work of men, but in which their gaze, undazzled by the sunshine of covetous days, wanders sometimes as far as the stars. The perfect stillness around him had something solemn in it, but he felt it was the lying solemnity of a temple devoted to the rites of a debasing persuasion. The silence within the discreet walls was eloquent of safety but it appeared to him exciting and sinister, like the discretion of a profitable infamy; it was the prudent peace of a den of coiners – of a house of ill-fame! The years would pass – and nobody would know. Never! Not till death – not after. . . .

'Never!' he said aloud to the revealing night.

And he hesitated. The secret of hearts, too terrible for the timid eyes of men, shall return, veiled for ever, to the Inscrutable Creator of good and evil, to the Master of doubts and impulses. His conscience was born – he heard its voice, and he hesitated, ignoring the strength within, the fateful power, the secret of his heart! It was an awful sacrifice to cast all one's life into the flame of a new belief. He wanted help against himself, against the cruel decree of salvation. The need of tacit complicity, where it had never failed him, the habit of years affirmed itself. Perhaps she would help. . . . He flung the door open and rushed in like a fugitive.

He was in the middle of the room before he could see anything but the dazzling brilliance of the light; and then, as if detached and floating in it on the level of his eyes, appeared the head of a woman. She had jumped up when he burst into the room.

For a moment they contemplated each other as if struck dumb with amazement. Her hair streaming on her shoulders glinted like burnished gold. He looked into the unfathomable candour of her eyes. Nothing within – nothing – nothing.

He stammered distractedly.

'I want . . . I want . . . to . . . to . . . know. . . .'

On the candid light of the eyes flitted shadows; shadows of doubt, of suspicion, the ready suspicion of an unquenchable antagonism, the pitiless mistrust of an eternal instinct of defence; the hate, the profound, frightened hate of an incomprehensible – of an abominable emotion intruding its coarse materialism upon the spiritual and tragic contest of her feelings.

'Alvan . . . I won't bear this . . .' She began to pant suddenly, 'I've a right – a right to – to – myself. . . .'

He lifted one arm, and appeared so menacing that she stopped in a fright and shrank back a little.

He stood with uplifted hand. . . . The years would pass . . . and he would have to live with that unfathomable candour where flit shadows of suspicion and hate. . . . The years would pass – and he would never know – never trust. . . . The years would pass without faith and love. . . .

'Can you stand it?' he shouted, as though she could have heard all his thoughts.

He looked menacing. She thought of violence, of danger – and, just for an instant, she doubted whether there were splendours enough on earth to pay the price of such a brutal experience. He cried again.

'Can you stand it?' and glared as if insane. Her eyes blazed too. She could not hear the appalling clamour of his thoughts. She suspected in him a sudden regret, a fresh fit of jealousy, a dishonest desire of evasion. She shouted back angrily—

'Yes!'

He was shaken where he stood as if by a struggle to break out of invisible bonds. She trembled from head to foot.

'Well, I can't!' He flung both his arms out, as if to push her away, and strode from the room. The door swung to with a click. She made three quick steps towards it and stood still, looking at the white and gold panels. No sound came from beyond, not a whisper, not a sigh; not even a footstep was heard outside on the thick carpet. It was as though no sooner gone he had suddenly expired – as though he had died there and his body had vanished on the instant together with his soul. She listened, with parted lips and irresolute eyes. Then below, far below her, as if in the entrails of the earth, a door slammed heavily; and the quiet house vibrated to it from roof to foundations, more than to a clap of thunder.

He never returned.

The Lagoon

The white man, leaning with both arms over the roof of the
little house in the stern of the boat, said to the steersman —

'We will pass the night in Arsat's clearing. It is late.'

The Malay only grunted, and went on looking fixedly at the
river. The white man rested his chin on his crossed arms and
gazed at the wake of the boat. At the end of the straight avenue
of forests cut by the intense glitter of the river, the sun appeared
unclouded and dazzling, poised low over the water that shone
smoothly like a band of metal. The forests, sombre and dull,
stood motionless and silent on each side of the broad stream.
At the foot of big, towering trees, trunkless nipa palms rose
from the mud of the bank, in bunches of leaves enormous and
heavy, that hung unstirring over the brown swirl of eddies. In
the stillness of the air every tree, every leaf, every bough, every
tendril of creeper and every petal of minute blossoms seemed to
have been bewitched into an immobility perfect and final.
Nothing moved on the river but the eight paddles that rose
flashing regularly, dipped together with a single splash; while
the steersman swept right and left with a periodic and sudden
flourish of his blade describing a glinting semicircle above his
head. The churned-up water frothed alongside with a confused
murmur. And the white man's canoe, advancing up stream in
the short-lived disturbance of its own making, seemed to enter
the portals of a land from which the very memory of motion
had for ever departed.

The white man, turning his back upon the setting sun, looked
along the empty and broad expanse of the sea-reach. For the
last three miles of its course the wandering, hesitating river, as
if enticed irresistibly by the freedom of an open horizon, flows
straight into the sea, flows straight to the east – to the east that
harbours both light and darkness. Astern of the boat the
repeated call of some bird, a cry discordant and feeble, skipped
along over the smooth water and lost itself, before it could
reach the other shore, in the breathless silence of the world.

The steersman dug his paddle into the stream, and held hard
with stiffened arms, his body thrown forward. The water

gurgled aloud; and suddenly the long straight reach seemed to
pivot on its centre, the forests swung in a semicircle, and the
slanting beams of sunset touched the broadside of the canoe
with a fiery glow, throwing the slender and distorted shadows
of its crew upon the streaked glitter of the river. The white man
turned to look ahead. The course of the boat had been altered
at right-angles to the stream, and the carved dragon-head of its
prow was pointing now at a gap in the fringing bushes of the
bank. It glided through, brushing the over-hanging twigs, and
disappeared from the river like some slim and amphibious
creature leaving the water for its lair in the forests.

The narrow creek was like a ditch: tortuous, fabulously deep;
filled with gloom under the thin strip of pure and shining blue
of the heaven. Immense trees soared up, invisible behind the
festooned draperies of creepers. Here and there, near the glistening blackness of the water, a twisted root of some tall tree
showed amongst the tracery of small ferns, black and dull,
writhing and motionless, like an arrested snake. The short
words of the paddlers reverberated loudly between the thick
and sombre walls of vegetation. Darkness oozed out from
between the trees, through the tangled maze of the creepers,
from behind the great fantastic and unstirring leaves; the darkness, mysterious and invincible; the darkness scented and
poisonous of impenetrable forests.

The men poled in the shoaling water. The creek broadened,
opening out into a wide sweep of a stagnant lagoon. The forests
receded from the marshy bank, leaving a level strip of bright
green, reedy grass to frame the reflected blueness of the sky. A
fleecy pink cloud drifted high above, trailing the delicate colouring of its image under the floating leaves and the silvery blossoms of the lotus. A little house, perched on high piles, appeared
black in the distance. Near it, two tall nibong palms, that
seemed to have come out of the forests in the background,
leaned slightly over the ragged roof, with a suggestion of sad
tenderness and care in the droop of their leafy and soaring
heads.

The steersman, pointing with his paddle, said, 'Arsat is there.
I see his canoe fast between the piles.'

The polers ran along the sides of the boat glancing over their
shoulders at the end of the day's journey. They would have
preferred to spend the night somewhere else than on this lagoon

of weird aspect and ghostly reputation. Moreover, they disliked Arsat, first as a stranger, and also because he who repairs a ruined house, and dwells in it, proclaims that he is not afraid to live amongst the spirits that haunt the places abandoned by mankind. Such a man can disturb the course of fate by glances or words; while his familiar ghosts are not easy to propitiate by casual wayfarers upon whom they long to wreak the malice of their human master. White men care not for such things, being unbelievers and in league with the Father of Evil, who leads them unharmed through the invisible dangers of this world. To the warnings of the righteous they oppose an offensive pretence of disbelief. What is there to be done?

So they thought, throwing their weight on the end of their long poles. The big canoe glided on swiftly, noiselessly, and smoothly, towards Arsat's clearing, till, in a great rattling of poles thrown down, and the loud murmurs of 'Allah be praised!'* it came with a gentle knock against the crooked piles below the house.

The boatmen with uplifted faces shouted discordantly, 'Arsat! O Arsat!' Nobody came. The white man began to climb the rude ladder giving access to the bamboo platform before the house. The juragan of the boat said sulkily, 'We will cook in the sampan, and sleep on the water.'

'Pass my blankets and the basket,' said the white man curtly.

He knelt on the edge of the platform to receive the bundle. Then the boat shoved off, and the white man, standing up, confronted Arsat, who had come out through the low door of his hut. He was a man young, powerful, with a broad chest and muscular arms. He had nothing on but his sarong. His head was bare. His big, soft eyes stared eagerly at the white man, but his voice and demeanour were composed as he asked, without any words of greeting—

'Have you medicine, Tuan?'

'No,' said the visitor in a startled tone. 'No. Why? Is there sickness in the house?'

'Enter and see,' replied Arsat, in the same calm manner, and turning short round, passed again through the small doorway. The white man, dropping his bundles, followed.

In the dim light of the dwelling he made out on a couch of bamboos a woman stretched on her back under a broad sheet of red cotton cloth. She lay still, as if dead; but her big eyes,

wide open, glittered in the gloom, staring upwards at the slender
rafters, motionless and unseeing. She was in a high fever, and
evidently unconscious. Her cheeks were sunk slightly, her lips
were partly open, and on the young face there was the ominous
and fixed expression – the absorbed, contemplating expression
of the unconscious who are going to die. The two men stood
looking down at her in silence.

'Has she been long ill?' asked the traveller.

'I have not slept for five nights,' answered the Malay, in a
deliberate tone. 'At first she heard voices calling her from the
water and struggled against me who held her. But since the sun
of to-day rose she hears nothing – she hears not me. She sees
nothing. She sees not me – me!'

He remained silent for a minute, then asked softly—

'Tuan, will she die?'

'I fear so,' said the white man sorrowfully. He had known
Arsat years ago, in a far country in times of trouble and danger,
when no friendship is to be despised. And since his Malay friend
had come unexpectedly to dwell in the hut on the lagoon with
a strange woman, he had slept many times there, in his journeys
up and down the river. He liked the man who knew how to
keep faith in council and how to fight without fear by the side
of his white friend. He liked him – not so much perhaps as a
man likes his favourite dog – but still he liked him well enough
to help and ask no questions, to think sometimes vaguely and
hazily in the midst of his own pursuits, about the lonely man
and the long-haired woman with audacious face and triumphant
eyes, who lived together hidden by the forests – alone and
feared.

The white man came out of the hut in time to see the
enormous conflagration of sunset put out by the swift and
stealthy shadows that, rising like a black and impalpable vapour
above the tree-tops, spread over the heaven, extinguishing the
crimson glow of floating clouds and the red brilliance of depart-
ing daylight. In a few moments all the stars came out above the
intense blackness of the earth, and the great lagoon gleaming
suddenly with reflected lights resembled an oval patch of night
sky flung down into the hopeless and abysmal night of the
wilderness. The white man had some supper out of the basket,
then collecting a few sticks that lay about the platform, made
up a small fire, not for warmth, but for the sake of the smoke,

which would keep off the mosquitos. He wrapped himself in his blankets and sat with his back against the reed wall of the house, smoking thoughtfully.

Arsat came through the doorway with noiseless steps and squatted down by the fire. The white man moved his out-stretched legs a little.

'She breathes,' said Arsat in a low voice, anticipating the expected question. 'She breathes and burns as if with a great fire. She speaks not; she hears not – and burns!'

He paused for a moment, then asked in a quiet, incurious tone—

'Tuan . . . will she die?'

The white man moved his shoulders uneasily, and muttered in a hesitating manner—

'If such is her fate.'*

'No, Tuan,' said Arsat calmly. 'If such is my fate. I hear, I see, I wait. I remember . . . Tuan, do you remember the old days? Do you remember my brother?'

'Yes,' said the white man. The Malay rose suddenly and went in. The other, sitting still outside, could hear the voice in the hut. Arsat said: 'Hear me! Speak!' His words were succeeded by a complete silence. 'O Diamelen!' he cried suddenly. After that cry there was a deep sigh. Arsat came out and sank down again in his old place.

They sat in silence before the fire. There was no sound within the house, there was no sound near them; but far away on the lagoon they could hear the voices of the boatmen ringing fitful and distinct on the calm water. The fire in the bows of the sampan shone faintly in the distance with a hazy red glow. Then it died out. The voices ceased. The land and the water slept invisible, unstirring and mute. It was as though there had been nothing left in the world but the glitter of stars streaming, ceaseless and vain, through the black stillness of the night.

The white man gazed straight before him into the darkness with wide-open eyes. The fear and fascination, the inspiration and the wonder of death – of death near, unavoidable, and unseen, soothed the unrest of his race and stirred the most indistinct, the most intimate of his thoughts. The ever-ready suspicion of evil, the gnawing suspicion that lurks in our hearts, flowed out into the stillness round him – into the stillness profound and dumb, and made it appear untrustworthy and

infamous, like the placid and impenetrable mask of an unjusti-
fiable violence. In that fleeting and powerful disturbance of his
being the earth enfolded in the starlight peace became a shadowy country of inhuman strife, a battle-field of phantoms
terrible and charming, august or ignoble, struggling ardently for
the possession of our helpless hearts. An unquiet and mysterious
country of inextinguishable desires and fears.

A plaintive murmur rose in the night; a murmur saddening
and startling, as if the great solitudes of surrounding woods had
tried to whisper into his ear the wisdom of their immense and
lofty indifference. Sounds hesitating and vague floated in the air
round him, shaped themselves slowly into words; and at last
flowed on gently in a murmuring stream of soft and monotonous sentences. He stirred like a man waking up and changed
his position slightly. Arsat, motionless and shadowy, sitting
with bowed head under the stars, was speaking in a low and
dreamy tone—

'. . . for where can we lay down the heaviness of our trouble
but in a friend's heart? A man must speak of war and of love.
You, Tuan, know what war is, and you have seen me in time of
danger seek death as other men seek life! A writing may be lost;
a lie may be written; but what the eye has seen is truth and
remains in the mind!'

'I remember,' said the white man quietly. Arsat went on with
mournful composure—

'Therefore I shall speak to you of love. Speak in the night.
Speak before both night and love are gone – and the eye of day
looks upon my sorrow and my shame; upon my blackened face;
upon my burnt-up heart.'

A sigh, short and faint, marked an almost imperceptible
pause, and then his words flowed on, without a stir, without a
gesture.

'After the time of trouble and war* was over and you went
away from my country in the pursuit of your desires, which we,
men of the islands, cannot understand, I and my brother became
again, as we had been before, the sword-bearers of the Ruler.
You know we were men of family, belonging to a ruling race,
and more fit than any to carry on our right shoulder the emblem
of power. And in the time of prosperity Si Dendring* showed
us favour, as we, in time of sorrow, had showed to him the
faithfulness of our courage. It was a time of peace. A time of

deer-hunts and cock-fights; of idle talks and foolish squabbles between men whose bellies are full and weapons are rusty. But the sower watched the young rice-shoots grow up without fear, and the traders came and went, departed lean and returned fat into the river of peace. They brought news too. Brought lies and truth mixed together, so that no man knew when to rejoice and when to be sorry. We heard from them about you also. They had seen you here and had seen you there. And I was glad to hear, for I remembered the stirring times, and I always remembered you, Tuan, till the time came when my eyes could see nothing in the past, because they had looked upon the one who is dying there – in the house.'

He stopped to exclaim in an intense whisper, 'O Mara bahia!* O Calamity!' then went on speaking a little louder.

'There's no worse enemy and no better friend than a brother, Tuan, for one brother knows another, and in perfect knowledge is strength for good or evil. I loved my brother. I went to him and told him that I could see nothing but one face, hear nothing but one voice. He told me: "Open your heart so that she can see what is in it – and wait. Patience is wisdom. Inchi Midah* may die or our Ruler may throw off his fear of a woman!" . . . I waited! . . . You remember the lady with the veiled face, Tuan, and the fear of our Ruler before her cunning and temper. And if she wanted her servant, what could I do? But I fed the hunger of my heart on short glances and stealthy words. I loitered on the path to the bath-houses in the daytime, and when the sun had fallen behind the forest I crept along the jasmine hedges of the women's courtyard. Unseeing, we spoke to one another through the scent of flowers, through the veil of leaves, through the blades of long grass that stood still before our lips; so great was our prudence, so faint was the murmur of our great longing. The time passed swiftly . . . and there were whispers amongst women – and our enemies watched – my brother was gloomy, and I began to think of killing and of a fierce death. . . . We are of a people who take what they want – like you whites. There is a time when a man should forget loyalty and respect. Might and authority are given to rulers, but to all men is given love and strength and courage. My brother said, "You shall take her from their midst. We are two who are like one." And I answered, "Let it be soon, for I find no warmth in sunlight that does not shine upon her." Our time came when the Ruler and all the great people went to the mouth of the river to fish by torchlight. There were hundreds of boats, and on the white sand, between the water and the forests, dwellings of leaves were built for the households of the Rajahs. The smoke of cooking-fires was like a blue mist of the evening, and many voices rang in it joyfully. While they were making the boats ready to beat up the fish, my brother came to me and said, "To-night!" I looked to my weapons, and when the time came our canoe took its place in the circle of boats carrying the torches. The lights blazed on the water, but behind the boats there was darkness. When the shouting began and the excitement made them like mad we dropped out. The water swallowed our fire, and we floated back to the shore that was dark with only here and there the glimmer of embers. We could hear the talk of slave-girls amongst the sheds. Then we found a place deserted and silent. We waited there. She came. She came running along the shore, rapid and leaving no trace, like a leaf driven by the wind into the sea. My brother said gloomily, "Go and take her; carry her into our boat." I lifted her in my arms. She panted. Her heart was beating against my breast. I said, "I take you from those people. You came to the cry of my heart, but my arms take you into my boat against the will of the great!" "It is right," said my brother. "We are men who take what we want and can hold it against many. We should have taken her in daylight." I said, "Let us be off"; for since she was in my boat I began to think of our Ruler's many men. "Yes. Let us be off," said my brother. "We are cast out and this boat is our country now – and the sea is our refuge." He lingered with his foot on the shore, and I entreated him to hasten, for I remembered the strokes of her heart against my breast and thought that two men cannot withstand a hundred. We left, paddling downstream close to the bank; and as we passed by the creek where they were fishing, the great shouting had ceased, but the murmur of voices was loud like the humming of insects flying at noonday. The boats floated, clustered together, in the red light of torches, under a black roof of smoke; and men talked of their sport. Men that boasted, and praised, and jeered – men that would have been our friends in the morning, but on that night were already our enemies. We paddled swiftly past. We had no more friends in the country of our birth. She sat in the middle of the canoe with covered face; silent as she is now; unseeing as she is now – and I had no regret at what I was leaving because I could hear her breathing close to me – as I can hear her now.'

He paused, listened with his ear turned to the doorway, then shook his head and went on.

'My brother wanted to shout the cry of challenge – one cry only – to let the people know we were freeborn robbers who trusted our arms and the great sea. And again I begged him in the name of our love to be silent. Could I not hear her breathing close to me? I knew the pursuit would come quick enough. My brother loved me. He dipped his paddle without a splash. He only said, "There is half a man in you now – the other half is in that woman. I can wait. When you are a whole man again, you will come back with me here to shout defiance. We are sons of the same mother." I made no answer. All my strength and all my spirit were in my hands that held the paddle – for I longed to be with her in a safe place beyond the reach of men's anger and of women's spite. My love was so great, that I thought it could guide me to a country where death was unknown, if I could only escape from Inchi Midah's fury and from our Ruler's sword. We paddled with haste,* breathing through our teeth. The blades bit deep into the smooth water. We passed out of the river; we flew in clear channels amongst the shallows. We skirted the black coast; we skirted the sand beaches where the sea speaks in whispers to the land; and the gleam of white sand flashed back past our boat, so swiftly she ran upon the water. We spoke not. Only once I said, "Sleep, Diamelen, for soon you may want all your strength." I heard the sweetness of her voice, but I never turned my head. The sun rose and still we went on. Water fell from my face like rain from a cloud. We flew in the light and heat. I never looked back, but I knew that my brother's eyes, behind me, were looking steadily ahead, for the boat went as straight as a bushman's dart, when it leaves the end of the sumpitan.* There was no better paddler, no better steersman than my brother. Many times, together, we had won races in that canoe. But we never had put out our strength as we did then – then, when for the last time we paddled together! There was no braver or stronger man in our country than my brother. I could not spare the strength to turn my head and look at him, but every moment I heard the hiss of his breath getting louder behind me. Still he did not speak. The sun was high. The heat clung to my back like a flame of fire. My ribs were ready to

burst, but I could no longer get enough air into my chest. And
then I felt I must cry out with my last breath, "Let us rest!" . . .
"Good!" he answered; and his voice was firm. He was strong.
He was brave. He knew not fear and no fatigue . . . My
brother!'

A murmur* powerful and gentle, a murmur vast and faint;
the murmur of trembling leaves, of stirring boughs, ran through
the tangled depths of the forests, ran over the starry smoothness
of the lagoon, and the water between the piles lapped the slimy
timber once with a sudden splash. A breath of warm air touched
the two men's faces and passed on with a mournful sound – a
breath loud and short like an uneasy sigh of the dreaming earth.

Arsat went on in an even, low voice.

'We ran our canoe on the white beach of a little bay close
to a long tongue of land that seemed to bar our road; a long
wooded cape going far into the sea. My brother knew that
place. Beyond the cape a river has its entrance, and through
the jungle of that land there is a narrow path. We made a fire
and cooked rice. Then we lay down to sleep* on the soft sand
in the shade of our canoe, while she watched. No sooner had I
closed my eyes than I heard her cry of alarm. We leaped up.
The sun was halfway down the sky already, and coming in
sight in the opening of the bay we saw a prau manned by
many paddlers. We knew it at once; it was one of our Rajah's
praus. They were watching the shore, and saw us. They beat
the gong, and turned the head of the prau into the bay. I felt
my heart become weak within my breast. Diamelen sat on the
sand and covered her face. There was no escape by sea. My
brother laughed. He had the gun you had given him, Tuan,
before you went away, but there was only a handful of powder. He spoke to me quickly: "Run with her along the path. I
shall keep them back, for they have no firearms, and landing
in the face of a man with a gun is certain death for some. Run
with her. On the other side of that wood there is a fisherman's
house – and a canoe. When I have fired all the shots I will
follow. I am a great runner, and before they can come up we
shall be gone. I will hold out as long as I can, for she is but a
woman – that can neither run nor fight, but she has your heart
in her weak hands." He dropped behind the canoe. The prau
was coming. She and I ran, and as we rushed along the path I
heard shots. My brother fired – once – twice – and the boom-

ing of the gong ceased. There was silence behind us. That neck
of land is narrow. Before I heard my brother fire the third shot
I saw the shelving shore, and I saw the water again: the mouth
of a broad river. We crossed a grassy glade. We ran down to
the water. I saw a low hut above the black mud, and a small
canoe hauled up. I heard another shot behind me. I thought,
"That is his last charge." We rushed down to the canoe; a man
came running from the hut, but I leaped on him, and we rolled
together in the mud. Then I got up, and he lay still at my feet.
I don't know whether I had killed him or not. I and Diamelen
pushed the canoe afloat. I heard yells behind me, and I saw my
brother run across the glade. Many men were bounding after
him. I took her in my arms and threw her into the boat, then
leaped in myself. When I looked back I saw that my brother
had fallen. He fell and was up again, but the men were closing
round him. He shouted, "I am coming!" The men were close
to him. I looked. Many men. Then I looked at her. Tuan, I
pushed the canoe! I pushed it into deep water. She was kneeling forward looking at me, and I said, "Take your paddle,"
while I struck the water with mine. Tuan, I heard him cry. I
heard him cry my name twice; and I heard voices shouting,
"Kill! Strike!" I never turned back. I heard him calling my
name again with a great shriek, as when life is going out
together with the voice – and I never turned my head. My own
name! . . . My brother! Three times he called – but I was not
afraid of life. Was she not there in that canoe? And could I not
with her find a country where death is forgotten – where death
is unknown!'

The white man sat up. Arsat rose and stood, an indistinct and
silent figure above the dying embers of the fire. Over the lagoon
a mist drifting and low had crept, erasing slowly the glittering
images of the stars. And now a great expanse of white vapour
covered the land: it flowed cold and grey in the darkness, eddied
in noiseless whirls round the tree-trunks and about the platform
of the house, which seemed to float upon a restless and impalpable illusion of a sea.* Only far away the tops of the trees
stood outlined on the twinkle of heaven, like a sombre and
forbidding shore – a coast deceptive, pitiless and black.

Arsat's voice vibrated loudly in the profound peace.

'I had her there! I had her! To get her I would have faced all
mankind. But I had her – and——'

His words went out ringing into the empty distances. He
paused, and seemed to listen to them dying away very far –
beyond help and beyond recall. Then he said quietly—

'Tuan, I loved my brother.'

A breath of wind made him shiver. High above his head, high
above the silent sea of mist the drooping leaves of the palms
rattled together with a mournful and expiring sound. The white
man stretched his legs. His chin rested on his chest, and he
murmured sadly without lifting his head—

'We all love our brothers.'

Arsat burst out with an intense whispering violence—

'What did I care who died? I wanted peace in my own heart.'

He seemed to hear a stir in the house – listened – then stepped
in noiselessly. The white man stood up. A breeze was coming in
fitful puffs. The stars shone paler as if they had retreated into
the frozen depths of immense space. After a chill gust of wind
there were a few seconds of perfect calm and absolute silence.
Then from behind the black and wavy line of the forests a
column of golden light shot up into the heavens and spread over
the semi-circle of the eastern horizon. The sun had risen. The
mist lifted, broke into drifting patches, vanished into thin flying
wreaths; and the unveiled lagoon lay, polished and black, in the
heavy shadows at the foot of the wall of trees. A white eagle
rose over it with a slanting and ponderous flight, reached the
clear sunshine and appeared dazzlingly brilliant for a moment,
then soaring higher, became a dark and motionless speck before
it vanished into the blue as if it had left the earth for ever. The
white man, standing gazing upwards before the doorway, heard
in the hut a confused and broken murmur of distracted words
ending with a loud groan. Suddenly Arsat stumbled out with
outstretched hands, shivered, and stood still for some time with
fixed eyes. Then he said—

'She burns no more.'

Before his face the sun showed its edge above the tree-tops,
rising steadily. The breeze freshened; a great brilliance burst
upon the lagoon, sparkled on the rippling water. The forests
came out of the clear shadows of the morning, became distinct,
as if they had rushed nearer – to stop short in a great stir of
leaves, of nodding boughs, of swaying branches. In the merciless
sunshine the whisper of unconscious life grew louder, speaking
in an incomprehensible voice round the dumb darkness of that

human sorrow. Arsat's eyes wandered slowly, then stared at the rising sun.

'I can see nothing,' he said half aloud to himself.

'There is nothing,' said the white man, moving to the edge of the platform and waving his hand to his boat. A shout came faintly over the lagoon and the sampan began to glide towards the abode of the friend of ghosts.

'If you want to come with me, I will wait all the morning,' said the white man, looking away upon the water.

'No, Tuan,' said Arsat softly. 'I shall not eat or sleep in this house, but I must first see my road. Now I can see nothing – see nothing! There is no light and no peace in the world; but there is death – death for many. We were sons of the same mother – and I left him in the midst of enemies; but I am going back now.'

He drew a long breath and went on in a dreamy tone.

'In a little while I shall see clear enough to strike – to strike. But she has died, and . . . now . . . darkness.'

He flung his arms wide open, let them fall along his body, then stood still with unmoved face and stony eyes, staring at the sun. The white man got down into his canoe. The polers ran smartly along the sides of the boat, looking over their shoulders at the beginning of a weary journey. High in the stern, his head muffled up in white rags, the juragan sat moody, letting his paddle trail in the water. The white man, leaning with both arms over the grass roof of the little cabin, looked back at the shining ripple of the boat's wake. Before the sampan passed out of the lagoon into the creek he lifted his eyes. Arsat had not moved. He stood lonely in the searching sunshine; and he looked beyond the great light of a cloudless day into the darkness of a world of illusions.*

Author's Note

Of the five stories in this volume, 'The Lagoon', the last in order, is the earliest in date.* It is the first short story I ever wrote and marks, in a manner of speaking, the end of my first phase, the Malayan phase with its special subject and its verbal suggestions. Conceived in the same mood which produced 'Almayer's Folly'* and 'An Outcast of the Islands', it is told in the same breath (with what was left of it, that is, after the end of 'An Outcast'), seen with the same vision, rendered in the same method – if such a thing as method did exist then in my conscious relation to this new adventure of writing for print. I doubt it very much. One does one's work first and theorises about it afterwards. It is a very amusing and egotistical occupation of no use whatever to any one and just as likely as not to lead to false conclusions.

Anybody can see that between the last paragraph of 'An Outcast' and the first of 'The Lagoon' there has been no change of pen, figuratively speaking. It happens also to be literally true. It was the same pen: a common steel pen. Having been charged with a certain lack of emotional faculty I am glad to be able to say that on one occasion at least I did give way to a sentimental impulse. I thought the pen had been a good pen and that it had done enough for me, and so, with the idea of keeping it for a sort of memento on which I could look later with tender eyes, I put it into my waistcoat pocket. Afterwards it used to turn up in all sorts of places – at the bottom of small drawers, among my studs in cardboard boxes – till at last it found permanent rest in a large wooden bowl containing some loose keys, bits of sealing wax, bits of string, small broken chains, a few buttons, and similar minute wreckage that washes out of a man's life into such receptacles. I would catch sight of it from time to time with a distinct feeling of satisfaction till, one day, I perceived with horror that there were two old pens in there. How the other pen found its way into the bowl instead of the fire-place or wastepaper basket I can't imagine, but there the two were, lying side by side, both encrusted with ink and completely undistinguishable from each other. It was

very distressing, but being determined not to share my sentiment between two pens or run the risk of sentimentalising over
a mere stranger, I threw them both out of the window into a
flower bed – which strikes me now as a poetical grave for the
remnants of one's past.

But the tale remained. It was first fixed in print in the *Cornhill
Magazine*, being my first appearance* in a serial of any kind;
and I have lived long enough to see it guyed most agreeably by
Mr Max Beerbohm* in a volume of parodies entitled *A
Christmas Garland*, where I found myself in very good company. I was immensely gratified. I began to believe in my public
existence. I have much to thank 'The Lagoon' for.

My next effort in short-story writing was a departure – I
mean a departure from the Malay Archipelago. Without pre-
meditation, without sorrow, without rejoicing, and almost without noticing it, I stepped into the very different atmosphere of
'An Outpost of Progress'. I found there a different moral
attitude. I seemed able to capture new reactions, new suggestions, and even new rhythms for my paragraphs. For a moment
I fancied myself a new man – a most exciting illusion. It clung
to me for some time, monstrous, half conviction and half hope
as to its body, with an iridescent tail of dreams and with a
changeable head like a plastic mask. It was only later that I
perceived that in common with the rest of men nothing could
deliver me from my fatal consistency. We cannot escape from
ourselves.

'An Outpost of Progress' is the lightest part of the loot I
carried off from Central Africa, the main portion being of course
'The Heart of Darkness'.* Other men have found a lot of quite
different things there and I have the comfortable conviction that
what I took would not have been of much use to anybody else.
And it must be said that it was but a very small amount of
plunder. All of it could go into one's breast pocket when folded
neatly. As for the story itself it is true enough in its essentials.
The sustained invention of a really telling lie demands a talent
which I do not possess.

'The Idiots' is such an obviously derivative piece of work that
it is impossible for me to say anything about it here. The
suggestion of it was not mental but visual: the actual idiots. It
was after an interval of long groping amongst vague impulses
and hesitations which ended in the production of 'The Nigger'*

that I turned to my third short story in the order of time, the first in this volume: 'Karain: A Memory'.

Reading it after many years 'Karain' produced on me the effect of something seen through a pair of glasses from a rather advantageous position. In that story I had not gone back to the Archipelago, I had only turned for another look at it. I admit that I was absorbed by the distant view, so absorbed that I didn't notice then that the *motif* of the story is almost identical with the *motif* of 'The Lagoon'. However, the idea at the back is very different; but the story is mainly made memorable to me by the fact that it was my first contribution to *Blackwood's Magazine* and that it led to my personal acquaintance with Mr William Blackwood whose guarded appreciation I felt nevertheless to be genuine, and prized accordingly. 'Karain' was begun on a sudden impulse only three days after I wrote the last line of 'The Nigger', and the recollection of its difficulties is mixed up with the worries of the unfinished 'Return', the last pages of which I took up again at the time; the only instance in my life when I made an attempt to write with both hands at once as it were.

Indeed my innermost feeling, now, is that 'The Return' is a left-handed production. Looking through that story lately I had the material impression of sitting under a large and expensive umbrella in the loud drumming of a heavy rain-shower. It was very distracting. In the general uproar one could hear every individual drop strike on the stout and distended silk. Mentally, the reading rendered me dumb for the remainder of the day, not exactly with astonishment but with a sort of dismal wonder. I don't want to talk disrespectfully of any pages of mine. Psychologically there were no doubt good reasons for my attempt; and it was worth while, if only to see of what excesses I was capable in that sort of virtuosity. In this connection I should like to confess my surprise on finding that notwithstanding all its apparatus of analysis the story consists for the most part of physical impressions; impressions of sound and sight, railway station, streets, a trotting horse, reflections in mirrors and so on, rendered as if for their own sake and combined with a sublimated description of a desirable middle-class town-residence which somehow manages to produce a sinister effect. For the rest any kind word about 'The Return' (and there have been such words said at different times) awakens in me the liveliest gratitude, for I know how much the writing of that fantasy has cost me in sheer toil, in temper, and in disillusion.

J.C.

NOTES

(Along with these notes, a number of foreign names and other terms have been itemised in the Glossary, to which readers are directed.)

As are all who come after, I am much indebted to the work of other Conradian scholars. Cedric Watts has been extremely generous in directing me towards work on some of these stories, and through him the information provided by Hans van Marle has been very helpful. I would particularly mention the following sources (referred to in the notes under the indicated abbreviations):

ABr: Andrzej Braun, 'The Myth-Like Kingdom of Conrad', *Conradiana*, 10.1 (1978), pp. 3–16.

ABu: Andrzej Busza, 'Conrad's Polish Literary Background and Some Illustrations of the Influence of Polish Literature on his Work', *Antemurale*, 10 (1966), pp. 109–255.

CEW: Norman Sherry, *Conrad's Eastern World* (Cambridge: Cambridge University Press, 1966).

CLJC: *The Collected Letters of Joseph Conrad*, edited by Frederick R. Karl and Laurence Davies (Cambridge: Cambridge University Press, 1983–).

CW: Cedric Watts, *'Heart of Darkness' and Other Tales* (Oxford: Oxford University Press, World's Classics, 1990).

CWW: Norman Sherry, *Conrad's Western World* (Cambridge: Cambridge University Press, 1971).

FF: Yves Hervouet, *The French Face of Joseph Conrad* (Cambridge: Cambridge University Press, 1990).

p. 1 Epigraph: 'Be it thy course to busy giddy minds with foreign quarrels.': from Shakespeare, *II Henry IV*, Act 4, Scene 5, l. 181. This political advice is offered to Prince Hal by his dying father, King Henry IV: engage the country in foreign wars when you succeed to the throne, the king urges, to prevent your potential political enemies from having time to conspire against you. A misquotation crept into later standard editions of the *Tales* (including the Doubleday and the Dent Collected

Editions): 'Be it thy course to *being* [rather than *busy*] giddy minds/ With foreign quarrels.' This ungrammatical sentence suggests that Hal's mind is unrestful.

Dedication: To Adolf P. Krieger: Conrad had known Adolf Krieger, one of his first friends in England, since the early 1880s. Krieger helped Conrad get maritime postings – including that to the Congo – and lent him fairly large sums of money, though Conrad's indebtedness probably led to a cooling off of their friendship after 1897. It is true that in a letter to Edward Garnett of 14 August 1896, written at the height of the composition of *Tales of Unrest*, Conrad had implied that the collection would be dedicated to Garnett himself: 'I must explain that that particular story ['An Outpost of Progress'] was no more meant for You than the *Idiots* – that is *all* the short stories (*ab initio*) were *meant alike* for a vol inscribed to *you*' (CLJC, vol. 1, p. 300). That was not to be. Perhaps the actual dedication was thought to be more judicious.

Karain: A Memory

'Karain: A Memory' first appeared in *Blackwood's Magazine* (Edinburgh), in November 1897. Though divided into parts, as at present, it appeared in one issue of the 'Maga', as the journal was widely known.

p. 5 native risings in the Eastern Archipelago: the story is set on the island of Celebes (now Sulawesi, in Indonesia) in the Malay Archipelago. From the 1840s to the 1880s (when merchant seaman Conrad sailed in these Eastern waters) there was considerable internal unrest, both between rival kingdoms in the region, and also against the colonial presence of the Dutch, the Spanish and the Portuguese.

p. 6 Karain: Conrad was fascinated by the life of James Brooke, 'The White Rajah of Sarawak', whose journals, published in Captain Robert Mundy's *Narrative of Events in Borneo and Celebes* (London: Murray, 1848, in two volumes), provided important source material for Conrad's 'Malay works'. In it, a 'rajah Karain' is mentioned as ruler of the Wajo (Wadjo) region of south-west Celebes (Mundy, vol. 1, pp. 110–11). 'Karain' is derived from 'Kara-eng', which in Macassarese means 'lord, descendant of rulers'.

p. 6 the middle of the bay: Andrzej Braun identifies this as Palu Bay in Donggala (Dongkala), Celebes, where Conrad's ship sometimes stayed in the 1880s (ABr, p. 13).

p. 7 **Mindanao:** the second largest island of the Philippines.

p. 8 **Spanish gun-boats:** the Philippines were still under Spanish colonial rule in the nineteenth century.

p. 9 **Bugis:** Indonesian inhabitants of southern Celebes (Sulawesi).

p. 10–11 **a kriss ... which he would politely conceal:** (see Glossary). Watts cites another Conrad source, Frederick McNair's *Perak and the Malays: 'Sarong and Kris'* (London: Tinsley, 1878):

> Considered an almost indispensable article of his dress, the Malay always wears his kris on the left side, where it is held up by the twisting of the sarong, with which during an interview it is considered respectful to conceal the weapon. (CW, p. 245).

p. 12 **a small Bugis state:** according to Braun (ABr, p. 11), Conrad probably used for his model the historical figure of the Queen of Boni, Banrigau Sultana Fatimah, who also appears fictionally in *Lord Jim* as 'the chief ruler of Wajo States [. . .] a fat wrinkled woman (very free in her speech, Stein said)'.

p. 13 **His mother ... the Gulf of Boni:** the Gulf (now called Teluk Bone) lies in the southern part of Celebes, extending deep inland. Braun, citing B. H. M. Vlekke, *Nusantara: A History of Indonesia* (Brussels: A. Manteau, 1961), says that in 1859,

> There was fighting on Celebes where a proud queen of the Buginese had ordered her skippers to display the Dutch flag upside down on their ships. Batavia [(Djakarta) the main town and governmental centre of the Dutch East Indies] retaliated with armed force, and the campaign gave the Dutch the opportunity to renew their old alliance with the Aru Palacca of Bone. (p. 299; ABr, p. 13)

The Times (29 March 1860, p. 11), reporting on Dutch forces putting down the Queen of Boni's uprising in 1859–60, says: 'The people have submitted, the Queen has taken to flight, and her successor will hold office as a vassal of Holland' (cited in CW, p. 257).

p. 13 **Korinchi man:** a middle-class Muslim Malay from Western Sumatra, who would not carry the same social status as a Buginese queen. Hans van Marle suggests it would be equivalent to Queen Victoria marrying John Brown (CW, p. 257).

p. 20 **at all hazards:** probably from the French, *à tout hasard*, 'in any case'.

p. 22 **running water:** the magazine version has 'flowing water'.

p. 23 **the great trouble . . . the alliance of the four states of Wajo:** Wajo (Wadjo) lies in the central and eastern part of the southern peninsula of Celebes (Sulawesi). There were a number (actually six, not four, as Conrad has it) of confederated, vassal states under the suzerainty of Wajo chiefs. Conrad may have gleaned their history either from the *Diaries* of James Brooke, or first-hand when he was in Donggala, Celebes, in the 1880s. Four of the states, Wajo, Boni (Bone), Soping (Sopeng) and Si Dendring (Sidenring), fell into dispute in the late 1840s over the succession to the rajah of Si Dendring, and the Dutch took advantage of this civil strife to assert and extend their own colonial influence. The semi-independent states then fell under Netherland East Indies control during the 1860s and 1870s.

p. 23 **Pata Matara:** 'Pata' means 'Lord' (a noble title); 'Matara' was the name of a Bugis nobleman, Dain Matara, who was befriended by and accompanied James Brooke on his travels in the Archipelago in the 1840s. Conrad may well have drawn the name and something of the relationship from that source.

p. 25 **a great mountain burning in the midst of water:** Cedric Watts suggests this might be Gunung Api ('Fire Mountain'), a volcanic island located 8°12′ south, 119° east, near the meeting point of the Selat Sape and the Flores Sea. Another Gunung Api lies a little further east at 6°38′ south, 126°40′ east. A further candidate, much more famous, would be Krakatoa, on the small volcanic island in the Sunda Strait between Java and Sumatra, which in 1883 erupted to spectacular and massively devastating effect. The event itself must have been sharp in Conrad's mind when he was sailing in the Archipelago in the 1880s. In the temporal setting of Karain's story (about 1860), Krakatoa in its dormant state would have been merely one more 'fire mountain' in the area.

p. 26 **those Dutchmen are all alike:** in similar form but different versions this is an abiding *anti-racist* joke in Conrad's writings. He is inverting the English/European racial slur that 'all "Chinamen"/"niggers" (etc.) look the same', to give those who employ it a taste of their own medicine. For a similar though politically more potent moment, see my account in *Heart of Darkness* (Milton Keynes: Open University Press, 1989), pp. 45–50.

p. 27 **Bajow people, who have no country:** the Bajow (Bajau), also known as 'Orang Lauts', a nomadic maritime people in the eastern Malay Archipelago, were traders who tended formerly to be regarded as 'sea gypsies'.

p. 27 Goram men: Muslim traders from the Goram islands (Kepuluan Seram and Seram-Laut) in eastern Indonesia.

p. 28 Atjeh: in the Atjehnese (or Achinese) wars of 1873–1904, the Dutch pursued an ultimately successful colonial campaign to conquer the Muslim state of Atjeh (also known as Achin, now Aceh), which formed the northern extremity of the island of Sumatra.

p. 28 Delli (Deli): Watts suggests that this is a reference to a region of north-eastern Sumatra (CW, p. 280). It might otherwise refer to the island of Pulau Deli, off the north-western end of Java, near Krakatoa; or indeed to Dilli, in eastern Indonesia (now East Timor). Karain's travels take him all over the Eastern Archipelago – 'We went West, we went East' – and exact geographical specification is not at issue.

p. 28 Selangore (Selangor): a state of Peninsular Malaysia, on the Strait of Malacca.

p. 28 planting tobacco on conquered plains: the Dutch had widespread control of the islands in the Eastern Archipelago, forming the Netherlands East Indies under whose government fell numerous vassal states. Other semi-independent states were 'allied' to the Dutch. G. J. Resink, who offers a very informative historical account of the region in 'The Eastern Archipelago Under Joseph Conrad's Western Eyes', *Indonesia's History Between the Myths* (The Hague: W. van Hoeve, 1968), cites Conrad as referring to tobacco plantations but adds 'there were few, if any Western agricultural or mining enterprises' in the area at the time; trading in high-quality native products was the primary commercial activity (p. 321).

p. 29 scraped the flint with his thumb-nail: Andrzej Busza cites this phrase as a reference to 'Czaty' ('The Ambush'), the ballad of the renowned Polish Romantic poet Mickiewicz. The plot of the ballad closely resembles the central episode of 'Karain: A Memory'. At one point in 'Czaty', the Governor orders his henchman to 'pour in some priming and scrape the flint with your nail', in order to shoot his unfaithful young wife (ABu, pp. 209–15).

p. 30 Perak: a small state on the Malay Peninsula, lying north-west of Selangor.

p. 32 Greenwich Time: from 1852 time measurements within Britain were made uniform based on the time/longitudinal zero line of the Royal Observatory, Greenwich, which lies on the south side of the River Thames in London. In 1884, an international conference in Washington, D.C., agreed upon the Greenwich longitudinal line as the zero-degree meridian for determining international standard time and longitudinal lines for maritime, cartographic and communications purposes.

p. 34 Sultan of Sula: the Sula (now Sulu) are islands lying eastward of Celebes.

p. 38 dash home through the Canal: the Suez Canal in Egypt links the Red Sea (and thus the Indian Ocean) with the Mediterranean Sea. Built 1854–69, the canal effectively halved the distance for ships travelling from the Far East to Europe, which previously had to take routes rounding the Cape of Good Hope, at the southern tip of Africa.

p. 38 a likeness ... an engraved image: according to one tradition of Islam, the religious and cultural belief which held a dominant place for many inhabitants of the Malay Archipelago, the artistic representation of any human or animal figure was forbidden. Hollis is therefore anxious that giving Karain an image of Queen Victoria (in the form of the coin) may be offensive to him, if he is a very strict Muslim. Because this tradition is not universal within Islamic belief, though, not all believers would be averse to icons in the way Hollis sensitively fears.

p. 39 a Jubilee sixpence: to celebrate the fiftieth anniversary of Queen Victoria's coronation, new coins were issued, bearing the likeness of the Queen on one side, the royal coat of arms on the other. Watts notes that the silver sixpence, which was of relatively low value, bore 'a close resemblance in size and design to the gold half-sovereign, which was of relatively high value; so it was often gilded in order to be fraudulently passed as the half-sovereign' (CW, p. 259).

p. 39 Suleiman the Wise: Suleiman (Solomon) the Wise was, according to the Koran (Sura XXXIV, 11, 13), served by djinn or genii (spirits). 'They made for him whatever he pleased of palaces and statues and large dishes like fish ponds.'

p. 42 Bland's window: Bland's was a well-known gunsmiths, at 430, West Strand, London, which lies east of Trafalgar Square in an important shopping, business and theatre street of central London.

p. 43 caballeros: gentlemen, cavaliers (in Spanish). Here the term refers to the Spanish colonial presence against whom Karain is reportedly fighting.

p. 44 a line of yellow boards: 'sandwich men', carrying two advertisement boards suspended from their shoulders, one in front, the other behind ('sandwich boards'), would walk along streets advertising the name of a product or a firm. Alternatively (as here) the boards would be carried on a frame above the head of the bearer for greater visibility. Often the board might carry only one individual letter, a line of such sandwich men thus together 'forming' a word or product name.

The Idiots

'The Idiots' was first published in the *Savoy* in October 1896. Of all the stories in this volume, it is the most naturalistic, in the manner of Maupassant. It draws much of its detail from Conrad's own experience of Brittany.

The story was finished in May 1896, soon after Conrad's marriage to Jessie George (24 March) and their departure for a honeymoon in northern France. They stayed first in Lannion, a small port on the north coast of Brittany, and then moved (7 April) to a small cottage on the Ile-Grande, where they lived for six months. Conrad drew on the landscape of Brittany and aspects of its peasant life for this, his first short story to be published:

> The coast is rocky, sandy, wild and full of mournful expressiveness. But the land at the back of the wide stretches of the sea enclosed by the barren archipelago, is green and smiling and sunny – often even when the sea and the islets are under the shadow of the passing clouds. From beyond the rounded slopes of the hills the sharp spires of many village-churches point persistently to the sky. And the people that inhabit these shores is a people of women – black-clad and white-capped – for the men fish in Iceland or on the banks of Newfoundland. Only here and there a rare old fellow, with long white hair, forgotten by the successive roll-calls of the sea, creeps along the rock bestrewn beeches [*sic*] and looks sad and useless and lone in the stormy landscape. (Letter to Ted Sanderson, 14 April 1896 [*CLJC*, Vol. 1, p. 274].)

Although the plot of the story was invented, Conrad drew upon a considerable level of local Breton detail. Place-names, topology, cultural character, as well as strong French literary influences imbue the rather extraordinary tale with a prevailing naturalism. Jessie Conrad's account also suggests that the story was drawn from Conrad's experience.

> It was during our drives on the mainland that we came across the idiots, who became the subject of one of the short stories written on the spot. It was not usual for my husband to use material so close to hand and at the time of finding it, spread out as it were before him. In his story, 'The Idiots', which has sufficient relation to actual truth to need no explanation by me, he has not given quite the full number of unfortunates. I pointed out to him that there were two more at least and was quite startled by his unexpected violence: 'Good God, my dear, I've put enough horror into that story in all conscience. Two more! More than enough of them without, to my mind.'
>
> It was indeed a dismal spectacle to see those creatures meandering up and down that narrow lane, shuffling aimlessly in the deep ditches or lying in the long grass bordering the road, their staring eyes fixed and a silly grin on their formless mouths. One only, I think the second in age, a youth of about seventeen, had sufficient intelligence to smile when he saw me, but even that smile would become a fixed grin if you happened to look back after you had driven past his motionless figure. Many times we have had to make a wide detour, even going on the grass the other side of the road, to avoid knocking one of these poor things down. Our coachman would start cracking his whip and shouting as soon as we turned into the lane if he caught sight of them. 'The Idiots', he would declare, pointing at them with his whip. (*Joseph Conrad and his Circle*, [London: Jarolds, 1935] p. 37).

Jessie continues:

> It was on the return drive from Lannion the next day that I saw again the whole of the family of idiots together, and noted to my surprise that one was a girl. In repose her face was exceedingly pretty, but catching a glimpse of our driver a most diabolical expression came over the young child's face, she yelled and shouted abuse until she was forced to stop to draw breath. The man retaliated by making violent show of his whip and aiming a slash at the slim figure as we passed. The girl was dressed exactly like the boys, in long black shapeless garments, from the bottom of which their lean shanks protruded a few inches. They usually had their hands thrust into the loose sleeves and their bare feet in wooden sabots. These sturdy youths and the well-grown girl were the children of a small farmer, or rather peasant retainer, of a Marquis who owned a considerable property, and the parents were employed, we were told, in the fabrication of the famous Camembert cheese. They had a certain allowance from the State to keep these children out of an Institution.
>
> There were other unfortunates, men and boys mostly, misshapen in mind and body, who inhabited those lanes, shuffling sideways in the deep ditches under the hedges, sometimes almost out of sight, by the side of the road.

> One heard almost unbelievable stories of hardship and injustice done to these creatures due to family greed.
>
> Drink also provided a good deal of the misfortune and not a little amusement to the casual observer because the drunken objects were for the most part ridiculously dignified. (p. 40)

p. 45 Treguier/Kervanda/Ploumar: Tréguier is a medieval cathedral city and small port on the north coast of Brittany, France. The fictional **Kervanda** and **Ploumar** may correspond to Kervégan and Pleumeur, small villages on the road from Lannion to the peninsula of Ile-Grande, the Conrads' home for the first six months of married life.

p. 45 undulating surface: Hervouet (*FF*, p. 34), citing Milton Chaikin ('Zola and Conrad's "The Idiots"', *Studies in Philology*, vol. 52, 1955, pp. 502–7), finds in this phrase and others echoes of Zola's novels, *La Terre* (*The Earth*) (1887) and *La Joie de vivre* (1884). Zola's influence is also revealed in the opening topological description and in the story's thematic concerns with the land.

p. 47 It's the mother: an instance of Conrad's non-standard use of the definite article in English. This is a good idiomatic French construction, however.

p. 47 spring-cart: a cart hung, or suspended, on springs.

p. 47 On the road . . . groups: Hervouet (*FF*, p. 33) cites this sentence and the rest of the paragraph as evoking, indeed borrowing from, the description of Emma and Charles Bovary's wedding party in Flaubert's novel *Madame Bovary* (1857). In the details of local dress, the gargantuan wedding feast and the bird-scaring fiddler, Conrad's description echoes elements of the earlier work.

p. 48 biniou: Breton bag-pipes.

p. 50 sabots: wooden clogs.

p. 51 Marquis de Chavanes: a marquis (and his wife, the marquise) belong to the minor French aristocracy, below the rank of duke and above that of count.

p. 51 toilette: dress.

p. 51 enraged republican: 'enraged' suggests the French *enragé*, meaning in this context 'fanatical'. Following the French Revolution, when the Republic was established, nineteenth-century France saw much constitutional change with the re-establishment of monarchy. But in

1871 the Third Republic was re-constituted. Characteristic of republicanist supporters was their fervent anti-clericalism and hostility to the establishment (Roman Catholic) Church.

p. 52 Channel Islands: Jersey and Guernsey and other British islands which lie some forty to sixty miles off the northern coast of Brittany.

p. 52 liberal: republican, and hence anti-clerical, supporters.

p. 52 One yet: a Gallicism, from '*Alors, un*', meaning 'Now, one'.

p. 52 *soutane*: a priest's cassock.

p. 53 insist for: from the French '*insister pour*' ('insist on something').

p. 53 was viciously muttering: this verbal inflection demonstrates the influence of Polish verbal forms and tenses on Conrad's English usage. Mary Morzinski's *Linguistic Influence of Polish on Joseph Conrad's Style* (Eastern European Monographs, New York, 1994) gives a very full account of this influence.

p. 54 crows: here, and subsequently, the derogatory references to 'crows' allude to priests, in their black garb, or more generally to the Church.

p. 54 Allez! Houp!: (as an interjection) 'Upsadaisy!'

p. 54 Malheur!: 'Bad luck!'

p. 55 Having to face alone: Hervouet (*FF*, p. 35), citing Chaikin, finds a verbal and thematic echo of Zola in this concern with the immensity of the land and the need for and anxiety over continued family possession of it. (See note p. 45 above.)

p. 56 On stormy nights: Hervouet (*FF*, pp. 35–6) cites Zola's *La Joie de vivre* as the source for this description, anticipating in its atmosphere the death of Susan on the rocks.

p. 57 Lotharios: libertine lovers; from the rakish character, Lothario, in Rowe's tragedy, *The Fair Penitent* (1703).

p. 58 Her husband: heredity and inherited insanity are also major preoccupations of Zola's novels.

p. 62 cold caress: Hervouet (*FF*, p. 36) finds an echo of Zola's *La Joie de vivre* here and elsewhere in this description.

p. 62 Molène sands: the 'Ile Molène' lies off the west Brittany coast, near Brest. Like 'Fougère' and other geographical locations in the story, it corresponds to an actual Breton place-name but is used with fictional licence.

p. 63 Morbihan: a department of south-west Brittany, a rugged farming and coastal region.

p. 66 consecrated ground: an allusion to the fact that the Church would not allow someone who had committed suicide to be buried on 'holy ground'.

An Outpost of Progress

The letter of Conrad to T. F. Unwin, 22 July 1896, gives a good sense of the origins of the story:

> It is a story of the Congo. There is no love interest in it and no woman – only incidentally. The exact locality is not mentioned. All the bitterness of those days, all my puzzled wonder at masquerading philanthropy – have been with me again, while I wrote. The story is simple – there is hardly any description. The most common incidents are related – the life in a lonely station on the Kassai. I have divested myself of everything but pity – and some scorn – while putting down the insignificant events that bring on the catastrophe. Upon my word I think it is a good story – and not so gloomy – not fanciful – alas! I think it is interesting – some may find it a bore! (*CLJC*, vol. 1, p. 294).

The tale was completed in July 1896, and published in two parts in *Cosmopolis* (June–July 1897). In 'My Best Story and Why I think so', an article solicited by *Grand Magazine* (March 1906), Conrad was later to declare it his best story.

p. 67 Kayerts . . . Carlier: according to Norman Sherry (*CWW*, pp. 21, 43), one Alphonse Keyaerts, a commercial agent for the Belgian Société Anonyme du Haut-Congo, for which Conrad also worked, travelled up the Congo river with Conrad on the *Roi des Belges* from Stanley Pool to Stanley Falls in 1890. Sherry comments that he may also have been the model for the figure of the 'pilgrim in pink pajamas' in *Heart of Darkness* – receiving Conrad's scorn as 'a fat little man, with sandy hair and red whiskers, who wore side-spring boots and pink pajamas tucked into his socks'. A Captain Carlier was master of the steamer *Lualaba*, which sailed from Antwerp to the Congo in the early 1890s. There seems to be a distinct homophony between the names 'Kayerts' and 'Kurtz': a literary forerunner, Kayerts shares Kurtz's belief in ivory and progress.

p. 67 **Sierra Leone nigger:** a British colony on the west coast of Africa, Sierra Leone was largely populated by freed former slaves. The implication here is that Henry Price is not from a local (Congo) tribe but is a displaced, de-tribalised native working for the company.

p. 67 **Henry Price:** in the original *Cosmopolis* magazine version of the story, Henry Price was named James Price.

p. 67 **Makola:** perhaps named after Makala, a village in the Eastern Province of the Congo Free State on the Lindi river tributary of the Congo. It was the site of the defeat of the last of the Arab traders, who had been in long-standing conflict with European (here Belgian) powers over the slave-trading of native labour.

p. 67 **about the country:** after this sentence, the magazine version has: 'Everyone called him by it.'

p. 67 **Loanda** (Luanda): town on the Atlantic coast of southern Africa, capital of present-day Angola.

p. 67 **dried-grass roof:** the magazine version has 'palm-leaf roof'.

p. 67 **torn wearing apparel:** later editions have 'town wearing apparel', which would suggest inexperience. The present edition prefers 'torn', which confirms the men's shabby decline, given that at the story's outset they seem to have been at the station for some time.

p. 68 **sardine box:** this is one of a number of features echoed in the later novella, *Heart of Darkness*, where Marlow's boat is described as being like 'an empty Huntley & Palmer biscuit-tin'.

p. 68 **Carlier was told off:** 'to tell off' (a quasi-military term) means 'to be detailed or deputed to a particular task'.

p. 68 **He made a speech:** Sherry suggests that the managing director is based on Henry Morton Stanley, the explorer, coloniser and 'rescuer' of David Livingstone. Sherry cites Stanley's advice to agents he is putting in charge of a trading-post:

> The instructions, few and simple, to him are: See now, sir, this is your domain, legitimately acquired. It has become, by the power invested in you as chief, your estate, over which you have absolute control, subject to none other than myself. I must leave you as master and sole arbiter in all questions. Let justice attend your dealings; be kind to your people, for remember you

are their father and their mother. Show me on my return that a fit choice was made when I selected you. (*CWW*, p. 127)

The upshot of this is no better for Stanley than for the fictional director:

I [Stanley] am absent ten months from the scene, but I find on my return that the condition of the place is far worse than when I departed. The warm promises made by him created in me an ideal paradise; but instead of my bright, and, alas! too florid an ideal, I see the wild grass has overrun our native village, so that it is scarcely visible . . . famine beleaguers the garrison . . . the stores are empty . . . The natives leave him and his station so severely alone that he is in actual risk of starvation. (*CWW*, p. 128, citing Stanley, *The Congo*, II, p. 244)

p. 68 in an army guaranteed from harm by several European Powers: the magazine version has 'an army guaranteed harmless', later corrected by Conrad to the present version. Glossing this, Cedric Watts notes (CW, p. 254) that by the Treaty of London (1839), guaranteed by Britain, France, Prussia, Russia and Austria, Belgium was declared 'an independent and perpetually neutral state'.

Conrad was later to remark in a letter of 1903:

Kayerts is not a French name. Carlier perhaps, but as soon as I name him, I hasten to say that he is a former cavalry n.c.o. of an army *protected from all danger by several European powers*. I took the trouble to make a soldier out of that animal deliberately. They are gallant Belgians – God bless them: and they were recognized as such here and in Brussels when the tale appeared. (*CLJC*, vol. 3, p. 94)

p. 68 to begin: after this sentence the magazine version inserts, 'The two most useless men I ever saw', and at the start of the next paragraph repeats, 'The two useless men watched', amended here to 'The two men watched'.

p. 70 they were very active: Hervouet (*FF*, p. 37) citing Wallace Watson, argues for Conrad's indebtedness to Flaubert's posthumously published *Bouvard et Pécuchet* (1881), particularly in the ironic treatment in this scene of collegial comic domesticity.

p. 71 He regretted the streets: from the French *regretter*, 'to miss' (as in 'to miss old times'). Subsequent occurrences of 'regretted' in this paragraph imply the same sense.

p. 71 the sense of the idleness: the magazine and later editions have 'the sense of idleness'.

p. 71 nowhither: the magazine version has 'nowhere'.

p. 71 spears in their hands: the magazine version has 'handfuls of spears in their hands'.

p. 72 fetish: the *Oxford English Dictionary* does not record a use of 'fetish' as referring to the *storehouse* in which the collected ivory ('bone') and fetishes ('rags') are held. 'Fetish' normally refers to an inanimate object believed to hold magical properties and irrationally worshipped as such.

p. 72 palaver: a conversation or conference, especially between tribespeople and traders. Like 'fetish' it is of Portuguese etymological origin, the Portuguese being early traders with and colonisers of sub-Saharan Africa. Only gradually did the more colloquial meaning of 'empty, useless talk' arise in English usage.

p. 73 made the acquaintance of Richelieu ... people: later editions have 'made acquaintance of'. Richelieu and d'Artagnan appear in *Les trois mousquetaires* (*The Three Musketeers*) by Alexandre Dumas the Elder (1844). Dumas's is a fictionalised version of Cardinal Richelieu, the great French statesman (1585–1642). Hawk's Eye is (presumably) Conrad's reference to Hawkeye (Natty Bumppo), the central character in *The Last of the Mohicans* (1826) and the other Leather-Stocking Tales by James Fenimore Cooper (who, like Conrad, was a professional sailor before he started writing). Father Goriot is the eponymous hero of Honoré de Balzac's *Le père Goriot* (1834) and appears in others of his sequence of novels, *La comédie humaine* (*The Human Comedy*). Conrad's ironic play with levels of reality and fiction here and the naïve reactions of Kayerts and Carlier to these characters also echo Flaubert and his satirised characters, Bouvard and Pécuchet.

p. 73 high-flown language: the Berlin Conference of 1885 which 'legitimised' the European powers' 'Scramble for Africa', dividing it up into different areas of economic interest, confirmed King Leopold II of Belgium as the sole possessor of the 'Congo Free State'. Leopold pursued the brutal economic exploitation of a million square miles of Central Africa, setting up trading concession companies controlled by his representatives. His frequent speeches, reported in the press, justified this colonial expansion in the name of Christian philanthropy and civilisation:

> The mission which the agents of the State have to accomplish on the Congo is a noble one. They have to continue the development of civilisation in the centre of Equatorial Africa, receiving their inspiration from Berlin and

Brussels. Placed face to face with primitive barbarism, grappling with sangui-
nary customs that date back thousands of years, they are obliged to reduce
these gradually. They must accustom the population to general laws, of
which the most needful and the most salutary is assuredly that of work.
(Cited in R. Kimbrough's edition of Conrad, *Heart of Darkness* [London,
1988], p. 79.)

p. 73 Gobila: Henry Morton Stanley (whom Norman Sherry specu-
lates could be a model for the Director of the trading company in this
story) set up a trading station in 1882 in Mswata, Upper Congo, where
the tribal chief was one Papa Gobila, who held daily palavers with the
station manager:

> This old gentleman, stout of form, hearty and genial in manner, came up
> breathlessly and held out his fat hands, and welcomed Bula Matari [a native
> sobriquet given to Stanley, meaning 'Rock-breaker'] after his long absence
> . . . Gobila, genial, aldermanic Gobila – Papa Gobila. (H. M. Stanley, *The
> Congo and the Founding of Its Free State: A Story of Work and Exploration*
> [London, 1885, in two volumes], vol. 1, p. 510, cited in Sherry, p. 131.)

Gobila's skinny physique and paternal manner in Conrad's fictionalised
version may imply a higher valuation of the native chief over his portly
white counterparts. Here and in *The Secret Agent*, where there is a
fleeting echo of the Gobila figure, fatness seems associated for Conrad
with duplicity and physical and moral laxity.

p. 77 told off to: see note p. 68.

p. 78 carried the big calabashes: a kind of gourd, the dried shell of
which can be used as a drinking or cooking vessel. Later editions have
'carried big calabashes'.

p. 83 exterminating all the niggers . . . habitable: the phrase prefigures
Kurtz's scrawled postscript to his report to 'The International Society
for the Suppression of Savage Customs' in *Heart of Darkness*: 'Exter-
minate all the brutes!'. The magazine version has 'could be habitable'.

p. 83 Melie: another allusion to Flaubert's *Bouvard et Pécuchet*, where
Mélie appears. The magazine version describes her simply with 'long
tresses'.

p. 86 swooned: the magazine version has 'fainted'.

p. 86 Come along, Mr Kayerts. He is dead: an uncanny prefiguring of
one of the most quoted phrases in *Heart of Darkness*, ' "Mistah Kurtz
– he dead." '

p. 87 with his right eye blown out: the magazine version has 'with half his face blown away'.

p. 88 a heavy mist: for 'mist' the magazine version has 'fog' throughout this paragraph.

p. 89 incontinently: archaic, meaning 'without delay', 'straightaway'; in French, *incontinent* still carries this meaning, rather than the more current English physiological one.

p. 89 toes: the magazine version has 'feet'.

The Return

Alone of the present collection, this tale was not previously published in magazine form, although Conrad thought of placing it in the avant-garde *Yellow Book*. First mention of it is made by Conrad in April 1897, when he envisages it completing the volume which was to become *Tales of Unrest*. He estimated its length at some '5–7,000 words'. When he had completed it, in September 1897, it ran to 23,000 words.

p. 91 The inner circle train: the Circle line of the London Underground system (until the 1930s called the Inner Circle) serves the central part of London, running from the City (London's financial centre), westward through Westminster, Victoria and Kensington, then north and east via Paddington, King's Cross and Liverpool Street back to the City. It thus linked wealthy residential areas in central London as well as all the great mainline railway termini north of the Thames and was an important commuter route. Electrification of the Circle line started in 1906, sixteen years after the electrification of the system first began. The steam engines add to the hellish atmosphere Conrad wants to create. It evokes Dante's Inferno, where the lower circles are reserved, appropriately enough, for those guilty of deceit and treachery.

p. 91 West-End: a fashionable upper- and middle-class residential and shopping area to the west of Piccadilly in central London. From late 1889 to 1896, Conrad rented lodgings in Victoria, but in less fashionable quarters.

p. 91 greenish, pinkish, or whitish colour: although 'whitish' was the normal colour of newspapers, some were characterised and marketed through the use of other colours. Thus *The Globe*, the oldest London evening paper (started in 1806), adopted pink as its colour in 1863; and the *Westminster Gazette* (started in 1893) decided on green.

p. 91 band of brothers: in the context, Conrad makes a piercingly ironic allusion to the famous speech of Henry V before the Battle of Agincourt in Shakespeare's *Henry V*:

> We few, we happy few, we band of brothers:
> For he to-day that sheds his blood with me
> Shall be my brother . . .
> (Act IV, sc. 3, ll. 60–2)

p. 94 band of men: as if escalating the irony, this alludes again to *Henry V*, IV, 3, and the Shakespearean motif of brotherhood (see note p. 91 above). The phrase is echoed a third time (p. 105) even more negatively as 'a band of veiled malefactors hastening to a crime'.

p. 95 a marble woman. . . cluster of lights: this image prefigures that depicted in a painting by Kurtz in *Heart of Darkness*, which Marlow describes as 'representing a woman, draped and blindfolded, carrying a lighted torch'. Cedric Watts (CW, note to p. 169) points out that traditionally the goddess of justice, Astraea, is often depicted as blindfolded (implying the impartiality of justice); the figure of Liberty frequently holds a lighted torch. Conrad's exploitation of this symbolic motif is as ironic in *Heart of Darkness* as it is here. Various forms of blindness – which are neither gender specific nor judiciously benign – are crucial thematic preoccupations in the tale.

p. 95 pier-glass: a tall mirror, originally filling the 'pier' wall between two windows.

p. 97 a sinister loom: Conrad has brought nautical terminology to land. See *Oxford English Dictionary*, where 'loom' is cited as a seaman's term for the indistinct and exaggerated appearance of land on the horizon, or for an object seen through mist or darkness. The phantasmagoric change of city into sea at this point justifies the appropriate, if obscure, verbal usage.

p. 103 Yes, long-time ago: another of Conrad's Gallicisms, likely to be a too literal translation of '*longtemps*'.

p. 103 faltering fear . . . into a handful of dust: a possible source for this allusion is Meditation IV of John Donne's *Devotions Upon Emergent Occasions* (1624), where Donne reminds us of the vanity of human pretensions:

whats become of mans great extent and proportion, when himselfe shrinkes himselfe, and consumes himself to a handfull of dust?

Donne, in turn, is echoing Ecclesiastes 12:5,7, where we are warned about the mortality of human life:

and fears shall be in the way . . . Then shall the dust return to the earth as it was.

Conrad reiterates the image in *Youth* where Marlow expresses his nostalgia for the lost illusions of youth, 'the triumphant conviction of strength, the heat of life in the handful of dust'.

There are prefigurings here of T. S. Eliot's *The Waste Land*, 'I will show you fear in a handful of dust' (l. 30), and the title of Evelyn Waugh's novel. In Eliot's poem, the image of the commuter as inhabitant of the infernal city is also exploited – a motif for which 'The Return' has already fully prepared.

p. 103 woke up . . . peopled by monsters: this seems to be a ghosting (not quite a quotation), which inverts the optimistic sentiments of Wordsworth's sonnet, 'Composed upon Westminster Bridge, September 3, 1802':

> The City now doth, like a garment, wear
> The beauty of the morning; silent, bare,
> Ships, towers, domes, theatres, and temples lie
> Open unto the fields, and to the sky
> All bright and glittering in the smokeless air. (ll. 4–8)

p. 105 band of veiled malefactors: see notes on pp. 91 and 94 above.

pp. 106–7 She was mysterious . . . She had lifted her veil: this develops, indeed animates, the image of the marble draped female figure who 'blindly' brings the light into the house. (See note on p. 95.)

p. 112 made love: in 1900, 'to make love' did not necessarily imply sexual intercourse, but rather usually meant 'to express amorous affection towards, to woo or make advances towards'.

p. 116 toilettes: a Conrad Gallicism, referring to summer dress or fashion.

p. 117 He saw her shoulder touch the lintel: critics, concerned with the acrobatics involved here, have been much exercised over Conrad's use of the term 'lintel'. Jacques Berthoud's account in *Conradian*, Vol.

12.2 (1984), itemises the (linguistic) contortions, suggesting that Conrad appears to mean 'door jamb' rather than 'architrave'. Jeremy Hawthorn, commenting on Berthoud's account, has also alluded to other examples in Conrad's works. The explanation may lie in the fact that in Polish, 'próg' or 'proze' is used to name what in English refers to (the whole) 'door frame'. As in other Slavic languages, there is in Polish no immediate distinction made between what in English are variously 'lintel', 'door jamb' and 'door sill'/'threshold'. Thus, when specificity is required, 'lintel' in English is rendered in Polish as 'nadproze' (something like 'above- or over-doorpost'). From the viewpoint of English house-building terminology, Conrad was being horizontally challenged, even sloppy; but his usage reflects the complexity of his linguistic and cultural heritage.

pp. 129-30 **Perhaps her face . . . of the gods:** this image makes explicit the analogy to the marble figure, already mentioned. (See note to p. 95.)

p. 137 *portière:* a heavy curtain hung over a door, or doorway, to prevent draughts, or to serve as a screen or for ornament.

p. 138 **conscience:** in this context 'conscience' should be read as 'consciousness', 'intellectual awareness'. Up until the twentieth century, these words were fairly interchangeable, referring to mental awareness. 'Conscience' was not necessarily limited to the contemporary meaning, which tends to refer to the awareness of the moral quality of actions or motives, or a sense of moral duty.

The Lagoon

'The Lagoon' was written in August, 1896, and was accepted for publication in the *Cornhill* magazine (January 1897). Commenting to Edward Garnett on his submission of it, Conrad says, 'It's a tricky thing with the usual forests river – stars – wind sunrise, and so on – and lots of secondhand Conradese in it. I would bet a penny they will take it' (*CLJC*, vol. 1, p. 301). They did.

p. 143 **'Allah be praised!':** a common Muslim saying, this registers the dominant religious presence of Islam in the Eastern Archipelago. Its religious and social ethic pervades this and Conrad's other Malay stories.

p. 145 **'If such is her fate':** hesitantly muttered, paradoxically by the white man, this clause perhaps takes up again the Muslim motif with its emphasis on Divine Providence. This belief in fate is of course not confined to Islam, as the cleric in 'The Idiots' demonstrates.

p. 146 **After the time of trouble and war:** in the 1840s and 1850s the states of Wajo, Boni (Bone), Soping (Sopeng) and Si Dendring (Sidenring) were in dispute over the successor to the Rajah of Si Dendring. (See the note to p. 23 on the Wajo wars in 'Karain: A Memory'.)

p. 146 **Si Dendring:** Conrad's conversion of the name of the Kingdom into that of its ruler.

p. 147 **O Mara bahia!** (bahaja): a Malay exclamation meaning, roughly, 'What terrible misfortune!'.

p. 147 **Inchi Midah:** a name possibly drawn from a powerful Buginese princess Immudah.

p. 149 **fury ... haste:** the magazine version has, respectively, 'spite' and 'fury'.

p. 149 **sumpitan:** a blow-pipe made by the Malays from a hollow cane, from which poisoned arrows are shot.

p. 150 **murmur:** the magazine version has 'rumour', a likely French linguistic influence.

p. 150 **Then we lay down to sleep:** the magazine version has 'Then we slept'.

p. 151 **illusion of a sea:** the magazine version has 'illusion of a sea; seemed the only thing surviving the destruction of the world by that undulating and voiceless phantom of a flood. Only far away . . .'

p. 153 **Arsat had not moved ... world of illusions:** the magazine version has 'Arsat had not moved. In the searching clearness of crude sunshine he was still standing before the house, he was still looking through the great light of a cloudless day into the hopeless darkness of the world.'

Author's Note

This Note was written along with a number of others, in 1919, at the instigation of Doubleday, Page (New York) for their Collected Edition (1923). It subsequently also appeared in the Collected ('Uniform') edition by Dent (London). The present text is taken from the Double-day edition.

p. 155 **earliest in date:** in fact the writing of 'The Idiots' and of 'An Outpost of Progress' pre-date that of 'The Lagoon'.

p. 155 **'Almayer's Folly':** Here and in subsequent references to Conrad's works in the Author's Note, no consistent typographical distinction between the titles of novels and short stories is made by Conrad. My text retains this original version of titles.

p. 156 **my first appearance:** referring to the *Cornhill* magazine [sic!] publication in January 1897, and continuing his autobiographical re-fashioning, Conrad also overlooks the earlier publication date of 'The Idiots' (October 1896) in the *Savoy*.

p. 156 **Max Beerbohm:** the brilliantly witty artist and critic wrote a parody of Conrad caricaturing the stylistic features of 'The Lagoon', in particular. See Max Beerbohm, 'The Feast. By J*S*PH C*NR*D', *A Christmas Garland* (London: Heinemann, 1912), pp. 127–34.

p. 156 **'The Heart of Darkness':** Conrad is alluding to his trip to the Congo in 1890 and his experiences there – his 'loot' – which formed the basis of *Heart of Darkness* [sic!], his searing critique of European colonial exploitation.

p. 156 **'The Nigger':** *The Nigger of the 'Narcissus'* was completed by early February 1897 and published at the end of that year.

GLOSSARY

ad patres: 'to the fathers'; 'send (them) *ad patres*' thus implies: kill them.

amuck (amok), **run amuck:** to be seized with a violently uncontrollable, murderous frenzy (a phrase of Malay origin).

amulet: a charm, often inscribed with a magic incantation or symbol to aid or protect the wearer against evil.

Atjeh: also known as Achin (now Aceh), a territory which formed the northern extremity of the island of Sumatra.

attap: palm fronds (especially of the nipa palm), used for thatching.

Bajow (Bajau): also known as 'Orang Lauts', a nomadic maritime people in the eastern Malay Archipelago, traders who tended formerly to be regarded as 'sea gypsies'. They traded in the coastal areas of Celebes, Borneo and the southern Philippines.

Batavia: on the north coast of Java, the administrative capital of all Dutch settlements.

buckler: a small shield.

Bugis: inhabitants of a realm in the south-western part of Celebes (Sulawesi), now in Indonesia.

bulkhead: an upright partition separating compartments in a ship.

caballeros: gentlemen, cavaliers (in Spanish). The use in 'Karain: A Memory' (p. 43) is ironic, and refers to the Spanish colonial presence in the Archipelago.

campong (kampong): a native village, normally enclosed with defensive palings, from which 'compound' derives.

chased hilt: an ornamentally engraved or embossed handle of a dagger.

cortège: a formal procession of attendants.

cuddy: on a small boat, a shelter or locker in the bow; on larger ships (such as in 'Karain: A Memory'), a room or cabin used as a common room, especially for meals.

curé: a parish priest (in French).

Inchi (Encik): Malayan term of polite address, 'Mr' or 'Mrs'.

juragan (djuragan): captain, master (of a boat).

kriss (kris, creese): a Malay or Indonesian dagger, with a blade which has wavy edges.

nibong palms (nibung): a Malaysian stemless palm, also known as 'cabbage tree'.

nipa palm: a semi-aquatic creeping palm, indigenous to Australasia. Its leaves are used for mats and thatching roofs.

plantain-patches: plantain is a tree-like tropical plant bearing fruit closely resembling bananas.

prau (proa): a Malay boat, usually without a deck (like a canoe), propelled by sail, oars, or paddles, and capable of being sailed forwards or backwards.

Rajah: a Malay ruler or prince.

rattan: (Malay) a climbing palm with long, thin and pliable stems, used in furniture-making or as a walking stick.

sampan: (Malay) a flat-bottomed boat, usually propelled by oars.

sarong:(from the Malay) a skirt-like garment, a long strip of cloth worn tucked round the waist.

schooner: a two-masted, swift sailing ship with fore-and-aft rigging.

serang: a native boatswain.

shoaling water: shallow area of (sea) water, often caused by sand banks.

sumpitan: (Malay) a blow-pipe, made from hollow cane, from which poisoned arrows are shot.

sternports: a port or opening in the stern of a vessel, used for the loading of cargo, ventilation, etc.

Tuan: 'Lord', a common form of polite address in Malay.

CONRAD AND HIS CRITICS

Of the daunting number of monographs, critical essays and reviews registered in bibliographies on Joseph Conrad's works, comparatively few are devoted to *Tales of Unrest*. This selection of critical responses has two aims. It indicates the range of early review opinion about the strengths and weaknesses of the collection; and it illustrates Conrad's thematic and stylistic preoccupations in *Tales*, as later critics have discerned them, and the ways in which recent literary theoretical concerns have offered fresh perspectives on the stories.

The earliest newspaper and journal reviews of *Tales of Unrest*, on both sides of the Atlantic, are very mixed. They range from the laudatory to the decidedly negative. From the outset, *Tales* produced a critical unrest that has not abated. Thus one reviewer announces that Conrad is the only living writer to approach Kipling in his 'reticence, dramatic power, mastery over both ideas and language' and his disregard for sentimentality (*Cosmopolis*, August 1898, p. 412). But he is also quite capable of writing a disagreeable book, emphasising the seamy side of life and displaying a mania for treachery – so thinks the reviewer in the *Literary World* (New York, 25 June 1898, p. 204). Conrad 'adopts an air of mystery with reference to locality and character and even language itself, the reason for which is inexplicable', complains the reviewer in the *Cleveland Leader* (15 May 1898, p. 17).

The *Daily Mail* review (12 April 1898, p. 3) sees in *Tales of Unrest* 'great breadth of view, much power and a conspicuous lack of literary training'. Sounding rather like a school report, however, it adds: '[It] is sufficient testimony to Mr. Conrad's power that we accept and enjoy him as we do, considering the continual weakness of his grammar and the frequent slipshodness of his general method.' 'The Return' comes in for special praise for 'the sheer force of the author's psychological insight and his unusual ability to see common things in an uncommon way'.

For others, the *Daily Telegraph* reviewer for example (9 April 1898, p. 8), the finest story is 'Karain: A Memory', in which Malaya was real and 'drawn to the life'. But the 'sheer morbid horror' of 'The Idiots' and 'An Outpost of Progress' ('gloomy [. . .] and morbid to a fantastic degree') leads the same reviewer to conclude that Conrad should choose more pleasant themes in the future. (With this advice no doubt in mind, Conrad went on immediately to write *Heart of Darkness*.)

The Academy did a great deal to establish Conrad's early reputation. Its earliest review of *Tales of Unrest* (16 April 1898, pp. 417–8) praises his artistic control and, as if answering objections about choice of subject matter, defends Conrad's 'realistic' observation:

> Mr Conrad has seen strange things in strange lands, and he can describe what he has seen impersonally, incuriously, without senti- mentality, and without wailing. He is not eloquent, and hysteria is unknown to him; but he has grit, and the epithets 'nervous, artful, buxom' also describe his English. These tales [. . .] march straight on; where they are tragic the tragedy is inevitable. The artist selects and tells. That selection is his concern and his alone. Things horrid and inexplicable may happen, and it is not his affair to suggest why heaven remains sealed and unanswering any more than it is his business to explain why illusions are often better aids to living than the naked truth. He tells, and the critic's business is with the sincerity and method of presentment, not with the choice of subject. We rise from the reading of these *Tales of Unrest* strengthened, not depressed. For the work is sincere, and it deals in realities. Mr Conrad is a writer's writer [. . .] with *Tales of Unrest* he becomes [one] to be reckoned with.

Edward Garnett, the great champion of Conrad in his early writing years, also writes enthusiastically and discerningly about the collection in *The Academy* (15 October 1898):

> What is the quality of his art? The quality of Mr Conrad's art is seen in his faculty of making us perceive men's lives in their natural relation to the seen universe around them; his men are part of the great world of Nature, and the sea, the land and sky around them are not drawn merely as background, or something inferior and

secondary to the human will, as we have in most artists' work. This faculty of seeing man's life in relation to the seen and unseen forces of Nature it is that gives Mr Conrad's art its extreme delicacy and its great breadth of vision. . . . We find life's daily necessity in Mr Conrad's art, we find actuality, charm, magic; and to demand inevitability from it is perhaps like asking for inevitability from Chopin's music. . . . His power [in *Tales of Unrest*] of making us *see* a constant succession of changing pictures is what dominates the reader and leaves him no possible way of escaping from the author's subtle and vivid world. He throws a mirage magically before you; he enmeshes your senses, you are in his universe, you accept it all. (pp. 82–3)

A landmark in the reception of the *Tales* was established when *Tales of Unrest* received an award from *The Academy* in 1898. Under the general title 'Our Awards for 1898. The "Crowned Books"' (14 January 1899, pp. 66–7), *Tales of Unrest* received this accolade. Although it is unsigned, Owen Knowles has persuasively argued that it was written by Arnold Bennett. (See Knowles' article in *The Conradian*, 10.1, 1985, pp. 26–33.)

Mr Conrad, in the five years or so that he has spent on land, setting down for our beguilement some of the stories that had come to him during his life at sea, has produced only four books; but they have been, in the fullest sense of the word, written. It might be said that the work of no novelist now working gives so much evidence of patient elaboration of style, without, however, leaving any sense of elaborateness. Mr Conrad's art conceals art. With the nicest precision of epithet (a precision the more remarkable when we recollect that he lived so long at sea) Mr Conrad tells his tales of strong men fighting the elements, of emotional crises, of settlers in foreign lands among alien people, by the conflict of the East and the West, of savagery and civilisation. This contrast between his own calm and the turbulence of his subject-matter lends his work a peculiarly impressive character. If his work reminds us of anyone it is Turgenev. His aloofness is Turgenev's. But his poetry, his outlook on life, his artistic conscience – these are his own.

Another of Mr Conrad's distinguishing qualities [is] that he keeps man in his place. He has an eye ever vigilant both for the transitory persons of his drama and for the permanent forces at their back. He blends human beings and nature. The puppet never fills the universe, as with certain other novelists. Everything is related and harmonised.

This comprehensiveness of vision, this amplitude of outlook, makes Mr Conrad more than just a story teller. He seems to us to have some of the attributes of the Greek tragic dramatists. He has their irony. He sees so much at once, and is so conscious of the infinitesimal place a man can fill. Hence his work belongs never to cheerful literature; it is sombre, melancholy, searching. Yet Mr Conrad is poet too. At the same time that he is aware of man's shortcomings he is profoundly in love with his capacities for grandeur, with his potential nobility. [. . .] He is one of the notable literary colonists. He has annexed the Malay Peninsula for us. With him it is not merely an array of names and ethnological facts, it is the real transference to paper of something of the very heart of the country, the nation, described.

Critical opinion over the subsequent decades has been equally mixed. In Albert Guerard, *Conrad the Novelist* (Cambridge, Mass.: Harvard University Press, 1958), Conrad's work is seen in terms of a Jungian mythic-psychological 'night journey':

'The Lagoon' is a distinctly less coherent story [than 'An Outpost of Progress'] which may well have deserved Max Beerbohm's amusing parody. And yet it has the very originality and personal accent that provoke parody. It is indeed an eccentric dream. [. . .] The story of Arsat, like that of Karain, is interesting as part of [Conrad's] misogynous pattern and even more interesting as an early version of the essential Conradian crime. But the unnamed white man, who seems indirectly responsible for the pretentious 'Conradese', gives us greater pause [. . . He is] present to occasion the rendering of a highly subjective landscape. A Jungian reading might well find another night journey into the unconscious in his movement from the broad river, through the fabulously deep creek, to the lagoon and its house on pilings. [. . .] There is no need to argue that this writing (which is certainly bad writing) is markedly subjective and even compulsive. [. . .] The uncertainty of impulse behind 'The Lagoon' – at once symbolist prose-poem, story of crime and punishment, and exotic local-color story – makes it the incoherent performance it is. (pp. 65–7)

In the case of Thomas Moser, *Joseph Conrad: Achievement and Decline* (Cambridge, Mass.: Harvard University Press, 1957; reprinted Hamden, Conn.: Archon Books, 1966) the argument for Conrad's 'decline' in his late works and his thesis that

Conrad's weakness is his inability to treat convincingly the 'Uncongenial Subject' of sexual psychology have been very influential. Of 'The Return' Moser comments:

> It appears from Conrad's letters to Garnett and from the patches of rather crude irony which occur in the story that Conrad *thought* that he was satirizing Hervey, thought that he was rendering him ironically. Yet somehow Conrad became so confused about Hervey that try as he might he could not judge and condemn Hervey's despair.
>
> Conrad's confusion seems to arise from the fact that 'The Return' is more about Hervey's sexual difficulties than about his bourgeois ideas. An examination of his reactions to his wife's desertion and return may illuminate the central meaning of the story. When Hervey finds that his wife has left, he does not care so much about losing her as about the personal insult that she had found another man sexually preferable to himself. (p. 73)

Moser then discusses the closing scenes of the story, and concludes:

> Hervey [is left] alone in the darkness to make his discovery that nothing matters. The darkness and the discovery are both intolerable, and he goes, as always, to his wife for help. [. . .] He finds no help there, of course, and runs out of the house, into the night.
>
> So ends the only serious direct treatment of a sexual subject that Conrad finished during his early period. One may well ask why we have dwelt so long on such a bad piece of writing, [. . . 'The Return'] provides us with a kind of *locus classicus* for the near paralysis of Conrad's creativity when dealing with a sexual subject. [. . .] it is significant that Conrad's one extended study of a sexual subject should center in an inadequate male who sees female sexuality as an inescapable menace. (p. 77)

Edward Said's early work, *Joseph Conrad and the Fiction of Autobiography* (Cambridge, Mass.: Harvard University Press, 1966), and his subsequent thinking through, and at times against, Conrad (in *Orientalism* and *Culture and Imperialism*) have not only informed Conrad scholarship, but have also profoundly affected what is now called post-colonial studies. Here, Said discusses *Tales of Unrest* in terms of a dialectic between immediate experience and the fictional narration of it:

The retrospective mode of so many of Joseph Conrad's shorter works can be understood as the effort to interpret what, at the time of occurrence, would not permit reflection. And, most of the time, the action that has already occurred not only troubles the present, but also calls itself to immediate attention. Conrad's very first tale, 'The Idiots', explicitly accounts for itself in this manner. [. . .] Between the recollecting narrator and the actual tale there is a barrier that is eternally closed. (p. 88)

The characteristic, idiomatic twist in every Conrad story is that the attempt to see a direct relation between the past and the present, to see past and present as a continuous surface of inter-related events, is frustrated. [. . .] It is almost impossible not to remark that acting first and reflecting afterwards is always the problem, with reflection hopelessly far behind, hopelessly leading one further away from an inscrutable surface of action into a confusing 'beyond'. (p. 95)

Lawrence Graver, *Conrad's Short Fiction* (Berkeley: University of California Press, 1969), comments:

Tales of Unrest is inchoate yet typical Conrad – inchoate in the sense that it is marked by daring, diffuseness, energy, uncertainty, and all the signs of the apprentice hand; yet typical in that most of the stories are based on memory and reminiscence, make use of situations of murder and mayhem to examine problems of conduct, and are enlivened by Conrad's theatrical sense of history. Although in none of the early stories does Conrad achieve more than a partial success, one can nevertheless trace a development in his experiments. This development is generally a matter of trying a form and finding it in one way or another restrictive [. . .]. But in two stories, at least, the development is clearly positive. 'The Lagoon' suggests that a symbolic setting can, if held in check, amplify theme; while 'Karain' shows that the use of several narrators can add moral complexity to a melodramatic situation. [. . .] Although two of the stories were summarily written with specific writers and magazines in mind, the failures in *Tales of Unrest* are mainly of judgment and execution. 'An Outpost of Progress' has a forced ending, 'Karain' dissolves into a trivial anecdote, and 'The Lagoon' is overwritten; yet there is no need to dismiss them as mere potboilers. They are too intense and varied to come from the hand of a writer primarily concerned with money. (pp. 39, 41)

Dale Kramer, in 'Conrad's Experiments with Language and Narration in "The Return"' *Studies in Short Fiction*, 25 (Winter 1988), pp. 1–11, suggests:

> Seldom does Conrad disguise the broad targets of his observations nor does he in this early story about a class of English society about which he knew little directly. Conrad's target in 'The Return' is stereotypes – stereotypes about ourselves that we accept, partly for convenience and partly because we cannot tell what is real from what we have always unquestioningly understood to be the case. The course of 'The Return' portrays Hervey's unwilling, slow, circumlocutory, self-resistant journey to an evaluation of the real and the understood [. . .]. The isolation of the individual cannot be broken unless he or she is willing to recognize another's true rather than understood self *and* unless that other person simultaneously makes a similar recognition. Little wonder, the story suggests, that so much of human life is loneliness, given the odds that two people linked arbitrarily will be able at the same time to recognize each other as something other than an appendage to self-concern and be able to find the words in their impoverished vocabularies to express states of feeling and mind they had until moments before never conceived of. (p. 4)

Jeremy Hawthorn's *Joseph Conrad: Narrative Technique and Ideological Commitment* (London: Edward Arnold, 1990) is a subtle and detailed understanding of Conrad's writing, which successfully links a close 'formalist' analysis of Conrad's narrative strategies with a broader (well-disposed, Marxist-oriented) reading of major works, including 'An Outpost of Progress'. Referring to Kayerts's and Carlier's 'reading' of newspapers and novels, Hawthorn comments:

> Carlier and Kayerts lack the ability to read literature critically, and this is directly related to their helplessness. They have never had to explore the relationship between language and reality, have never had to be on guard against the duplicities of language. [. . .] Conrad suggests a connection between the ability to read critically and the ability to distance oneself from one's surroundings, to escape from the imprisoning power of custom, authority and social control. [. . .] Imperialism is able to lie and deceive about what it actually involves, because its servants are either unable or unwilling to question the reports they are given.

Revealingly, 'An Outpost of Progress' itself cannot be read in the manner in which Kayerts and Carlier read the discovered novels. [. . .] Able to enter the world of the novels they read, they are incapable of distinguishing between novelistic world and real world. The reader [. . .] cannot enter the world of the tale in this way [. . .] Carlier and Kayerts are *apart* from us, separated from our world by a narrative technique that forces us to observe and analyse them. (pp. 162, 165–6)

Daphna Erdinast-Vulcan, *Joseph Conrad and the Modern Temper* (Oxford: Clarendon Press, 1991), suggests that there is a tension in Conrad's works between a pre-modern (but not 'primitive') mythic discourse and the pressures of modernity. Of 'Karain: A Memory' she argues:

Many of the features of the mythical mode of discourse are encapsulated in 'Karain'. [. . .] The figure of Karain can be seen as the prototype of Lingard [of *The Rescue* and other Conrad Malay novels] or of [Lord] Jim in Patusan; he is the essential mythical hero, an embodiment of heroic virtues, larger than life, holding the life of his people in his hands. [. . .] Like a true mythical figure, Karain commands the faithfulness not only of his people but also that of nature [. . .]. Karain's story is [. . .] a version of the story of Cain, a man guilty of fratricide, haunted by guilt and remorse, and its denouement is also brought about by a charm. [. . .] Unlike Jim or even Lingard, Karain is clearly not 'one of us', and the narrative frame of the story erects a clear division between this likeable but primitive other, and the modern civilised outlook of the white people, drawn together to form a cohesive cultural unity by the first-person plural of the narrative. (pp. 31–2)

Hugh Epstein's ' "Where He Is Not Wanted": Impression and Articulation in "The Idiots" and "Amy Foster" ', *Conradiana*, 23.3 (1991), locates Conrad's frequently mentioned 'impressionistic' style in a broader context of contemporary theories of language and knowledge:

Moments of pure sensation [which impressionism seeks to capture] are, in themselves, meaningless; and if life really is no more than a succession of perceived moments, it cannot be a shared story: we are fundamentally alone. But against this decomposing quality of prose 'pointillism', it is characteristic of Conrad to oppose the efforts of a narrator actively seeking to confer meaning on what he sees. [. . .]

However, in 'The Idiots' the major artistic impulse is towards the depiction of those moments that confirm only isolation and exile. [. . .] the narrator's attempts to site the idiots in a moral universe is stridently naive [. . .]. The tale, when at last it stands before its narrator, will indeed reveal heaven to be empty [. . .]. Impenetrability is indeed the keynote of the vision in 'The Idiots,' where nature gives no corresponding sign to man's presence. [. . .] Language, meaning, is a matter of human imposition, and the chances of success are not very high. (pp. 220–1)

Surveying the critical literature on *Tales of Unrest*, I have found it evident that over the last fifty years the changing pattern of attention paid to particular stories has followed broader cultural and interpretative trends. Thus 'The Lagoon', often read as a psycho-mythical story, was in favour in the late 1950s and early 1960s. In the 1970s and 1980s, anxieties surrounding Western imperialism and forms of colonial practice have highlighted 'An Outpost of Progress' as a rich and complex text for critical debate, often as a preface to *Heart of Darkness*. More recently, interest in theories of narrativity, modern memory and its discontents, and post-colonialism and the clash of cultural difference has generated rewarding critical consideration of 'Karain: A Memory'. This new and welcome attention attests to the fact that Conrad's *Tales of Unrest* can nourish – and, indeed, demand and survive – the needs, questions, and answers we bring to them as readers.

SUGGESTIONS FOR FURTHER READING

The formidable number of books, articles and reviews on Conrad is a measure of his enormous impact on twentieth-century literature. Three bibliographies give an invaluable guide and commentary to critical works on his writing, fully covering the period from the late 1890s to the 1990s.

Bruce E. Teets and Helmut E. Gerber, *Joseph Conrad: An Annotated Bibliography of Writings About Him* (De Kalb: Northern Illinois University Press, 1971).

Bruce E. Teets, *Joseph Conrad: An Annotated Bibliography* (New York & London: Garland, 1990).

Owen Knowles, *An Annotated Critical Bibliography of Joseph Conrad* (Hemel Hempstead: Harvester Wheatsheaf, 1992).

Conradiana (Lubbock: Texas Tech University) and *The Conradian* (London: Joseph Conrad Society, UK), excellent sources in their own right for articles on Conrad, also provide regular bibliographical updates on and reviews of Conrad scholarship.

Biographies of Conrad

Given the challenging mixture of high adventure and high artistry which figured in, indeed determined, Conrad's life, it is not surprising that biographers of Conrad have found rich material for their own inspired histories of his life and works. Among the most important are:

Jocelyn Baines, *Joseph Conrad: A Critical Biography* (London: Weidenfeld & Nicolson, 1960; reprinted Harmondsworth: Penguin Books, 1971).

Frederick R. Karl, *Joseph Conrad: The Three Lives – A Biography* (London: Faber & Faber, 1979).

Zdzisław Najder, *Joseph Conrad: A Chronicle* (Cambridge: Cambridge University Press, 1983).

Historical Contexts

For biographical and historical background to Conrad's writing, the works of Zdzisław Najder and Norman Sherry are extremely useful starting points:

Zdzisław Najder (ed.), *Conrad Under Familial Eyes*. Trans. Halina Carroll-Najder (Cambridge: Cambridge University Press, 1983).

Norman Sherry, *Conrad's Eastern World* (Cambridge: Cambridge University Press, 1966).

Norman Sherry, *Conrad's Western World* (Cambridge: Cambridge University Press, 1971).

Other very useful, historically orientated works specific to the *Tales of Unrest* include:

Andrzej Braun, 'The Myth-Like Kingdom of Conrad', *Conradiana*, 10.1 (1978), pp. 3–16.

G. J. Resink, 'The Eastern Archipelago Under Joseph Conrad's Western Eyes', in *Indonesia's History Between the Myths* (The Hague: W. van Hoeve, 1968).

Anthologies

For wide-ranging anthologies, containing reviews and articles relevant to *Tales of Unrest*, readers should consult:

Keith Carabine (ed.), *Joseph Conrad: Critical Assessments*, in 4 vols. (Robertsbridge: Croom Helm, 1992).

Norman Sherry (ed.), *Conrad: The Critical Heritage* (London and Boston: Routledge & Kegan Paul, 1973).

Introductions and Guides

The following works offer good introductions to Conrad's writing:

Jacques Berthoud, *Joseph Conrad: The Major Phase* (Cambridge: Cambridge University Press, 1978).

Owen Knowles, *A Conrad Chronology* (London: Macmillan, 1989).

Norman Page, *A Conrad Companion* (London: Macmillan, 1986).

J. H. Stape (ed.), *The Cambridge Companion to Joseph Conrad* (Cambridge: Cambridge University Press, 1996).

Cedric Watts, *A Preface to Conrad* (London: Longman, 1982; rev. ed., 1993).

Cedric Watts, *Joseph Conrad: A Literary Life* (London: Macmillan, 1989).

Publishing History

For a fuller account of the publishing history of Conrad's short stories, see:

J. D. Gordan, *Joseph Conrad: The Making of a Novelist* (Cambridge, Mass.: Harvard University Press, 1940).

Elmer A. Ordoñez, *The Early Joseph Conrad* (Quezon City: University of the Philippines Press, 1969).

George W. Whiting, 'Conrad's Revisions of Six Stories', *PMLA*, XLVIII (1933), pp. 552–7.

Critical Works

Given the relative scarcity of scholarly work on *Tales of Unrest*, the following studies, which have substantial chapters on the collection, are to be noted:

Andrzej Busza, 'Conrad's Polish Literary Background and Some Illustrations of the Influence of Polish Literature on his Work', *Antemurale*, 10 (1966), pp. 109–255.

Daphna Erdinast-Vulcan, *Joseph Conrad and the Modern Temper* (Oxford: Clarendon Press, 1991).

Lawrence Graver, *Conrad's Short Fiction* (Berkeley: University of California Press, 1969).

Albert Guerard, *Conrad the Novelist* (Cambridge, Mass.: Harvard University Press, 1958).

Jeremy Hawthorn, *Joseph Conrad: Narrative Technique and Ideological Commitment* (London: Edward Arnold, 1990).

Yves Hervouet, *The French Face of Joseph Conrad* (Cambridge: Cambridge University Press, 1990).

John Lester, *Conrad and Religion* (London: Macmillan, 1988).

Jakob Lothe, *Conrad's Narrative Method* (Oxford: Clarendon, 1989).

Thomas Moser, *Joseph Conrad: Achievement and Decline* (Cambridge, Mass.: Harvard University Press, 1957; reprinted Hamden, Conn.: Archon Books, 1966).

Edward Said, *Joseph Conrad and the Fiction of Autobiography* (Cambridge, Mass.: Harvard University Press, 1966).

Daniel Schwarz, *Conrad:* Almayer's Folly *to* Under Western Eyes (London: Macmillan, 1980).

Andrea White, *Joseph Conrad and the Adventure of Empire: Constructing and Deconstructing the Imperial Subject* (Cambridge: Cambridge University Press, 1993).

Mark Wollaeger, *Joseph Conrad and the Fictions of Skepticism* (Stanford: Stanford University Press, 1990).

Critical Articles

Much fresh and welcome work on *Tales of Unrest* is appearing in journals, the most important of which are *The Conradian*, *Conradiana*, and *L'Epoque Conradienne* (Limoges: Société Conradienne Française). Among useful critical articles on *Tales of Unrest* are the following:

Mark Conroy, 'Ghostwriting (In) "Karain"', *The Conradian*, 18.2 (1994), pp. 1–16.

Deirdre David, 'Selfhood and Language in "The Return" and "Falk"', *Conradiana*, 8.2 (1976), pp. 137–47.

Hugh Epstein, '"Where He Is Not Wanted": Impression and Articulation in "The Idiots" and "Amy Foster"', *Conradiana*, 23.3 (1991), pp. 217–32.

Gail Fraser, 'Conrad's Irony: "An Outpost of Progress" and *The Secret Agent*', *The Conradian*, 11.2 (1986), pp. 155–69.

Adam Gillon, 'Shakespearean and Polish Tonalities in Conrad's "The Lagoon"', *Conradiana*, 8.2 (1976), pp. 127–36.

Wray C. Herbert, 'Conrad's Psychic Landscape: The Mythic Element in "Karain"', *Conradiana*, 8.3 (1976), pp. 225–31.

J. C. Hilson and David Timms, 'Gobila in London: A Note on "An Outpost of Progress" and *The Secret Agent*', *Conradiana*, 9.2 (1977), pp. 189–92.

Robert W. Hobson, 'A Textual History of Conrad's "An Outpost of Progress"', *Conradiana*, 11 (1979), pp. 143–63.

Reynold Humphries, '"Karain: A Memory". How to Spin a Yarn', *L'Epoque Conradienne* (1983), pp. 9–21.

Owen Knowles, 'Arnold Bennett as an "Anonymous" Reviewer of Conrad's Early Fiction', *The Conradian*, 10.1 (1985), pp. 26–33.

Dale Kramer, 'Conrad's Experiments with Language and Narration in "The Return"', *Studies in Short Fiction*, 25 (Winter 1988), pp. 1–11.

Joseph Martin, 'Edward Garnett and Conrad's Reshaping of Time', *Conradiana*, 6.2 (1974), pp. 89–105.

Catherine Rising, 'The Complex Death of Kayerts', *Conradiana*, 23.2 (1991), pp. 157–69.

Daniel Schwarz, 'Moral Bankruptcy in Ploumar Parish: A Study of Conrad's "The Idiots"', *Conradiana*, 1 (1969), pp. 113–17.

Karain: A Memory

The tale is narrated by an (unnamed) English sailor, gun-running with fellow British sailors (Hollis and Jackson) in the Malay Archipelago. Over years they have traded with Karain, a Malay prince, establishing a close friendship with him. A masterful, dignified but pensive personality, Karain has established his own rule in an isolated corner of the Archipelago, living in exile from his home state. His constant attendant is an old sword-bearer who functions as his spiritual protector. On a subsequent visit, the white men learn of the old man's death and find Karain now distracted by fears, ghosted by a secret past. He tells them his full story.

Long ago, Karain and his friend and brother-in-arms Matara had spent years searching the Archipelago for Matara's sister, who had dishonoured her family by going off with a Dutch planter. Matara's intention was to hunt down and kill the lovers, but, over the years of pursuit, Karain created and was secretly sustained by an image of Matara's lovely sister. The couple is eventually discovered, but the ambush goes awry: Karain cannot bring himself to carry out the plan of shooting the Dutch planter while Matara stabs his sister. Instead, to save the sister, Karain shoots Matara. The sister afterwards claims not to know Karain. Desolated and guilt-stricken, Karain is haunted by the ghost of his friend until protected by the benign presence of the old sword-bearer. The latter's death opens up all the old fears and drives Karain to seek spiritual asylum with the white men. After Karain completes his story, Hollis gives him a talisman – a gilded silver Jubilee sixpence – which exorcises Matara's ghost and enables Karain to return to rule his people.

Years later, a chance meeting in London brings the narrator and Jackson to reminisce about Karain. The former, forever confident of superior Western values, scoffs at Karain's superstitious naïveté. But Jackson demurs, more impressed by the alternative reality and the spiritual world Karain represents.

The Idiots

The story's setting is the wild north coast of Brittany, the (nominal) narrator a visitor foreign to the area. He comes across a group of 'idiot' children in a country lane. It is their family's story he gathers and relates. Jean-Pierre Bacadou, who stems from a rich and influential local family, returns from military service and takes over his elderly parents' now dilapidated farm. He decides marriage will ensure a new generation of sons and thus a future for the family farm. However, Susan, his chosen wife, first bears him 'idiot' twin boys. The third child, another boy, also proves an 'idiot'. Jean-Pierre succumbs to the persuasive pressure of Susan and her mother, Madame Levaille, a powerful and independent businesswoman in the region. Though a staunch anti-cleric and republican, he decides to go to mass to appease Divine Providence. Business (in the form of Madame Levaille), Church (the local priest) and Polity (the royalist Marquis de Chavanes, the local mayor) are delighted at this 'conversion'. But the fourth child, a girl, also turns out an 'idiot'. Humiliated, defeated, and embittered at fearing the farm will revert to undeserving, distant relatives, Jean-Pierre turns to drinking, abusing Susan and blaspheming at the church gates. Eventually, in a violent argument, Susan stabs and kills Jean-Pierre. She searches out her mother, confesses to her, then rushes to the rocky shoreline. Tortured by guilt and remorse, she imagines she is being pursued through the rocks by her dead husband. (In fact it is a local seaweed-gatherer, who, worried for her, calls after her.) There, she stumbles (or jumps) to her death. As epilogue, in response to his friend Madame Levaille's sad news, the Marquis says he will declare the death an accident (rather than suicide) so that Susan can be buried in consecrated ground. He also plans to have Madame Levaille appointed trustee of the farm.

An Outpost of Progress

Kayerts (as chief) and Carlier (his assistant) are appointed as managers to the isolated ivory trading-station of a large European colonial concern in the Congo. Makola is their African station clerk, and with his family, he and ten native labourers form the station's community. The Europeans begin work cherishing sentimental notions of friend-ship, high hopes of progress, and fine colonial slogans. As their stay lengthens, boredom and futile activity take their toll, and they become increasingly irascible. Furthermore, after Makola trades the ten workers to an itinerant group of African slave-traders for ivory, the local tribal villagers and their leader, Gobila, withdraw from social contact and the exchange of food and ivory. They naturally fear for their own well-being. At first sanguine about Makola's dealings, the two Europeans grow increasingly fraught as their local trade dwindles and their food supplies run short. Over months the tension rises and a petty quarrel leads to Kayerts's ludicrous shooting of Carlier. Makola suggests that Carlier be buried – as a fever victim. The next day, the much-delayed Managing Director of the Company finally arrives at the station with supplies – to find that Kayerts has hanged himself from the cross erected by Makola to mark the grave of the previous station manager, who had died, we hear, of fever.

The Return

Upper-middle-class businessman Alvan Hervey returns home one evening from his London office to find a letter from his wife. They have enjoyed a comfortable though disengaged five-year marriage, full of material luxury, prudent bliss and philanthropic good works. But the letter tells him she has left him for another man: a social-climbing literary type whose society paper Hervey has been financing. He is shocked out of his habitual complacency into waves of fear, anger, nausea and disbelief. Recovering into indignation, however, Hervey starts worrying about the social impropriety and embarrassment his wife has involved him in. Within hours she returns, admitting the letter was 'a mistake'. The rest of the tale is taken up with their (rather one-sided) dialogue, Hervey upbraiding her for her dishonesty, unaccountable behaviour, failure of duty and lack of self-restraint, and she seeking (but failing) to explain her position to him. After a brief stony interlude for a formal dinner in front of the servants, the couple resume their altercations in private. Hervey wants to 'forgive and forget'; she refuses to 'forget'. The impasse is broken and the story ends with Hervey leaving the house, never to return.

The Lagoon

A white trader moors his small boat to spend the night at the house of his Malay friend, Arsat, who lives in an isolated lagoon somewhere in the Malay Archipelago. He finds Arsat tending his ill and dying wife, Diamelen. Unable to help her in her final hours, the two men sit by a camp fire, the white man listening to Arsat's story of their great love against the backdrop of a starry tropical night. Years before, with the help of his brother, Arsat had run away with Diamelen, a servant to his ruler. The three steal away by night in a canoe but are soon pursued by the ruler's guards, who discover them on a lonely beach. Arsat's brother offers to give fight; Arsat wants simply to flee. While Arsat and Diamelen run off, his brother tries to hold off the advancing enemy guards. Overtaken, his cries for help unheeded by Arsat, he is killed; Arsat and Diamelen escape. Since then, Arsat has been stricken with guilt and remorse over his brother's sacrifice.

At day-break, Arsat's story at an end, the two men go back to the house to find Diamelen in her death throes. Afterwards, Arsat says he will return to his homeland to avenge his brother's killing. The white man departs from the lonely Malay.

ACKNOWLEDGEMENTS

I would first like to thank Cedric Watts. As the General Editor for the Everyman Conrad series, he has offered me patient and meticulous advice for my own edition. His work on Conrad has been especially helpful for my notes and glossary. I thank also Hans van Marle, of Amsterdam. All Conradian scholars will know how much his learning and enthusiasm, selflessly shared, contribute to our understanding of Conrad.

I have cited the following works in the section on Conrad and his Critics, for which I thank both scholars and publishers.

Hugh Epstein, ' "Where He Is Not Wanted": Impression and Articulation in "The Idiots" and "Amy Foster" ', *Conradiana*, 23.3 (1991), pp. 217–32.

Daphna Erdinast-Vulcan, *Joseph Conrad and the Modern Temper* (Oxford: Clarendon Press, 1991).

Lawrence Graver, *Conrad's Short Fiction* (Berkeley: University of California Press, 1969).

Albert Guerard, *Conrad the Novelist* (Cambridge, Mass.: Harvard University Press, 1958).

Jeremy Hawthorn, *Joseph Conrad: Narrative Technique and Ideological Commitment* (London: Edward Arnold, 1990).

Dale Kramer, 'Conrad's Experiments with Language and Narration in "The Return" ', *Studies in Short Fiction* 25 (Winter 1988), pp. 1–11.

Thomas Moser, *Joseph Conrad: Achievement and Decline* (Cambridge, Mass.: Harvard University Press, 1957; reprinted Hamden, Conn.: Archon Books, 1966).

Edward Said, *Joseph Conrad and the Fiction of Autobiography* (Cambridge, Mass.: Harvard University Press, 1966).

Karen Edwards, with her searching calls for clarity and patient help has been unstinting in her support. For their insights and contribution I would also like to thank Daphna Erdinast-Vulcan, Robert Hampson, and Owen Knowles. In Heidelberg, Brigitte Flickinger's generosity and warm support in my research and preparation of the edition were invaluable. It is, though, to Rudolf Sühnel, on his ninetieth birthday, that I would give particular thanks for friendship and conversations, Conradian and otherwise.

p 69